MW00379628

VIGILANTE
PRIEST

By

Joe Gallagher and Dan Bowden

For permission requests, write to the publisher of this work. Please submit all inquires to rukiapublishingus@gmail.com.

PRINT PAPERBACK ISBN: 978-1-7378472-4-3
PRINT HARDCOVER ISBN: 978-1-7378472-3-6
eBOOK(ELECTRONIC BOOK) ISBN:978-1-7378472-5-0
1ST EDITION 2024
TINTON FALLS, NJ
LIBRARY OF CONGRESS CONTROL NUMBER: 2024910629

This book is dedicated
to the strongest person we know,
my wife and Dan's niece,
Dena Gallagher.

TABLE OF CONTENTS

ACKNOWLEDGMENTS

Thank you to all our friends, colleagues and family who helped us put together Vigilante Priest for you the reader.

Mickey Bayard, Brian Buckley, Jamie Carroll, Joe Castelluccio, Cathy Duffy-Heller, Linda Dunphy, Matt Eitner, Bob Fazio, John Fray, Eddy Garcia, Lope Lesigues, Jerry Lyons, Alice McGillion, Tommy Millin, Kevin Murphy, Paul Pliester, John Shea and Gene Slattery.

A special thanks to Artie Grix and his wife Dr. Maureen Grix. Artie for his tremendously helpful insights into the workings of the New York City Police Department. Maureen for her greatly appreciated and much needed constructive feedback.

Additionally, we would like to thank Dan Petrosini, USA Today and Amazon Best Selling Author, for holding our hand throughout the process.

And finally, we'd like to thank Sandy Bowden who put in endless hours, editing, offering suggestions and being a tiebreaker for major decisions involving the direction of the story. If there is a hero to the story, it would be Dan's wife, Sandy.

PROLOGUE

Seventeen Months Ago

FATHER TONY

Sipping my Tuscan red, I stared blankly out my Vatican office window into the throng of tourists in Saint Peter's Square. I knew wine and sleeplessness were a bad combination, but I wanted to steel myself. Or perhaps numb myself.

My nights had grown increasingly restless over the last five years. I had known about the Vatican's sad, dark secret since arriving in Italy four decades ago—in fact, the secret, or some twisted version of it, had brought me here. But five years ago was when I saw the actual list for the first time. I wondered then what the right thing to do was, and whether I could do it. I was a coward.

My cell phone rang. The call was fifteen minutes late.

"Pronto." I answered.

It was Daniel O'Malley's driver. His boss was a remarkable man, a great supporter of the church, who shared my roots in the Bronx, New York's famous-yet-floundering borough. O'Malley, a hyper-focused billionaire, once told me that "On time is late," so I was surprised his driver was calling behind schedule.

———

The driver, a stocky man with an olive complexion, was dressed in an expensive suit. This was juxtaposed with the electric mini FIAT he was driving. Whatever O'Malley had to tell me, he wanted it to be low profile.

"Father, I haven't been to church for a while. How should I address you? Is it Father Morelli, Father Anthony, or Father Tony?"

"Any one of them is fine."

Sitting in the back, I began to open the mini bottle of Pellegrino placed in one of the cupholders.

"Father Morelli, if you could please not open that, I would appreciate it." My driver's voice was pure New York City, my old home.

As I put it down, I noticed the heavy tint on the windows. "Where are we going?"

"Actually, Father, it's better that you don't know."

I was about to say something when the driver continued, "Do you see the plastic bag on the back seat, the one from the pharmacy?"

It was the only other thing in the back seat besides me and the Pellegrino. "Yes."

"I need you to put it on."

Opening the plastic bag, I could see the black fabric inside a clear plastic bag and assumed it was a surgical mask. I remembered that Daniel did not sound like his robust self during our previous conversation. "Is he sick?"

The driver didn't answer.

When I opened the inner bag, I was shocked. It wasn't a mask, but a full hood. There was a single hole, presumably for my mouth.

This was meant to cover my entire head. I saw the driver's eyes staring back at me in the rearview mirror.

"Won't this call attention to us? I mean, if other drivers see me?"

"Put it on, lie low, close your eyes, and relax, Father."

I donned the hood which turned my world pitch black as the fabric covered not only my head but went to the base of my neck.

I took his advice. I closed my eyes and tried to nap.

The driver gently tugged my right arm. I had fallen asleep. Immersed in the darkness, I reflexively went for the hood as the driver grabbed my wrist to stop me.

"No. No, Father. Just a few steps now."

He helped me sit up. Then guiding me by my arm, steered me out of the car, across cobblestones, up some steps, and into a corridor with a hard floor where our steps echoed. Finally, we turned into a room with a carpet, and I heard a familiar voice.

"You can take that off, Father Tony," Daniel said.

I pulled off my hood. We were in a huge, elegant room. A palazzo, I guessed, from the stately windows. Growing up in a New York family, as a Centeno, I recognized the aesthetics of the home of a connected Italian family. There were not many O'Malleys that you would see in a place like this.

Danny, as I had called him since childhood, looked pale and unhealthy. I quickly ran to embrace him.

His wide eyes stopped me.

I had forgotten about his haphephobia. He avoided being touched at all costs. Even to the point where he refused communion. My heart hurt for him.

"Daniel!" I sobbed.

"So I look that bad?" The normally vibrant O'Malley sighed.

I nodded. "It's a shock. You—" I searched for the right words. "You are a man who exudes positive energy."

"But not anymore?"

I cursed myself for my insensitivity. "May I ask about your condition?"

"I'll spare you the details. But it's terminal."

I was stunned.

"But I have some time." O'Malley brightened slightly. "Doctors say a year, maybe two."

"I pray there will be more."

"Regardless, I'm here about you, Father. There is nothing I can do regarding me, but you… I want to fix what happened to you." O'Malley sipped some whiskey from a short glass.

He continued, "You remember when we met?"

My friend was going to die, and here he was thinking of helping me as his dying wish. I could barely speak. "Of course," I sputtered. "You had quit the football team. I remember Sandro Accardi was furious at you. You were his star receiver."

O'Malley swirled his drink. I heard the clink of ice cubes.

"And then you told me why. You told me you didn't like one of my fellow priests, one of the football coaches. The one that my nephew accused much later."

"There was no way you could have known. I didn't name names, and there were four coaches."

I shook my head. I had revisited that scene many times. "We weren't as aware as we should have been. But I should have seen the signs. You gave up something you loved. It was obvious, in retrospect, what you were trying to tell me. I should have investigated. And then..."

"And then you were falsely accused."

I nodded. I had insisted on my innocence. "I met with my bishop and explained that this was a shrewd fabrication. With my linguistics background and fluency in multiple languages, including

Italian and Latin, they had other plans for me. Many years later, my accuser privately admitted that he had lied about the accusation, but I was already settled.

"I took my vows to help, never to harm. I was fortunate. I had an exemplary record. My school, St. Francis, was well regarded. It was not far behind the esteemed Jesuit-run Regis High School, in terms of getting our students into top colleges. I was moved to the Vatican. I worked in the public affairs division, and studied and worshiped at the sacred center of Christ's church. Leaving my nephew Angel, his assigned protector Sandro Accardi, and you behind."

O'Malley finished his drink. "Your family is with me on this, the Centenos and the other New York families, for that matter, not to mention your accuser. He will tell the world that what he said about you was a lie. I have the mayor willing to make an official statement on behalf of the city and tell the story of how you were falsely accused. I've donated enough money to the church and the city. I can ask for a favor like this."

This was a sign. I would no longer be a coward.

We took a break for a late lunch and decided to lighten the conversation. We laughed about how Accardi, the quarterback he had abandoned in high school, had become his closest friend years later.

We laughed about the fight that broke out between the police precincts, between my nephew and Liam Hannigan and how that all got sorted.

After lunch was finished, and the table was cleared, O'Malley had another drink and steered the conversation back to forcing an apology from the church and allowing the stain to be removed from my name. "So what do you think? You ready to fly back to the Big Apple? Get the key to the city, maybe—"

"I have a list," I said, interrupting a man who was not used to being interrupted. "A very secret list. It relates to your very kind project."

"A list?" He was irritated.

"A list of protected priests."

O'Malley was dumbfounded. "You mean priests who…" His anger was rising. "Molesters? We are talking about molesters, right?"

I nodded. "Accused priests who have been moved to new parishes or banished to desk jobs. But they are still part of the Holy See, despite the stain they carry and risk of recidivism."

O'Malley fell back into his seat in shock.

The silence hurt. It was a weight. A weight I bore for my cowardice. "I'll make it public. That's the least I can do. I can do that. We will tell your story. You know, officially."

O'Malley was silent.

It was more than just a rumor that O'Malley had been molested. It was an accepted fact by those in power in New York City. The city as a whole didn't know. It didn't matter. I just wanted my friend to speak to me.

His voice was measured. "You know I wanted to be a doctor, right?"

I did, but I didn't answer him.

"My parents knew I was a genius as a young boy. They kept me on grade *for my benefit*! So I could socialize. There was no way for them to know what would happen to me at a religious high school. I mean, how could they? Children of God," he spat.

I bowed my head.

"Did I tell you what happened on my wedding night?"

He hadn't.

"I could barely touch Maria. For years, because of what

happened, I wondered about myself. Was I like him? Maria and I, we didn't have a normal courtship. She was a good Catholic and tolerant about my condition. We would kiss and neck, but it was work for me. I had to explain; I had to introduce her to my shrink! And then, when it was time, when we were married, on my wedding night... Well, I couldn't. He took that from me, the son of a bitch. And the church hid him and so many others!"

"Danny..."

He turned angrily toward me. I worried that he equated me with those who had wounded him. But instead, he sat back into his chair and finished the rest of his whiskey, the ice cube long gone.

"So you have a list." He looked into the empty glass. "Well, reporting this to the press won't do much good. They'll just deny it. We need to make this bigger. We need to send a message. No longer can we allow children to be hurt. If we make the message big enough. If we make it clear enough. We can change everything."

Daniel O'Malley stood and walked around the small hundred-year-old wooden table toward me. "You would do this with me, wouldn't you?"

I didn't know what my friend was asking, exactly. But I agreed with him. Something had to be done. I nodded. I was in.

VIGILANTE PRIEST I
Not The Beginning I Wanted

FATHER TONY

I remember the first time I saw total, absolute terror in a man's eyes. The fear that he was going to die. It was at a family wedding. It wasn't where I would have expected to see such a thing.

At the wedding, Salvatore made a toast. He praised his daughter and the groom; he talked about love and honor. And then he talked about friendship, trust, and decency. "Everyone here is family to me," he said. "Except for one guest."

Then he paused. He always commanded attention, but now even the waiters filling water glasses froze in place. "Can you imagine that on this very special day, the biggest day of her life, someone here, a friend of ours, burdened Anna Maria with a tale of his own stupid debts. And then this snake bad-mouthed me to my own daughter, as if I were responsible for his drug habit, alimony, gambling problem, and stupid business deals. And he begged Anna Maria to ask me for mercy."

The whole thing seemed surreal. Salvatore stared at a man at the table next to mine, and everyone followed his gaze. I saw the man's eyes grow wide as he realized what was about to unfold. He was paralyzed. He knew he was a dead man.

As three men in dark suits approached the table, my cousin and table mate, Luca, grabbed my arm and said, "Father Tony, you don't want to be here for this."

But it was too late.

"No, no, no!" the man cried, as one of a trio pulled his seat away from the table.

Another blocked the guests' view and got very close to the man's face, demanding his silence, while the third dragged him from the table and quietly ushered him out through the back.

"My sincere apologies," Salvatore's wife said, raising a champagne flute. "To family!"

The image of the marked man has stayed with me.

Now I was like Salvatore. I was the bringer of death.

For the wages of sin is death, I thought, not wanting to finish the verse in my head.

Sandy Accardi, my nephew Angel and I watched Father Charlie make his way to a coffee shop. I had told him to meet me there. That we had things to discuss best addressed outside of the church. It wasn't technically a lie.

He left the church, and we followed in a white van. Two blocks from the coffee shop, he waited for the light to change. Sandy stopped the van in front of him, Angel pulled a black surgical mask over his face, hopped out, and greeted Father Charlie with a 9mm Glock. "You're coming with me," Angel said as he pointed into the open side door of the van. He then pushed the portly priest in.

"Why are you doing this?" Father Charlie looked confused.

No one responded, so Father Charlie spoke again: "I am a priest. Why would you do this?"

I sat up front. There was no way I was going to respond. Although my heart wanted to scream at him. "You should know exactly why we're doing this! You have brought this on yourself. The only shameful miracle is it's taken this long to erase the permanent shadow you have brought into this world."

But I couldn't say anything until it was over.

I had a hat and a mask on. We all did. It was the one upside to COVID; it provided a bit of cover for our daylight operation. But Father Charlie might recognize my voice. He knew I was an emissary of the Vatican, and it wasn't the time for him to put things together.

"This makes no sense," Father Charlie said. "I am penniless. I was on my way to meet a senior member of the Vatican. There will be a manhunt as soon as I am late."

"You are going to be very late," sneered Sandy. "Now shut the fuck up or we'll put a bullet in your head."

Father Charlie began to sob.

I thought about his many delusions. That he was safe. That he was protected. That he thought the meeting I'd arranged was aboveboard.

A truthful witness saves lives, but he who utters lies is treacherous.

Me not telling Father Charlie I was here was a lie by omission. It felt wrong.

"I—" I had to say something.

"You shut up, too! Not another fucking word," Sandy said.

"Hey, cool it," Angel said. "Show some respect."

"Sorry, Fa— sorry."

He was absolutely right. I looked back down in shame.

Once Cardinal Uelichar told me there was a list, more than five years ago, I should have acted immediately. Now, after much anguish and speaking with Daniel O'Malley, I was committed to the process.

I had been appointed one of three watchers over the troubled priests. I was given access to all the names in the United States. There was a dossier on each of them. Many in the Vatican regretted letting the sinners and their transgressions go unpunished but turning a blind eye had become a generational process. The process was meant to preserve the sanctity of the Church while also protecting the public. I was given access and trusted with this information, because regardless of what I said, I was believed to be one of them.

Decades ago, I accepted the judgment of the Vatican and stayed in Italy from that moment on. But I had never been at peace.

Nobody spoke until we got to the warehouse. We drove in, and Angel pulled Father Charlie out of the van and sat him on a chair in the middle of the floor. Sandy shoved a rag in his mouth and tied him up.

The architect was there when we arrived.

Once a strong, athletic man, a billionaire, triathlete, he was now frail. But his fury animated him.

"Do you know who I am?" he seethed at Father Charlie.

The priest made a muffled sound, and Sandy pulled the rag out of the prisoner's mouth.

"Daniel O'Malley?" Father Charlie was stunned. O'Malley had given so much money to the Catholic Church, he seemed destined for sainthood. "There must be some mistake. Please, help me."

"We know your past," O'Malley said, sitting down on a chair provided by Sandy.

Let he who is without sin...

"My past?" Father Charlie questioned.

"Lie to me. I want you to lie to me." O'Malley's face turned sinister. He had a lot to be angry about. The cancer was destroying his body and his future, after a past he had fought so hard to recover from.

Father Charlie licked his lips. "Let me explain myself."

"Go on." O'Malley smiled. It was a wicked smile.

The one who conceals hatred has lying lips.

"It's just... It's just..." Father Charlie was defeated.

"Take him," O'Malley spat.

There is only one Lawgiver and Judge, the one who is able to save and destroy.

"Wait!" Father Charlie screamed, then mumbled, "I'm gay."

This infuriated Angel. "Gay! Who the fuck cares if you are gay? This isn't about being gay. This is about corrupting innocence. It's about fucking—"

"No. That's what I am saying. The ones that you are concerned about. They were also... gay."

"They were fourteen and sixteen!" O'Malley roared. I worried for the frail man's health.

"I know," Father Charlie mumbled. "But it's not like I corrupted them."

O'Malley almost whispered, "Then why did John Danvers kill himself at age seventeen?"

"What?" Father Charlie looked shocked. Was this the first time he'd heard about the damage he'd caused? It seemed impossible.

"Take him," O'Malley said. He shook his head and looked at me in commiseration, as if looking for approval.

"Dear God," I breathed out. I was horrified. I had wanted to get the names to the people in power to protect the innocent. Now I wondered who, exactly, was innocent. *Was I?*

CHAPTER ONE

Life 2.0

EDDIE

My half-brother, Paul, didn't want an honest answer to his question.

"It went better than expected," I responded.

Paul had booked the vaccination appointment. But both my brothers rarely visited our mumbling, fading father. And by default, I had become the old man's chaperone.

I drove him to the appointment in the back of my unmarked cop car. Technically, it was against department regulations. But my ancient beater was barely running, and necessity, as a fellow cop once told me, is the mother of corruption. As violations go, this wasn't going to get me in much trouble.

My dad stank of piss, cigarettes, and alcohol. He was seventy years old and hadn't been able to take care of himself, except to light up and pour drinks, for the last ten.

He avoided throwing up or soiling the car, and none of the three or four words he uttered were insults about my manhood or racial slurs, so the drive went better than expected. The appointment also went better than I imagined. The federal government had upped its game. We were done in thirty minutes.

"That's great, Eddie," Paul said. Paul wasn't a failure like me or a loser like our brother, Steve. He was just an inconsiderate prick. If I needed money, he'd send me money. If I asked for help with Dad, he'd half-ass something. He was a Wall Street sellout who had made enough money that he could leave the city and do his grift remotely from Maryland.

"Well, that's great, Eddie. I'm sure he appreciates it." I could hear Paul shuffling through some papers. He had better things to do. He didn't enjoy talking to his fuck-up of a brother, not to mention his dad, whom he affectionately called "he" as opposed to "dad" or "father." Paul wasn't going to waste any more time on me. "All right, then. I'll talk to you soon." With that, the line went dead.

I knew I could count on Mr. Busy. I only had five minutes to get to my meeting with Internal Affairs.

———

"You shot a kid."

Internal Affairs never started with batting practice. Edna James, a tall African-American woman in her mid-forties was a veteran slugger at IA. She didn't even offer a hello.

"I didn't shoot a kid. I shot in the direction of a kid." I had been down this road before.

"So, because you missed, does that make you a better cop?"

"I didn't miss. I shot directly where I wanted."

"Ballistics says you were no farther than four feet away from hitting him. Cutting it a bit close, if you were intentionally trying to miss him."

I thought I was done with this. They had taken my gold shield. For me, there was no bigger punishment. I had worked hard for that three-inch piece of metal. Receiving it, along with being made an anti-crime-unit detective was one of the happiest days of my life. I was one step closer to becoming a detective in Homicide.

But not anymore after the demotion came. Captain Broward reassigned me. I'd no longer be working active, in-the-thick-of-it cases, instead I would be in Missing Persons, supporting my old colleagues as a regular officer. At least I didn't have to wear a beat-cop uniform to work in Missing Persons. Captain Broward said in eighteen months we could try to get my gold shield back. Nobody said IA wasn't going to continue working on me, not even Bill, my union rep.

"You've already got me demoted! Do you want me out? Is that what you want? You really think I was trying to shoot some kid? You motherfuckers in your cozy offices are doing nothing to help the violence out there. Just finding new ways to jam us up, like videotaping us as if *we're* the fucking criminals. You doing that got me a fucking warning on some bullshit thing already. Why don't you use the cameras to stop scumbags selling fentanyl to seven-year-olds in the street? Cops like me are trying to keep some law and order in this city."

"Do you think all Black people are scumbags?" James was trying to goad me. It was working.

"No, and you know that's not what I am saying. I didn't bring up anything about race. You are trying to spin things because you hate cops. I'd appreciate a simple thank-you for patrolling the neighborhood so someone doesn't shiv you for the fifty dollars in your purse."

"Thank you." Her voice dripped with sarcasm. "Thank you so much, Mr. Rodriguez. You and your buddies wearing your Confederate T-shirts on the weekends are a blessing to all of us."

"You do realize I'm Latino, right? I'm not some hillbilly from Appalachia, and my T-shirts have rainbow flags, so get a clue with your stereotypes, bitch!"

Bill, my union advocate, jumped in. "Eddie didn't mean that, Ms. James. He's just angry because you are taking potshots at him."

She turned her full attention to my advocate. "Mr. Wagner, I wouldn't trust him separating recyclables at the dump. I am going to recommend removal from the force."

"Good luck with that," I seethed.

"Eddie, allow me to do my job and shut the fuck up," Bill snapped at me, then he turned to my nemesis. "Ms. James, these are not good times for police officers, and Eddie has been under a great deal of stress. He has shown remorse. He's already been demoted. He's not working violent crimes anymore. He's in Missing Persons. Just let him be, and he'll be fine."

"You going to be fine, Mr. Rodriguez?"

"Yes." The fire had subsided for now.

All three of us were screwed. The force had been depleted by about 30 percent in the city. I blamed the liberals and bogus politicians for shit like this. Edna James blamed systemic racism and toxic masculinity for breeding scumbags like me. Bill, well, he was stuck between both of us.

I wanted to be out on the street stopping crime, not picking up the pieces. That's what it felt like in Missing Persons in the 41st Precinct, Fort Apache. I'd heard stories about how the cops who worked this beat in the seventies used to carry machine guns. Crime was so out of hand, one member of the force would spray the street with bullets to announce his arrival. That was the story, anyway. Things had gotten tamer over the years, but there was still action to be had.

If you were young enough, pretty enough, rich enough, or connected enough, you would get one of the senior officers at Missing Persons. Everyone else was stuck with me. I got the cases in the 41st Precinct no one cared about. The lost causes. Most of my cases evolved from the same lead. The one that ended at the morgue. And then, if it looked like the misper—that's what we called them—landed in the freezer under suspicious circumstances, I had to pass it off to Homicide.

There were stacks of cases of people who managed to survive into their twenties while trying as hard as possible to kill themselves through drugs. Now and then, some civilian, who obviously ditched their spouse, would disappear. In my first month, only one case interested me: a missing priest in his seventies. I was surprised that this case fell to me and wasn't viewed as a higher priority, being connected to a local church.

The holy misper was named Father Charlie Rhodes. He was from St. Dominic's which was within walking distance from the precinct. He had vanished into thin air, and his fellow clergy hadn't been very helpful. As I understood it, he was the parochial pastor, not the head of the church but an elderly number two. His boss, the monsignor, seemed to be annoyed by Father Charlie, but I couldn't tell if it was personal or he was pissed off by the inconvenience of a staff member disappearing.

I was shown Father Charlie's basement studio in the rectory at the side of the church. It was neat and sparse. Everything seemed in order. I ran my eyes over the lone crucifix on the otherwise bare walls, the small, old-school tube TV with antenna, the half-filled bookcase with a stack of *People* magazines, and a decades-old photograph of a young man with a shag haircut. There wasn't much to put out of order.

I sighed. It was depressing. I figured God would want his staff to enjoy themselves at least a little. "Has he lived here long?"

"About five years."

"Any idea who he was meeting or where he was headed?"

"He told me he was going out for a walk. I assume on his own. He might have been meeting with one of our parishioners, but he would usually let me know. As an older priest, he mostly spends time in contemplation and helping out with the services. I checked with Constance the next day when he didn't return to see if he called in or if she had talked to him before he left, but he hadn't and she didn't."

"Constance?"

"She works in our office."

"Did he do that often?"

"No. I mean, he'd leave now and then to run errands, but he was always back in the parish by nighttime. I don't recall him ever not being here since he's arrived. When I realized he hadn't returned the following morning, that was when I called the police."

"Did he seem nervous or different in any way lately?"

"Not particularly. If I would have known something like this was going to happen, I would have been paying closer attention."

The list of parishioners he might have visited was slow in coming, as were any other church files on Father Charlie. While I waited, I caught an unsolicited call from another cop, Brian Vargas who worked the 17th Precinct in Manhattan. He had a missing priest case, too. Our cases had matched in the misper database. One of us would call the other every day or two just to check in since the cases were similar.

"Anything new?" I asked. I was getting ready to wrap up for the day.

"Nah. Typical shit. I feel like the priests are jerking me around. I go in there and I talk to a few of them and they answer some basic questions but never have anything specific. The monsignor doesn't seem to want them to talk to me. Maybe the missing priests were pervs, and they sent them off somewhere before any charges came."

"Maybe, but then why the hell alert us that they are missing?"

"Good question. No priors on your guy, right?" Brian asked.

"Nope. I'm stuck. You played the Catholic card, right?"

"Yeah, I wouldn't have passed any tests if they gave me one, though. One of the priests offered to pray with me, but in terms of going over the misper's past, forget it," Brian said.

"Yeah, I got a similar vibe, but I thought it was because they view me as a total lost cause."

"You never know. A young, gay cop? They might really want to save you. Or God knows what else." Brian laughed. Not at me, at them, I assumed.

I laughed, too. I had gotten in the habit years ago of letting people know early on that I was gay. It prevented me feeling duty bound to bring it up when someone called another officer a "fag" or something like that. "Anyway, let me know if you find anything."

"All right, Eddie. You also."

As I was getting ready to leave, John, one of the people I liked the most back when I was in Anti-Crime, stopped by, insisting I get a beer with him at Pauline's. Like the last five generations of cops before us, Pauline's was our watering hole of choice.

"Okay," I said. "I can use a drink or ten."

"One of the old guard, Sandy, is up from Florida."

"Oh yeah. I think I met him briefly once, a while back."

"Get ready for Fort Apache in the eighties' war stories."

John had always been nice to me ever since I joined Anti-Crime years ago. Initially, I thought he might be interested in me. Then one Friday I met him for a drink, and he was there with a girl. "Girl-friend?" I asked. "Yep, we've been dating for a couple years now." Not the response of someone who was still trying to figure things out. Regardless, I enjoyed hanging out with him. It was better than going home and feeling sorry for myself.

CHAPTER TWO

Pauline's

EDDIE

I hadn't been in Pauline's since the latest COVID surge hit. The bar was packed, but that didn't mean much, considering how small it was. There were about ten of us cops and ten or so locals, most of them women. Sandy was standing there, all six feet three inches of him, pointing to the moose head on the wall, and I knew the story without hearing it.

Once, at closing time, a cop named Ferreli was getting razzed as the worst shot in the precinct. Everyone joked about his eyesight, and when the bartender jokingly asked if he could see the exit sign, Ferreli said, "Fuck you. Keep an eye on your goddamned moose." He squeezed off six shots at the moose head hanging on the far wall.

"And only one of them hit the freaking thing!" Sandy boomed.

Sandy's real name was Sandro Accardi. I knew this because his name was on two different plaques in the station for acts of courage.

Young Officer Accardi had barely turned twenty-one when he joined the force in 1978. He was prideful and quick tempered, going by Sandro to his fellow officers and by Officer Accardi to everyone else.

So, unfortunately for Officer Accardi, the movie *Grease* came out the same year he joined. Shortly afterward, a few of his fellow officers started calling him Sandy after the female lead in the movie. There were a few fights in the precinct, some pushing and shoving, and everyone decided it wasn't worth the hassle to bust his chops.

A couple of weeks later, Officer Accardi went on a routine bust on some three-strike drug dealer and started reading him his rights. His partner, in an act of insanity yelled over, "Hey, Sandy. Don't forget to Mirandize him." Sandy had tackled him and was working on getting the cuffs on.

Needless to say, the perp thought this was hilarious. He started yapping and quoting the song from the movie, like he was John Travolta, "Yeah! San-dee, ba-bee, read me my-eye-eye rights." So then Officer Accardi starts reciting the rights, and the fucking perp said, "No, sing it to me, Sandy baby!" At that point, Officer Accardi whacked him across his face with his nightstick and broke his orbital bone.

When Precinct Captain "Whispering" Jim Carroll heard this, he went ballistic. People could hear him berating Sandy even before they entered the station. Breaking perps' faces might feel good, but it is not good for business. The captain was getting some uncomfortable questions, and the precinct was looking at a possible lawsuit. Luckily for Sandy, the perp got popped in another drug deal before he could sue the department and the City of New York. But as punishment, Captain Carroll made it mandatory for all fellow officers to call Officer Accardi Sandy from that point forward. Eventually Sandy got used to it.

"Hey, Pauline, get me a Dos Equis." The waitress's real name was Angelique, but everyone called the waitresses in this bar Pauline, in homage to the long-since-gone proprietor.

"Hey, Eddie. How goes it?" Angelique got well within the six-foot barrier that most people kept since COVID began years ago.

"It's good."

"Well, you look good, Poppi!"

She was pretty and definitely interested but not my cup of tea. I always liked feeling attractive to women even though I was gay. They graded on a different scale.

"So, get your shot yet?" she purred. She was talking about the latest COVID booster shot.

"No, not yet. I will get it soon," I lied, thinking my unboosted status would be a good deterrent.

"Well, I got mine, and I can tell you from experience—"

"Hey, Eddie," Sandy cut her off. "You mind coming over here and having a beer with me?"

"What are you drinking?" Sandy asked before I sat down.

"Dos Equis."

"Pfft," Sandy scoffed. "Two Budweisers."

As Pauline worked the tap, Sandy nodded at her and lowered his voice. "I got a son who's gay. He'd have the same thing happen to him all the time. In my day..." He shook his head. "Hey, it's a free world. All of us have the right to be miserable with whomever we damn well please."

"Well, thanks for that." He was already pissing me off, legend or not. I wondered why he was citing my sexual preferences. Or his son's.

"I heard you are dealing with some IA bullshit. We didn't even know what IA was when I started. It was like they all hatched out of some lizard eggs in the eighties. Different breed. We are out there serving and protecting, and they are finding clever ways to shit all over us. Am I right?"

Our drinks came, and I tapped my half-finished Dos Equis bottle against his mug. "You'll get no argument from me," I said.

"I hear you are in Missing Persons. What are you working on?" He took a big swig of Bud, forcing me to talk.

"Well, the usual. Frustrated housewives and meth heads, but I do have at least one case that is somewhat interesting."

"I always found frustrated housewives interesting," he said, flashing a predictable leer. "What's the interesting one for you?"

"A case involving a priest."

"A priest, really? What's interesting about it?"

"There is another priest missing in Manhattan."

"Hmph." He took a quick sip before adding, "How'd you hear about that?"

"Everything goes in a database nowadays, and the computer surfaces connections for us."

"Interesting. What does it sort by?"

"Well, professions. All kinds. Clergy are flagged, as are cops, Wall Street types. Any data point, really."

"Any links between the priests?"

"Nothing yet."

"I get cops, and I get the money, but what's the deal with priests?"

I wondered if Sandy was bullshitting me. "Come on, Sandy. There's always the shadow of pedophile shit on these guys. Even during your time, right?"

Sandy narrowed his eyes for a moment. "Yeah, that's true. That wasn't the focus for Fort Apache, though. We were too busy with the murders and the semiautomatic weapon fire in the streets."

This overly friendly q-and-a was bothering me. "No disrespect, Sandy, why all the interest in Missing Persons, especially the cases I'm involved in? I mean, most people are more interested in the missing kids more than anything else. Not to mention, you got John from Anti-Crime here who has some crazy stories. Why you wasting your time with me?"

Sandy sat there staring at me.

I had dug a hole. I kept digging. "I mean, don't get me wrong. I appreciate you buying me a beer and talking with me. Everyone talks about you, and I'm sure there's a lot that I can learn. It's just that..."

"I'm not just here checking out the sights. I'm here checking on my friend."

I stared back at him blankly, not sure if he was going to punch me or just walk off. Neither would have surprised me, based on his reputation.

"Your friend?"

"Yeah, O'Malley. Daniel O'Malley."

That got my attention. Daniel O'Malley was an investment guru turned heart-of -gold philanthropist. But he'd been in the headlines most recently because he had been missing for the last three weeks.

"Daniel O'Malley," I repeated, trying to process why the prick sitting next to me had brought this up.

"Yeah, we went to high school together."

"I had no idea. You realize he's not one of my cases. He's being handled by the feds, I believe." I couldn't believe I just said that.

"No shit."

"So I take it you're worried about your buddy and came back to the old precinct, thinking about him. That got you thinking of talking to me in Missing Persons?" I was the only one in my division here.

"Something like that." I could tell he was calculating before he continued. "Now, I'm concerned about the missing priest. I'm Catholic, and I take it he is from St. Dominic's?" He had a fifty-fifty shot on that one, being that there were two Catholic churches in our jurisdiction.

"Yeah, that's right. St. Dominic's."

"And now you are saying, there is another priest missing." He paused for a second. "Well, let me know if you get stuck. I might be able to help. I know some people in the community who might be willing to talk." With that, he handed me a business card with his name and below it, "Retired Detective." "That's my cell number. Call me if I can help in any way or if you find out anything."

CHAPTER THREE
Always Starts With A Smile

E**DDIE**

Next morning, the precinct was tense. IA was harassing Harris at his desk, letting him know that he was under formal investigation. Turned out he shot someone. Harris worked with John and me back when I was in Anti-Crime. He was a decent guy, and from what I had seen, a straight arrow.

"Morning, Captain." I tried to sound upbeat, not sure what type of mindfuck he was going to lay on me this morning.

"Morning, Officer Rodriguez." He parroted me, swirling his coffee, staring and trying to read me. It stung to no longer be called detective.

I needed to change the focus. "What's up with Harris, Captain? Is my pal Edna James bothering him now?"

Captain Broward gave out a loud sigh. He used to teach at NYU before getting into law enforcement. Instead of remaining a professor, he decided to change the world. At forty-five, with seven years on the force, he made captain. His fast rise pissed off a lot of people and led to lots of whispers about friends in high places.

The captain looked down and fiddled with his papers before turning his attention back to me. "He should be okay. It looks like it was gang related. Someone took a pop at him and he responded."

After the bullshit I had been through, I had to watch what I said, so I went with, "Now and then, things escalate. That's unfortunately part of the job."

"That may be so, but people want us to stop shootings, not be part of them." Captain Broward sighed. I figured that was partly about the raft of paperwork and partly the bullshit coming down the pike for him. "You know. We are here to protect and serve. Violence is never the answer."

I thought but didn't say, *Violence is* never *the answer. Then why the hell do we carry these shooty things and nightsticks? Are we supposed to hug perps to death, or would that be violence since we were invading their personal space?* Even so, the perceptive captain could tell what I was thinking.

"You know what I mean, Eddie." He was regretting what he said but didn't want to take it back. "It's a new world, whether we like it or not. We've been cracking heads in the city for hundreds of years and nothing ever changes. We need to try something different. People don't want to be bad. Some of it is their environment."

He looked at me again, reading me, and seeing I was unmoved.

"Just keep your shit together out there. I'm not the enemy. I would do anything for any of you, including Harris and you."

I decided to take him at his word. "Okay, Captain. Listen, I get it. Thanks. So what can I do to help?"

"Well, two more priests have been snagged."

"Shit," I breathed. I was shocked at the fact that it might be a serial but also shocked that he was telling me directly instead of through my lieutenant. I would get my answer with his response.

"They aren't local. One is Tennessee and one is Florida. Long story short, the feds aren't messing around, and they want to quar-terback this. You follow?" He looked at me with an arched eyebrow. It took me a second to realize why. He wanted to be sure I got the quarterback analogy.

I laughed. "I'm gay, Captain. But I understand football clichés as well as the next straight guy. Not all of us sit around all day listening to disco and going to musicals."

"Right, of course." He was red-faced. "Anyway, the FBI is running this. Agent Murray is coordinating the case. She wants a call from you A-S-A-P. Hopefully, if it is a serial, we can help by putting together any specifics we have so far."

"Okay, I'm on it. Give me a name and number, and I'll get her a write-up."

"You know what, Eddie? Why don't you just give me every-thing you have directly? Call her. Find out what she wants. And then tell her I'll check in with her later. That way we can be doubly sure we give them what they want."

I wasn't sure if he didn't trust me or he wanted to get tight with the Bureau. But either way, it was no big deal. I needed him on my side if I was ever going to get out of Missing Persons.

"Sure thing, Cap."

After generations of shitty police coffee, we finally had a Nespresso machine in the precinct. It took a grieving mother to get it. We found her daughter's body two blocks from a meth lab that cut in fentanyl. This was a surprise in the Bronx. We had more than our share of users, but usually the labs were found Upstate. They were too hard to conceal in the city with the distinct smell they made.

Anyway, the mother, Mrs. Gennero, who had been stopping by daily to check on whether we found anything on her daughter, had heard a few of the officers complaining about the coffee. Amazingly, she bought the precinct a pair of machines, not to mention two hundred pods *after* we found her overdosed daughter. It was a great gesture, although we all joked that it felt like we were rewarded for not doing our job. We chipped in and sent Mrs. Gennero a huge order of flowers.

I sat in my cubicle admiring the foam on top of my coffee for a moment before looking down at the number the captain had given me. I had written up everything this morning. Now, three hours later, the FBI's Agent Murray wanted to chat. I dialed.

"Murray." Not even a ring and she had answered.

"Oh, hey. Sorry about that. I thought I'd have a moment to sip—"

"Rodriguez or Vargas?" Her voice was monotone.

"What?"

"Rodriguez or Vargas?" she repeated.

"What? Wait. What makes you think that I am either—"

"I have five active cases, not all of them are based in New York. I can tell you are calling from a New York area code, and you have a voice I don't recognize. Are you saying that you are not Rodriguez or Vargas?"

"What? No."

"Then are you Rodriguez or Vargas?" I sensed a hint of annoyance. This was about one thousandth of how annoyed I was.

"Rodriguez. But, hey, listen. I know you are the feds, but there is a way we can do this pro—"

"So, Officer Rodriguez, can you tell me what you have so far?"

"Agent Murray, I am a professional as are you. Can't we be professional and help each other for Chrissake?"

"Officer Rodriguez, I apologize if I come across as curt. Like I said, I am running five separate investigations. All of them have a clock connected to them. Yours and Vargas's priests are most likely dead. We are forty-eight hours in on the two other priests—"

"I get that. I only want—"

42

"Let me finish, please. As you are aware, the first seventy-two hours are vital. It is extraordinarily likely that this call is going to be a waste of time, but if you can get through my questions, we will have a better chance of saving one or two lives. I hope that is important to you."

"Fine." Bitch or not, she had a point.

"Your captain sent over the notes and current photos of the priest, you shared with him. I hear that the church wasn't much help. The photos of the priest have been cataloged and it has been noted that there are no scars or other distinguishing marks on him. You reported the last place he was spotted was at the church. As for friends of the priest, you just stated that 'He's a priest.' Is this a joke?"

"No, it's not a joke. That was a literal quote from the monsignor when I asked the question."

"Do you really think that priests don't have friends? He must have friends in the community, maybe a deli he visited often, maybe a widow that he is consoling. Maybe someone else he is consoling who is not a widow. You know that some priests have had affairs with married women, right?"

"I got it. But if the local priests and monsignor won't help, it is kind of tough to get a full picture—"

"Do your job."

What the fuck was I supposed to say to that?

She went on: "With the family, it looks like you contacted the priest's mother and sister but, and I quote, 'There was nothing that came from these conversations.' Is that the best you can do?"

I had enough. "Listen, yes, that's the best I can do. I don't need to be browbeat by you. I get here at seven thirty every morning to work for a city that thinks I'm a piece of shit. You try talking to these priests who're obviously telling me as little as possible or to a worried mother and sister."

The line was silent.

"Hello?"

Finally, she said, "Are you finished?"

Fuck you! "Yes, I'm finished."

"I've seen two of my partners die. I have been called a traitor for the simple fact that I'm in law enforcement." She paused. "We don't do this job for the accolades or 'atta boys.' If you want to be adored, be a teacher, a coach, or a civil rights activist. We do this because we want to make a difference. We do this for the families that are hurting. We are held to the highest standards because we can take a life or save a life on any day.

"If you need a merit badge or constant positive reinforcement, you chose the wrong profession, Officer Rodriguez. Move aside. If you want to live a life that matters with the ability to truly change the world for the better, then stand beside me and we will do that. Regardless, I don't have time for pep talks. I understand, as I am damned sure most of your fellow officers understand, there is no room for coddling in what we do. You can still be a good man but go elsewhere."

The silence built as she waited for my response.

"Okay, Agent Murray. You win. I will make another pass at the priests and the family."

With that, she hung up the phone. I hadn't even gotten her first name.

CHAPTER FOUR
Vaya Con Dios

EDDIE

I promised myself I was not going to leave the church until at least an hour went by. Agent Murray wanted me to think I was a shitty cop, that I didn't care. But I did care. Once again, I had rolled snake eyes with the priests and Constance, and now I was being escorted into the monsignor's office.

"We miss Charlie terribly, Detective Rodriguez. You must know this," the monsignor said, repeating a favorite refrain. He also consistently called me detective, even though I corrected him.

I looked down at my watch. Only ten minutes left until I could check this box off with a clear conscience.

The monsignor indicated that Father Charlie was a bit of a shut-in, a recluse. I had already checked his room again. It was meticulous, almost too clean and precise.

"So the last time you saw him was around four p.m.?"

The monsignor nodded.

"And he never seemed particularly stressed or elsewise occupied around the time he disappeared?"

"Like I said, nothing out of the ordinary. Now and then, he would argue with other priests about certain ecumenical issues, or like all of us, he wouldn't have a particularly good day."

I looked at my watch again. Ugh. Still eight minutes. It was like time had stopped.

I decided to push on this. "Which priest would you say he would have had an ecumenical argument with in the last two weeks?" I wasn't completely sure what ecumenical meant, but it had to mean something regarding Catholicism or the Bible.

The monsignor seemed hesitant. "I hope you are not thinking that an argument about the Council of Trent would cause one of our priests to vanish."

With multiple priests missing, probably not. But the monsignor didn't know about those other missing priests. "No, it's just that if there was something on his mind, or there was a tense discussion, I need to know about it. Maybe he decided to conduct his own research about the topic of disagreement."

"Without telling me? Doubtful."

"I'd like to talk to this priest that he had this argument with. We cast a wide net in cases like these. I'm sure you understand." I felt like this would be a decent enough olive branch and would give the monsignor the incentive to let me do my job. Not to mention, I would be way beyond the hour I promised to myself.

The monsignor sighed. "Unfortunately, the last person he had an argument with is not here."

"When is he coming back?"

"I don't think he is coming back any time soon." The monsignor stared down at his large mahogany desk, almost like a child who knew he had been caught in a lie.

"So was the argument serious enough that the priest left the church?"

"It was not one of my priests." He looked like he was going to continue but then stopped and looked down again.

What was with this guy? Is he fucking with me?

"Monsignor, you have to help with what I am missing. You said Father Charlie rarely left the church except for basic errands, and he got into an ecumenical argument with one of your priests. So are you telling me now that the priest he had the argument with left, and he is no longer considered one of your priests? Are you trying to get me on semantics? Is there something I'm missing?"

"When did I ever say he was one of *my* priests? He had an... I don't like to use the word argument. Let's call it a difference of views. He had a difference of views with Father Anthony, a priest visiting New York from the Vatican."

I stared at my notes. That was better than sneering at the monsignor. His priest disappeared, and all he cared about was protecting senior management. I kept my cool.

"Where can I find Father Anthony?"

The monsignor arched his eyebrow. "Let me find out where he is, and I will get you a number for him and his email. Would that suffice?"

"Sure. Thank you for your time." I got up to leave the monsignor's office.

Before I got to the door, he blurted, "I am sure that he will allay any fears that you might have regarding this. Hopefully, it will renew your faith. May God be with you."

After my third voice message to Father Anthony, he finally texted me, asking if we could set a time for us to have a call due to his schedule. I told him I'd rather meet in person but would settle for a call in the very near future. I was investigating a serious matter. Time was of the essence. He agreed to talk at 6:00 p.m. Technically,

I was off the clock at six, but I remembered my scornful pal at the FBI and sucked it up.

"I really didn't know Father Charlie all that well." Father Anthony talked with a heavy Italian accent.

"Really? The monsignor said you asked to meet with him."

"A friend of a friend recommended I look him up."

"Who was that?"

"Someone in the Holy See offices. My visit is part of a large operation involving a cross section of the church."

"I see," I said, even though I didn't. "According to witnesses at St. Dominic's, there was a bit of a heated discussion between you and Father Charlie."

I had to watch what I said here. If it was anything, I didn't want to tip my hand.

"The monsignor said this?"

"I'm not at liberty to say."

"A spat with Father Charlie, let me see..."

He was using a talk-to-yourself voice, so I could imagine him thinking hard. I decided to give him a hint. "Someone thought it might have been an ecumenical argument."

I had written the word down and looked it up. It meant promoting unity between Christian religions. Since both men were Catholic, it seemed like a strange thing to argue about.

"Ecumenical?" Father Anthony said. "Oh! I remember now."

Father Anthony cleared his throat. "Well, first I would not call this an ecumenical argument. I mean, disagreements like this happen all the time in the secular world. If anything, it is more epistemological." He stopped talking.

"Epistemological," I repeated. Another word to Google. "Uh-huh."

"Well, it had to do with ordination and the imprint. This is all very deep-in-the-weeds-type things." *I could swear his accent was leaving him.*

"That's fine, Father. Please continue. An imprint?"

"Yes, right. So it is believed that certain steps we take in our Catholic journey leave us with indelible marks or imprints on our soul." He cleared his throat again. "Whereas this is commonly agreed upon, there are differences regarding its importance and whether or not this grants us, as priests, a certain status in God's eyes. I'm sure this type of thing seems quite silly to you."

"What do you believe?"

"Well, I believe it does not."

"And Father Charlie?" I prompted.

"And Father Charlie believed it does."

"You just said 'believed,' not Father Charlie believes. Do you think he is dead?"

The line was silent for a few seconds. "Well, of course. Why else would he not have checked in with the church after all this time? I think we all have to fear the worst. Don't we?"

I paused before answering. I wondered if there was some reason Father Charlie needed God to regard priests as special. "I prefer to remain hopeful. Sometimes we find people in hospitals, or they just go off the grid and come back. Other than your argument—"

"I would call it a spirited discussion."

"Other than your 'spirited discussion,' did Father Charlie seem upset? Did he mention going anywhere?"

"No. Nothing like that. It was mostly just about his work and his views. The Holy See is trying to be more inclusive in our outreach, not just to the parishioners but those who serve them."

"Thank you for your time, Father. I may need to reach you in the future."

"May God be with you." Father Anthony hung up the phone.

CHAPTER FIVE
Sticks and Stones

EDDIE

On my walk back from St. Dominic's to the precinct, I stopped off at *CVS*. I needed to refill my meds. Running out of my antidepressant sucked; I got instant headaches. It was only a couple blocks off course. It had been a long time since I had thought about church. It was my mother's parents who got my family to go most Sundays. After my mom got shot, her parents drifted away. As for my dad, he needed a bottle more than he needed God.

I remember wanting to be part of the 44th Precinct, where my mother had been killed, so badly. I had wanted to be where it all happened. Where my life began to disintegrate. I was beyond disappointed when I was assigned to the 41st, Fort Apache. Thinking about it now, I was glad to be on the other side of the Bronx.

Per NYPD policy, we had been asked to wear our masks even when outside until further notice. It didn't matter if we were up to date with our vaccinations or not. We were sending a message to the community. Message or not, it was uncomfortable in the summer, and I ditched the mask. I decided to make good use of my walk, while trying to distract myself from the heat and my thoughts.

I popped in my headphones and decided to call Vargas, my counterpart in Manhattan, handling the missing priest case.

"Hey, Brian. How's it going?"

"Not bad, Eddie. What's new?"

"I got something, but it's pretty thin."

"If thin is all we got, Eddie, I'll take it. I might have something small for you also."

"All right, so you might want to ask around your church about a Father Anthony. He's visiting from the Vatican and doing the rounds at various churches. It sounds like he and my missing priest got into some sort of biblical scuffle a day or two before my guy went missing."

"Shit! The Vatican guy punched your priest?"

"No, not that kind of scuffle. A hurt-them-with-your-words scuffle versus hurt them with your fists."

"Oh. Ha!" I could hear him breathing heavy on the other line. Not sure if he just got back from running or if he was out of shape.

"Like I said, it's thin. But if Anthony met your guy, then we have an angle. You said you might have something for me?"

Vargas laughed. "Well, sort of. I take it you talked to that Agent Murray already, right?"

"Yep. She's hard to forget."

"She strolled into my precinct with her partner."

"Her partner?"

"A guy named Cooper. Hold on." I heard a door shut, and he said, "Sorry. It's noisy out there."

"Do you have an office?"

"Yeah. I share it with two other guys."

"Nice. I'm in a cubicle like I'm a fucking telemarketer."

"Ah, that sucks. I'm sorry. But listen, she's something to behold, Agent Murray. Tall, dark, and good looking. But what a ballbuster.

The two of them come into the office dressed like they should be in a *Men in Black* sequel, and she immediately is on me. 'Did you ask this?' and 'Why did you do that?'"

"Yeah, I got the same treatment," I said.

"I gotta tell you; I almost didn't mind. That's how, um, equipped she is. Wait until you see her, a real Jackie Brown look-alike. I bet you think the same. Or, I mean, if..."

"Yeah, I know. If I was straight. Did they share any insight?"

"They are pushing the perv angle. Four of the five priests have been moved from different parishes in the past, including yours. The one in Tennessee was the only exception."

"Five? When I talked to her yesterday, she said four. I'm sure she will be reaching out to me shortly to keep me up to date on the case," I added sarcastically, unsure if it came through.

"Yeah, I'm sure she will."

The sarcasm hadn't come through.

"Did she ask you to look for anything special?" Maybe I could stay ahead of her.

"No. She basically just told me to do a less-shitty job in the future."

I was getting ready to hang up when I remembered something he had said earlier. "Oh, what about the other one? What did you say his name was... Cooper?"

"Oh yeah, him. He was a treat. He looked like some dopey white guy who was more distracted with what was in the conference room we were in than what I was saying. But every now and then... 'Did you dust his car for prints?' or 'What size shoe does he wear?' It was like he was autistic or maybe just fucking creepy. Anyway, I got to run. See ya."

"Hey, Brian, don't forget to ask about Father Anthony."

"Oh yeah, I got it. Thanks, Eddie. Take care."

I got my meds and put my mask back on two blocks from the precinct. Hustling up the steps, I nearly bumped into the captain, his face maskless.

"Don't forget your mask, sir." I loved getting my superiors on this shit.

"Oh crap. Thanks, Eddie." He grabbed his mask out of his pocket. "Any update on your priest?"

"I found something today, but it is pretty thin."

"Whatever we can do to help with the case." Sometimes his sappy Dudley Do-Right talk made me nauseous.

"There's this priest from the Vatican who is checking in on some of the New York churches."

"Okay… and...?"

"It looks like he might have had an altercation with our missing Bronx priest."

"A fistfight?" The captain's eyes got wide.

This again? Shit. "No, not like a slugfest. They basically had a verbal argument."

The captain nodded and walked past me. "Well, it's something. Good work, Eddie. Don't forget to tell Agent Murray. I hear she gets really pissed if she is not kept in the loop."

I decided I'd leave a message for her before walking into the precinct.

Her phone rang once. "Rodriguez?"

It took me a second to realize what she was doing and that this stood as a proper greeting on her planet.

"Yes, it is I," I replied, trying to counter her brusque manner.

There was a pause.

"You called *me*, Rodriguez." Murray already sounded impatient.

"It looks like our missing Bronx priest had a run-in with a priest visiting from out of town."

"Go on."

"So this priest is from the Vatican, a Father Anthony, and he is visiting some of the New York churches. He had a run-in with our missing priest before he left the Bronx church." It took me a second to realize I basically just repeated myself. *Damn, she made me nervous.*

"Verbal or physical?" She didn't miss a beat.

"Verbal. Anyway, I thought you should know."

"Okay. Thank—"

"I let Vargas in Manhattan know also. So he will check to see if Anthony visited his priest or his church." I couldn't help myself. I was like a proud son showing a good report card to my parents.

"Please refrain from doing that in the future." She was her normal monotone.

"Doing what?"

"I don't think you and Vargas should be discussing your case threads. I would like you and him to discuss them with me. This way there would be no chance for the two of you discussing something material, or even worse, something that you don't realize is material, without me being looped in."

"Are you saying you don't want me to talk to Vargas?"

"Yes," she said flatly.

Well, fuck that. "Okay, then. Well, I hope the Anthony lead helps. I'll call soon."

"We're not done yet. I have some questions. Did you personally talk with Father Anthony?"

What a bitch. "Yes."

"Do you know when Father Anthony arrived in New York?"

"No."

"Do you know what other parishes he visited so far?"

"No."

"Do you know when he is planning on going back to Italy?"

"No."

"Did you let him know that you wanted him to check in with you if he was planning on leaving the city?"

"No."

"Can you give me his contact information?"

"I will email it to you as soon as I get into the office."

With that, she hung up the phone.

VIGILANTE PRIEST II
Pride

FATHER TONY

The first call from the local cop, Rodriguez, I was prepared for. When I heard the voicemail from an Agent Murray, I was shocked. How had the FBI gotten involved so quickly?

I called Accardi once I digested the message. I was supposed to call her as soon as possible.

"Shit!" he said. Then he said, "Sorry, Father."

"I confess I was thinking along similar terms."

"I know this looks bad. But we are still on track. So let's keep our cool."

"What do you mean, 'on track'?" I recounted her voicemail to Accardi, stressing that Agent Murray was very aggressive and should not be taken lightly. We went through the game plan with our contacts, and I prepared myself for any contingency.

Accardi told me that O'Malley had things under control. The FBI and police were just doing their jobs. But O'Malley had friends in high places. Friends who could stall or redirect investigations.

I didn't find this particularly comforting. O'Malley was engaging in abuse of power. Ironically, our operation was tied to punishing abuses of power. I wondered, as I had so many times over the last few weeks, if this was truly the Lord's work. *He who is a hired hand, and not a shepherd, who does not own the sheep, sees the wolf coming and leaves the sheep and flees, and the wolf snatches them and scatters them.*

"I still have to deal with Agent Murray."

"Tell her you can't discuss Vatican business," Accardi said. "Shut her down, Father."

I called Agent Murray back after her fourth message in two days. I imagined the call was routine since I was a variable in this situation. I just needed to remain calm. I could say I was busy, but I didn't want to raise any suspicion.

The phone was answered on the first ring. "Murray."

"Agent Murray, I am glad I reached you. This is Father Anthony. How can I be of assistance?" I used my Italian accent, but I needed to remember not to slip.

"Thank you for returning my call, Father Anthony." Agent Murray waited for me to say something, but since there was no question, I waited. She then followed with two questions. Actually, the same question twice. "However, why the delay? Where have you been for the last forty-eight hours?"

"The church keeps me very busy. I am only in New York for a limited time. I—"

"How limited, and you did not answer my original questions?"

She was very rude. I could use this. "Agent Murray, I am not sure what you believe you know, but if you know something specific—"

"I do not believe anything. I am trying to do my job and find your priests. I asked you to come see me at the FBI in person, but instead you called. I would be happy to come to you. I'm very concerned: two priests have gone missing shortly after you spoke with them. Naturally, I'm worried that someone may be following you."

She did not know about the others. That was a small relief. What wasn't a relief was that Murray was the opposite of Rodriguez. All business. She could do the higher math of investigation a lot faster than Rodriguez. I had to watch every word.

She wanted to know everything: where I was staying, who I was visiting, what my mission was. I put her off as best I could. I was on assignment from the Holy See; I couldn't possibly discuss Vatican business. Surely she understood. As for my itinerary, I promised to send her the details when I had the time. She continued to push.

"So when can I see you? And once again, where have you been these last two days."

"I was on a retreat."

"Where? With who?"

"I'm not at liberty to say."

"Father Anthony, before we go any further, I need to advise you that lying to a federal agent is a crime punishable by up to five years in prison."

"Are you accusing me of lying?" I said, feigning shock and outrage.

It was the only moment that gave her pause. But she recovered quickly. "I'm just making sure you are aware of American laws."

"Thank you for the lesson. I must go. I have another appointment."

She jumped on this. "Okay, let's schedule another one. What time can you arrive here? I can be here as late as you like. Give me an address, and I can pick you up personally."

"Sounds good, Agent Murray. Let me check with my superiors and see what they can do about adjusting my schedule. I can call you back in twenty-four hours to set something up. Would that work for you?"

"No," Agent Murray responded coldly. "The first seventy-two

hours are critical. We are already beyond that for these two missing priests. We need to check on all the other priests and individuals that you have met with since you arrived in New York."

She was good, dogged, but so was I. "All of the people? Agent Murray, there are many. So many that I—"

"Give me one," Agent Murray interrupted yet again.

I couldn't overthink this. "Monsignor Angelos," I blurted, knowing that she would already have this name.

Agent Murray scoffed at this. "Okay, that wasn't hard. Keep going."

"Keep going with what, Agent Murray?" I let out some genuine annoyance.

"The names. Keep going. Who else?" she coaxed me.

I had to end the call here. "I am sorry, Agent Murray. I have tried to be cooperative and responsive. Both of us care—"

"No, you haven't."

"Agent Murray, I will do all I can in my power to help you and more importantly, my missing priests. However—"

"Then you should—" Agent Murray tried to interrupt again, but this time I kept going. "However, I am on a tight schedule, and thanks to you, now I'm worried about myself and the other priests that I have met. I need to discuss things with the archdiocese about what I can do to ensure their safety."

"You could—" Agent Murray tried again.

"I promise I will give you a call as soon as I can find anything pertinent to your investigation. Good day."

"You—" Agent Murray was beginning as I hung up the phone.

She immediately called back. I turned the ringer off and pondered my next move. This was taking a toll on me. *A truthful witness saves lives, but one who breathes out lies is deceitful.*

We met in a row home in Douglaston Queens. One of O'Malley's "friends," most likely connected, had rented it. It was a lot nicer than the warehouse where we had taken Father Charlie and the other two priests.

Has Father Mahoney recovered?" I asked.

When Father Mahoney was forced into the black van at the north end of Manhattan, the sight of Angel's gun did not have the intended effect. The priest started screaming, and Angel clocked him with a hard blow to the back of his head. It knocked him unconscious, and I saw a line of blood leak out of his right ear. After that, Sandy dropped me off at the subway and instructed me to return to my hotel.

Mahoney was the last of the three priests targeted in New York City. We had gotten the one in the Bronx without much of a problem. The retiree in Queens, who'd had multiple incidents and been removed from the public, but was still getting a pension, came along without incident also. And then there was Father Mahoney, who changed parishes with such alarming frequency, I wondered if he was a charming conman or had the goods on someone higher up in the church. I wanted to find the answer.

Accardi and Angel were still getting settled. They had been making it a habit to drink every time we got together. Accardi sat down first on the couch leaving a space for Angel, next to him. It was the kind of code that can only come from working in life-and-death situations for decades.

Angel had one Budweiser open and the remaining four in tow in his right hand, hanging from the plastic.

"What's going on?" I asked. "A blind man could see something has happened." *Be sober-minded; be watchful. Your adversary, the devil, prowls around like a roaring lion, seeking someone to devour.*

Angel frowned and nodded. He turned toward Accardi. "He's going to find out sooner or later."

"Find out what?" I felt sick. *For the wages of sin is death.*

61

"I hit him too hard," Angel said. "With the Glock."

"In the wrong fucking spot," Sandy said.

"A one-in-a-million accident," Angel added.

I was confused. "What are you saying?"

"I'm saying Mahoney's dead," he snarled. "I hit him, and he never came to."

"Oh no."

"Oh no? Really, Father?"

"What did you expect to happen? I mean did you expect this all to go smoothly? Unless, you have something else on your mind." I could see Angel's hands shaking as he put his beer down. "Are you telling me you are questioning the list? Is that what you're saying?" Angel slowed to force me to respond.

"No," I said flatly. "I was just thinking about his last rites, and that it was a sudden, painful end."

"Last rites? Are you kidding me, Father? You realize what we are doing here."

"It is a reflex. Part of my job."

"And what happened in the van is now part of your job. At least, this job."

"That is not a reflex," I said. "Stopping these men, that is natural. But the precise method of stopping them... Let's just say it is not part of my training."

Angel continued, "That's right. No. I mean, the Church doesn't put that much time and effort into putting a list together unless they are sure. Right?" He paused, waiting for me to respond, but this time I didn't.

He slowed for a second before speeding back up to make his point. "This doesn't end for any of them except this way. I mean, I mean there's a good chance this is the way it ends for all of us. Have you thought of that?"

I let him continue. "Jesus. I don't mean to use His name in vain. I'm just trying to say... I'm trying to say that is the whole point of this… we… us… you know, and the others. We are trying to make things right. We can't let things continue the way they've been, right?"

Accardi looked over at me and I looked back at him and we both looked down. Accardi took a slug of his beer and made a face. He put the can down on the table next to Angel's. I got the feeling it had soured for him.

Before leaving, Accardi gave me a fresh burner cell phone. I had ditched my old one outside my hotel after checking out.

Angel told us that he would take care of Father Mahoney's body. He tried to play it off as a tough guy, that he "had it handled." My Angel, my nephew, was not a tough guy. My Angel was a sweet, young boy who became a conflicted man. This would be the fourth person who had been killed by his hands, and all but one had been by accident. My Angel wasn't a killer. He was one of God's children. A child struggling to do the right thing.

I had brought my bags to the row home. I would be here until tomorrow when I would be picked up by a blue car. I would never be in New York again. I would never be able to go back to the Vatican again. I would never be a priest again, at least in a formal sense. I knew months ago when I took that initial phone call that everything was about to change for me. But that was all theoretical. Today was the day everything became real.

CHAPTER SIX
Lies and Omissions

EDDIE

Captain Broward leaned into my cubicle. "Hey, Eddie, you mind heading to the break room with me? It is looking pretty thin for Detective Juarez."

It was already four thirty, and my shift ended at four, but I wasn't going to miss my fellow Latino's send-off. He was being forced to retire. Like it or not, at age sixty-three in New York City, you needed to go somewhere else to be a cop. Miguel Juarez had gotten divorced years ago, and as far as I knew, the job was the only thing he had. I wondered if I'd be in the same boat in thirty years and thought, just shoot me.

"Yeah, sure thing, Captain. Let me just log out."

There were only eight of us in the break room. On a Formica side table was a standard yellow cake that had the word "Congratulations" written on it. This was an unintentional irony. No one was less happy than Juarez about his retirement.

We took turns paying tribute to Juarez and razzing him about retirement. This was required protocol before someone handed him a knife to cut the cake.

"Miguel," his partner for the last three years, Mark McCoy, said, "I know you are worried about a gringo like me going into the hood without you. But I'm pretty lucky. Google Translate works great—and doesn't stiff me on lunch."

Everybody laughed. Then McCoy started being serious. He started yammering on about how much he'd learned from his partner. I thought Juarez might tear up. Fortunately, the TV in the corner was still on, so I looked up at the screen. A photo popped up of billionaire Daniel O'Malley in a tuxedo. I moved closer to listen. "The worst is feared regarding billionaire philanthropist Daniel O'Malley. His yacht, *Fortune's Folly*, vanished six weeks ago after leaving Perth, Australia, setting off an international search. Today the family issued a short statement to the 'many people whose lives Daniel O'Malley touched' that indicated the search is over, and the family believes its beloved patriarch was lost at sea."

The broadcast cut to a very good-looking woman standing in front of a mansion. "'We will all miss Daniel dearly. You only knew his public face, but privately he was many times the man that you have seen. He was an adoring father and uncle. We appreciate all that law enforcement is doing, but we know our Daniel. There is no way he would not have checked in with us if he was still alive. Thank you all for your loving messages and support for our family and his legacy. The family is asking for privacy at this time and will hold a private Mass at St. Patrick's Cathedral. Then a celebration of his life will be held at Rockefeller Center." I clicked off the TV, so the focus could be on Juarez at least for a few minutes.

It was my turn to say something. "Hey, Miguel, I'll miss you, buddy. I know I'm supposed to make a golf joke or something, but just know we all mean it when we say, 'Don't be a stranger.'" I felt like I was talking to someone who had a terminal illness.

"Thanks, Eddie. You keep doing your thing, my friend. You

have to keep us Latinos looking good." I thought he might be taking a shot at me getting demoted, but there was no humor in his response.

McCoy, Juarez's partner, returned to comedy. "You know, Juarez isn't going to have it easy retiring. I took him golfing, and everybody thought he was the fucking caddy."

Miguel laughed. Then he looked down at his polished police uniform shoes. He had shined them himself. They were like mirrors.

"But seriously," McCoy said, "my partner refused to talk about his plans. So I want to know: when are you moving to Vegas so I can come visit?"

Juarez exhaled. "I got no plans. Just gonna figure it out."

"Don't worry about it, Miguel. McCoy, myself, and the others will keep you busy. Just let us know what works and we can hang out, do whatever; just let me know?" The words sounded hollow coming out of my mouth.

"Nothing more depressing than an old retired cop hanging around the precinct still trying to mix it up. Nah. I'm not going to be one of those guys."

"Then what about Detective Accardi?" I said. "He was just here. Did you get to talk to him? I think he's retired in Florida, but there have to be tons of Fort Apache guys around."

He looked at me, and his face brightened slightly. "Yeah, Sandy is a good guy. He was a take-no-prisoners type, unlike his partner, Barney. What a fucking odd couple. *Dios mio.* Yeah, I think they both retired to Florida. I don't know if that place is for me." He shook his head.

I tried again. "Well, yeah, Miguel. You have that pension now. If I was you, I would take a trip down there and see some of those guys. Or treat yourself to Vegas. You gotta do something."

"Yeah, Eddie. I'll be fine. I'll think about Sandy. It's not a bad idea."

Then a light bulb went off in my head. "I'm pretty sure he will be here for that Daniel O'Malley event they just announced."

"Did they find him? I heard all they were getting were BS tips, trying to collect the reward money," the captain said.

"No, the family just announced they think he's dead," said Rosalie, a Latina beat cop.

"I heard O'Malley and Accardi were pretty close," I said, turning the attention back to Miguel.

That got a laugh out of Miguel. "Pretty close? Sandy used to own that guy; he used to ride him like a rented mule. I mean, at least that was what he said."

"What? Own O'Malley?"

"Once O'Malley hit it big in the early nineties doing something with foreign bonds, or some shit like that, that was all Sandy would talk about. How he basically bossed the guy around in high school. Sandy turned out to be a good guy later on, but he was a *pendejo* in his early days."

No reason to bring up what I had heard from Sandy. *Why would he lie about the two of them being friends?*

"Okay." I gave up. "It was just an idea."

"Thanks, Eddie. I'll figure it out. I really appreciate your kind words."

That was my cue. I didn't have any interest in the standard yellow sheet cake. I shook his hand and clapped him on the shoulder. "Stay in touch, amigo," I said and walked out of the break room.

My phone started ringing. An unknown number flashed on the screen. Just what I needed, some yahoo trying to sell me a car warranty or tell me I am due a Microsoft refund. A while back, I used to pick up and lead them on for a while. Then I thought, why mock some poor soul in Mumbai doing this shit seventeen hours a day for ten bucks a day? I felt my phone vibrate in my pocket. The mystery caller had left a voicemail.

I checked out my beat-up beige Tercel from the lot and got my Bluetooth set up for the five-mile drive to my condo overlooking the river. The voicemail was from Monsignor Angelos.

The Tercel had three hundred thousand miles on the odometer. I was keeping it more out of loyalty than not being able to afford another car. It was burning a lot of oil at this point but still started with little effort. I placed the return call to the monsignor, then put the car in drive.

"St. Dominic's," a nun or a receptionist answered.

"Good evening. This is Officer Rodriguez. Is Monsignor Angelos available?"

"I'll check. Hold, please."

Usually I was excited when I turned onto 161st Street. Crossing the Macombs Dam Bridge, which separated the Bronx on the east from Manhattan on the west, represented a break from my past. The Bronx side of the bridge was my youth-filled memories of my dad's restaurants and, of course, my mother. The Manhattan side—I was a Washington Heights resident now—represented a transition, aspiring to better things. Not everything went as planned; discarding the Yankees for the Mets had been a mistake, for example.

Normally, I was just thinking of getting home, relaxing, and drinking a beer, but seeing Juarez retire had me spinning.

After a full minute, the monsignor picked up the phone. "Good evening, Detective Rodriguez. I hope all is well with you. It was a beautiful day today, wasn't it?"

"It was."

"I called because I think you must have misunderstood our last conversation."

"Did I? What did I get wrong?"

"Yes. I wanted to clarify things. I certainly do not believe that

Father Anthony is any way involved in Father Charlie's disappearance. This is a terrible misunderstanding."

"I know that," I said.

"You do?"

"Sure. You said the two men had an argument. You never accused Father Anthony."

"Oh." He paused. "I just heard... I was concerned you might have drawn the wrong conclusion. I know it does not look good from a law officer's perspective that he had visited both churches. I certainly can understand your predilections but something involving hermeneutics, well, I just think this is not a good path for your case."

I wasn't sure about predilection, but I was 100 percent on hermeneutics. This prick, monsignor or not, was trying to talk over me.

Fucking Father Anthony must have put pressure on this guy or more likely I bet my number one fan, Agent Murray, must have yanked his chain.

"You know what, Monsignor? I think it would be a good idea if I stopped by. We could discuss this face-to-face. You know, sort all of this out."

That got his attention. "Ha! No. No. That wouldn't be necessary, Detective. It is already late, and I don't believe you are understanding my—"

"I insist," I said coolly.

There was a pause. "Insist? Do you mean you insist in a legal sense?"

I paused. I was not going to answer that. I wanted him to talk next.

"Okay, then, if you must."

I turned around and headed back to the station. When I got there, I parked the Tercel and told the station attendant I needed another car. The closest one reminded me of what I used back in Anti-Crime. It still had the magnetic siren on the top. I quickly signed the docket to release the car and headed to the church. It couldn't hurt for me to get the extra hours, and I didn't have any dinner plans.

The monsignor sat in his office looking like he'd rather be at a funeral. Investigators can have that effect on people. But in this case, I thought his anxiety was misplaced.

I certainly didn't think he was involved in whatever happened to my missing priest.

"So, Monsignor, Father Anthony from the Vatican visited both your church and the church in Manhattan where there is another missing priest?"

"I already discussed things with Agent Murray."

"Monsignor, I don't want you to get in trouble. But investigators are going to start pushing hard, and they are not going to appreciate being misled or discovering you weren't fully cooperative. For example, it would be an issue if we discovered allegations had been made against either one or both of these priests by a parishioner or someone in the community at some point. Because that would have been something material and important to know. Is that the case with Father Charlie?"

It was a shot in the dark.

A shot that made the monsignor's eyes widen for a second. He looked down as he said, "Yes."

Bull's-eye! This one felt good. Now we finally had motive. All we needed now was to find a perp that—

"As you are aware, I went over this in great detail with Agent Murray earlier today. I told Agent Murray, these are just allegations, ever since, well, you know... the problems the Church had decades ago. Now, we have very strict protocols. Not every allegation is true as I am sure you are aware... Detective... I mean, Officer Rodriguez? Are you listening to me?"

I was. I just didn't know what to say. *How could Agent Murray not let me know this?*

"Yes, of course. Just to double-check, Father Charlie's history... were there recent allegations? Or was that why he was moved here?"

"As I thought I told Agent Murray, they surfaced at a previous assignment. He was strictly on widow-and-elderly duty here."

"Right, right. Thanks. I'm juggling a lot of information. I appreciate the clarification."

The monsignor had just spelled it out for me. Father Charlie was suspected of being the worst of the worst: a pedophile priest. I thought about the stack of *People* magazines in Father Charlie's studio apartment. The top issue blasted a "Sexiest Man Alive" cover line. Not that there's anything wrong with that. Pedo-priests, on the other hand...

"Well, we are very appreciative of law enforcement, and we will cooperate however we can, but we would appreciate it if you would leave Father Anthony out of this. He is most certainly one of the 'good guys,' to use your parlance."

Yeah, my parlance. Hmph. I was derailed at this point. "Thank you, Monsignor. I will see what I can do."

All I wanted to do was call Agent Murray, but I knew that was a bad idea.

CHAPTER SEVEN
Definitions and Misunderstandings

Eddie

Hermeneutics (noun)—the branch of knowledge that deals with interpretation, especially of the Bible or literary texts.

It was almost six o'clock, and now I was starving. I needed to return the unmarked car to the station before I could grab something to eat. I lingered at a red stoplight before waiting for a space in the traffic to turn left once it went green.

With the bubble on the top of the car, I thought about turning on the siren and blowing through the red light, but instead I waited for it to turn green. I signaled, swung into the intersection, then slammed my brakes mid-turn for three teenagers running across the street. I hit my horn. Fucking morons. They had the light, but they had bolted in front of me.

"Hey," said the teen closest to the car. "Who you beepin' at, motherfucker?!" He slammed his hand against the hood. His friend behind him winged a glass bottle at my windshield. The bottle shattered, blocking my vision.

"Fuck you, pig!"

"All cops should burn in hell!"

"Justice for Julian." At least, I think I heard the name Julian. I wasn't even sure who Julian was.

Another bottle hit the driver's side window, and with my windshield cleared I hit the gas. Immediately, I heard a distinctive thud come from the right front panel.

"Motherfucking bitch hit me!"

Then all hell broke loose.

One of the teenagers rushed the car grabbing the front door handle. It was locked. So he began beating on my driver's side window with his fist. The third teen jumped on the hood of the car.

"This fucking cop hit us!" he yelled to the world. "Don't let him get away!"

The car behind me was blasting its horn.

That was when the crowd began to form.

I grabbed my radio and placed the call. "This is Officer Rodriguez..."

The next forty minutes were a blur with police coming in from all directions, followed by SWAT. It made the eleven o'clock news and the morning papers the next day. Luckily, I had only clipped the kid. It didn't appear that he had any life-threatening injuries, his left hip was bruised.

Two days later, I was back with Internal Affairs.

"So we have sworn testimony that says you tried to run over three teenagers. When you missed them, you put your car in reverse. You then went back in drive and slammed on the gas and this time clipped a teen separate from the first three. You then stopped because one of them threw a beverage at your windshield so you couldn't see to drive off," Ms. Edna James stated matter-of-factly.

"Hmmph," I breathed.

"Officer Rodriguez, this is very serious. As you are aware, you are already on probation."

I needed to stay in control. "So you have sworn testimony that I just casually reversed back onto Prospect and magically there was no traffic? So I could, what? So I could hit some random kid? All while being recorded by at least one iPhone?"

"So you are agreeing with this testimony?" Ms. James asked flatly.

Luckily, Bill, my advocate, put his hand on my arm before I could respond. "Ms. James, obviously Officer Rodriguez is questioning the veracity of this story. There is no need to be unnecessarily confrontational."

"Unnecessarily confrontational? This precinct is set for a multi-million-dollar lawsuit because, at best, your officer can't keep control of his vehicle. I am asking for an immediate suspension, and you best believe we will get it this time. Officer Rodriguez should be happy he's not being terminated."

"I'm thrilled," I seethed.

"You see? Do you sense any remorse there?"

"Remorse?" I looked down to gather my thoughts for a tirade. She's IA. I'm a cop. Bill's doing his job. Nothing is personal. Suddenly, I was just tired. "I was making a turn, and they bolted in front of me. Then they literally attacked my vehicle, throwing bottles at the car. When I tried to pull away, one of the assailants got clipped. I regret clipping him."

"Well, that's something, I guess." Ms. James turned off her recorder and walked out in disgust.

I turned to Bill and finished my thought:

"To be honest, I regret clipping him and not running him over."

Bill knew it was just dark humor, but I should probably reel it in, considering the depth of shit I was in.

Edna James was right. I got two weeks suspension without pay. No one believed the story, how it was told, but I should have made sure there was no one there before stepping on the gas. I could have sworn I checked.

I tried not to go stir-crazy. My cases got moved on to others. I watched a lot of TV and went to Connecticut for a few days. I was the only one visiting my father at this point; without my visits, the old man would be completely alone. I should have reached out to my brother in Jersey, but that never turned out well.

I never got into the whole TV binge-watching thing. So I found myself just clicking around a lot. Whenever I would click on the news, they would bring up the memorial for Daniel O'Malley. I guess that's why I called my captain with a plan. He called me back an hour after I left him a message.

"Hey, Eddie." Captain Broward was wary.

"Hey, Cap." Besides my temper, I also hated having to use formal titles. *I have to reel myself in.* "I wanted to ask you for a favor."

"A favor? Now might not be the best time for one of those, Eddie." He paused. "You need to be careful. IA is looking at you hard, and it looks like the city is going to be out a few million on that kid you hit." Another pause. "I'm just happy he's okay."

I had to play this right. "Yeah. Very sorry about that, Captain. I am glad the kid is good, too." Hmmm. "It got me thinking that I wanted to do something for someone else. You know how Miguel didn't want to retire, right?"

"Uh-huh."

"Well, do you think you can get me and him on the list for the

76

Daniel O'Malley memorial. That is technically my fourteenth day. It sounds like we are going to have a pretty good representation from our precinct like the other city precincts because of all the things O'Malley did for the NYPD. It might be nice for him to see that we haven't forgotten about him."

A longer pause this time. "Okay, Eddie. Call Miguel first and see what he says, and then I will see what I can do."

I called Miguel and then quickly hung up, thinking of a different angle. I pulled the business card that I had gotten recently, out of my wallet.

"Hey, Detective Accardi. It's Eddie Rodriguez from Fort Apache." I tried to sound upbeat.

"Oh. Officer Rodriguez. How can I help you?"

"Well, I was hoping you could do me a favor. You remember Officer Juarez?"

He perked up. "Yeah, how's Miggy doing anyway? I'm surprised he's still around. Some of us never learn. I left the force at age fifty and felt like that was ten years too late."

"That's just why I'm calling. He just aged out."

"Aw… Shit. Well, tell him to give me a call. I hope he's not all alone."

Sandy got points in my book for that comment, but I still wanted to know why he lied about his relationship with O'Malley. "Are you coming up this weekend for your friend O'Malley? And by the way, my sincere condolences."

"Thanks. Yeah, I'm definitely flying up."

"What do you think about seeing if Miguel wants to go?"

Sandy did not respond.

"If possible, I'd like to go also. I think it would be nice for him."

"You will be there also?" That seemed to get his attention.

"Yeah. I mean, if I can get in."

"Okay. I'll call the family and take care of that. Give me Miggy's number. I can only imagine how he's handling retirement. I'll have to coax him into going. See you soon."

That went better than expected. I called the captain back, letting him know I didn't need him to pull any strings after all.

CHAPTER EIGHT
The Silver Medal

EDDIE

It was two thirty. The official ceremony began at one. The family had spoken. The mayor had spoken also. While cameras flashed, he gave the family a silver medal for distinguished service to the city. Miguel and I were both ready to go at this point; the captain was talking with someone I didn't recognize.

Detective Accardi had left Miguel and I outside the front entrance with our dicks in our hands. I had called four times and texted seven. We had arrived at twelve thirty as planned, but Accardi never showed. At one, we walked up to the attractive young lady with the clipboard and gave her our names. We were not on the list. I was surprised that flashing my badge worked. It works in a lot of situations, but the crowd control was tight here with all the VIPs. I figured maybe Accardi had gotten here earlier than us and just went inside, but he was nowhere to be found.

The captain was wrapping up as we approached.

"Hey, Captain, we are getting ready to go."

"Well, it will be good to see you again on Monday, Eddie. I have a big stack of paperwork with your name on it."

"Oooh, I can't wait."

"Hey, it's for your own good to stay desk-bound for a while. You have two strikes, and IA is looking at you hard." He paused for a moment. "You know they have a job to do. I'm glad they are looking out for us."

I laughed out loud and was rewarded with a frown.

I didn't want to leave things on a down note.

"Hey, Captain, I'm really sorry about all this. I feel like I'm a magnet for bad luck. But I want to turn things around. Really. Whatever I can do to help. I know that priest case must be giving people fits, especially dealing with the feds. Let me know who got stuck with that one, or any of my cases, and I'll help however I can."

The captain laughed appreciatively. "The priest case has already been put to bed. Well, at least at our level."

"Put to bed?"

"Yeah, René Centeno got assigned the case, and he wrapped up the remaining pieces and packaged them up. The feds got what they needed, and we were told to stand down."

"Centeno? The transfer from Manhattan? I thought he was a beat cop. And what do you mean we were told to stand down? We're here to assist them, right? They should be thankful for our help, fucking pricks."

"Well, Eddie, not that I have to report to you, but Centeno happened—"

"Centeno," Miguel interrupted. "Like Angel Centeno's nephew?"

Hearing the name one more time jogged my memory. Centeno. I had heard about them back in high school. They were a local mob family in the Bronx. I'd hear the stories from other kids about drug dealers, violent beatings, all kinds of shit. But it was impossible to know what was true when your source was an acne-scarred four-teen-year-old trying to impress everyone.

"Yeah, he's Angel's nephew, if you can imagine that." The captain smiled. "I guess the apple sometimes does fall far from the tree."

Miguel smiled and nodded. "Thank you, Captain. Thanks to both of you. It really means a lot, you guys looking out for me."

Fucking Accardi.

"No problem, Miguel," I said. "Look, Captain. Sorry about my anti-fed rant. I'm just passionate about the job. I want to make sure we get the bad guys. I'll see you Monday." I held my hand out.

He shook my hand, which was odd nowadays especially during COVID season. The fist bump had replaced the traditional hand-shake. He gave Miguel one of those.

There was only one way in and out for security reasons. As we got close, Sandy waved his hand jovially toward Miguel and me.

"Phone broke?" I asked flatly.

"Fuck you," retired Detective Accardi snarled. "I don't fucking report to you. I'm sorry I was late. Something came up."

Then, like he hadn't talked to me at all, he turned to Miguel. "Miggy!" A broad smile crossed his face as he broke all COVID protocols and gave former Officer Juarez a warm hug. Sandy was still a physical specimen even at his age, and he smothered the much smaller Miguel.

"Hey, Sandy. I was worried you weren't going to make it."

"Miggy... never worry about that. You are part of a new broth-erhood now. Me and every other retired cop are here for you." He paused and reached into his sports coat and handed him one of the business cards that he had given me earlier. "Here's all my info. If you ever need anything, don't hesitate to call."

He then turned back to me. "So, kid." He was trying to own me now. "You never called me on that priest case."

"I didn't realize I not only reported to my captain and lieutenant but also to every cop that retired from our precinct."

Sandy stared at me hard.

Miguel smacked me on the back. "Hey, settle down, *idiotas*! What's wrong with you two?"

"Eddie, one day you are going to realize that I'm one of the good guys. You would be much happier having me as a friend. Trust me."

I turned to Miguel. "Hey, Miguel, you ready?"

I could tell by his eyes he wasn't. For whatever I thought of the "Retired Detective," Miguel missed his buddy Sandy.

"Don't worry about it, Eddie. I got him," Sandy said.

I stared at Miguel. "Is that okay with you?"

Miguel shrugged.

If Miguel wanted to hang out with this douchebag, so be it. "Sure thing, Miguel. I'll give you a call next week."

CHAPTER NINE

Someone Has To Be Wrong

EDDIE

Captain Broward wasn't lying to me about the paperwork. On Monday, there was a big stack to be organized and filed. All depressing stories on the cases that had wrapped up in Missing Persons. I was happy when I got a phone call from Detective Vargas in Manhattan.

"Hey, Eddie, how's it going?"

I didn't answer immediately, so he continued, "Yeah, bad question, right? I heard you've had some trouble."

"It's my fucking middle name. Anyway, I came back from suspension, and all my cases just wrapped up on their own."

"Oh man. I didn't realize you got suspended. I wasn't sure what happened. I heard there was an accident."

"Yeah, accident is one way to put it. One more strike, and I'm gone."

"Oh. Whoa. Sorry about that." I was making him uncomfortable.

"I'm sure I'll be fine. What's up?"

"Yeah. Right. So that tidbit on that Father Anthony seems to have paid off. I'm not sure why you aren't getting some credit for that."

"What happened?"

"Doesn't your captain share this shit with you? Anyway, the feds have him fingered on the missing priests, and that's not even the shocking part."

"Yeah. What's that?"

"The Vatican said they would help." Vargas paused for emphasis. "Can you believe that shit? This guy must be the dirtiest priest in the world."

"Yeah, maybe." Something wasn't adding up, but I wasn't sure what.

"Shit, man. I guess technically I shouldn't be telling you this."

"Hey, I appreciate it, Brian. Don't worry about me. I'm a desk jockey now. Who can I tell?"

"Okay, man. Don't be a stranger."

Vargas hung up.

After a long day of paperwork, my brain was fried. I'm sure most filing jobs become rote: you just see the names, dates, and page numbers, and organize them. But every one of these files involved a life, a life that had been permanently altered for the worse—either dead or damaged.

Now and then, I would recognize a name. Even though I grew up in the northern Bronx, and this was the southern Bronx, it wasn't like the place was *that* big. Not to mention, my dad had a restaurant in both the northern and southern Bronx. The southern one was right on Longwood Avenue on the same road as the precinct. Now I would drive down Longwood every day multiple times, but the real estate had turned over so often, I couldn't even place where the restaurant had been. Seeing Longwood on a report always stirred up memories. To some extent, missing is worse than dead. The uncertainty.

Driving to my condo, my mind spun through the things I had read: a few of the cases I'd been personally involved with, but most were just names and numbers. So many people making the same fucking mistakes.

I refocused as I passed a church on my right, some sort of Presbyterian thing. I wanted to call Agent Murray, but there was a good chance she would just jam me up. I was concerned about Detective Accardi's interest in this case but not enough to call that prick. He'd just jerk me around. So I settled on Miguel.

"Hey, Miggy. It's Eddie." Ugh. I just accidentally called him Sandy's pet name.

"Ha." Miguel paused, not sure what to say.

"Sorry about that. I mean, Miguel. Not sure why I did that. I guess it seemed you liked it when Sandy called you that."

"No problem, Eddie. You know, I think you would like him if you gave him a chance. He's really a good guy."

"Pfft. Yeah, a real charmer, especially when he was in high school picking on his fellow teenagers." I was remembering how Miguel told me at his retirement how Sandy treated O'Malley like shit early on.

"Yeah. Nah, it wasn't like that. It wasn't like he was still... Oh, never mind."

There was a pause between us while both of us thought of what to say. He went first. "So, Eddie. What's up? You called me. Everything, okay?"

"Yeah, I'm good, Miguel. Just checking in."

"Yeah, everything is good. I think you gave me some good advice."

"Really?"

"I'm going to Florida. Miami. Sandy, his partner, Barney, and someone else from my past, Angel, all live down there. It will be like—"

"Wait, what? So Sandy is—" I didn't finish my thought.

"Sandy is what, amigo?"

"Gay?" I mumbled.

"Gay?! Ha! Hell, no. He had two divorces! I remember him banging cocktail waitresses two at a time back in the day."

"Yeah, like I said. He sounds like a saint. I really need to spend more time with him."

"No, that was before—"

"What do you mean by partner, then?"

"Yeah, his partner, like, his partner on the force. I think I already told you about him before. Sandy worked with some other guy for a couple years when he started. After that it was him and Barney until they both retired. Barney moved there with his wife to be near Sandy, and I guess Sandy and Angel just moved down there for the weather."

Angel again. "Wait, Angel, like Centeno's uncle, Angel?"

"Si! Now you are putting it together. Yeah, all of them were on the force together. I guess Angel was only on the force for a few years before everything went down, but still, Accardi always treated him like a little brother."

"What about Angel?"

"Well, you heard the stories, right? The Mafia? Cop shooting. I mean, *mierda*. It was a long time ago, but this was a really big deal."

The story started to come back to me. "The Mafia cop! I forgot," I said. Amazing how much cop lore we all carry around.

"That was never proven."

"Wait, are you telling me that is Angel's story? What happened? Being from a mob family made it tough for him, right? Then there was a hit?"

"It was fucked up. Somebody set him up. It was never clear who. In the chaos, Angel and his partner got jumped, and somehow Angel's partner got shot with Angel's gun."

"Fuck, and I thought I had bad luck."

"He was arrested, then released, but got canned from the force as part of a plea agreement. The case ripped the department apart with different cops taking different sides."

"I thought the guy behind that story died out in California, right? How can it be Angel, then?"

"Died? No, it was Angel, and he didn't die. He stabbed a guy to death in a pool hall. Did ten years in Chino."

"Well, that sucks." I was trying to connect all the pieces.

"Damn right. It's total mierda. Shit." Miguel had a way of passively trying to teach me and everyone else Spanish.

"So they all just happened to get together after all those years?"

"I guess so. As Sandy said, the bond is unbreakable."

"All right, Miguel. Let me know what works for coffee next week."

"You got it, Eddie, because after that I am in Florida."

I got to the precinct twenty minutes before my shift and knocked on the captain's partially opened door.

"Hey, good morning, Captain. Don't worry, I'm very excited to get to my paperwork. Look, I even got here early."

Captain Broward didn't smile.

"Hey, I'm just joking, Captain. I really appreciate you looking out for me."

"There's only so much looking out I can do. The grapevine says IA is continuing to review your case or actually, your cases. The mayor is getting grief about police brutality and aggressive practices."

"So I'm going to be made an example of?"

"I'm not saying anything, Eddie; nothing is done yet. They will be having at least a couple more interviews before anything formal comes through."

I didn't say anything at first. But I wanted the captain to see it from my angle. "Those fucking kids. They attacked me. I would never have encountered them if I wasn't working on the priest case."

"Hey, Eddie, I get it. Listen, if anyone can bounce back from a situation like this, it's you. Plus, you've got..." He drifted off.

"Were you going to say money, Captain?" He knew I lived in a condo in gentrified Washington Heights. The place was well beyond what a young single cop would normally be able to afford. My father at his height owned five restaurants and the properties where they were located. Once my mom died, he spiraled downward and we sold everything, which left us with a fair amount of money.

My middle brother, Steve, the attorney, who's close to my age, handled things initially. The eldest, my half brother, Paul, was around twenty years older than me. I didn't know his exact age. Paul ended up handling the money and distributions for us after Steve got in trouble.

Steve had gotten disbarred and divorced. He was even homeless for a bit. Afterward, he completely lost it and had never fully recovered. He had been haunted by demons ever since.

The captain hadn't responded to what I said. I remembered there was another precinct cop who was in the shithouse.

"What about Harris? He actually shot a kid, and he's white as snow. That should be your fucking example. Am I right?" I pushed harder.

Captain Broward breathed out almost as if he was in pain. "Eddie, it's not a contest, and that was Harris's first strike. Not to mention, it was completely unintentional."

"Like mine wasn't?"

We both just let that hang in the air before I played my last card.

"You remember why I joined the force, right, Captain? If I hadn't lost someone early in my life, I'd have never taken the test."

The captain looked defeated. "I know, Eddie. I know. I'll see what I can do."

I walked back to my desk, paperwork waiting. Suddenly, I thought about Miguel and how lost he was. *What would I do if they took this away from me?*

Mierda.

CHAPTER TEN
Too Much Coffee

EDDIE

Hearing I was on the chopping block threw me off my game with the captain. I hadn't asked a single question about the priest case. Instead, I bombarded Miguel with them.

Miggy. I was disgusted with myself. I had started using the nickname that asshole Sandy had come up with.

"Miggy, you have to agree it's odd for Centeno to get the priest case, right?"

I had already walked through how odd it was for a beat cop to get moved into Missing Persons so quickly and then for him to wrap up the priest case in under a week. Not to mention that he had just gotten transferred from Manhattan around six months earlier because he decked some suit and they didn't trust him downtown anymore. And then for him to specifically ask to be transferred to Fort Apache when he was told he needed to be moved out of the Manhattan precinct?

"That's a lot of coincidence, right?"

Miggy sipped his coffee, a café Americano, no sugar, no milk. It was juxtaposed with my vanilla latte made with foam and almond milk. The sort of drink my cop friends would love to hear me order so they could needle me with gay jabs. I didn't feel threatened by that stuff, though. I like to think I gave as much shit as I took. Telling gay jokes was the number one sign of those of us not brave enough to step out of the closet.

Miggy wasn't buying any conspiracy theories. "Not sure there, Eddie. Sure, Centeno was a bit of an odd choice, going back to his uncle's precinct. But he had a clean record, and from what I hear is very smart. When he was in Manhattan, they wanted to keep him running taps and doing research because of what he could do with the computers. Dios mio. Anyway, so what if he was an odd choice? I've seen odder things."

"Well, what if someone knows something? I mean, between Sandy and the Centeno connection with the nephew business. You telling me it doesn't seem fishy?"

"Fishy? Okay, so let's say that both Sandy and Angel Centeno have a hard-on for pedo-priests. Sandy wants to make sure no one is putting pressure on the precinct to sweep it under the rug. Accardi gets someone to put young Centeno on the case because of the juice he has with the city and particularly Fort Apache. He knows young Centeno will make sure shit is done by the numbers. I mean, what's the big deal?"

He was right. It wasn't like this was being swept under the rug. If anything, things had intensified with the feds getting the green light to go after the Vatican priest. But wait... "But, wait a second. When's the last time you've heard of the Vatican giving the green light for law enforcement to go after one of their own?"

Miggy thought for a moment. "What? I'm not even sure what you are saying. Are you saying some Vatican priest started going all Liam Neeson on these pedo-priests, like a vigilante or something, and what, the Vatican is, like, that's a bridge too far, and now they want to reel him back in?"

I laughed out loud at the Liam Neeson reference and the thirty different remakes of his kids getting kidnapped. At some point, you have to accept he's just a shitty father.

"Yeah, I guess it's a stretch."

I tried one more angle. "So Sandy comes out of nowhere and chats me up about this priest case and wants me to call him with any updates. Then Angel Centeno's nephew gets put on the case, and my captain tells me he wrapped it up. But Vargas, a cop in Manhattan, tells me it isn't wrapped up, and that after I talked to the monsignor, the shit got real. You telling me that's nothing?"

Miggy put down his coffee, and now he looked irritated. "Eddie, I'm not saying nothing is nothing. I'm just not sure what you are saying. You saying that Sandy has some juice with the Vatican, and he calls up Italy and says, hey, send your assassin to get these guys? *Muy loco, mi amigo.*"

I got the point. Maybe I needed to examine my motives. I thought Sandy was a prick, and I wanted him to somehow be dirty. It wasn't rocket science.

"Okay, last thing, Miggy." I couldn't help myself. "You told me about Sandy beating O'Malley's ass all the time, so then why didn't you know they made up and became best buds later on? What's up with that?"

Miggy's face had relaxed, and he now had a smirk, amused at how hard up I was to pin something on Sandy. "Well, first, I never said he beat his ass. It was more just talk, from what I understand. As for them becoming tight friends, not that I know of. Once O'Malley became a big shot, Sandy would joke with the other cops about how he'd bullied him. Nothing serious, just high school stuff. As for their current relationship, I'd say… no, they aren't tight. I don't think it would be good for either of us to speculate…"

"Come on, Miggy. You can't do me like that."

"This stays between you and me." He was serious. "I've seen this sort of thing many times over during my forty years in the precinct. Dealing with big money is a stressful job, just like being a cop. Now and then, both cops and high-powered money types need something to help them cope. Sometimes, it's booze. Sometimes, it's something a little heavier. It's probably an AA or maybe an NA thing —you know, drugs. But like I said, I don't know shit. Are we clear?"

"Yeah, we're clear, Miguel." I personally saw Sandy pound four Budweisers in about twenty minutes. If it was AA, he wasn't getting any tokens for a while. I guess it could be drugs, but that didn't seem right, either.

If this was the only angle I had, I would still look into it.

"Hey, Centeno. Do you have a moment?" I had been keeping an eye out for my Missing Persons replacement the last couple of days and finally happened to corner him near the coffee machine.

"Maybe."

"Can I buy you a cup of coffee?" I pointed toward Mrs. Gennero's donated Nespresso machine.

Centeno was younger than me, slightly taller, with a middleweight wrestler's build, wiry and strong. He stood there with a frown, waiting for me to get to the point.

Well, screw him. I stuck out my hand. "Eddie Rodriguez."

He shook with a hard grip. "You already know my name."

"Yeah, I do. I just wanted to tell you how impressed I was by how quickly you got the priest case wrapped up."

Centeno started working on his own cup of coffee ahead of me. "Thanks," he said. "Wasn't much to do. Just get the feds a full report. Your notes were helpful."

"Yeah, but some things didn't get in my notes."

"Really? Like what? How to embarrass the precinct in the *Daily News*?"

What a prick.

"Close," I said. "The links to your uncle and Detective Accardi and even the recently deceased Daniel O'Malley."

With that, Officer Centeno put down his paper cup and stared hard at me. "What are you saying?"

"I'm not saying anything exactly. It's just some curious coincidences."

With that, I confirmed that the younger Centeno was a wrestler. He swept my legs out from under me. I got my hands out to soften the landing, but was pressed into the floor when he stuck a knee into my back. Then he wrenched my head back, putting one arm around my neck and got me in a choke hold. NYPD cops were banned from using this lethal maneuver, but he obviously wasn't too concerned about best practices at this point.

"Listen, Mary, I know why you love these priests, but you are done. Done with this case or worse if you don't start shutting the fuck up."

"Hey, break it up!" Good. Someone had seen us.

Centeno let go of his hold and got off me. "No worries. Just a little misunderstanding," he said to the three approaching cops.

I stood up, massaging my neck. "Rodriguez, you okay?" It was Milton, a desk sergeant.

"Fine, fine," I said.

"Centeno, that didn't look fine. You guys are both cops. I don't want to see that again."

Centeno stared at me for another moment. Then he looked at Sergeant Milton. "There is zero chance of that ever happening again." Then he walked out on us.

"What the fuck was that?" Milton asked.

"Must have been something I said," I cracked. "I wish I could tell what it was, but I got no idea. Thanks for seeing and saying something."

I went to my locker. It was time to clock out. My throat was aching. *Fucking Centeno.* If he thought I was going to be intimidated by him, he was mistaken. There was something wrong here. I needed to figure out who would have some answers.

VIGILANTE PRIEST III
Sloth

FATHER TONY

O'Malley owned a huge mansion on Fisher Island, a sliver of land in Biscayne Bay off the southern tip of Miami Beach. Sandy Accardi told me this was the most exclusive zip code in America.

We boarded the *Charlotte*, one of O'Malley's old boats, a 1960 fifty-three-foot Hutchins Fairform Flyer, to head to Fisher Island. The *Charlotte* was docked on Rivo Alto Island off the pier of a McMansion that was owned by O'Malley under a fictitious name. We left the white van here as well as an old BMW that we could use to ride into town. The two neighbors were fellow New York money and never there.

Before boarding, Accardi asked me to change, worried I'd stick out on the island, "Put away your priestly garb, Father. This land follows a different religion."

Centeno laughed. "Yeah, you need to be anointed with billions of dollars."

Even though they were trying to keep things light, I couldn't. I frowned at their sacrilege.

We needed to load the priests onto the small lower deck of the *Charlotte,* like cargo, to move them to Fisher Island and store them in O'Malley's bomb shelter.

The cargo. I remembered a Psalm.

The Lord hears the needy and does not despise his captive people.

I was in murky waters indeed.

O'Malley's other boat, the yacht, *Fortune's Folly,* now renamed *Dreamscape*, which would be used for the final trek, was docked half a mile away from Rivo Alto, in clear view of a large Coast Guard station. Accardi had someone at the Coast Guard station who could let us know if it was getting any attention. We couldn't dock it right outside O'Malley's Fisher Island mansion, or someone would almost definitely recognize it even though it had been refitted and painted.

It was Barney Fergusson's boat that pulled the threads together and created the ruse for their fishing alibi. His boat was on the other side of a thin strip of water that separated Fisher Island from Miami Beach. Fisher Island could only be reached by private boat or ferry, and we had that area watched for police. We wouldn't be surprised by someone who decided to just snoop around. We weren't the only ones on Fisher Island who preferred the police to not be checking in on them.

We intentionally did not take Barney's boat to Fisher Island. We would only take the *Charlotte*. Barney's boat was too small to hide any "cargo," and we wanted any onlookers to get used to seeing the *Charlotte* outside of the mansion anyway.

On most visits, the others would dump their regular cell phones off on Barney's boat so they couldn't be tracked. Then Barney would typically head out to a nearby reef or elsewhere. If any questions were asked on why they were in the area, fishing the reefs was their alibi.

As for me, my regular cell phone was kept in a lockbox in downtown Miami at this point. If Accardi was alerted from one of our sources that someone was onto us, I would go to *Fortune's Folly* myself. This would be where I would take the fall. All of us were expendable depending on different scenarios.

While on Fisher Island, we rarely went inside O'Malley's mansion except to check on the priests in the bomb shelter. We had to watch drawing any additional attention. It wouldn't be odd for Accardi, a friend of the O'Malley family, to be there looking over the property or the boat, but it would be better if the FBI or local police didn't ask any questions.

Fergusson and the new guy, Miggy, were out getting supplies. There was a heated discussion on bringing Miggy in this late, but Sandy swore by him.

And Sandy, from his connection to O'Malley, was our leader.

Which meant he was my leader. Priests take vows of obedience, poverty, and chastity. Obviously, these priests broke their vows which brought this mission together. I vowed to serve my bishop at ordination. Not Sandy. Or O'Malley.

More murky water.

I felt restless. A glass of dark Tuscan red didn't settle me. Accardi was smoking topside, and Angel was barking into his phone.

"No, I don't understand what you mean," Angel said. "I can tell you it wasn't him. Just let it go... and don't call him that. None of that matters; we all have jobs to do. So do yours and don't fucking let us down."

"He's talking to his nephew," Sandy said. "All in the family!"

"René. You realize I'm related to him also, right?"

"Yeah, but not René anymore. He thinks it sounds effeminate.

He's back to Renato, even though he thinks his mom might as well have named him Spaghetti-head."

Angel hung up the phone. "It looks like that young cop in Fort Apache is still causing problems."

Angel looked to me, then Sandy. "I think we need to make another phone call about it."

Accardi frowned and shook his head.

A few hours later, Miggy and Barney returned. We all went below deck and sat around the center of the *Charlotte*.

"It's tight, but we should probably all stay here tonight, agreed?"

Everyone shrugged.

Sandy said, "Angel has some news. Miggy, maybe you can help."

"Sure. What's up?"

"That fucking cop Rodriguez is connecting the dots. If that moron has gotten this far, God help us."

"What do you need me to do?" Miggy responded, all business.

"So next time he calls, let him know what the Centeno name means. It still means a lot, that I can assure you." Angel gritted his teeth. I could feel his anger. "He's got family, right? People he cares about. You tell him that—"

"No," Accardi stated with finality.

"What the fuck do you mean 'no'?"

"I mean, don't do that."

Angel stood up.

I finally said, "Listen, you two, whatever you think you are about to say next—don't. We have a purpose here, and at worst, this purpose needs to be a noble one. Let us focus on completing our mission."

Angel nodded. "Father Tony, I am not trying to show some sort of false machismo here. We need to close this leak, and we need to close it off by any means possible. Like I said, this is not going to go smoothly. We are already looking at a tropical storm, potentially a hurricane, coming, and we are dealing with the FBI. We don't need any other variables."

"There are other methods, surely. Logic, money, compassion. Love conquers all things."

"Not everything can be boiled down to a Bible verse, Father. I mean no disrespect. It is just a matter of strategy."

I laughed. "First, that is not a Bible verse, it is Virgil. I have been contemplating him often. Second, I'll remind you that Eddie Rodriguez is his own worst enemy. Didn't city hall tell us he was being removed? With this, our best move is to have Miggy tell him the truth."

Everyone's eyes got wide. Sandy said, "Father Tony, are you nuts?"

"I'm sorry. Let me be clearer: Not the truth of what we are doing now, but the truth about the injustice that happened to Angel and then the further injustice that happened to me. There is no way possible that Eddie Rodriguez is not going to find out what happened to Angel in the past. You know what, don't bring me up. There's still a chance he doesn't know that Angel and I are related.

"I understand there is a risk that he makes the O'Malley connection, but if we give him a reason wrapped in a bow, maybe he stops digging. It has to look odd that Centeno's nephew is on the case. So let Rodriguez get that small victory. Complete the circle for him by having Miggy let out that maybe Accardi did use some pressure through O'Malley to get your nephew on the case. That should close the threads for him, right?"

The others nodded their heads in agreement with me after I spoke. Angel looked numb and detached.

I was creating a web of half truths to cover our tracks. *The heart is deceitful above all things, And desperately wicked; Who can know it?*

We needed to get the cargo out of the bomb shelter and onto the *Charlotte,* which had been refitted with a tightly locked room below deck, then in open water about twenty miles offshore, we would get the cargo onto *Fortune's Folly,* now renamed *Dreamscape,* for the longer journey.

With the death of Father Mahoney, I wanted to stay with our current number of eleven and make this transfer now. We didn't need more variables. Accardi didn't want to hear any of it.

"One of these pricks is right here in Miami, and the other is less than fifty miles away." Accardi looked at me, confused.

"Is it really worth risking things to get the final two?" I said with authority, feeling cramped in the center of the *Charlotte.* There were five of us, and we were all standing. No one was calm enough to sit.

"They are there for the taking."

"I realize that, but I know of many more targets. Once we are done, I can talk about the others and remove the stain that has marred our Church for years. If we get caught before we can complete our ultimate task, all is for naught."

"We are better off being on the move for the next few hours anyway. We can use one of our contingencies if either of the marinas are compromised," Accardi said. Then he pressed his case again: "At this point, it would be foolish to change the plan."

"We can still be on the move without taking any more risks," I replied.

"We stay the course," Accardi shot back calmly but with finality.

The others blathered on as I tuned out. *How had the world*

gotten to such a despicable place? How was I now part of the mess and part of the solution? We would have thirteen. Thirteen governments that Man created were inspired by Satan in outright rebellion against God, and it was Nimrod himself, the thirteenth of Ham's line that tried to take the place of God. His name had been synonymous with foolish tasks ever since, and now here we were. No wonder—

"Father Tony?" It was Miguel. He had pulled me out of my stupor, and then I realized the mistake we were making. I ignored Miguel. I was more concerned that we were discussing all the details with Barney Fergusson around. We had kept him out of these, so he would have plausible deniability.

I addressed Barney directly: "Why are you here?" But he was already arguing with Accardi. This was taking a toll on me.

"What? How the fuck did this happen!" exploded the normally jovial Barney Fergusson. "I thought I was just going to be an operational guy! Now the fucking feds are calling me?"

"That was the plan, Barney," Sandy Accardi said. "I don't understand how they found you."

I bit my tongue. If I waited long enough, I'd figure out what I missed.

"Three fucking messages. All from today! From Special Agent Murray."

"That's not good."

"You think?" It was Angel, snark oozing.

"It must have been one of our phones."

"We've been using burners."

"They must have gone back a few months. Or they could just be taking stabs in the dark. NYPD vets in Florida?"

Barney was on the verge of tears. "I won't tell them anything. I mean, what do they have on me? I haven't done anything."

"Yeah, we all know that, Barney," Accardi said. "It's your decision to make. It's just that they also will ask for the log of your boat.

If you stay and take the heat, you may be fine but on the other hand you may not. If you join us, we have it set up where only one person takes the fall, and he very clearly is happy to do this."

Barney shook his head.

Miguel looked at me, no doubt thinking I had volunteered to take the fall for all of this. While my life was already permanently changed, I was not the person Accardi was referencing. "So what is the plan? How do we get out of being tracked by the police and the FBI?"

Accardi turned to him without emotion. He must have already thought of the plan. "Well, if there is a storm coming, we do what O'Malley did."

Miguel's face turned white at that. "But he's dead."

CHAPTER ELEVEN
False Impressions

EDDIE

"Hello?" He was waiting for a response, and I had frozen.

This wasn't some small mistake like misfiling a report. This could be a major fuckup, especially with the amount of heat on me. The priest case was wrapped up at the precinct level. There was no need for me to be involved at this point. I shouldn't be talking to him.

"Hello?" he had repeated into the void.

"Monsignor." I paused.

"Yes, Officer Rodriguez." He knew it was me. I had to get through his secretary to get him on the line.

I stayed mute.

"Officer Rodriguez, I think it would be a good idea if we got together and had another talk."

That stunned me. "Okay, sure, Monsignor."

"Can you come over now?"

I had already pushed my chips into the pot at this point. I said, "Yes. See you in fifteen minutes."

I decided to walk. No one would see my car in front of the church. And no teenagers would pelt it with bottles, either.

The monsignor went through his normal pleasantries. This time I accepted a cup of Earl Grey tea.

"So, you called *me*, Officer Rodriguez. How can I help?"

"I wanted to apologize. Do a little community outreach. I felt like maybe I was too harsh on you during my last visit. I really just want to make sure that we get the bad guys and protect the good guys. I'm sure with what you do, you can understand this."

The monsignor took a moment to study me before responding. "Well, you were most gracious, compared to the officer who replaced you. I mean, why would the powers that be put him on this case? Aren't detectives supposed to do their jobs devoid of emotion?"

I nodded my head.

The monsignor continued, "When I called in with additional information, he wouldn't even talk with me. He told me the case was closed on his end and hung up on me. If not for that FBI agent, I think this case would have just been buried."

"Agent Murray?" Had to be her.

He brightened at that and even gave a slight laugh. "She is something. A little curt but she is noble. A Christian."

"So how did that go?"

"Well, I am sure you've been informed about this already, right?"

"How can I put this, Monsignor. There are caste systems everywhere. Even in law enforcement. The FBI doesn't have to give the NYPD the time of day."

"About Father Anthony, I am restricted to a certain degree on what I can say, but the Vatican believes it is necessary for us to work with law enforcement here." The monsignor took a sip of his own tea before beginning. "Well, Father Anthony used to be called Father Tony. He was a priest. His parish was in Queens. His case—the monsignor used air quotes—"had some gray areas, but ultimately, it appeared to be true. At that time, the Church hoped to redeem these priests, so Father Tony was sent to Italy." He paused for a second and looked at me with sad eyes.

"Go on," I prompted.

"Well, needless to say, many more cases surfaced, the overwhelming majority of them were spurious. I mean, even our own parish was caught up with this. And Father Tony, as I understand it, has steadfastly maintained his accuser was lying."

If he wants to make me feel like an idiot, fine! At least I was getting somewhere. "What does spurious mean?"

His cheeks reddened at that. "Oh, I'm sorry, my son. It means without truth."

Something was still not right here. "So, the Vatican, after taking in this Father Tony, is now okay with the feds and the entire US government going after him?"

His eyes widened but only for a moment. "Times are changing. I know it's different for all of us."

"So if Father Tony is the bad guy, then what is the point of him going after these other priests? Especially with them doing the same stuff as he had."

The monsignor bristled at that. "Officer Rodriguez, I would hope that you would not buy into these fantasies regarding the allegations about these priests. I assure you these are only allegations. They are moved with an abundance of caution. If I told you how many of these cases are reported annually with absolutely no merit, you would—"

This was not the track I wanted to be on... listening to Vatican

PR bullshit. "Okay, okay, I got it, but then, still, say that all of these allegations are as you said, spurious, then that makes even less sense. Why go after these priests?"

The monsignor smiled and pointed at me proudly. "That's the righteous question. Because their perceived sins reflect his real sin. Father Tony never admitted fault. He never confessed for the awful things he had done. He had told everyone that the stories were fabricated. As I understand it, Father Tony knew in his heart he was a liar and refused to believe that these other priests could be telling the truth. It only augmented his own sin."

Okay, but how does this link into what I want to figure out? "So who was the kid that he molested?"

"My God." The monsignor looked shocked.

Now I reddened at my bluntness. "I'm sorry. It's just that there are a lot of people putting pressure on this case, and I'm not seeing the whole picture."

"Well, you obviously know about Centeno, that's why I was so surprised that his nephew wouldn't—"

"Wait. What about Centeno?"

"Officer Centeno is Angel Centeno's nephew. I recognized the last name. And after he was so brusque with me, I looked into it."

I couldn't care less how he found out that Angel was Centeno's uncle. "Right. That's okay, but can you refresh my memory about what happened with Angel Centeno?"

"That's an old story, Detective Rodriguez. I wouldn't feel comfortable talking about something that I wasn't part of, so many years ago that... Frankly, it created a lot of strain between us and your precinct."

"Monsignor, I could really use this. If you care about your missing priest, you would let me have as much information—"

His eyes narrowed at that. "You don't even remember his name. Do you, Officer?"

I froze. I didn't. I had been going over so much paperwork over the last couple of weeks and then with IA hassles, I had completely lost the plot.

"I think we are done for tonight. May God be with you."

The monsignor opened his arm wide, and I slowly walked toward the exit to his office, trying to think of something else to say until the door closed behind me.

CHAPTER TWELVE
Subtraction Through Addition

EDDIE

I had left three messages for Vargas and heard nothing back. He might have gotten spooked by my bad mojo. Or he might have been told to put this to bed like I was and he was following orders. Regardless, unless I wanted to drive down to his precinct and walk in on him, he was going to be a dead end.

My other option wasn't much better. I had left Miggy a voice message early in the day. He didn't get back to me until late afternoon.

"Eddie? It's Miguel. What's up?"

"Just checking in to see how you are doing. You excited about leaving for Florida in a couple days?"

"Doing well. And I am already here. I had no reason to wait."

"Bien, bien." I tried to ingratiate myself.

"Well, thanks for calling, Eddie. I'll check in with you if I come back."

"*If* you come back?"

"I'm kidding. *Relajar*. Relax. Although it's nice down here. Lots of ladies… and guys, too, I suppose."

I laughed.

"So you want to tell me the real reason you called me, pendejo?"

"Honestly, Miguel, I'm so spun around, I don't know what to ask. This young gun Centeno put me in a fucking choke hold when I asked him a question."

"What do you want, Eddie?"

"I heard something weird."

"Perfecto. What do you have now?"

Fuck. I took a deep breath. "Was Angel Centeno molested?"

"Dios mio, Eddie. You need to let this shit go. Where did you hear this? You are going to start to piss off the wrong people. Who have you been talking to?"

"So it's true, then, right?"

"Eddie, as your friend, I will tell you what I heard. You will get yourself in trouble at best by bringing this up, or worse if you say it to the wrong people. Anyway, here's what I've heard. Angel Centeno goes home and tells his parents that something happened. You know his family is connected. You know what I mean?"

"Yes, I know what you mean by connected." He was right. I felt uncomfortable already.

He continued, "So he goes on about how some priest touched him inappropriately and, his dad sits there taking it in all calm and collected, but Angel knew his old man. He was an enforcer. He was going to go and whack the priest that did this to him. Angel was only fourteen at this time. Anyway, what Angel didn't count on was how religious his dad was. Not to mention, Angel was a wildcard as a kid: shitty grades, bad reputation in the community, fights, lying about ditching school, the whole nine. You with me, Eddie?"

"Yeah, Miggy, go on."

"So Dad ends up talking with the priest and the monsignor, and instead of getting justice, Angel gets an ass-whipping from the old man."

"Shit," I breathed.

"Shit is right. It actually gets worse. Angel then takes a bat to the priest, and the cops have to get involved. Papa Centeno and the cops decide to work it all out. The mob and the cops had an on again off again relationship back then. They make an agreement to send Centeno out to military school, and the old man basically writes him off. He had two other sons and a daughter to worry about, if I remember correctly. Use that detective brain of yours to figure out the rest."

"So this is why things went bad with Angel Centeno, like you told me in the past. This is why he decided to become a cop. To piss off his old man, and then everyone gets jumpy. But then Angel Centeno gets set up, or at least that's what his friends presume, and then he leaves the state without a family and no longer able to be a cop so he hits rock bottom in California."

Miggy snorted. "Well, you are missing a few things here and there but close enough."

"So what happened to the priest?"

"Ha. Good question. They wound up finding him dead in a dumpster while Angel was away in boarding school. Story goes that the priest got frisky with another young parishioner, and that was that—the mob took him out. He was stabbed to death with a pock-etknife. Lots of easier ways to kill someone. This was personal."

"Is that what you think? It was the mob?"

Miggy took a sip of something before answering. "What do I think? It really doesn't matter what I think. The case was never solved."

"C'mon, Miggy."

"He was friends with a few of the sons of the cops in our precinct."

"Who was friends with a few of the sons of the cops in our precinct?"

"The kid. The other kid that got molested, and Angel, for that matter. It was never proven, but there weren't a lot of resources dedicated to the case. If you ask me, what do I think? I think it was us. Not the father of the kid or the mob. It was some of the other cops in the precinct. Like I said, nothing was ever proven."

"Wow, thanks, Miggy."

"I don't want your thanks, Eddie."

I knew where he was going, but I was once again angry. "Well, then, what do you want, Miggy? I mean, I'm trying to do the right thing here. What would you do if you were me? Would you just walk away?"

"Walk away?" Miggy parroted. "Eddie. News flash. This is not your case. And even if it was your case? What are you doing? You are spending all of your time trying to connect this back to old friends of mine, my partners, my amigos... *mi hermanos*. What are you trying to prove?"

"Nothing, Miggy. I ain't trying to prove nothing. There's just something wrong here and—"

"You keep saying that, Eddie. You keep saying that over and over again, but what am I supposed to do with that? There's no motive, and not that it matters to you, but these are my friends."

"I know, Miggy. I know."

"You say you know, but then you stick with this." He stopped cold. He was thinking. "Eddie?"

"Yes, Miggy."

"I think I need you to stop calling me."

"Stop calling you?"

"Yes. I need you to stop calling me. I mean, at least until you stop viewing my friends and, by connection, me, this way."

"Aw, c'mon, Miguel. I never said anything about you."

"Listen, Eddie. I like you. I'll tell you one last time. These are not bad guys. Now get smart or get a case of amnesia, but back the fuck off."

I listened to the dead air on the line for a few seconds. My circle was continuing to get smaller.

CHAPTER THIRTEEN
Our Darker Angels

EDDIE

"Not sure if I am going to remain a cop, Ma," I said. "I am trying to do the right thing here. But the odds are against me."

Clouds filled the sky. It was chilly out. I sat on the fake marble bench and focused on her name: Rosalita Rodriguez.

My mom was the true love of my dad. He had fallen in love with her when he had just turned forty. She was only in her mid-twenties. It was his second marriage.

My father came to the United States from Cuba. His wealthy family was on the wrong side of the Cuban Revolution. They saw the writing on the wall and got a lot of their money out of the country. Avoiding the chaos in Miami, they moved to New York City.

It was a Chinese friend of my dad's who gave him the idea of setting up a restaurant in New York. My dad was a decent cook, and many Chinese who had immigrated to Cuba were now leaving and starting new lives in New York. Many of them opened restaurants. My dad's friend was having success, so my dad figured why not.

For his twenty-first birthday, his parents helped him open his first restaurant. Explicitly saying they did not want it to compete against their fellow refugees, my father created his first restaurant, advertising it as serving Mexican cuisine. Regardless of how it was listed, this restaurant and all the others he opened still retained some of his ancestral Cuban flair.

My dad married an Irish Catholic girl from the Bronx named, of course, Mary. They were both young. She was pretty but poor, a blue-eyed, red-headed, lily-white girl. I have the impression she was my brown-skinned father's dream girl. She made him more Americanized. After Paul was born, the marriage lasted for six more years.

Mary made it very difficult on my father after they separated. She was embarrassed about being divorced, which was not normal for those times. She blamed my father for everything. She demanded a house in the suburbs where nobody from the neighborhood could judge her.

My father started drinking. He drank a lot before, but now he upped his game. Luckily, my grandparents were there to keep the restaurants going.

My mother saved my father from his first battle with alcohol and himself. Five years after the divorce from Mary, another local girl, a waitress with dark eyes lightened by a gleaming smile, met my dad and dragged him from his despair. She was smart. "I knew the way to his brain was through his heart," she told me. She got that right. *What forty-year-old drunk wouldn't put his boozing on pause when a beautiful, much younger woman seemed within reach?*

Well, maybe quite a few. Alcoholism, judging by the NYPD divorce rate, is a powerful antidote to love.

But my mom, Rosa, was fifteen years younger and a lot more disciplined. They got married and shortly afterward had my brother, Steve. I was born five years after that.

"I wish you would still talk to me, Mom. I miss your voice."

I rubbed my fingers over my badge. I had brought flowers, but maybe this was what I should leave with her. Would that simplify things or complicate them?

I knew her answer: Don't be ridiculous, Eddie.

"You're right," I said. "I will make you proud. I became a cop for you. If they take that away from me, I will not change. I will still strive for justice. You deserve that. I love you."

I always visited my mother first. It was less depressing for me to spend time with her than with my dad. When I was younger, I would bring a six-pack of beer. Now, I would just bring a bottled water and sometimes a book. And flowers.

When no one was around, I would rest my head on the smooth marble headstone and close my eyes. In the past, I cried. Now, I would smile. It soothed me. I would read to her sometimes. Other times, I would just sit there and remember.

There was so much to remember: joyful events, hopeful moments, and the hard stuff, including why I had become a cop.

My father was in his usual form.

He hadn't been able to stand since I walked through the door. I was pretty sure he was sleeping in the La-Z-Boy that was surrounded by old mail and trash. The place reeked of piss, and the air was heavy with dust. But the worst was the smoke. It stung the eyes and forced me to blink rapidly. His pants and shirt were covered in holes. Some of the holes were cigarette burns, others seemed like the clothes were disintegrating right off his body.

"Don't have time for me anymore?" he seethed.

"I called a couple times, Dad. I'm not exactly retired," I said. It had been a few weeks since my last visit.

I tried to respond as little as possible to him.

"You use your firearm again? You almost got one of them, but you couldn't even do that right."

My father had been a racist as long as I could remember. People would find it shocking that a Latino, especially a dark-skinned Latino, could think like this. The death of my mother completely removed any reservations. Now there was no one to keep his anger in check. He had gotten so much worse. N-word-this and Jew-that. I guess that might be why I predominantly dated Black guys if I wanted to psychoanalyze myself—yet another way to get back at him.

"I'd have Black bastards running out on checks or stealing from me directly and your goddamn pig friends stealing from me saying I had to pay for protection. Do you know they were collecting most of that money for the fucking Mafia?"

"You've told me a thousand times, *Papi*. You haven't been taking your medicine?"

"Papi? Don't you speak that language to me. You don't have the work ethic to be Latino! You could have been someone... like your brothers."

It caught me off guard, the don't *speak that language* line. *The only word I had said in my limited Spanish was "Papi" but that was one word too many from his least favorite son.*

"My brothers. Which one you want to talk about first, the Wall Street shyster who refused to keep your name or the one that got disbarred and has filed for bankruptcy twice?"

"Well, it's a more honest living than yours. You went and joined the pigs. The sons of bitches that didn't do anything to find your mother justice. You should have just joined a street gang with the spooks."

I wasn't going to be able to last much longer on this visit. I wondered how much of his anger lay in the loss of my mom.

"What is that? You looking at me with pity? Pfft, I can still kick your ass, Nancy. Come on! Prance over here."

"Dad." I didn't know what else to say.

"Don't worry, son. I'll die soon enough. I'll die, and you and your brothers will get the rest of my money. It's always been the money, hasn't it?"

"Oh, Papi." I turned away. That fucking hurt.

He tried to speak but instead convulsed with a heavy smoker's cough. He grabbed a disgusting, soiled handkerchief and coughed into it.

"Eddie, Eddie," he said, catching his breath, "please don't come and see me anymore. Let me be. I know what I am. I know what I was. I know what I'm going to be." He broke into another convulsive cough.

"I will be back shortly, Papi. With your groceries and your prescriptions." I had gotten in the habit of stopping by first and then heading out and picking things up for him. I didn't want to admit it, but I was checking to see if he was alive before picking up groceries and prescriptions. I started doing this after I had seen the prescriptions that I had delivered to him shoved into his overflowing mailbox when I visited. Even picking them up, I wasn't sure he was taking them and not just tossing them. He wanted to die.

Saying goodbye to my dad was momentarily liberating. It was a joy to leave his gloomy reality.

I drove back to my condo feeling exhausted. I wasn't sure I'd be able to continue visiting once a month.

I was so deep in my head that when my phone rang, I answered it without seeing who was calling.

"Officer Rodriguez?"

"Yes."

"I have some additional questions for you regarding Father Charlie Rhodes and Father Anthony Morelli."

"Ah, Agent Murray! I was wondering, does FBI training include a phone call etiquette course?"

"One guess, Officer Rodriguez."

"Do they have any etiquette courses? Is the word 'politeness' in any manual?"

"Eddie, please. I am very busy. I apologize if my manner offends you."

"Wow. Thank you."

"Great. Now, my questions."

"Isn't it Saturday?"

"So?"

"It's just that. It's been a long day... my day off, in fact... and I'm not even on this case anymore. You know that, right?"

"I know. But you are still a cop, right?"

"For now."

"What does that mean?"

"Never mind. Agent Murray, what exactly can I do for you?"

"You can help me solve a crime. So it looks like after your accident, you were put on leave. That seemed to be a little excessive, even based on your previous history."

"Checking up on me behind my back, Agent Murray?"

"Yes. And it seems somewhat strange. Patrolman Centeno gets on the case and gives me a bunch of supporting evidence pointing to Father Anthony Morelli. I was curious how some random street cop can take a few minutes to review the file and do all that? Is he that much more intelligent or perceptive than you, Officer Rodriguez?"

I literally saw red, then completely lost it. "Fuck you! Fuck you, you crazy bitch! You have no idea what I've done or what I have been through." I could feel myself cry and that angered me further. "I am still fucking working on this case even though it's not even mine anymore, and I can tell you that you don't know everything. You... you all are trying to just wrap up this fucking case, and you are the noble one? You psycho fucking robotic bitch."

"Are you okay, Officer Rodriguez?" Her voice was measured and calm.

I laughed. I laughed and couldn't stop laughing. I could swear that for that brief moment she cracked just in the slightest way, and I heard a chuckle back.

"Sure. Sure. Whatever I can do, Agent Murray, just let me know." I was snorting, my nose running.

"It's okay, Eddie. I agree. Something is off. What can you tell me about this Officer Centeno who was assigned to this case and, more importantly, his Uncle Angel Centeno?"

CHAPTER FOURTEEN
Cautious Companion

EDDIE

I could tell before the captain said anything. He looked beyond me, outside his office, as if checking that no one had seen me enter.

"Shit, Eddie, you're early. Close the door."

"I've come in early every day since I landed in the shit."

"There's no good way to say this. I am so, so sorry, Eddie. I'm telling you it is out of my hands."

"You realize that I am Latino and gay? Right, Captain?" I had been mulling over this since he first let me know this was a possibility.

"Well, dear God, Eddie. Don't tell anyone I told you anything yet. I just heard myself from—" He stopped cold.

"From who?"

"Well, I'm not sure that's important."

"Not important! Well, that's just fucking great! Why don't you tell me what is important, then?"

"Eddie, you'll see what is what soon enough. As soon as it's official. I understand this is brutal. But I can't tell you any more. I don't know any more. Speak with Bill, your union rep. That's the best move. I think he's probably on his way here."

I was stunned. "The best move," I repeated.

"Just keep it together. I am really sorry about this, Eddie."

"Thanks, Captain." It was hard for me to stay mad at Captain Broward. This bullshit was coming from someone else. IA. Or city hall.

Unless he was the biggest phony of all time, I really believed the captain had my back.

"As for now, I need you to leave the precinct. Come back at one and Bill, you, and I will talk it over."

Bill Wagner, Captain Broward, and I all met in the conference room at 1:00 p.m. However, there was one extra person, my good friend Edna James. It was Ms. James who had the pleasure of officially telling me that I would no longer be a cop. Bill Wagner and Captain Broward looked nervous, and Ms. James, well, Ms. James looked confused.

She began. "Officer Rodriguez, effective immediately, you are no longer a member of the New York Police Department. Please relinquish your side arm and your badge to your captain."

"You realize we will be contesting this," Bill said.

There were some formalities that needed to be discussed regarding time frames for my appeal, handing over my nonexistent cases, and confidentiality issues regarding my termination. The "separation" terminology they used was the least damaging if I wanted to look for other jobs.

Ms. James held out her hand to me as she was wrapping up. "Mr. Rodriguez, I wish you well. I truly do." I could swear she looked embarrassed as she exited the conference room.

Captain Broward and Bill stayed behind, offering me support. The final insult came when I asked Bill if we could start working on my appeal and my wrongful termination lawsuit.

"Sorry, gentlemen," Captain Broward said, standing up. "This discussion will have to happen somewhere else. Mr. Rodriguez needs to clear out his cubicle and leave. Or we can ship his property. But, Eddie, you need to leave. Effective now. Let's go get your stuff."

I quickly boxed up everything and walked out of the precinct toward my car with my head down, my captain and my advocate following me until I exited the building.

The whole thing felt surreal. I imagined this was true for everyone who had something like this happen to them. It was a quarter to three on a Monday, and my entire life was over.

I slept in until eleven the next day. Slept in might be a stretch. I forced myself to lie in bed until eleven. I decided I'd give myself one day to wallow and then a week to party and enjoy myself. I thought about the upside. I no longer was going to have to be stuck in that alpha-male, misogynistic world where I knew my homosexuality was being snickered about behind my back. My dad was dying. I could start living my life for myself, not in spite of him.

I checked my cell for messages. I had two calls, one from Bill, my advocate, and the other from John. I guess he had heard the news. I poured some instant coffee into a mug, added water, and tossed it into the microwave. I could handle shitty coffee for the weekend, but if I was going to spend more time at home, I'd need to get a machine.

I spent a few minutes thinking of John and how my interest in him echoed what appealed to my dad about his first wife. John was a blond, blue-eyed American. That was not my standard fare, but I definitely found him attractive, regardless of his level of interest. I also remembered that it was John who inadvertently started my latest run of bad luck.

He had invited me out for drinks that night, the night when I met the great Sandy Accardi. Oh well. I grabbed the coffee out of the microwave, added an excessive amount of almond milk, and sat down in the kitchen to call him.

"Hey, John. Thanks for calling."

"Hey, Eddie, I feel bad about not calling you earlier and now this." He sounded nervous.

"It's okay."

"Hey, I know it's short notice, but would you be up for going out to dinner? There's a great Mexican place near me that I think you would like. It's in the West Village."

I laughed. "Are you trying to appeal to my gay side or my Latino side? Sure, that would be fine. Just let me know the name of the place and the time." *Is he making a pass at me?* Things were looking up potentially.

John was right. The place, Sierra, was nice. I had gotten there early, dropped John's last name, and was seated at the table for four.

He arrived fifteen minutes late and he wasn't alone. He was with a girlfriend again. I was pretty sure it was the same girlfriend he had been with the last time when I thought it would be just the two of us. I wracked my brain for her name but came up empty.

I stood up to greet them. "Hey! Great to see you," I said, offering handshakes. "I was wondering about them seating me at a table for four. But now I get it."

"Oh, sorry about that. I thought I said there was going to be three of us."

"Uh, no. I don't think so. But this is great. The more the merrier."

"Oh, Eddie. Great. I really thought I mentioned it. I was just worried that... Well, I'm not sure what to say."

Worried?

Did he really not trust me with him alone, because I was gay? I was surprised by how angry I got. "Worried? Worried about what? Did you think that I'd follow you into the bathroom, lock the door, shove one of my old tube socks in your mouth and take you over the sink?"

Both of their eyes widened at that. I also was getting some looks from the table next to us.

"What, Eddie?! Jeez, no. I mean the rumors at work. And then I saw your cubicle empty. I'm not sure what I should say or shouldn't say. I heard some things, or at least I might have heard some things. Uh, you know, maybe this is a bad idea. Not sure how this changes anything."

Oh shit.

"Oh what? No, go ahead. I'm not sure what's wrong with me. I am sorry, John. I really am. I am just pretty beat up over getting let go, and I am so sorry to you also." I had turned my focus directly to John's girlfriend, intentionally avoiding John. "I apologize... What's your name again?"

"Debbie. We met before." She stared at me wide-eyed as if I had just been let out of an asylum.

The rest of the evening was a kind of a beer-heavy therapy session for me. Whatever he was going to tell me was not going to be discussed. He had something sensitive he heard that I would like to know, but now he didn't trust me with the information. He was scared it would get back to someone. He had brought the girlfriend as a cover in case anyone saw us together.

John's girlfriend settled down a little after John told her about my freak attack by drunken teenagers. I was fishing for some sympathy to smooth things over.

"That is *so* unfair!" Debbie responded, sounding genuine.

"And it was my third strike."

"I'm so sorry, Eddie," she said, reaching out to squeeze my arm. Then she stood up to go to the bathroom.

I immediately grilled John about the precinct and Captain Broward. At the roster, Broward had warned against discussing "Dearly departed Eddie Rodriguez."

"He said that? 'Dearly departed'?"

"Oh yeah."

"Did he get a laugh?"

John shifted in his seat. "What do you care?"

"Of course he got a laugh. Fuck that guy."

We ended the evening a few Dos Equis later, with Debbie giving me a full-body, breasts-to-my-chest hug that was wasted on me, and John giving me a firm handshake and a much looser hug. These were remnants of a time past, a time pre-COVID replaced nowadays with a fist bump.

CHAPTER FIFTEEN

You Win Some. You Win Some

EDDIE

I returned Bill's call the next day. We discussed fighting my termination. He felt confident that we certainly could at least get a hearing. I wasn't sure that was the way I wanted to go, and after a couple minutes, Bill threw me a curve.

"So, Eddie. Captain Broward called me. He has a job opportunity for you or at least an interview."

"What?"

Bill paused and then spoke quietly over the phone. The one thing I hated about him was his habit of talking low. I think he did it as a power move. To force me to listen. "Well, you know he has connections, Eddie? I think he feels bad about how things went down, and he probably reached out to a few folks."

"I don't need anyone's charity." It came out sounding defensive, but I meant it as a point of fact. Paul was giving me a generous allowance from my dad's savings through some sort of trust.

"I don't think it's like that, Eddie. As captains go, he's a good guy. You know that, right?"

That was the second time he had tried to gauge me, and suddenly I felt that cold tingle I got when something wasn't right. I had felt it with the priest case and a few times during my career as a cop before. There was something wrong about this.

"Are you not telling me something, Bill?"

"Nah, Eddie. Why would you ask that?" His response was smooth. If he was hiding something, he was hiding it well.

"What's the job?"

"It's a security gig at BDQ Investments. I think I got the initials right. Good money from what I hear. Twice as much as what you make as a cop. And good bennies."

"Twice as much?" Now I was on high alert. "That seems odd, right?"

"It's a finance company. Those guys are swimming in cash. Like I said, I think he felt bad and wanted to set you up."

"Set me up or shut me up?" I couldn't help myself.

To Bill's defense, his last answer before he hung up the phone definitely sounded honest. "Maybe both."

The appointment was off Park Avenue on the forty-third floor of the kind of high-rise office building New Yorkers pass and never really pay attention to. I arrived fifteen minutes early and got a mug of coffee from the receptionist, who asked if I wanted milk, cream, or almond milk.

"Wow, someone must have told you about me," I joked.

She gave me a weak smile, a visitor's clipboard, and a pen. I signed in.

At two o'clock, a young Black lady, Ms. Igwe, in an impeccable, formfitting business suit, asked me to follow her. I noticed she had a lot of form to fit. So far, the gig felt like a movie set.

"Mr. Rodriguez, thank you so much for coming in today." Ms. Igwe nodded at me, and I nodded back. This was another odd thing that started post-COVID, when the fist bump seemed too casual.

She went through the basics of the job. It was a standard security gig. I would vet scheduled visitors before they arrived. I would monitor unscheduled visitors. I would navigate and collaborate with the building's security firm. The company wanted one security professional in the office at all times, and had a team of six on staff. That meant lots of fill-in hours when someone got sick or went on vacation.

"Was that a problem?"

"No, Ms. Igwe," I said. "I mean, I still have a few questions."

"I think you will find it a step up from the NYPD," she said, placing a form on her desk.

She asked a barrage of questions and made a series of checks, circles, and cross-outs on the sheet in front of her as I answered. Was I good with computers? Yes. Did I speak Spanish, French, Chinese, Japanese, Arabic, or Russian? Very little Spanish. Had I ever been arrested? No. Did I have a license to carry a gun? Yes. Had I undergone security training? Yes. Did I have martial arts skills? Tae Kwon Do.

In the end, she had a sheet with many more circles than scratch-outs.

I frowned at the obvious. "Hey, listen, I get it. I appreciate your time. Is there something—"

"Where do you see yourself in five years, Mr. Rodriguez?"

"Well, as you know, I just left the NYPD, so I'm getting my bearings." I wasn't too sure about any of this. "At this point, I am still trying to figure out where I would fit in at your company."

"Well, you got a pretty good recommendation from your

captain. This will require you to change your focus. It's fairly different than being a cop."

"Okay," I said.

"Can you start Monday?"

"Well, I was planning on taking care of some— " I wasn't even sure how I was going to finish the sentence when she interrupted me.

"Well, the following Monday would be fine. Of course, we'll need to do a deeper background check and contact your references. And then HR would draft your offer letter. Of course, right now, I'd like you to meet Mr. Kennedy, the head of our HR Department, to get the preliminary paperwork taken care of."

"What?"

"The next step would be for HR to handle your benefits and other paperwork."

I thought for a second of running for the exit, but I figured I'd let this play out a little further. I knew Captain Broward had some connections. It made sense that the NYPD wouldn't want a disgruntled gay Latino cop shaking trees. But what if this had something to do with Angel Centeno and Accardi? I couldn't shake it. What if they were trying to get rid of me, so I didn't look into whatever it was they were up to? What if they somehow put pressure on the NYPD to get rid of me in the first place? None of this was lost on me.

"Sure." I smiled. "Let's do it."

Kennedy, the head of HR was an older white gentleman.

"So, Mr. Rodriguez, I have your packet for you, and I'd be happy to answer any questions."

He might regret saying that.

"I am grateful for the job, Mr. Kennedy. I really am, but I have to ask. Why me?"

"Can I see your cell phone, Mr. Rodriguez?" *What the fuck?*

"Excuse me."

"Can I see your cell phone?"

I decided not to go back and forth with him. I handed him my cell phone.

He looked at it, pressed the button on the side to get the screen to appear and then looked at the back of it. Instead of handing it back to me, he placed it with the screen face down just slightly out of my reach.

He then handed me a piece of paper. "Can you sign this?"

It was a one paragraph statement attesting that on today's date, between the hours of noon and five p.m. Eastern Standard Time, I would not record any conversations between myself or any employee or agents of BDQ Investments.

I bristled at this. "Are you serious?"

"I take it you want us to have an honest and open conversation, Mr. Rodriguez. I can't do that currently."

"Are you recording me?"

"No, I am not, and I can assure you that there are no recording devices active in this room right now."

I signed the form. I wasn't taping this geriatric jerk, so what did I care.

"I apologize about the formalities, Mr. Rodriguez. I assume you have questions about the job and the compensation."

"Well, I'd like to know all that, yeah. But mainly I'm wondering why I am being offered a job at what I'm told is a hefty raise after being basically fired from the police? I'd also like to know—"

Mr. Kennedy interrupted. "It might be better if I answered your questions one at a time. Is that okay?"

"Sure."

"So you want to know why all of this is being done for you? I get it. We did a thorough check of your background. You have some obvious anger issues. If there will be a downfall to your career here, that will be it. Well, as for the rest, it's basically politics of one form or another."

"What do you mean?"

"Ultimately, everyone is concerned about the optics. With you gone from the NYPD, the mayor, on one hand, can spin that they fired a racist cop who had two altercations with people of color. On our side, we get a competent person who is not only a person of color but also gay. We strive to be diverse here. On the other hand, we were told about your anger issues; it's a concern. We don't need any problems here. We expect that you will keep that under wraps. Regardless, we believe in second chances."

I was in a blur. Ironically, I went for my default reaction: Anger. "So I get a job, the NYPD gets rid of a headache, and you get to check boxes for your corporation, and not look like a bunch of bigots?"

Kennedy started to laugh, then realized I was serious. "Mr. Rodriguez, we are a significant minority ownership company. Our CFO is transgender. We don't have any boxes to fill. We think that you would fit perfectly here, and when we hire, we try to hire for the long run."

I sat back. I should have done my own research on the company.

I shrugged off my own idiocy—my primary survival mechanism. Finally, I said, "What's the offer?"

"A hundred and fifty thousand dollars a year, plus a fifty percent bonus."

I nodded thoughtfully. But I was actually more shocked than anything.

"Fifty percent bonus?"

"Welcome to the finance world. If you were a trader, you'd be eligible for a hundred percent bonus."

"I don't know what to say."

"I take it that's a good thing. Are those terms okay?"

If I was going to be a sellout, these numbers would help me get over it. "I can't see why they wouldn't be."

He laughed. "I'll get the papers. But one last thing. We really need you here this Monday. I know that doesn't give you much time, but we need to get you up to speed, and as you realize, you have a lot of ground to cover. Once we get you running, we can be very flexible with your schedule from there."

I thought for a moment, wondering what the rush was. "I was going to spend some time away, visiting my dad..."

Kennedy frowned. "We really are short-staffed. Can I offer you a signing bonus? Say, five thousand."

What could I say?

"I guess I'll visit him on the weekends."

"Great."

He handed me a stack of forms to sign before I left. "Leave them with Nancy, the receptionist," he said, giving me a fist bump. "Great to have you aboard. See you Monday!"

I read through all the forms thoroughly. They all seemed fairly boilerplate. I signed them and headed home to my condo, gainfully employed.

CHAPTER SIXTEEN
Blood Is Thicker Than Agua

EDDIE

I had received an email late that night from BDQ. They sent me a computer-knowledge assessment and my benefits packet with a bunch of forms. I was supposed to complete them by Monday morning at nine. There were questions about health insurance, the 401k plan, supplemental coverage, life insurance. I needed to talk to someone who knew about this stuff. I might as well kill two birds with one stone. I had to call Paul, anyway; I needed money.

Around 10:00 a.m., after refilling my mug with more shitty instant coffee, I steeled myself and dialed his number.

He answered on the second ring. "Hey, Eddie. How's it going?"

"You know me."

"Yeah. That I do, Eddie."

"Thanks, Paul." I guessed he had seen the stories on the web. But that made me feel lousy. If I'd seen stories about him, I'd have reached out for sure. We were a sorry bunch.

"I know I haven't reached out. It's been a bit crazy here lately. I just interviewed someone. It might finally be three of us… not just Heidi and me."

I was fairly sure Paul's wife's name was Mary. *I had no clue who the hell Heidi was.* "Great, Paul. Hey, I was hoping you could send me my quarterly distribution a little early." We received quarterly distributions based on the trusts Paul administered for us to shield and share in our old man's holdings.

"Sure thing, Eddie. I'll ACH it to your bank tomorrow. Everything okay?"

ACH? Jesus, even the way he talked bugged me. He didn't realize that in the real world…"Yeah… I need a car."

"Good for you, Eddie. What was it that you've been driving, a Toyota, right? I assumed you didn't want to talk about it. I read about what happened with you online. Did everything work out?"

I hadn't even told him I'd been demoted from detective. He was going to love this. "Nope… the other way, Paul… I was fired."

"Fired?" Paul paused for a moment. "I'm sorry to hear. You loved that job."

"I did. But it's a fucked-up place, and I didn't help myself, either."

"Sorry about that. I am sure you will figure it all out."

"Wow, when you put it that way, I guess everything is just fine, then." I was dripping sarcasm.

"All I'm saying is I am here. Let me know how I can help."

"Thanks," I said. He was always so sure of himself, always ready to lord over his half brothers. This pissed me off. I could figure out the 401k crap on my own. "Listen, I have to go."

I hung up the phone. He immediately called me back, and I let it go to voicemail. I was getting ready to turn the ringer off when I surprised myself by hearing Mr. Kennedy in my head talking about my anger issues. I was getting ready to call him back when he called again.

"Eddie?" He sounded concerned which made me angry at myself.

"Yeah, Paul, I'm sorry."

"I am, too, Eddie. Sorry if I offended you somehow."

Suddenly, I was pissed again. "Jesus Christ, Paul! Who are you trying to impress? I was the asshole for fuck's sake. I call you up asking you for money and then hang up on you. *I* am the asshole."

He laughed, then said softly, "I know, Eddie, but you are still my brother. I worry about you."

I wasn't going to cry. I had too much pride to do that; however, I wasn't going to be a dick anymore, either. "Thanks, Paul. I really needed to hear that."

We spent a few minutes catching up. I let him know about my new job, and he told me which funds I should contribute to. He was actually the big brother I needed for once. Then I heard a voice in the background. "You need to go?"

"Uh, yeah. I'm sorry, Eddie. I have to get this. If you need anything else, let me know."

I hung up with a smile on my face.

It's funny how the mind works. I found myself craving Mexican for lunch. I didn't want to psychoanalyze myself, but I was fairly certain I was embracing my Latino background in the face of talking with my Irish-looking half brother.

I ordered some tacos, trying my broken Spanish on the street vendor, and started walking back to my condo. This got me thinking of Miguel. After the tacos, I gave Miggy a call. Unfortunately, it went to voicemail.

When I got home, I searched the internet for info on my new employer. They were certainly more than legit. On the website, it said they managed more than half a trillion dollars in assets. Started around ten years ago. I couldn't help myself. I typed into the Google search field "BDQ Investments Daniel O'Malley." I knew someone with influence had to have called to get me the new job, and with Accardi's apparent connections to the O'Malley family, that seemed to be a likely option.

There it was. Daniel O'Malley was one of the seed investors and a member of the board.

I changed my search and went down a rabbit hole with O'Malley and Kennedy. Kennedy had joined O'Malley about twenty years ago. He was hired to do HR stuff for one of O'Malley's hedge funds and then ten years later was installed as the HR head when BDQ launched.

Kennedy's was the only lily-white face I could find on the corporate website besides the transgender CFO, and she was new to the company. I had little doubt Kennedy was doing a favor for someone. Either city hall or the NYPD or both. Regardless, with the O'Malley connection, it probably involved that asshole Sandy Accardi. I was bought and paid for. Or they thought I was.

What a fucking sellout.

I looked at the clock. I'd been plodding away at this for a while. *Fuck it.* I jumped in the old Toyota and went to find the answer in my old precinct.

There were more than a few eyes on me as I walked through the precinct. I was surprised no one told me I wasn't allowed in or at least told me to stop. John was on the phone and did a double take when he saw me, gesturing for me to stop. But I was on a mission. I knocked on the captain's door. He saw me through the glass and came running to open it.

"Get in here! Come on, Eddie. You know you are not supposed to be here."

"Why not?" It came out more scared than menacing.

"Why not? Why not? What do you mean, why not?"

"BDQ was funded by Daniel O'Malley."

"So?"

"Well, Accardi and him were friends. Did he broker this with you to get me to back off?"

Captain Broward got red-faced at this. "Yes, that is exactly what it is supposed to do. Get you to back off. You have to quit fucking around with other people's lives, especially in areas that won't do anyone any good." That was the first time I had ever heard *that,* Captain.

"You need to leave Angel Centeno and Accardi alone." *Centeno? He's the key.* "They were good cops. They are good people. They've done a lot for this city."

"But what about the priests?"

"What about the priests? The feds are on it. They don't need your help. There are lots of scars among all of these people. O'Malley's family wants this put to bed. There are powerful people that just want things back in order. The priests and this precinct particularly have a complex history. There is nothing left for you to do."

"I'm not sure—"

"You're not sure?" Captain Broward now stood within two feet of my face. This was not normal for him, but I could tell he was unnerved. "You're not sure? Well, maybe you should try to get sure. You couldn't save yourself when you had a badge, Eddie. How're you going to defend yourself without one? Listen, I'm trying to help you. Besides the police and the church, there are other elements that might be connected to the Centeno name that also want you to back off. There is nothing good that will come out of you digging into this any further. Am I clear?"

I was stunned.

"Am I clear?" he yelled.

I nodded my head.

I walked out, left the precinct, and went home more confused than ever.

The Centenos. Until this case, I had forgotten about them. Growing up, they were just a local mob name, part of Arthur Avenue, which was nowhere near Riverdale, where I grew up. Even being a cop, it was rare to hear something that was mob-related nowadays, but back when I was young in Riverdale, you knew certain people were untouchable.

I tried Miggy's phone yet again. I couldn't even remember the last time we had talked. As the phone rang, I tossed ideas around.

Could it be as simple as the Mafia didn't want it to be public knowledge that one of their sons got molested? Then what about O'Malley? Was O'Malley molested? And Accardi? But if O'Malley and Accardi were both molested, presumably in high school, then why would Accardi have been such a prick to him? None of this was making sense.

Miggy called.

"Hey, Miggy? How was Florida?"

"It is good, Eddie. It is very good. I thought I told you not to call. Why are you calling me?"

"Aw, c'mon, Miggy. I thought we were past that. I took a new job and everything."

"Then why are you still pursuing this stuff, Eddie? You are hurting the people I care about."

"What?" *Did the captain call Miggy and let him know about our conversation?*

"You are still going after my friends. This is goodbye, Eddie." There was none of his Spanish that he'd throw in to lighten the conversation. He was serious.

"Hey, come on, Miggy, lighten up," I laughed.

"It doesn't matter, Eddie. Listen, I'm moving to Florida. I'm going to be here with my police family. *Vaya con Dios.*"

WTF? *Did he say "here"? Was he still down in Florida? Had he not been back to New York yet?"*

I caught him before he hung up. "So Captain Broward called you and told you what I said. That's what you are telling me."

"The captain didn't call me."

"Right, so he called Accardi. Big difference."

"No. The captain didn't call Sandy. Bye, amigo."

I was hurt but still thinking. *Then it was… John? Wait, no. Then it hit me. It was that shitbird psycho nephew. Fucking Renato Centeno.* Word definitely would have gotten around the precinct that I had talked to the captain. I was down another friend. I was more and more alone every day.

VIGILANTE PRIEST IV

Gluttony

FATHER TONY

The reflection of light from the spinning silver necklace had awakened me. Barney couldn't stop fidgeting with his chain. I could understand his nervous tic, but I had barely slept during our first three days crossing the Atlantic. We had been able to move the prisoners from the *Charlotte* to the *Dreamscape* in the eerie calm before the storm. We then scuttled Barney's favorite possession, his boat, in the approaching hurricane.

Our prisoners were isolated in the soundproofed bottom deck of the yacht. There was so much that weighed on us. Or at least me, and judging by his jittery nature, Barney. I spent hours in my cabin performing moral calculus and failing. It all caught up with me in the massive main cabin of O'Malley's former yacht.

"Can you please stop spinning that fucking chain?" I growled. I started to fade back to sleep before realizing what I had said and snapping back awake. "I'm so sorry, Barney." I caught a glimpse of Saint Christopher before Barney breathed heavily and walked to the opposite side of the cabin. I wanted to apologize more fully, but I was too groggy.

Instead, I fell deep into that strange space, a haze of being barely awake. Barney was like Saint Christopher, a giant of a man. From there my thoughts became more introspective. Saint Christopher died saving the baby Jesus by helping him across a river. Was I dying bringing down men I didn't really know and being judge, jury, and executioner to my fellow clergymen.

For judgment is without mercy to one who has shown no mercy. Mercy triumphs over judgment.

The others seemed fine with the chaos below decks. I was not. One of the priests, Father Charlie, the Bronx priest, cut the main electricity line to the lights in their rooms, which were nothing more than heavily padded cells. He saw the power line, barely visible above the thick white plastic padding, and had severed it. All the lights went out on the priests' level, but the power remained on in the rest of the boat. I volunteered to go down and fix the wiring. My initial repair job didn't last long as the wires were again cut. The others had decided to let them be in darkness for a day before repairing it again.

Miguel had asked me. "Why would the priest do that? Doesn't he realize that it will just make things worse for him?"

"I don't know."

"Father Tony, do you think they even grasp what they've done?"

"I think so, but if you twist the Bible and get too deep into the traditions of the clergy, you can find excuses and sometimes even reasons for doing evil.

"We are taught that we are the voice of God on Earth. We are taught to communicate effectively with others, to debate and win. Those are powerful tools that enable a predatory priest to lie to himself. In the wrong hands, this is very dangerous. In Father Charlie's mind, the incidents were consensual, so he has convinced himself he hasn't done anything wrong."

"Amazing. As a cop, you see some bad stuff. But you also see remorse, at least once in a while. But these guys..."

"He still thinks he's innocent, or no worse than anyone else."

I knew this because a day earlier, when I brought him a meal tray, Father Charlie used his broken Italian to ask, "Why are you doing this?"

"This is not just about you or me," I replied in English.

"Let he who is without sin cast the first stone," Father Charlie retorted.

I looked back at him, furious. He was quoting John 8:7 to me. Every sinner's denial of responsibility. He still thought I was a pedophile, the charge that had motivated me for this mission. I had never been like him. *How could he still think that, considering the lengths I was going through to remove this abomination from the Church?*

"Unlike you, I was falsely accused. But I, and the Church I love, have suffered because you and others like you have spent your life enmeshed in mortal sin."

He could not return my gaze. And so, in my anger, I chose a Bible verse only a couple of lines down from the one he had quoted to me. "Though I bear record of myself, yet my record is true: for I know whence I came, and whither I go; but ye cannot tell whence I come, and whither I go."

The smile left my face as I locked the door behind me, leaving Father Charlie to his thoughts. I had quoted the words of Jesus as if they were my own. This too was a sin. Frightening words to a captive. I was too angry to ask for forgiveness.

We had left Florida on the *Dreamscape* four days ago, after we found out that O'Malley was truly dead. At that moment, all our alibis died with him.

It was a grim moment for all of us. There was no going back. Poor Barney had joined us, thinking he'd be away from his family for a few months. Now his absence was most likely permanent. He looked broken as he accepted his fate.

Angel called his nephew in the Bronx.

"He's dead, René," Angel said. "O'Malley is fucking dead. We no longer have a protector, so watch your ass." I winced hearing O'Malley's name, not just because I missed my friend but also if anyone was listening to Renato's call, there wouldn't even be the slightest bit of ambiguity. "Yeah, I'm sure. No reason I can think of for Liam Hannigan to lie to us about that."

Angel listened to his nephew Renato Centeno and shaking his head he finally said, "Renato, listen to me. No, no, and no. Just back the fuck off. At this point, lay low. We're almost done. Rodriguez? He will soon be busy with his new gig and forget about all this. Just don't even bother.

"We barely have support for what we are doing now. Do not get the family any more involved. Do you understand? Yes or no? I'm asking a simple question." Apparently, Renato said yes, but Angel was still shaking his head.

The conversation Accardi and Angel had next didn't make me feel any better.

"I flat out don't trust Hannigan, Sandy," Angel began.

"Well, I get that, but he has been the person who has been there with O'Malley all this time. He holds a lot of cards. I mean, besides the local contacts. There's also—"

"The money," Angel said.

"Who?" Miguel asked.

"It's not important." Angel turned to Sandy. "We need to man up and be ready for anything; that's what I am saying."

"Wait a second. I thought the island was all settled and all we had to do was get there," I said.

Sandy turned to me and gave me a half smile, hoping to lower some of the tension.

"Things just got a little more complicated. Basically, O'Malley held a lot of details close to the vest. The mole in the FBI, his insiders at city hall, and the NYPD. You know, his plan was to protect us. He had to tell Hannigan about these things with the two of them on the island together. Luckily, I have some of the necessary pieces, like for the sale of the *Dreamscape* and contacting Hannigan to help us with funding and logistics. Other things, like paying the yacht's crew once we get to the island and handling things when we get there, we will have to manage ourselves."

"But—" I began.

"Don't worry, Father. I'll take care of it." Sandy smiled. But it looked forced.

When we had boarded the *Dreamscape* in Florida, there were four new members in our group. These were the men who were going to have to be paid. They had been on the yacht since it had been refitted in Cape Town to come to Miami. They did not talk to me much, but they had talked to Accardi a few times in the past and often since we all came aboard. It was agreed that they would be paid by the selling of the yacht.

They knew how to operate a big boat and had been the ones who had scuttled Barney's boat in the storm, allowing Accardi, Centeno, Barney, and Miguel to disappear. They also felt comfortable handling the sale of the yacht.

The four new members were rough-looking fugitives who had been hired on once a plan had been put into place to turn *Fortune's Folly* into *Dreamscape*. They were clearly American and appeared to be ex-military. All of them had some connection with the

Centeno family and the broader New York Mafia, even though only one of them looked slightly Italian.

Whatever affiliation they had with my family or Accardi, they did not show much warmth. It was clear they were doing this for the money. They kept mostly to themselves, talking about women and drinking.

Whoever walks with wise people will be wise, but whoever associates with fools will suffer. Disaster hunts down sinners, but righteous people are rewarded with good.

———————

Miggy's last call with ex-Officer Rodriguez was about two weeks ago. He'd be out of the picture with his new job keeping him busy. There wasn't much that could be done with the FBI. We had a resource that could help deprioritize the case, but he couldn't get it squelched. The O'Malley family and the mayor had pressured them under the guise that no one wanted to besmirch the Catholic Church any further. They assured the feds that the Vatican would work on finding the missing priest, *me*, who would soon be the only living connection involved in their case. Of course, nobody has direct control over the FBI. Take a look at any of the past presidents to prove my point.

If all of the connections to the case were either presumed dead or had fled the country, it seemed safe to believe that we would be in the clear unless we made a mistake and I got on Interpol's radar.

This would just leave us with the endgame on the island. O'Malley previously had a plan for this, but now we were going to have to figure out what to do. I knew to achieve my goals I would need to get the stories of the priests, and how they were protected by the Church, out to the press. This would be my ending but hopefully a brighter future for my Church going forward.

My soul was pleading with me. I wasn't like this. I needed to return to an earlier time, before I had sullied myself, to when love, kindness, and compassion were my first responses.

The letters that make up the word silent are the same ones that spell the word listen. This was a favorite thought of mine. A reminder of how peace and quiet are essential to understanding. Out on the deck, amid the throb of the engine and rush of the wind, I thought about the misery below.

How could no one hear the screams but me?

I refused to wait twenty-four hours to turn the lights back on.

"Come on, Barney." He was a big man, and it seemed to me he had a bigger heart than the others.

We grabbed flashlights, electrical tape, and a stun gun, and went below deck. The prisoners—Accardi and Centeno had taken to calling them scumbags—were all locked in their cells. As soon as we descended, the screams intensified.

Barney bellowed, "Shut up!"

"We are here to fix the lights," I said.

"You should thank this man, the only real priest of God on this boat. The others wanted to keep you in darkness. Father Charlie, you pull any more shit, and the darkness is going to be permanent. Now, we don't want to hear another word."

We reconnected the severed wire and wrapped the tape around it, then Barney flipped the switch in the breaker box.

"Let there be light," Barney mumbled to himself.

No one was happy with me: Barney, the priests, the mercenaries that Accardi had recruited, or the original group who helped me plan this. As penance, I took a pillow and blanket and lay in one of the empty cells in the underbelly of the yacht with the fallen priests. There... there I learned a lot.

The yelling and whispering to me became a cacophony as I fell into a deep sleep. There, after not sleeping for four days, I saw the enormity of this entire situation.

First, my thoughts went to O'Malley telling me about his haphephobia—fear of being touched—that had haunted him since the incident. He had wanted to be a doctor. He was obsessed with helping other people. Being born a genius and excelling in everything he did, life came easy for him.

After the incident, his direction changed. He became obsessed with power and money. He felt if he collected enough money, he would be protected. He never reached a point where he felt completely safe. I remember the horror of realizing the rape had killed a brilliant boy. He could have cured cancer or been a world-changing teacher, but instead his last wish before he died was revenge. This bright light in the world had been snuffed out by an agent of God. What a perversion. And now he was dead.

Second, was the day we headed out under the ruse of killing ourselves. I was leaving everything important to me, being a priest, my love of knowledge and access to the Vatican library, while the others were going to be pronounced dead in the coming weeks.

Finally, the sky was the color of blood as we watched the sunrise, confirming the approaching storm that would add a modicum of believability to the sinking of Barney's boat and the pretended deaths of its four passengers. *Red sky in the morning, sailors take warning.*

In my sleep, it hit me. We were in the Phlegethon, the seventh layer of hell, crossing the river of blood. Large bodies of water were always treated with deference in the Bible, but this was much worse. It had worked out, on the third ring—the bottom of the boat —were those who committed crimes of violence against God, and if there is anything more emblematic of that than a servant of God raping an innocent, I do not have the imagination to think of what it would be.

On the first ring, or highest level of hell, were the ones who commit violence against one's neighbor. Accardi's four recruits had settled into the bridge. Only the good Lord above knew the deeds these ex-military men had done. They were handling the navigation and would be the face of the ship through the ports. The rest of us had to avoid any contact with law enforcement.

These four knew that. And that put us at a disadvantage. They had paperwork perfectly in order showing that the boat was being delivered to Malé, the Maldive capital, for sale. They knew we were up to no good. I wondered how they might extort us.

I hadn't trusted them from the second I laid eyes on them. But we had no choice but to trust them. My solution? Pray I was wrong and trust that my team could deal with them.

That left the rest of us—Sandy, Angel, Barney, Miguel, and myself—in the main lounging area with all the provisions and space. The decadence was hard to process and, for me, impossible to enjoy. The fine furniture, the digital TVs, the fully stocked kitchen and larder would have made an ideal holiday.

We were on the second level, the second ring. Here we were doing violence to ourselves. All of us had either reformed our lives, like Accardi and Centeno, or we had lived noble lives up until this point as had Barney, Miguel, and me. But now, now we were defiling our reputations, our humanity, our very souls.

It is not for you, Uzzah, to burn incense to the Lord, but for the priests, the sons of Aaron who are consecrated to burn incense. Get out of the sanctuary, for you have been unfaithful and will have no honor from the Lord God.

It was the opposite of a holiday. An unholy day.

I was awakened by a discordant scream. One of the priests had gone mad already. I had heard the crack as he had managed to break a bone even inside the padded cell. He howled loudly as I fumbled for a key to check on him. The living nightmares were beginning already, and we were still thousands of miles away from our final destination.

CHAPTER SEVENTEEN
Just Lunch

EDDIE

Sellout or not, it worked. I ended up getting into a routine at BDQ, and three weeks went by quickly. The people were nice. I was even dressing the part with my khakis and corporate sports coat. They even gave me a nice Italian leather shoulder holster. I may have gotten the job because of connections, but I felt like I was keeping up my end of the bargain. I had finished all of my new employee modules, and now they were enrolling me in an online university to get an information technology degree with a cybersecurity certificate. They had set an aggressive pace for me, one that I was matching.

After a few weeks, I rewarded myself. I bought a used Lexus and decided to reenter the dating scene. I'm sure it was frowned upon, but I ended up dating one of the analysts at work. I figured as long as I was clear about no strings, what could be the harm. Things were looking up.

That all changed when I discovered a voicemail on my phone. "This is Agent Murray. Please give me a call at your earliest convenience."

I was surprised. "Earliest convenience" did not seem like a phrase that Agent Murray was familiar with. Maybe she'd turned over a new leaf.

I stepped away from the reception desk at the main entrance and walked into our security office, next to the mailroom, to return the call. During my normal day, when I wasn't doing training or in meetings, I would be on the first floor. Visitors at our office had to go through a metal detector. It was like being part of the TSA at the airport. If anyone saw anything question-able, I would be brought over to assess the situation. I even had a kit to swab clothing or skin for bioagents. Needless to say, I didn't know when I'd use this kit. I suppose if a client named Osama Bin Laden Jr. walked in, I might break it out. But most of my down-time was spent at a station in the lobby, which had surveillance cameras of the elevators, the reception area, and the downstairs atrium.

"Hello, Mr. Rodriguez." She knew I had been canned as a cop. I expected that. "Would you be able to meet me for lunch tomorrow?"

She must be pretty hard up for leads on the priests' case. I hadn't even thought about it in weeks. "What?" I asked, surprised.

"I was hoping we could get together near the World Trade Center?"

"The World Trade Center?" There was no way. It would take me easily thirty minutes one way, if I was lucky, maneuvering through traffic or even by subway to get there. "Nah, that isn't going to work. I only get an hour for lunch."

"How about the weekend, then?" She was blunt as always.

"What's this about, Agent Murray?"

"I think you know what this is about."

If I had a brain in my head, I should hang up now, but I was hooked and couldn't let it go.

I had plans with the analyst for Saturday night. And Sunday was out. The pace at BDQ had made me enjoy a few lazy days on the weekend. "I could get together Saturday," I was mumbling to myself more than making a commitment.

"All right. Sounds good. What would you like to eat?" She was monotone.

I thought about pleading how busy I was, but I would regret not at least hearing what she had to say. I was still curious. "Whatever. How about anything Asian?"

"That'll work. I will see you at Twenty-Six Federal Plaza at noon. I'll be outside, wearing a blue pantsuit."

The World Trade Center was a few blocks away. Twenty-Six Federal Plaza was the Javitz building. The FBI HQ. I should have guessed.

Vargas, the Manhattan cop who was smart enough to step away from this bullshit, was right, she was a vision. She was standing outside the front of the building smoking a cigarette when I arrived. I had pictured Murray as a tough, butchy-looking agent. That was based on her macho, ball-busting attitude on the phone. But that was all wrong.

Special Agent Murray looked pretty damn special. She had the kind of body a navy-blue pantsuit couldn't ruin. She was tall and lean with curves that couldn't be cloaked. Her pixie-cut hair framed a fine-boned café-au-lait face with big green eyes.

"Special Agent Murray?"

She nodded and flashed her badge, then offered a handshake.

"I see you cut your hair," I said, glimpsing her ID photo. "It works."

"Thanks for coming down."

"Are we ordering in?"

Her hands were soft and smelled of lavender. *What the fuck? Was I getting turned on?*

"That's the plan."

"It's really nice to meet you. I'm sorry if we got off on the wrong foot," I fumbled.

Jesus. I couldn't believe the words coming out of my mouth. I had known I was gay from a young age. I didn't come out until after high school. I had kissed a few girls, came close to having sex with one but messed it up because I could tell it wasn't right. But this... this was something different.

"You okay, Mr. Rodriguez?" She could tell something was off.

"I'm fine. It's just... you didn't tell me we were meeting in the FBI building. I thought this was going to be informal. Do I need a lawyer? You know I am not a cop anymore. I'm still not exactly sure what this is about?"

"You know what this is about. But let's go upstairs."

"Yes, I know what this is about, but I don't know if that means you feel that I am somehow involved. If that's what this is about, I can first assure you I am not involved and second, I would like an attorney just in case."

"No, you are not implicated."

We went up to the twenty-third floor. I tried not to look at her. But it was hard. I was totally flummoxed. She was not my type. I liked dark men, not women.

She led me into a conference room. On the way, another agent walked by, and she made eye contact with him.

"Who was that?" Not sure if I was jealous of the well-groomed white guy getting some of Special Agent Murray's attention or if I just wanted to know what I was getting myself into.

"That's Agent Cooper. I work with him. He might stop in later. I ordered us some Indian food."

I didn't say anything to that, and it suddenly got very quiet. She sat there casually looking at me. I looked at my phone.

"How's civilian life?"

"Pretty sweet. I miss being a detective. But I don't miss being a desk jockey or being everyone's whipping boy."

"You had quite a streak."

"Don't believe everything you read. Or hear."

Finally, the food came. The curry was excellent. Now and then, I would think of leaving the city but, besides the nightlife, you just couldn't beat the food. No matter where in Manhattan, Brooklyn, or Queens you were, you could find great food from all over the world. Funny that the Bronx, where I'm from and my dad had restaurants, didn't match the food of the rest of the city, except for Arthur Avenue's Italian food.

We finished eating and cleared the table. She grabbed her briefcase off the floor and took out four different-colored folders... a basic manila, a green, a red, and an orange one.

She took a form out of the red folder and handed it to me.

"What's this?" I asked. She stared at me, and once again I felt my skin get warmer. "It's a CI form. It says you are a confidential informant and you are here to aid in an investigation and that you understand that lying to a federal agent is a crime."

"I'll talk to you, but I don't want to sign anything."

"Listen, Eddie. This case is no longer active on our end. If at any point, you don't want to talk, you can just let me know and we will skip to the next question, or if you'd prefer, you can just walk." She had called me Eddie. And what did she mean by "no longer active?" Like I said, I was curious.

"Look, I appreciate a free meal, but I can't sign anything without legal advice. I'm sure you can understand."

She didn't smile.

"Okay," I shot back uncertainly. I signed and dated the form. Immediately regretting doing so. Now there was something in writing that specifically linked me to this.

CHAPTER EIGHTEEN
Bad Judgment

EDDIE

She asked me if Agent Cooper could sit in. I wanted to say no. I said, "Sure."

Agent Cooper didn't sit close to me or Agent Murray; instead, he chose to sit at the other side of the table. He placed a thick, worn black leather binder on the table and a yellow pad where he had already scribbled something.

"I think there is a lot more than what we are aware of, Eddie," Agent Murray began matter-of-factly.

"A lot more, what? You mean priests?"

"Officially, we are only at ten missing, but"—she looked over at Agent Cooper who had been staring off into the distance and he shot back a shrug—"we both think there are others."

I was irritated with Cooper's familiarity with Murray. He was probably nailing her. I shook my head for a moment. *What the fuck is wrong with me?* My irritation with myself affected my response. "So?"

That sent Agent Murray back in her chair.

I worked to recover. "Sorry. I mean, I just don't know what I can do as a civilian. You know how hard I worked on this case. I'm pretty sure it cost me my shield for fuck's sake. The violence charges were bullshit. My work on the Father Charlie case is what got me bounced. What am I supposed to do with any of this?"

"I found a few things that link back to your angle." She started taking something out of the manila folder.

"I didn't realize I had an angle."

"Okay, ex-Detective Rodriguez, let's make a deal. I won't pretend that I am not trying to get you to help me with, frankly, something that I shouldn't be working on, and you don't pretend that you don't have some pretty interesting thoughts on this case. Does that seem fair?"

"Fine. But I prefer Eddie to ex-detective."

"So when was the last time you talked to your friend Miguel?"

"Juarez? What does he have to do with any of this?"

"He had a professional moving company that packed him up in New York and moved his belongings down to Miami."

"What are you saying? That he's involved? The guy retired. If he is involved, in what way?"

"I'm trying to put some threads together myself." She thumbed to another piece of paper in the manila folder. "So we know Accardi, Centeno, and Fergusson were down there in Miami, and Juarez came in later."

"Fergusson?" That was a new one.

"Yes, Barney Fergusson. Accardi's former partner on the force."

"So? And when you say Centeno, I take it you mean the uncle and not the young one, right?"

"All right, Eddie. How about we call the officer in your old precinct Young Centeno and the one down in Florida who worked with Accardi back in the day, Uncle Centeno?"

"Fine with me. Just trying to make sure we're clear."

"May I continue?"

I shrugged.

"So we also know O'Malley owned a property on Fisher Island, and that is where he kept his prized mega yacht, *Fortune's Folly*."

"Fisher Island?" This was going in too many different directions.

"Yes. Fisher Island in Florida. It's a hotspot for billionaires and their boats off Miami Beach." She looked over at me as if this were common knowledge.

Cooper, who had been quiet since we started, rapped his knuckles on the table twice.

She glanced over at him, nodded, and Cooper said, "So when was the last time you talked to Juarez?"

Now, I was pissed. "I don't know. Shit. Juarez, as you call him, I call him Miggy, he was a mentor of mine while I was on the force. He wrote me off because I was digging into this too much for him to be comfortable with—"

"That makes sense."

That angered me. "Fuck you. I'm not talking to you." I switched my gaze back to Murray.

"I didn't even know he was moving. It was me that put him in contact with Accardi and Uncle Centeno as we're calling him. I was worried about him being lonely. And then my conversations with him, they started getting confrontational. You saying this is why?"

"What happened, Eddie?" Murray asked.

"I guess he might have started buying into whatever Accardi was up to. Miggy told me to stop working on the case and asking questions.

"All I've gotten out of this is pain. If you don't start making sense and stop wasting my fucking time, I will take the option you gave me at the beginning and walk."

"Sorry about that, Eddie." I couldn't tell if Agent Murray was trying to be sympathetic, but it came across as hollow.

That was it. I started to stand up.

Cooper jumped in. "We think your ex-cop friends are gathering up these priests and torturing them or worse. There is obviously bad blood here."

"What?"

Murray shot a surprised look at Cooper.

Agent Cooper looked at her. "No, when we brought him in here, we had decided to show him our hand, so let's do it.

"Eddie, you gave Agent Murray the Father Anthony angle. Not sure how you came up with that, but it opened everything up for us. At that point, things got very difficult for you. It doesn't look like your hitting a pedestrian was staged, but we agree with you: the blowback you got was heavy-handed.

"Then we find out that they put young Centeno on the case. Someone not even in Missing Persons. This was a mistake by anyone trying to keep this hush-hush. We then do a search for Young Centeno and come up with some penny-ante stuff but nothing serious. However, who pops up in the computer search? The uncle. We started connecting more dots. Uncle Centeno was molested. This gave us a clearer motive, and we started looking at the ex-cops. Father Anthony flew into Miami International a few weeks earlier. Things started looking promising."

I sat back down as Cooper continued, "One of the least well-kept secrets was that O'Malley was molested also—"

"And Accardi," I added, to finish the trifecta. *So I was right on this.*

"No. Not Accardi," Cooper shot back. "Accardi is interesting. We are not sure if he did it because of a code or if he was given orders, being both Italian and part of the police force. I take it you figured out that he is the one rumored to have stabbed the original pedophile priest, Father Donovan, an unbelievable forty times."

Shit, I hadn't thought of that. I sat there, a bad poker player trying not to be read.

Cooper wasn't fazed. "The working theory is that they, the ex-cops, are finding these priests, potentially with the help of Father Anthony, who has his own baggage. Twenty-five years ago, he was Father Tony, a local NYC pedo-priest who skipped to Italy once the finger was pointed at him. Most likely the ex-cops coerced him to give them the names of the different pedo-priests throughout the country, and they started to snatch them up.

"But then there are still tons of questions like how do you store a bunch of priests in a place where they don't ask many questions? Well, how about Fisher Island in Miami? With all of the ultrarich there, you would think they'd have better cameras. Never seem to be able to get any video of anything that happens there when we ask. We have it on good authority that O'Malley owned a slip there under a shell company."

I looked back blankly at Cooper. "You know what I'm saying, Eddie? Whether some old rich dude is taking some girl out on his yacht and doesn't want the wife to know about it or other kinky crap, underage girls… boys… I mean, who knows all the stuff they get away with.

"However, even if we assume that they have no problem boarding the priests onto the yacht, there is still one obvious catch. It's crazy to think that this Father Tony would be able to know that many of them. Like it's public knowledge for anyone in the Vatican. Crazy. Your cop friends must have something good on him, because he was traveling and moving alone, to the best of our knowledge, until all of them disappeared recently.

"Another thing is the yacht. While buying a yacht could technically create a paper trail, isn't it still less risky than using O'Malley's existing yacht? Everything else being equal, they probably wanted to sink it, but where do you sink a billionaire's boat without getting a thousand people looking for it? If someone finds it, the jig is up when they don't find O'Malley's body.

"Forget what the family said about it being somewhere off the

coast of Perth. The family told us that the last contact was in the
Arabian Sea. They claim they didn't want to put more people at risk
getting close to the Somali pirates and other criminal activities, but
we think that's just a cover. Unbeknownst to them, we were able to
get a reasonable search of the area, and nothing came up showing a
sunken boat that size. So the working theory is that they refitted the
old yacht to transport the priests.

"Then you still have the problem of getting the priests somewhere where there are no eyes on you. Agent Murray has a theory,
but let's just say it isn't perfect." Agent Murray frowned at that but
not in an angry way, almost in agreement.

"I think they are taking them to the Maldives." She took
over.

"The Maldives? Like islands?" I was pretty sure they were
islands.

She answered, "Yes. Islands. There are close to twelve hundred
of them, and many of them are privately owned. Not to mention,
they are the farthest island chain from the Eastern United States.
This coupled with the Arabian Sea makes sense. Why would the
family say that to the FBI separately and not to the public unless
they wanted to control the number of eyes looking for the yacht? If
someone said they spotted a yacht that looks like O'Malley's near
the Maldives, they could claim, of course they did, that it was on the
way to the Arabian Sea."

"So?" I asked, curious to hear more.

Still, she bristled before answering, "So we made some calls to
places that have the capacity to refit boats this size around the time
of the claimed sinking of O'Malley's yacht, and we get a hit. One
week after *Fortune's Folly*, O'Malley's yacht, sinks, a boat by the
name *Iuvart's Ark* was registered out of Cape Town. The name was
quickly changed to the much more neutral *Dreamscape* out of the
Bahamas, but—"

Cooper laughed at this. "But they were basically giving law

enforcement the finger. They slipped up. If it hadn't been so obvious, we might have missed it."

This was exhausting. "I'm sorry what...Iu Wart... Am I supposed to have any idea what that is? It sounds like a fucking Harry Potter character."

Cooper gave a wry smile at that. "No, close but not that work of fiction... the other one."

I threw my hands up at that.

Agent Murray jumped in, "That's Cooper's attempt at a joke. He is talking about the Bible. Iuvart was a fallen angel. We think that the *Iuvart's Ark* was O'Malley's old yacht, *Fortune's Folly*." Murray tried to wrap up the pieces. "We have it on good intel that a yacht very similar to *Fortune's Folly* wound up in Cape Town and ended up getting refitted and reregistered. It's owned by a holding company out of the Caymans, but no chance of finding out who the principals are now, since we no longer have jurisdiction. Anyway, we have on reasonable authority it was ported in Miami until recently. Unfortunately, there are lots of yachts in that area, and while we think there is a slip owned by a shell O'Malley corp there, we don't know where it is.

"Regardless, we believe that O'Malley got dumped off with a small crew on an island in the Maldives to set things up while waiting for the others to show up later with the priests on the renamed and refitted yacht to mete out a sort of justice."

"Well... Jesus... that seems to be a stretch." This didn't seem right. "So, what... O'Malley just walked away from being a billionaire to do all this?"

Cooper started to speak, but Murray quickly interrupted. "Another well-known secret—O'Malley had advanced brain cancer and was dying. That's the reason for the relatively half-hearted search for him and the attorneys and insurance companies not putting up much of a fight while they were carving up his estate."

I looked at them both. "So what? His dying wish was to extract justice from a bunch of pedo-priests." Cooper shrugged. Murray, as per usual, didn't show any emotion at all.

I had to try to poke some holes in this. "So you really think that some random priest in the Vatican would know that many pedophile priests throughout the country? That doesn't sound odd to you?"

Cooper jumped in on that one. "Well, yeah, it's odd. This whole case is odd. Maybe, old Father Tony wanted to feel like he wasn't all alone as a priest who had screwed up. Maybe, he made it his mission to keep track of as many of them as possible to make himself feel better. It might explain why the Vatican is not offering any cover to protect Morelli and is fine with him getting thrown in jail and having the key thrown away: out of sight, out of mind. They sure as shit don't want a guy who can name names out there, and they certainly don't want to have to answer any questions. Make him look crazy to law enforcement, right?"

I ignored his leading question. "So what? These ex-cops somehow get clued in that some old priest who molested some kid, what, fifty some years ago is back in town. And then they, what? They grab him, and he says, *No don't hurt me. I have the names of a bunch of others*? I mean, come on."

Murray looked at me stone-faced. "Yeah. It's thin. That's what we are saying. It's thin."

"And Father Anthony is able to find the names? You still haven't convinced me of that. Do you think the Vatican keeps a list somewhere with bad priests on it… like Santa?" I laughed at that.

They both looked back at me, neither of them smiling. I took a breath to gather myself. "Wait. Why are you telling me all this?"

Murray leaned in. "Juarez is the newest one. If any of them are not committed, he would be the most likely. Everyone is missing at this point: the boat, Juarez, Morelli, Accardi, Fergusson, Angel Centeno. They are all gone.

"We tried leaning on the young nephew, Centeno, but he's claiming that he doesn't know anything. When we asked him about the calls he had been having with his uncle, he claimed they were just 'checking-in' calls. Lots of 'checking-in' calls since the two of them had only talked maybe ten times over the previous five years until recently."

"Who's Morelli?"

"The Vatican priest," Cooper said.

"Father Anthony," I said.

"Father Tony," Murray said.

"I can try to reach out to Migg— Juarez, as you call him, but he doesn't trust me and told me never to call him again."

Murray looked into my eyes. "Well, whatever you could do, it would be appreciated. We never were directly able to attach any of the ex-cops to the disappearances; they just happened to be in the wrong place at the right time."

"What do you mean by that?" I asked.

"Okay, so we were able to track both Accardi and Angel Centeno in New York, and we were also able to track them both in Florida."

"Great work. They live in Florida, and they still have ties here."

Cooper returned with a wry smile. "That's right, but what's interesting is that when the other allegedly pedo-priests were, by our theory, nabbed in Tennessee and South Carolina and Georgia, Accardi and Centeno seemed to vanish."

"What do you mean?"

"There're no cell calls, no credit card usage, no nothing. It's like they locked themselves up in their homes for a few days when these things were going on. Pretty suspicious. No doubt using burner phones and cash. The reason we think there are more priests is that we see other dead zones in their credit card and cell phone activity."

"So how did you get Accardi and Uncle Centeno?" I shot back.

"Centeno was easy. He has enough shit in his past we can tap him whenever. Accardi was a bit trickier, but we were able to get him because of his connection with O'Malley, and we know the guys that were on the O'Malley missing persons case. It was our fellow agents in Missing Persons who did the majority of the work, tracking the yacht and getting us a better timeline on O'Malley."

"This is all very interesting. And very gratifying. I knew that prick Accardi was up to no good. But other than calling Miggy, what can I do for you?"

Special Agent Murray sighed. "At this point, we aren't getting any additional resources, and we've been told to focus on other cases. I was able to at least get the case forwarded to Interpol because of the missing priests, Father Tony, and the help from the Vatican, but at this point, we are being told to wait until something pops up."

"Do you think someone higher up in the FBI is trying to cover this up?"

Cooper answered, "I doubt cover it up. But certainly the Catholic Church and the mayor, one of many of O'Malley's friends, want us to back off. But that could just be that both O'Malley and the mayor have been involved in the Church for years. Obviously, any press involving pedophile priests is press the Church wants to avoid. Anyway, our higher-ups don't want us to waste any more time on this until we have something specific."

"And you're hoping I can help dig up something specific."

"We wanted to put our heads together," Murray said. She smiled at me. That smile was a weapon that could send a gay man into an identity crisis.

"I'll try Miggy. And I'll think if there are other leads. How's that?"

"Great. Thank you."

I stood up feeling exhausted. The smarter part of me thought it's probably just best to forget about this entire afternoon. I walked out hoping to do that and get back to enjoying my new life.

CHAPTER NINETEEN
Boy Scout

EDDIE

I had taken an Uber to lunch. I didn't want to deal with finding parking and maybe I was overthinking it, but I also didn't want to have the *Lexus* I bought to be spotted next to the FBI building.

The Uber ride back was going to be paid by my signing bonus from the company whose only stipulation was they didn't want me to do what I was doing. On the elevator back down to the lobby I thought of a couple of things. Some of this was starting to make sense in a twisted way. Morelli, Father Tony the Vatican priest, was known to have visited at least two of these pedo-priests beforehand, and that's just what I knew from the New York cases.

Is it possible that one of the ex-cops knows about one or both of these NYC pedo-priests and grabs Father Tony and threatens him to tell them what else he knows? It was thin, but at least it was something. And the young Centeno—what benefit would he get from half-assing the back end of this case? He must have known some form of justice was going to be meted out. Or he was getting paid off.

The other thing was that this whole lunch was obviously just done to provoke me. They wanted to get "Crazy Eddie" to go shake some trees and see what would fall out. They couldn't give a fuck about me, sitting in their cushy FBI offices. If I burn on this, so be it. As long as they get this case resolved.

I left a message for Miggy anyway. The call went right to voicemail, no ring at all. If half the shit the feds told me was on the level, I wanted to check on him and make sure he was all right, regardless. I hit the gym for the first time in a month. It felt good. I went home and jumped in the shower. As the hot water and steam surrounded me, the image of Agent Murray smiling at me swirled into my head. I soaped up my face, in a half-hearted effort to erase it.

I had a date in a few hours. What the hell was I doing wondering if a painfully pretty FBI agent had the hots for me? Or if I had the hots for her. *WTF!* I was too young to be going through a midlife crisis. *So what was going on with me?* I had moved from not caring about money to having thirty-minute conversations with my brother about 401k plans, I had bought a Lexus, and I had started dressing less conservatively.

"Eddie," I said, toweling dry, "you're not a cop anymore. You've been through the fucking wringer. Give yourself a break."

That was the last bit of stress I had for the weekend. The rest of it was fantastic. I had been able to just unwind and not think about this garbage for at least a couple of days. And I was most definitely still gay.

At work I had gotten a parking space in the building. This was unheard of for jobs in the city. My Lexus blended in well with the garage full of luxury automobiles. On the drive downtown I thought about my strange interaction with Agent Murray, and I frowned, I had been excited by the adrenaline surge regarding a case like this. It was not so much her that I was attracted to, it was the job. I missed the buzz of the life-and-death nature of working a case. I was turned on by her getting me back in.

I got through a couple of days before I couldn't help myself. I tried Miggy again. I felt a rush of anticipation at being in the hunt. The call went right to voicemail. What a drag. I had dipped my toe in the water. Now I wanted to swim.

I called John. "Hey, John, it's Eddie."

I hadn't talked to John since our uncomfortable dinner in the Village.

"Hey, Eddie. I've been meaning to call." I knew it was a lie. But a lie was better than him telling me to get lost.

"No sweat, John. The phone works both ways. Sorry about when we went out to dinner. Things were still pretty fresh with me getting fired and everything. I have to tell you, I have been really curious about what you thought you heard."

There was silence.

Then he said, "You want to grab a cup of coffee or something?"

"Sure thing."

We met at an Ethiopian coffee shop near Columbia University. He had searched online for a coffee place with a good Yelp review but not any of the chains. He must be going for some sort of merit badge, helping the gay Latino and now the immigrant coffee shop guy. I laughed at the thought as he was arriving.

"What's so funny?" he asked.

"Nothing much, just remembering something at the office," I lied.

We settled outside. The weather was about as nice as it gets for the city heading into the end of September.

"How's the girlfriend?" I asked.

"Good, I think. We got engaged three weeks ago."

"Damn! We should be drinking champagne, not coffee. Congratulations."

"Thanks, Eddie."

"Man," I said, fighting off the urge to joke about the two of us never getting together. "Our worlds keep changing… for the better, in your case."

"I hope so. What about you? There's a rumor you came out of your nightmare living large."

"Life is good at the new company. Yep." I intentionally let the silence become awkward.

"I take it you want me to tell you what I heard," John finally said, wincing.

John looked around as if we were about to perform a drug deal, then took a deep breath. "Okay, so I am outside the precinct waiting for Debbie to arrive." If I hadn't taken a large swig of coffee and almond milk, I would have asked, who's Debbie? and almost certainly pissed him off again. *Debbie is the fiancée, you dickhead,* I scolded myself.

John continued, "And I see Renato Centeno talking on his cell phone outside, no earbuds; he's got it old-school, pushed up against the side of his head, and I'm pretty sure he's talking with his uncle, you know, Angel Centeno?"

I nodded.

"So he starts the conversation with 'A it's R.' This immediately grabbed my attention: well, that and having his phone shoved against his head. I mean, if he's using a burner, his earbuds wouldn't be synced, and the person he is calling wouldn't recognize the number, so he has to let him know who it is, right?"

I shook my head, impressed so far. Also, thinking the A could have stood for that asshole Accardi as much as it might have been his uncle.

"So he's talking about how, 'I will handle that,' then a gay slur. I take it, talking about you. Then a bunch of uh-huhs and buts from him. Anyway, based on this and other conversations I've overheard, I'm pretty sure that Centeno's uncle and some higher powers were the ones who got you off the force."

I couldn't believe this was it. I put on a broad smile and sarcastically said, "Well, no shit." I'm sure it wasn't just the Centenos; Accardi was also involved.

John surprised me by not smiling back and continuing, "It's the next part that really got me." He swallowed and began with his required disclaimer. "Like I said, I'm not one hundred percent I heard him right, but I think I heard the young Centeno say 'Dead?' Like it was a question. At that point, he started talking fast and loud: 'Well, then the deal is fucked. We need to bail on this immediately. There's no alibi, then!' As soon as those words were out, though, he must have realized he was talking out of school. He lowered his voice and moved farther down the block. I saw him turn and look at me, but fortunately, Debbie arrived, so I made a big deal about hugging her and headed her in the opposite direction from him."

I made the snap decision not to let John get any deeper into this hole. Centeno could cause him nothing but pain.

"That's pretty interesting. It jibes with some things I've heard," I said. "He was probably talking about getting my case. I was the one who was dead, so to speak. Everyone knew that. As for the alibi stuff, I'm pretty sure that's just something Angel got mixed up in. A tax thing. Sandy mentioned it to me."

"I'm pretty sure he said, 'We got no alibi,' Eddie. But you know, street noise. Maybe you are right. But why would he brag about getting your case?"

"Probably to show off. Kid was a fucking police officer, a beat cop before this. Sandy or his uncle pulled some strings. He wanted to let them know he was on his way. I really wouldn't worry about it."

John nodded. I wanted to put more distance between him, Centeno, and me. "I was wondering if maybe you heard anything about the captain? I think he really sold me down the river. Fucking guy always told me he had my back, meanwhile, my career moved in reverse, thanks to him."

"The captain? Not really. Although, one night at Pauline's after you left, some guys were talking about how we should start a betting pool on whether the captain gets a promotion or the heave-ho because of the headlines you generated."

"What was the consensus?"

"I think most felt he would get a promotion. You were the sacrificial lamb."

"Amen to that, John. I agree. Just a bunch of fuckheads. I'd steer clear of Centeno and the captain, and stay close to your fiancée."

John visibly brightened. A load had been taken off his shoulders. He smiled at me, stood up, and gave me a warm hug. "I'm really glad I talked to you about this. It had been keeping me up for weeks. Call me anytime, Eddie. We should do this again sometime."

He walked away and headed for his car. I felt proud of potentially getting my own merit badge: the not-ruining-some-poor-guy's-career-over-some-psycho-ex-cop's badge.

But I had a lot to think about. John's story was fascinating. Who was dead? A priest? Sandy's billionaire pal, O'Malley? What was the alibi for? Kidnapping? Murder?

All these were good questions. Especially if they led to answers. I felt that investigatory rush again. *God help me.*

CHAPTER TWENTY
Sins Of The Father

EDDIE

I needed to walk away. If I dump this on Murray, she can run with it. They would have to look into a phone call with the word "dead" in it if these ex-cops are considered suspects.

I tried to shake it, but now it was all I could think about. What if the ex-cops were working with Father Anthony, or for him? Or vice versa? But why would a pedo-priest help ex-cops catch other pedo-priests? Maybe it wasn't just O'Malley bankrolling the whole thing? I mean, yachts and an island? Lots of moving parts.

Also, the timeline was fucked. Let's believe the fantasy that Father Tony gets caught red-handed by the ex-cops and he even has this *Rainman*-type ability to remember pedo-priests and their locations. Still, how quickly can they get the operation moving? I mean, supposedly they had an island ready to go to and a refitted boat. That would take some time. How could they even know Father Tony would have names?

On the other hand, let's say that Father Tony gave names to the ex-cops to set all this up, but still that leaves us with the same why, not to mention how would this Father Tony stay connected with all these people? Also, if for some bizarre reason he wants to do this, why not just give the ex-cops the names instead of flying back to the US where he could be implicated? I mean, there can be holes in a theory, but this was Swiss cheese.

Then what about basic detective shit? Did they interview Fergusson's wife? Did they send any cops poking around Fisher Island? Talk to the dockmasters? There was a lot wrong here.

Murray was late answering my call. This time I actually heard it ring twice before she picked up. Maybe this was her version of playing hard to get.

"Murray."

"Hey, it's Rodriguez." She must be in the middle of something. Otherwise she would have seen my name.

She didn't say anything, so I decided to take the lifeline. "Hey, you know what, it's nothing. Just call me back—"

"Nope. Give me a second."

"Okay." I could hear her walking briskly and then opening a door.

"Are you done?" It took me a second to realize she wasn't talking to me.

I heard a muffled "What?" Another woman's voice.

"I need the room. Now."

I heard a door click and then Agent Murray, "What do you have, Eddie?"

Did she just kick someone out of a restroom? I decided to sit on my conversation with John and instead point out some of the shit that Murray and Cooper missed. "So I've been thinking, and there is no way that your theory could be correct."

"Really, why not?"

"Well, first off, even if by miracle you are right that the ex-cops squeezed Father Tony into giving them the names of other pedo-priests... I mean, how does O'Malley, the next day, have everything magically set up? He had to buy a fucking island, right?"

"Go on," she responded calmly.

"Well, then what about Fergusson's wife? Did you have a conversation with her? She's still down in Miami, right? Why didn't you or Cooper have a chat with her?"

"We did."

"And what about Father Anthony? Have you at least considered that he might be cooperating with the ex-cops and not just being manipulated?"

"Of course."

"Well, why didn't you two bring any of this shit up at lunch?"

"Well, Eddie. Don't blame Cooper. That was my idea. I figured that if you had any interest you would roll this around in your head, ruminate on things, and come back with questions. I'm glad you did. You are still a cop with or without the badge."

"Well, fuck you. I'm not looking for your approval." I took a breath. "I mean... you realize in no way is this shit good for me. There is not a single scenario where I become chief of police or have fucking Chris Evans playing me in the made-for-TV movie. The ending here is me getting fired from my current cushy gig or maybe Centeno's mob friends bury me in a fucking building, or maybe, and this is as good as it gets, I just get jerked around by you for the next six months or so, wasting my time and making me fucking miserable."

"Chris Evans?"

"What?"

"You think Chris Evans would play you?"

"The only one playing me now is you! What the fuck is wrong with you, are you drunk? I'm not fucking around. I'm done."

"Relax, Eddie. I'm trying to calm you down. It's a tactic to keep CIs calm. If you change the direction of a conversation, it can remove some of the tension and worry."

"CI? I'm just a confidential informant?"

"No, Eddie. You are not a CI, but the relationship we have is very similar. I mean, to the extent that I don't have a lot to offer you, besides the fact that you are helping others."

Her blunt honesty slowed me, but I couldn't help myself. "Great, I will be the savior of pedophile priests. My friends and family will be so proud."

"Wouldn't they?" There was no humor.

"Okay, Murray." I wasn't a cop anymore and she was right. Anything I was doing at this point was purely for her benefit. "So what else are you hiding from me?"

"Nothing. That is it, Eddie. As for the interview with Fergusson's wife, it went nowhere. She had already filed a missing persons report before we even got involved, and she was still hysterical when we talked to her. If she was faking it to cover for the husband, she deserves an Oscar."

I still wasn't on board fully, so I decided to sit on the Centeno conversation for now. "So, I am glad I passed your Detective 101 test. I will let you know if Miggy calls me. Other than that, I am done."

"Wait," she interrupted.

"Yeah?"

"Well, there is something else you could do if you wanted to help. The son still works in New York City. He's with the New York Fire Department."

"The son?"

"Yes, Fergusson's son. We tried to reach out and he stonewalled us. You know, kept on saying he's busy and keeping the conversation short. I threw in there if we find out anything about his father, would he want us to inform him, and of course he had to say yes to that. I didn't want to reveal to him what we had at the time."

"Okay."

"My thought is you could reach out to him and just talk broad-brush about how you talked with Accardi and Juarez. If he knows anything, and you play your hand right, he might assume that you are part of the enablers of the ex-cops and will give you something that we can use. If he doesn't know anything, you can just come across like you care. Right?"

"Right? No, not right. What if Accardi or Centeno or even Papa Fergusson said something to him like *Hey, there's this prick cop out there that we got fired who is snooping around in our business. Let us know if you see him doing anything fishy and we'll take care of it.* There's that, right?"

She was silent. Then she said, "Good point. Okay, I get it, Eddie. If you are scared of the potential repercussions, I understand."

"Fuck that. Don't try to play me. I'm not scared. I'm being smart... for about the first time in my life."

"Eddie, I get it. Listen, I will leave you with his name and number, and if you are up for it, great. If not, that's fine also. Whatever you can do. If you can keep on reaching out to Juarez to check on him, that would be appreciated also."

She gave me his name, Brady Fergusson, and his number.

CHAPTER TWENTY-ONE
Maybe Death Isn't Certain

EDDIE

I had gone back to my cushy gig, even taking the precaution of breaking up with the boyfriend, at least briefly. What we had was too important, especially with everything else going on. I did focus hard on work and made sure our relationship remained a secret in the office. I told myself I would never call Brady Fergusson, but the call from Captain Broward changed everything.

"Hey, Eddie. How're things going? I'm hearing good things." He was checking up on me. Obviously.

"Good, Captain. Glad to be someplace I'm wanted." I had paused for a moment thinking of calling him by his first name instead of captain.

"Come on, Eddie. I hope you know it wasn't like that."

It took me a second to understand what he meant. "Oh no. I wasn't picking on that, Captain. I meant the job itself. Didn't I hear that one of ours in Brooklyn got shot last week and the perp said he wanted to kill a cop?"

"Yeah. Yeah, that's right. Officer Johnson. He's going to pull through, but you are right; it's messed up."

"So, are you just checking in on me, Captain, or are you calling for another reason?"

"Well, yeah, of course I'm checking in, Eddie, but there is something else. How are you doing anyway? Anything new?"

"Everything is fantastic, Captain. Couldn't be better. So what's the something else?"

"Yeah, right." He cleared his throat. "Well, we are having a service at the church nearby. I think it would be good if you came."

What? "A service? I guess I appreciate the offer, but it's not like I am all that religious—"

"No, I got that, but it's a memorial for Accardi, Fergusson, and Juarez. I think it would be good for you to—"

"Wait… a memorial service? What the fuck? Are they dead? Miggy?"

"Jeez, Eddie. I'm sorry. I thought you knew."

"When did this happen?" I could feel my stomach turn. *Why the fuck didn't Agent Murray tell me?* I mean, if they were all dead, then that was it, the case was over. *Why the fuck wouldn't she have called?*

"Oh man. I'm really sorry. I thought you knew, Eddie. It happened a week or so ago."

"How the fuck would I know anything? I'm out, remember?"

"Yeah, anyway, sorry about that. It would still be great for you to be there. The service is Sunday at three at St. Dominic's."

Wait. Once again, something was off. "You mentioned Accardi, Fergusson, and Juarez, but no Centeno. Is Centeno around? Was he the one that—"

"What? No. No, we lost Angel Centeno also. His nephew is pissed we aren't recognizing him in the police funeral. Actually, it's not even an official funeral yet. We want to give it another month before we do that. It's just that the family should be allowed to grieve."

I got the Centeno part... "What do you mean, it's not official? Were the bodies"—the word was poison in my mouth—"mutilated that badly?"

"Mutilated?" Captain Broward sounded genuinely confused at that. "No, that's not it. They haven't found the bodies."

This was getting frustrating. "Wait. Find the bodies? What exactly happened?"

"Fergusson had a small fishing boat that they would take out on most weekends, not to mention a few times during the week. So, the last anyone saw them was right around tropical storm Oliver. You know in early September, it hit Miami pretty hard. Fergusson's Wellcraft 270 Coastal was found in pieces a couple weeks ago. No chance they could have survived this long."

I didn't buy for a minute they were dead, based on my conversations with Agent Murray. They must have destroyed the boat when they left on O'Malley's old yacht for the middle of nowhere. "Yeah, well, thanks. I'll try and make it," I said, trying to get off the phone so I could call Murray and lay into her.

"I know you didn't care for Accardi, but Juarez, I always thought you liked him."

"I sure did, Captain," I said, feeling like a dick, even though I was pretty sure they weren't dead. But Captain Broward didn't know that. "I'm sorry, Captain. I don't know what I am saying. I think I might be in shock." A broad smile crossed my face on that bit of acting.

It worked. "Nah, it's okay, Eddie. See you Sunday."

I sat down on my couch, took a sip, and counted backward from ten. I was trying to relax, but then something else began to bug me. Broward had been three steps ahead of me this entire time, and with all he knows, he's a hundred percent bought in that they are all dead, and there wasn't any funny business? I took another sip and placed the call.

"Murray," she answered.

"I thought you told me you weren't going to jerk me around anymore, Agent Murray."

"I'm not. So have you heard from Juarez?"

"What? Wait. Is that a fucking joke? Like, did I perform a fucking seance? You can't be telling me that you don't know that he is considered dead at this point, right?"

"That's the way I would have put it."

Damn she was annoying to talk to. "Listen, I don't want to play any fucking games with you. Why didn't you call me and tell me he's dead?"

She responded coolly as usual. "You said it yourself, Eddie: *he's considered dead.* I know you are not buying this. This is just another way to close the case."

She had me there. "Yeah, I guess. It's just that you should have called. I had to find out from my ex-captain."

"Well, sorry about that, Eddie. Anyway, just in case there is any doubt in your head about this, they found dark blue paint almost dead center on the starboard side of the craft."

"So what's the deal with dark blue paint?"

"It's the same color as *Dreamscape,* you know, O'Malley's refitted old boat. It looks like they ran over it to split it in half, dangerous move, but I guess they thought blowing it up would have been too suspicious and not given them proper cover to make it look like they died in a storm."

"So this has to be good news for you. If they connected the paint samples to *Dreamscape,* then they have to give you some leeway on opening up the case again."

"Nope, the opposite. The dark blue paint didn't make it into the report. I placed a call to the Coast Guard petty officer who spotted the debris and made the original call. He was the one who told me about the paint."

"Great. So did you tell your boss?"

"He said let sleeping sailors lie."

"I thought your organization always gets its man."

"That's the idea," she said. "Also, I probably should have let you know about the boat crash. That could have gone wrong for you depending on how you responded to your ex-captain. I owe you one. My first name is Amanda. Gotta go."

VIGILANTE PRIEST V
Greed

FATHER TONY

It was Father Gerald who had awakened me the night I had slept below deck. I had thought he had gone mad, but he had told me he had only tripped in the darkness. The elderly priest refused our assistance, barely moving from his bed, while his leg swelled to twice its normal size. I don't know whether it was a broken bone or a blood clot, but by the time he called out for help, a high fever had taken hold of him. We gave him antibiotics and anti-inflammatories, but based on the smell, some kind of sepsis must have taken over. He died two days later.

Accardi and Centeno removed his body and tossed it overboard. His empty cell interfered with the ability of the prisoners to communicate. The padded rooms were not completely soundproof, and if the priests were loud enough, they could hear their immediate neighbor. They passed messages from room to room to check on each other and discuss their fate and survival. But Father Gerald's room had been in the middle. And when Father Julio and Father Timothy both decided to protest with vows of silence, it split the remaining priests into two sets of two and two sets of three, where each set assumed the worst. They were all terrified.

The fourteen-room horseshoe on the bottom of the boat had become a burden for even Centeno who had been the most enthusiastic on enacting justice. While all the rooms had a sink and a sea toilet which was nothing more than a crude elevated hole with a seat that led to the open water, the whole level was musty and fetid, but worse than that, there was an eerie feeling of evil that all of us felt there.

We had finally reached our island in the Maldives. There was only a small stretch of beach with most of the island's shrubbery reaching to the ocean. The center of the island opened up with three main buildings of differing sizes. The one closest to the dock was the communications center. The smallest building was the entrance to where the priests would be kept. The largest building was the main living quarters. This is where the other overseers and I would sleep and eat.

Even though we were most exposed during the day when we unloaded our passengers, we still decided it was better than the night. The lights of the boat versus the blackness of night in the vast darkness was more likely to gain attention than our weary and beaten cargo being unloaded during the day. They cried and hugged each other, surprised only one had died during the journey.

I had heard stories about Hannigan, but now, months into the operation, I finally met him in person. We had to stay two hundred meters or so off the shoreline or risk running the yacht aground, so he came to us on a small speedboat.

Hannigan greeted us all with handshakes and swept his arm toward the island, declaring, "Welcome!" as if he owned the place. After that, he started scrounging through the supplies on board while the rest of us got to work. It would be dark by the time we finished unloading everything. We had to make multiple trips to unload the supplies we brought and, of course, our "passengers." After that, we would need to secure the yacht and get everyone settled.

Hannigan's thousand-yard vacant stare was constant. He was rarely engaged and would just walk off sometimes mid-sentence, mumbling at the end before finding a cigarette to smoke or something to drink.

Accardi noticed something off. We were supposed to have two speedboats because of the rule of redundancy that O'Malley had set for all things. There was only one.

Accardi asked Hannigan about this.

"It got fucking complicated, Sandy."

"What does that mean?" Accardi said.

"You don't know how much you two are fucking things up, do you?"

Accardi asked the same question, "What does that mean?"

"I am saying that there is way too much heat on this already and everyone is spooked. I'm not getting any response from the Centeno family or any of our friends in law enforcement. There is just too much heat. And when O'Malley got sick, I needed a little help."

"What does that mean?" Accardi stressed every word. "I am asking you about the missing boat."

"Our contact on the island of Malé. He's been bringing me stuff. He's the one with the other boat. The one with no electronics, so it can't be tracked. I had to trust someone. I was left all alone."

"So, wait. You were taking care of O'Malley while our contact was bringing you supplies? Did he bring you medical stuff also?"

"Well, yeah. When it got bad, he brought a nurse and a doctor?"

"A what? You telling me you brought other people here from outside? I mean, it's bad enough that you brought our contact, but—"

"Hey, fuck you!" Hannigan roared. "It's not me who fucked up here. It's you all with that bullshit with the police and feds.

"In the end, I did what he told me. Wrapped him in an American flag and tossed him into the sea."

Accardi tried to remain calm. "Well, I'm sure it didn't help when our Malé contact told our people back home that you brought outsiders on the island."

Hannigan got within three feet of Accardi. Centeno and Miguel came closer. Hannigan sounded defeated. "What the fuck was I supposed to do?"

That was the last thing said before we all went to bed. I prayed the next day would be better.

The next morning was worse. That was when I woke up to Accardi handing me a letter from his closest friend, Barney.

It began with his true first name, Sandro.

Sandro,

I feel like I am letting you down, but I don't know what to do. I was never prepared for this.

In my head, I thought I would help you all out and then get to head back to Janet and my kids and, of course, my grandkids.

You know I would die before telling anyone anything. I just need to make things right with my family.

I am not made for this type of work anyway. I would end up feeling sorry for all of them, regardless of what they did.

I'm certainly not judging you and the others. I respect all of you. This is on me.

I got a sign before I got off the boat. I no longer could find my Saint Christopher medal. The one my mother gave me when I took a Greyhound bus to go to college. The one that ensures safe travels. I searched everywhere.

Someone is telling me that I am more of a liability.

If anyone can make it through this, it's you.

I look forward to many more days in the sun with you.

Love you, brother,
Barney

I had taken the Saint Christopher medal. Barney had left it hanging like an ornament off one of the boat controls. I had felt bad for yelling at him about the medal on the trip across the Atlantic, so I had grabbed it off the boat and had planned to tell him about the importance of keeping Saint Christopher close to his heart, so he could protect him. Now, I would wear the medal until the day I died. Our mission and I needed his protection.

"Well, how did he..." I didn't even finish my own sentence. It was obvious. But Sandy spelled it out.

"He took our speedboat. He left us stranded."

We had been on the island for four days. Early on, when discussing the island, Angel Centeno wanted to name the island Azrael. He had heard or read somewhere that it was the name of the angel of death, and he was the one who judged. While in Judaism, there is reference to this name, there is no reference to this name in the Bible.

There is some discussion of Michael being an angel of death or a judge, but this is also somewhat disputed. I did not like to think of us as angels of death. I wanted us to be viewed more as teachers.

Regardless, O'Malley started using the name Michael as the name of the island. It was something that he would use in conversation, but I used the Latin Michaelus. I could not let my friend be the judge on his own. This was a burden on us all.

The sale of the yacht was supposed to be a simple transaction in the open waters between Michaelus and the Maldives' capital, Malé. I would imagine things like this could have some delays dealing with an Omani oligarch thousands of miles away and trying to get both boats to arrive at the same place at the same time. Still, there was no excuse for not getting a call on the radio or the satellite phone that we gave the four mercenaries, who had been our crew.

Accardi said optimistically a couple of days ago, that maybe after selling the yacht, the four goons who had been with the yacht since it had been refitted in Cape Town went and got supplies before coming back, but that would have taken an extra day at most, even if they had spent a night on the island before returning. Now there was no yacht, no money, and no boat. We were stuck on the island.

This was too much stress for all of us. When we arrived, our nerves were well beyond frayed. Besides the ghoulish task of having to deal with the prisoners with their age and failing health, we had to deal with the arduous northern coast of Africa.

We first went through the Strait of Gibraltar, where I remembered a fierce debate in the Vatican about whether or not it's referenced in the book of Isaiah.

From there, we were mostly worried about Interpol until we reached Egypt. Our prearranged deals came through, and we got refueled in Port Said. We made it safely through the Red Sea, then through the Gulf of Aden, a direct derivation of Eden where the human experiment had begun.

The most dangerous section for us was going past the coast of Somalia where there were still active pirates who would threaten to board. If that were imminent we would have called our Omani contact early, but only in an emergency. The purchaser of our yacht did not want any eyes on the transaction. Once past this, it was relatively safe and open waters to our island, Michaelus, in the Maldives.

My brooding was interrupted as Hannigan's hard stare had finally forced Accardi to speak.

"They might have been double-crossed by the Omanians," Accardi breathed.

Hannigan, who had been alone on the island for over a month, before dealing with this disaster, laughed out loud.

"Omanis," I said evenly, trying to change the course of the conversation.

"What?" Accardi fired back, confused.

"Maybe those ragheads took the yacht and shot your goons, but it's just as likely they just took the money and split," Hannigan barked back. He wanted to complain more about Barney again, but he was holding back. He knew it would only further divide him from the rest of us.

Even so, Hannigan looked feral, a wild animal who lacked direction. I imagined being on this island alone was a challenge. On the other hand, from what I had seen, it wasn't beyond the pale that he was always like this. It didn't matter which was true. I instinctively did not trust him. He made me nervous.

Accardi had not responded, and Hannigan's guilt was mixing with his anger.

"Well?" Hannigan yelled. "Should I have flown him home? Is that what you think? That he deserved a giant send-off? He didn't want it. This"—he waved at the island—"was the ending he wanted."

Accardi nodded. "I guess so."

"I fucking know so. The same way I know either the ragheads or your boys fucked us. Wanna bet on it?"

I could tell he was looking for a fight.

"I guess anything is possible. Greed drives people to do terrible things." Accardi leveled his eyes at Hannigan. It was hard not to think Accardi was sending a double message. Hannigan claimed that he had been locked out of the account of the remaining O'Malley money. Now that O'Malley was dead, there was nobody around to dispute this. Hannigan assured us he would go to Malé to secure additional funds. But all we had was his word.

Hannigan detected the nuance in Accardi's words. "If you have something to say, Sandy, say it."

Accardi measured the other man and then looked around, noticing it was just the three of us. Juarez and Angel Centeno were occupied with the ones we had taken. In my head, I had moved from thinking of them as priests to some form of livestock. I could hold this until I looked into their eyes again.

Let no man deceive himself. If any man among you thinks that he is wise in this age, he must become foolish, so that he may become wise.

Accardi could probably take the older Hannigan. The problem with pushing this was that Hannigan had leverage. He was the money man. Or "theoretical money man," as he was the only one who could attempt to access the money that O'Malley had put away. Not to mention, if the four people Accardi had brought on had abandoned us, and with the loss of Barney, then we were running really low on people to handle twelve captives while keeping a lookout and figuring out how to get supplies.

"I am agreeing with you. Robbers rob." Accardi stared back at Hannigan.

I couldn't suppress a smirk admiring how Accardi once again had twisted his words, implicating either Hannigan or his associates.

Hannigan shook his head and replied, "Well, you know what they say, 'Money is the root of all evil.'"

I couldn't help myself. "Actually," I said, "the quote is 'For the love of money is the root of all evil,' Timothy 6:10." I smiled once again, hoping to keep the peace.

"Up yours," Hannigan breathed out at me as he grabbed another cigarette and lit it before wandering away.

Accardi looked over at me warily.

Later in the evening, all of us got together. I was feeling more awkward than usual. I knew it had been a mistake for Sandy to give me a gun. I told him I was more likely to hurt myself than help anyone. Regardless, he ordered me to carry one from this point forward. He gave me his shoulder holster and told me to keep it under my shirt. With his recruits missing, and Hannigan's questionable behavior, he wanted me to be prepared for anything.

"Is that for me?" Hannigan sneered at the bulge under my shirt. "I'm not the one who fucked us."

"Hey relax," Accardi said. "You might be right about the guys I got to take us here, or maybe the Omanis double-crossed us. Be prepared for anything, right?"

Hannigan stared through Accardi and then turned back to stare at me.

I turned my head away and looked over at Miguel who had barely said a word since we had arrived. He was sitting at the foot of the eight-person wooden table with the four of us huddled at the other side. I was at the head. Hannigan was too close to me on my right side. I felt like I could feel the heat coming off him. Centeno and Accardi were to my left.

"Aw, fuck this," Hannigan finally said.

I attempted to calm him. "No. Like Sandy said, we need to protect ourselves. We need to be a team now more than ever."

Hannigan let out a snarky laugh at that. "All for one and one for all!"

Now it was Accardi and Centeno staring hard at him. They'd had enough of his bullshit.

"That would be nice," I said. "I mean, we have to worry about being double-crossed by the people we hired to bring us over and also by the Omani government, right?"

"What?" Hannigan let out another laugh. "The fucking government?" He screwed his face up in disbelief, then continued, "You thought that boat was for their fucking navy? Come on, Padre, you have to be shitting me. Right?"

"Hannigan, you need to sober up." It was Centeno.

Hannigan ignored Centeno. "Come on. Seriously?" He opened his arms up, then stood, having to use his right hand to balance himself.

Hannigan stumbled into the kitchen, looking for more booze.

"It doesn't serve any purpose," Centeno said.

"You know what? Fuck you. It does. I've been getting screwed over before you arrived, and ever since you all got here, things have gotten worse. I'm looking around this room, and I feel like I'm the only one who has to live with how deep the rabbit hole goes."

"Yeah, sorry you had to be stuck on a tropical island with fifty million while we had to kidnap fourteen people and take care of them for the last month or so. Sounds rough," Centeno said.

"It was rough. I had to take care of him. Every day. Watch him fade just a little more every day."

"Yeah, really convenient how that happened, isn't it?" Centeno came in strong but faded at the end, realizing what he was saying.

Hannigan came storming back to the table. "What the fuck are you saying?"

"I know. I know." The normally volatile Centeno stayed seated. "That was a little too much, even for me. I didn't mean it."

Hannigan looked at Accardi. "So tell him."

Accardi shook his head. But under Hannigan's unrelenting stare, Accardi finally said, "Hannigan thinks that the yacht we are selling might end up being used for nefarious purposes."

"Nefarious!" Hannigan laughed again. "You're getting soft, Accardi, you big pussy."

"Fuck you," Accardi shot back.

"There you go." Hannigan smiled at Accardi's aggression.

The enormity hit me. We had retrofitted the yacht with fourteen cells. "Human trafficking?" I gasped.

"Human trafficking?" Hannigan mocked my accent while putting a shot glass in front of Miguel, who looked like he was trying to sink into his seat and disappear.

"Not just humans, Padre," Hannigan continued. "How's this for irony? Little girls and boys, most likely."

"My God," I breathed. This was more than I could bear.

"He's just talking shit. Making things up as he goes along, Father Tony. He wants you to be miserable because he is such a miserable jerk himself." Accardi affected a smile and turned his head toward Hannigan, trying to lighten the mood.

Hannigan smiled back but sinisterly. "Oh, that's right, Father Tony. We are the good guys. We are going to have a nice little day camp here where everyone's needs will be taken care of. You can handle the arts and crafts." He put his hand on the back of my chair. "Yeah, everything you are doing is perfectly holy."

I nodded. He was right. No matter what I said or what I held myself out to be, I had become what I had feared.

What comes out of a person is what defiles them. For it is from within, out of a person's heart, that evil thoughts come—sexual immorality, theft, murder, adultery, greed, malice, deceit, lewdness, envy, slander, arrogance and folly. All these evils come from inside and defile a person. Mark 7:20-23

I thought of my mother. How she died of heartbreak when I was accused. Falsely accused. And how my father, left alone, drank and died, stumbling into traffic. Both dead before last rites could be received. And now this.

I stared at the table, watching Hannigan fill up shot glasses for each of us with a clear liquid. I didn't trust him, but there was no way his sleight of hand could be good enough in his current condition. If he was trying to drug all of us and faking his inebriation, he should win some sort of award.

Hannigan held up his shot glass with his left hand. "Come on, gentlemen. One last round."

Miguel mumbled something, got up, and raised a shot glass, standing to the right of Hannigan.

Hannigan slurred, "I don't want to drink alone. This is my last one! I'll shut up soon."

"Ah, fuck it." Sandy grabbed a glass and Centeno followed. I grabbed a glass, too.

Hannigan spoke evenly: "It's important for all of you to realize that I am in charge at this point. I know who our contact is in Malé, for supplies. I have access to the funds that we need, and most importantly, I know the rest of our friend O'Malley's plan. I won't allow any more screwups. This is not a threat. I am just stating the obvious. So, I need all of you to support me and help me, help us all to get to where we need to be."

I had no idea what he meant by that, but he ended abruptly, then held his shot glass toward all of us and jiggled it, waiting for us to toast. Accardi thought for a moment, then shrugged, and we all followed his lead and toasted Hannigan and took some of the clear liquid. I barely let it touch my lips, not trusting Hannigan in the least. On my lips, I tasted what seemed like fermented banana. Centeno, Miguel, and Hannigan drained their shots.

With that, Hannigan slammed his empty glass down and then clumsily went to the back of his pants with his right hand.

I felt so vulnerable sitting while Hannigan was standing above me with his gun. I guiltily felt lucky it was pointed at my nephew. Both Accardi and Centeno looked similarly uncomfortable pointing their guns up at Hannigan while being stuck in their seats. Miguel was the only one who didn't have a gun, and he looked almost relaxed. Well, not relaxed; he looked despondent. He was ready to accept his fate.

Accardi broke the silence as he calmly said, "Easy."

CHAPTER TWENTY-TWO
Rituals and Dances

EDDIE

I hadn't been to a Sunday church service since I was a kid. My mother's parents would take me and my brother, Steve, when they watched us on the weekends. They moved down to Boca Raton when I was twelve, and their visits were rare. Like most kids my age, I spent Sundays focused on the gospel of Nintendo.

After my mom got shot, they made a few attempts to see us, but they were older, frailer, and heartbroken. I guess we were all wrecked. Steve had already moved out and was going to college in Indiana. As for my dad, he was drinking hard, barely making it through the day.

They came one last time two weeks before my sixteenth birthday and told me they wished I could have had a better life, but they had no control over my father. They gave me three hundred dollars and left. I never saw them again. I think Steve still checks in with them now and then, but fuck 'em.

Paul was busy making his millions. He didn't have much time to check in with me, either. Things finally reached rock bottom when my dad crashed out on a bench in a playground and took a swing at the cops who tried to get him home. I called Paul from the police station, a social worker hovering over me.

Paul drove in from Maryland and began smoothing things over. He got my dad to give him power of attorney, and seized control of my dad's affairs. He gave social services a song and dance about making arrangements for me; I was almost seventeen at that point. One more year until I was, at least theoretically, an adult. He hired a woman to clean, cook, and shop two days a week, which made things a bit better. And he told me to hang in there.

He hired a restaurant broker to work on selling the restaurants, something that probably should have been done earlier. After the sales of the restaurants and the properties were done and the initial trusts were established, Paul disappeared, handing off the bill paying to Steve, who was heading to law school. It wasn't a great move. Steve, as we all found out the hard way, wasn't built to handle that level of stress.

The location made sense. St. Dominic's and the 41st Precinct wanted to show a face of unity for the community. It was hard enough to keep some level of order in the surrounding neighborhoods without additional infighting between the church and cops.

Monsignor Angelos had already started. If he noticed me entering, he did a good job of concealing it. I saw another of my fan club in the third row from the back: the young nephew, Renato Centeno. He wore his navy-blue uniform that the department designated for official events, but ignored the sign on the church door requesting attendees wear masks.

The place was standing room only when I arrived. I wedged in next to a moose of a man right at the entrance, he had to have been north of six six and close to three hundred pounds of ripped muscle. It was the right move. He was so big he could create space with just a slight movement; everyone backed off. Except, of course, me.

The Mass was as boring as ever. Then the priest prompted us to shake the hand of the person next to us.

The moose looked down at me, enveloped my hand with his, said, "Brady Fergusson," and gave me a pat on the shoulder.

I stared up at him, not sure what to say, so I just smiled.

He just nodded back.

He didn't seem that upset for a person who was mourning the death of his father. I wondered what he was doing in the back. Was there bad blood in the Fergusson family? *The families of the missing officers were up front.*

Monsignor Angelos mentioned Accardi, Fergusson, and Juarez. He said how admired they were in the community and how all of them and their families were in his and the church community's thoughts and prayers.

I watched Renato Centeno as the monsignor spoke. He was glaring at the priest, who had not included Angel Centeno's name. This was no oversight.

Based on my conversation with Miggy, it was Renato's uncle, Angel Centeno, who had been kicked off the force and suspected of killing his partner, who had been one of the first to start the pedo-priest conversations in New York. The church came out saying that was a lie and never admitted wrongdoing. With his history, both the NYPD and the Church viewed Centeno as a fucking disaster to be forgotten as soon as possible. Renato was delusional if he thought his uncle was going to be mentioned with the likes of the other police officers.

The service ended. The monsignor, the other priests, and the altar boys filed out first. The front rows followed suit. I wondered if this was a dick move meant to encourage people to arrive early so they could leave early, or if it had something to do with this type of service. As the moose breathed impatiently and uncomfortably in his mask, over my shoulder, I couldn't help but turn to him.

"Brady Fergusson? How are you related?" I wanted to ask *related to Barney Fergusson,* but at the moment, I had blanked on his first name. *Man, I really was a shitty cop.*

"I'm his son. What's your name again?"

I dodged the question the first time. This time I couldn't. If Brady and the young Centeno were friends, he might just kick my ass right here based on the stories he had heard. I felt relatively safe in the sanctuary of the church, but I couldn't help myself from making a slight adjustment.

"Ed Rodriguez," I mumbled.

"Well, Ed, it looks like we are in for a bit of a wait."

As usual, I couldn't help myself. "So, I hope it isn't rude for me to ask… why didn't you sit up front with the rest of your family?"

Brady opened his arms slightly to let me take a look at his massive frame, then said, "I hit traffic, and the first row was already filled when I got here. I have squeezed into too many church pews in my lifetime."

"I can imagine," I said, although it didn't make a lot of sense. People reserved space for family.

His eyes narrowed, not menacingly but curiously. "And… who are you again?"

"I used to be a cop. Actually, not that long ago, I guess I sold out and got a corporate security gig. While I liked the work, it got tough having people look at me as the enemy all the time."

Brady put his beefy paw on my shoulder again. "I feel for you, Ed. I love being a fireman. One of the reasons I didn't become a cop was how the men in blue are viewed. It must have been tough to leave."

This guy was just a big teddy bear. I relaxed, finishing my ruse. "I mean, it is one thing to leave the work, you know, taking care of the community, but it is a completely different thing to leave the band of brothers."

Brady's eyes had gotten wide as he was staring over my shoulder. I wheeled on my heel to face the young Centeno's eyes boring into me.

The procession had stopped behind him, waiting for him to move ahead. *Oh shit, we are going to do this right here and now.* I reflexively leaned back into Brady who caught me in his arms. With that, Centeno turned and exited the church.

"Yeah, friends for life." Brady chuckled derisively.

There's a trick that cops have pulled for generations. They station a rookie outside of an abandoned lot, and their fellow officers drive in, so they don't have to find street parking. Vacant lots were rare in the slowly gentrifying Bronx, but there was one available between the precinct and the church.

I spotted Centeno with the two guys he sat next to in the church, walking toward the lot. I hoped his friends were convincing him to head home instead of walking over to the middle-school gymnasium where the after-service gathering was being held.

When I got inside, Captain Broward was already talking to the woman I guessed was Accardi's ex-wife, since Mrs. Fergusson had embraced her outside the church. I doubted that it was Juarez's ex-wife, as I vaguely remembered her being Latino, and the woman Broward was talking to was not.

My new friend, Brady Fergusson, was surrounded by cops from

my old precinct. I looked around and couldn't find John, and I doubted my advocate, Bill Wagner, would be here. As I continued to scan the room, I spotted my old pal Edna James from Internal Affairs. She was walking right toward me.

"Mr. Rodriguez," she said.

"Is that a dig at me for my civilian status?"

"No. Not all. A sincere hello."

"What do you want?" *IA investigators are pariahs within the NYPD. And she was considered to be the worst of the lot. Her presence made me look good.*

There were many eyes looking at the two of us. We were being encircled. There was only one person who was clearly trying to avoid eye contact with me and that was my old friend Harris. That son of a bitch got to skate while I was fired from the force even though only one of us shot a kid. I had no idea how he was connected to any of this, but there were many people here who weren't close with Miggy and I can't imagine that close to any of the ex-cops.

"I knew you'd be here. Let's keep this brief. Call me. There is something off with Officer Centeno. I need you to call me." She shoved her business card with her handwritten cell phone number on the back, into my hand.

As she exited, a few people got back to their conversations. With that, I walked quickly out of the back exit of the gymnasium.

She was about to cross the street and was waiting for the light when I caught her.

"Why didn't you just call me and avoid making a scene like this?" I asked.

"Would you have answered if I had called, and more importantly, would you have realized how serious I was about me wanting us to talk?"

She quickly turned without waiting for an answer. The red hand flashed as she darted across the intersection.

Obviously, my sneaky move out the back door didn't fool anyone. When I turned around I saw no less than ten of New York's finest looking at me, including Captain Broward.

CHAPTER TWENTY-THREE
The Goat

EDDIE

"What the hell was that about?" Captain Broward asked.

"That bitch was digging at me. Called me Mister Rodriguez. I don't answer to her bullshit anymore."

"Well, this is not the time or place."

I had to think quickly. "She was covering her ass. Even by her standards, I was canned pretty quickly. She sounded like the dog that finally caught the car."

That worked better than expected. Captain Broward's eyes had widened once I mentioned my termination. He quickly looked from side to side at the other cops. "Well, you said you wanted a change anyway, the way I recall it." He was leading me.

If I was going to take a shot, now would be the time. I decided on something neutral. "It all worked out."

Back inside, I headed to the hospitality table. There was a coffee urn, a choice of teas, bottled water, and Bud Light.

"Slim pickings," a voice behind me said.

"Brady." I turned. "We meet again."

We both grabbed beers and popped the tops. "I was wondering, Ed, why are you here? There's a handful of cops who knew my dad or one of the other cops, who are missing. As for the others, it took me a while to figure it out, but I believe most of the cops are here because the captain told them to be here."

I wondered if someone planted that bug in his ear. But I had an answer and it was at least a partial truth.

"I was tight with Miguel. Not too many Hispanics in the precinct as detectives."

I had to handle this delicately. The word "missing" hadn't been lost on me. I wasn't going to dig too deep a hole, but did Brady not believe the story of his dad's death, either? "I was working on a case that Detective Accardi was interested in. It involved some priests and—"

I stopped mid-sentence as I saw Brady's eyes. He knew something. When he didn't say anything, I pressed just a little. "Hey, did your dad talk about what his friends were up to? Miggy wasn't much for fishing."

Brady hesitated. "Up to?" he said. "What do you mean?"

Even I wasn't stupid enough to dig any further with that response. "Never mind. Sorry for your loss."

Brady searched to change the subject. "So you were saying, you took a job with a security company?"

I thought of another angle. "Yes. I got a job with an investment firm, owned by a friend of a friend of Daniel O'Malley's. It really is sometimes who you know."

I looked around the crowd. "Accardi was tight with O'Malley. I'm surprised none of that family is here."

I could tell Brady was sizing me up.

I decided to punt for now with a football question I'm sure he'd gotten his entire life. "So, Brady… that's got to be a tough name for a New Yorker unless you are a Giants fan."

"Ha," he laughed. "Yes, you guessed it. I'm a Jets fan. I hate Tom Brady as much as the next guy. The name is actually a tragic story unto itself. My father's dad, Brandon, was a terrible drinker. He died of cirrhosis at an early age, leaving my grandmother to fend for herself. And Brandon's dad was named Brian after the last king of Ireland, Brian Boru. For some reason firstborn Fergusson sons got names with the initial B. When I was born, my dad wanted to pay homage to his mother, whose maiden name was Grady and he wanted to recognize her family. So he decided that Brady did the trick, even if it wasn't a typical first name. It used most of my grandmother's maiden name and kept the Fergussons' B tradition alive. And it's pretty fitting for me, since Brady means 'large chested' in old Gaelic."

I felt a hand on my shoulder. I quickly tensed, waiting for young Centeno to sucker punch me from behind but instead, as I turned, I saw Captain Broward.

"Hey, is it okay if I interrupt? Brady, can I grab you? There're a few other officers and detectives who would like to talk to you. You know, friends of your father's."

I was starting to realize that me being invited to this was at least partially a show for me to put this case to bed. However, between Ms. James from IA's spectacle and Brady Fergusson, one of the few folks not under the captain's command, chitchatting with me, I was making Captain Broward nervous.

Brady looked over at me, almost as if he were asking permission to go.

"You mind if I borrow your pen, Captain," I said.

He stared at me for a second, not sure how to respond, then handed it to me.

I clicked it and jotted my cell phone number on the back of my business card. "Great talking to you, Brady. Let me know if you are interested in going to a Jets game."

I would leave it in Brady's court if he wanted to continue our non-conversation.

"Sounds good, Ed. Great talking with you."

I headed for the exit.

The chill in the air wasn't unpleasant. It was going to be November in little over a week. In another month or so everyone would be cursing the cold.

I couldn't help myself.

I crossed the street and called Murray.

"Hey, Eddie," she answered pleasantly, not in her typical fashion.

"Agent Murray?" I asked.

"Have anything for me?"

"Well, I talked with Brady Fergusson."

"Good," she prompted.

"Yeah, I think so. He certainly didn't seem too broken up about his dad's death. His mom was shattered, but I think he knows something."

"What did he say?" I had her attention.

"Well, nothing direct. He did say his dad was missing instead of dead and—"

"Are you sure? What did you say when he said that? I mean, that was an obvious opening."

"It wasn't like he started a conversation with, *Hey, I don't think my dad is dead. I think he's missing.* It was more of a thing he slipped in when—"

"Eddie, listen. As you know, it's never that easy. If someone gives you a lead like that, stay friendly and casual, but keep in control of the conversation. You want to—"

"Hey, I gotta go."

"Eddie, wait, I—"

I hung up the phone.

Leaning against my Lexus was young Centeno.

CHAPTER TWENTY-FOUR
Frenemies

EDDIE

The phone buzzed in my pocket, begging for attention. Centeno and I just stared at each other. This was his move. The street wasn't crowded, but it wasn't empty, either.

I crossed the street. *Why the fuck couldn't some random pedestrians just be within eyesight?*

"Centeno," I said.

"You just keep showing up. Don't you, Eddie?"

I didn't say anything, so he continued, "You must have been laughing your faggot ass off, seeing how my uncle was disrespected today. Right?"

My opinion of Centeno kept on dropping. Gay jokes were one thing. But an old-school homophobic slur? It had been a long time since I'd heard one of those.

As he took a step toward me, I responded. "Officer—"

"Don't you fucking call me that, bitch," he seethed.

"Centeno?" I asked as a question. *What the fuck did he want me to call him? I knew for damn sure he didn't want me to call him by his first name.* "I obviously had no say in who was mentioned and who wasn't mentioned in the service today."

He didn't break his stare. "Nah, man. Yeah, you are so fucking innocent. Who's been spreading shit about my uncle for the last few months? Bringing up all types of shit that me or my family don't want revisited. To the FBI, no less. You were warned."

"I was doing my job."

He pushed his sneering face within six inches of mine. *Someone better show up soon.* "Doing your job, pfft. Listen, *maricon*, your job was to back the fuck off."

He had now made a homophobic slur to me in two separate languages.

"I did my job. Now, please, move. I came because of Miggy."

"Are you fucking kidding me?" I could feel the warmth of his breath.

Then he surprised me, looking over my shoulder. I heard people crossing the street toward us.

He leaned in with a false smile on his face as he said quickly, "I know a lot about you, Eddie. I know about your brother Steve, the disbarred attorney in Jersey. I know about your loser-ass father in Connecticut. I even know about your pompous sellout half brother in Maryland who didn't even have enough respect for your family to keep your last name."

The couple walked by us, and Officer Centeno politely waved to them as they went by with wide eyes.

If he thinks he can scare me... well, there he is right, but I can't let this threat stand against my family. "You better leave them alone, Centeno," I said, not even believing myself hearing my own voice.

"Which one?" he asked menacingly.

I didn't respond.

There was a group coming from the direction of the gymnasium.

It didn't appear to contain any cops, but it was enough to make Centeno back up. He wasn't going to do anything tonight.

"You don't want us to have another conversation, Eddie. Am I clear?"

I was so jittery, I fumbled for my fob, dropping it as I tried to unlock my door. I picked it off the sidewalk, scolding myself for forgetting that my Lexus could be unlocked with the fob in my pocket by simply putting my hand near the handle. I checked my voicemail as I drove off. It was an emotionless Agent Murray simply telling me to call her.

I was about to return the call when I thought, *Change of plan*.

I called Edna James and got her voicemail. "This is Eddie Rodriguez. I am calling you back as you demanded." I hadn't forgiven her for how she treated me, and if this recording turned up some day, this was something I could work with no matter who was listening.

Now, I called Agent Murray.

"Why did you hang up on me?" she said.

"I wasn't hanging up on you. I had—"

"Saying you have to go in the middle of a conversation and then clicking off is hanging up on someone, Eddie."

My phone beeped. It was Ms. James calling me back. "Oh shit," I said. "Bad timing. I've got to go."

"Eddie?" Ms. James asked.

"Yes, it's me."

"Thank you for calling. I really appreciate you getting back to me. Like I said…" She paused. "Are you alone? Is anyone else listening?"

"Yeah, I'm alone." Her nervousness was adding to my own fears.

"Can you meet me for a coffee?" *A coffee? It was six thirty, and I was starving.*

"How about you buy me a slice of pizza?" I replied.

She wanted to meet someplace out of the Bronx, far enough away from the precinct. She lived in Inwood, so we settled on a place I knew not far from my condo in Washington Heights.

Ms. James was already there when I arrived, sitting in a booth at the back of the small pizza place, with a bottle of water for company.

"Thanks for coming," she said as I sat down with a couple of slices and a Diet Coke.

"Yeah, no problem. What's up?"

"I'm not sure what I can say specifically. But just so you don't think I'm some kind of psycho, I wanted to let you know we have something in common. Sort of. My unarmed uncle was shot and killed in Bed Stuy when I was young. I know it's not the same as losing your mother, but..."

I wasn't looking at having a moment with Ms. James, so I just asked the obvious: "Did they catch the guy?"

"You mean the two white cops who said they mistook his plumber's wrench for a gun?"

"Let me guess: no time served, no termination."

"Bingo. I guess I'm saying I was born to be IA."

I sipped on my Diet Coke. "And I was born to be a cop. But I'm not anymore."

"It wasn't just me, Eddie. I was inclined to give you a pass on those kids. That was bad luck and outside pressure. The optics were bad. Somebody leaked your past history to the *Post*. And the mayor's office started leaning on us."

"I thought IA was like an untouchable secret society."

"Well, that's the thing," Edna James said. "Your case and

Centeno's involvement are the first time I've gotten any pressure from above. And my boss told me the same thing."

"What's up with Centeno?"

"He's a hothead with two civilian complaints against him. Suddenly, he's transferred to Fort Apache. And then we get word he jumped you in the precinct—"

"Somebody reported that?" I was amazed. Maybe I wasn't as unpopular as I thought.

"No comment."

"So how was he bumped up to take over my missing person case? Shit like that makes me wonder about Captain Broward."

"You are not alone."

I finished my second slice of pizza. "Actually, I am alone. I'm out, remember? I don't understand. What is bothering you so much?"

"This is the first time I've been told to stand down."

"Welcome to the club. You realize you are not telling me anything new. I am not a cop now, because there is something that they didn't want me to find... or maybe it was just opening old wounds for the department. I don't know."

"Well, what *do* you know? What was the case?"

"It had to do with two missing priest cases and a few retired cops showing a great deal of interest in the case."

"You mean the cops we just honored?"

"Yeah. And Centeno?"

"What would Officer Centeno have to do with that?"

"Not *that* Centeno. Angel Centeno, his uncle. He's missing, too, but he was bounced from the force. I think his nephew, Officer Centeno, was ordered to get me out of the picture."

"Why is that?"

"A source overheard him talking to his uncle. And even tonight, he was waiting for me by my car, threatening me. He made it clear that he knew about my family members."

"Well, he can't do that."

"He did."

She stared at me for a second. "What else?"

"Just the obvious. Why didn't Captain Broward hand an officer already in Missing Persons, the priest case?"

"Good. Good." She ignored my question and instead flipped back a few pages in a notepad she had sitting beneath her water bottle. "Has his father, Emilio, ever talked to you, or has anyone else from the Centeno family, or anyone who you think might be related to the New York Mafia ever talked to you?"

This was too much. "No and no. Listen, Ms. James. I appreciate—"

"You can call me, Edna."

"Okay, Edna. I appreciate you having a job to do, and I think you are right, but I just don't think I have anything substantial."

"Nothing substantial? You said a police officer threatened you."

I wanted to leave. "I think you might be reading into a couple of interactions a little too deeply."

She put the remaining bottled water into her handbag. "I would like to get a deposition from you. Let me know what days work." She had opened the calendar on her phone.

With that, I stood up. "No days work. If I am the best you have, I think you need to do more homework. Listen, Edna, I have to run. Good luck with all this."

"You can be compelled." She faded out as I walked out of the front exit, squeezing by a driver picking up a stack of deliveries.

I looked down at my phone, seeing seven missed calls from Agent Murray and two voicemails. Thinking of these two women in my life, I was happy to be gay.

CHAPTER TWENTY-FIVE
Loose Lips Sink Ships

EDDIE

I listened to Agent Murray's messages. The first voicemail was emotionless as normal. The second was also emotionless but contained a threat. "Mr. Rodriguez since you are not returning my calls and are acting erratic, I have to assume you are under duress. I don't want to cause you any inconvenience, but if you do not return my call by seven p.m., I will assume you are in danger and get someone from the local police department to check on you."

I looked down at my phone, it was seven fifteen. I gritted my teeth in the car and quickly called her.

"Eddie?"

"Was that a fucking joke about calling the local police department?"

"No."

"Are you trying to get me fucking killed? This isn't my job anymore. Hell, it wasn't my job beforehand. It was so not my job that I got fired for doing it."

"Killed? What do you mean, killed?"

"I mean killed as in fucking dead. Is there any other meaning?"

"Slow down, Eddie. If you are at risk, let me know how I can help." She almost sounded believable.

"I'm heading into my condo and need to pull into the garage. Were you serious about calling the local cops?"

"You know I didn't call them, Eddie."

WTF?

"Agent Murray, this is too much. Between IA coming after me again, my ex-captain hassling me, and death threats from Centeno, I really don't need fake fucking-veiled threats from you." I hung up as I pulled into the garage.

I walked out of the elevator and into my condo. I tossed the ringing phone on the couch and grabbed a Dos Equis out of the fridge. Instead of calling Agent Murray back, I walked out on the balcony and soaked in the view looking across at the Palisades on the Jersey side, looking south to the George Washington Bridge and then looking north toward the Cloisters. I technically lived in an area called Hudson Heights, but unless you knew the area, it was just easier to say Washington Heights. I took another sip, walked back inside and looked at my cell phone that had two new voicemails. I grabbed another beer for reinforcements, put in my earbuds, and walked back out on my terrace and called Agent Murray.

"Eddie, can we have a conversation at this point? Captain Broward, Centeno, IA? What's going on?"

I was trying to stay calm, looking out at the views.

"Well?" She was trying to sound calm while waiting for me to respond.

"You ever take a break from this, Murray? I mean, it's almost eight on a Sunday, and you are still going at it full speed. No vacations, no days off?"

I finished off the first beer and set it off to the side of the patio window. I opened the other Dos Equis.

Agent Murray had mistakenly taken this as me mulling over her response. "Two weeks a year. If that helps, two weeks a year, Eddie. I don't turn my phone off. I don't go somewhere so remote I can't be reached, but two weeks a year I take a vacation."

"That wasn't so hard, was it?"

Agent Murray bristled at that. "Actually, Mr. Rodriguez, it was. Now, can you get me up to speed on what is happening?"

"I can't. I just can't. Like I said, it is eight on a Sunday. Why don't we discuss this tomorrow? I'll call you at ten a.m." I needed to step away from this for a few hours.

"Ten o'clock, Eddie. Ten o'clock." She hung up the phone.

I had made the right call. Instead of dealing with an interrogation, the boyfriend came over. We drank some beers, hung out. It was just what I needed. At ten on Monday I went into the break room behind the main security desk at BDQ and called Agent Murray.

"Okay, Eddie. Captain Broward, Centeno, or IA?" she answered.

"No small talk, huh?" I quipped. "All right, all right. So, this Centeno is a macho hothead. He decked me when I still had a badge and asked him about the priests. At the church service he was really pissed that his uncle wasn't recognized as one of the cops. The fact is, both his uncle and me have something in common: we were both tossed off the force. But apparently, Renato hasn't made that connection."

"Probably can't imagine comparing you two."

"Yeah. He oozes homophobia." There. I had said it. I wanted Agent Amanda Murray to know I was gay. It was another strike against my weird crush.

With no response from her, I just continued, "I think he's pissed at a lot of people. I'm sure it's nothing, but if I end up missing one day that is who my money would be on for doing the deed."

"Uh-huh." She sounded bored.

"Uh-huh? That's your response?"

"His family is connected. We have an eye on him, or more to the point, the bureau has an eye on him and his family. However, it's a bit odd that Renato would be tight with Angel Centeno. Sources say Angel was written off by the family decades ago."

"I'll tell you one thing. Renato seemed to want to write off my family." By Murray underplaying things, I decided to give a little more. "He went through a short description of my half brother, my older brother, and what they do for a living, and my only surviving parent and his health status. He's been doing his homework."

Oh." She perked up at that. "I'm sure it's nothing, but what did he say?"

The turn in her voice made me nervous. "I mean, in theory he could have asked around the precinct and found this stuff out."

"Is that what you think?" She was calm.

"No," I responded flatly.

"Okay, I will see what I can find out internally. If he's talking about this with the family, someone might have heard something—"

"No. No deal. We're not even sure who the powers are that are pulling the strings to keep an eye on me. I don't want any record that I am still involved. With O'Malley's connection to the mayor, and therefore Accardi's connection to the mayor, there's a good chance the mayor is looking into me. I mean, we know my ex-captain is looking at me. Besides the Mafia, there could be all types of non-mob folks for me to be worried about."

"Okay, Eddie. Let's talk about something else. What do you think—"

"No. I don't want to change topics yet. What I want to hear from you is, 'You got it, Eddie. The fact that Centeno knows some shit on your family is something we will keep between the two of us for now.'"

"Okay, Eddie. I will not put into the formal file the fact that the younger Centeno knows things about your family that he shouldn't. Fine?"

I knew she was twisting the wording, but what else could I say? She could just lie to me and do whatever the hell she wanted anyway.

I continued, "Okay, the Centeno angle doesn't matter anyway. It will be handled. Young Centeno has the IA lady who fired me, on him."

"So that would be Edna James?"

"Do you have any idea how creepy you come across when you blurt out things that people think should be private?"

"That's my job. What about the captain?"

I paused before answering. "Nothing specific. I can just tell he has an eye on me. I get the feeling he really wants me to believe they are all dead."

"If they are dead, the priests probably are, too."

The word "dead" pushed a button for me. *Shit.*

"Murray, that reminds me: with everything going on, I forgot to tell you. A friend of mine from the precinct overheard a call between the two Centenos, you know the young officer one and retired Detective Angel Centeno."

"What! When was this?"

"Yeah, he thinks he overheard the young one saying the word 'dead.' I think it could be O'Malley who died. From there it is all conjecture, but he heard Officer Centeno saying to Angel something like he needs to bail on this and run. My assumption being that somehow O'Malley was planning to take the fall since he had a terminal disease. I guess more people than just the bureau knew he was sick. Not sure how it all adds up, but if O'Malley is involved and then dies, it changes things, right?"

There was silence on the other line.

"Hello?" Maybe I was lucky, and the call got dropped.

"How come you didn't tell me this before? We could have been tapping Officer Centeno's phone. When did you hear this? Who heard the call?"

"I'm sorry. I can't let you know that."

"Can't let me know that? Make no mistake, Mr. Rodriguez, we have a friendly relationship, but I have a job to do. I will get that name."

"Not happening, Agent Murray."

I wouldn't budge. She kept at me, but I told her she was wasting our time. I promised to work on getting back to her with the time of the call. She was not happy, but she let it go, at least for now.

"Call me soon, Eddie."

VIGILANTE PRIEST VI
Lord Of Lies

FATHER TONY

I started thinking of the mistakes each of us had made. Hannigan had to have been recalculating his move, but he was obviously drunk, and more importantly, he was broken.

I understood as a priest I should have been more sensitive to others and recognized better what Barney Fergusson was going through, but I couldn't help but blame Accardi for that. He bullied Barney into being more involved in this than he was comfortable with, and he didn't recognize the signs of his best friend detaching.

As for getting to the point of having Hannigan pull a gun on us, Accardi and Centeno had no excuses, being ex-cops. They had been on alert but still were probably hoping they could bring their old friend back.

What was most shocking was that everyone, including myself, had made one mistake as a group, we had discounted Miguel. We had forgotten that Miguel was and always would be *policia*.

When Miguel pressed his gun, the gun that none of us realized he had, into Hannigan's ribs, the dynamic changed.

"Get that off me before I deck you and beat you to death with it."

"Fuck you, Hannigan. You think you scare me? This is it for me. I have nothing to return to."

With that, Hannigan turned his attention briefly toward Miguel. This gave Accardi and Centeno enough time to jump up from their seats and stand. I was not as quick.

"Okay. Playtime is over." Hannigan's voice was wavering as he put his gun down on the table. "Let's just have a no-hard-feelings drink. I clearly lost my head."

Accardi nodded to Centeno while Hannigan put down his gun and began to pour another round.

"To moderation, cooperation, and eventually, copulation... except for Father, of course." Hannigan forced a laugh.

Everyone eerily sat back down and sipped their shots. I put mine down and stared at Hannigan's gun sitting on the table only a couple inches from his hand.

After a couple of minutes, Centeno stood up. "Anyone want anything?" He headed out behind me and Hannigan.

Hannigan looked up at him warily as Centeno began walking around my seat to go to the kitchen.

Accardi responded, causing Hannigan to look at him. "Yeah, see if you can find some sort of beer. This stuff could strip paint—and not one of those light ones. Something that has—"

Accardi stopped talking when Centeno hit Hannigan hard on the right side of his head with the butt of his gun. The first blow only shocked him.

By the third strike, Hannigan was laying on the ground, and Centeno had to bend down to keep hitting him.

Miguel finally grabbed Centeno's arm to stop him. "Enough."

Because conversations were limited—O'Malley thought it wise to operate on a need-to-know basis—Accardi and I both had knowledge gaps when it came to O'Malley's plans. But Sandy knew more than me. The initial thought for the island was to dump the priests here and then leave them on the island to fend for themselves, expecting some sort of *Lord of the Flies* reaction.

However, with our limited number of guards and not having any contact with our sources in the States, our targets would be spending their remaining days while never seeing the sun again.

O'Malley had hired military contractors. These people had a reputation for silence and secrecy. Even with this, they had to hire some specialists. Because of the water table, the military contractors subbed out some work to a tunnel building company. The equipment was heavy, expensive, and hard to hide.

Even in the middle of nowhere, this kind of traffic and activity was noticeable. Essentially, this decision turned one of the most obscure tropical locations we could think of into a known entity, at least locally. The cover was that the island was for an unnamed Russian oligarch.

Our plan should have been fine. The excitement of the locals over some rich thug would have waned shortly. And there would be no reason for uninvited guests to show up.

But when O'Malley began to run high fevers, Hannigan brought in the doctor and nurse toward the end to help O'Malley and try to keep him alive.

This clearly was against O'Malley's wishes no matter whether, as Hannigan had said, O'Malley demanded it or not. If O'Malley was, in fact, demanding this, he was no longer in a clear frame of mind, and like I said, all of this had definitely been stated and planned out beforehand.

If there was potential heat on this location, as Hannigan suspected, it was either one of the medical people or their support staff who had gotten us on the radar. The only other option was someone from the tunneling crew who built the underground bunker. Supposedly, the military contractors and our contact in Malé were trustworthy.

———————

Underground, we had twenty holding cells—steel-barred cages with automated retractable one-way, mirrored, plexiglass walls. If we wanted to isolate a prisoner, we could do so with the push of a button. The priests, who had now traveled across the globe, realized there was no escape.

Centeno told them where they were and that we had floated around the world on a falsely registered boat without a single harbormaster giving us a second look.

This is when the horror took hold.

And do not fear those who kill the body but cannot kill the soul. Rather fear him who can destroy both soul and body in hell.

Father Bob was the first. He renounced God. "Our Lord has forsaken us!" he cried out. "And why? Why did he give us life and love and fill my life with temptation? It is God's fault. He has betrayed me from the beginning."

Father Bob had a list of grievances, and spouted them in detail, babbling about his earliest memories and disappointments. He would confess to many crimes in his rants. But on this day, it was impossible to listen through his gurgling tear-filled diatribes.

The others who had changed were in two sets of three. Father Julio, Father Timothy, and Father James had taken vows of silence. Or so it appeared, they just stopped talking. One couldn't be sure if this was madness, resignation, or a way to atone to God. When I asked them, they said nothing, refusing to look me in the eye.

The other three were loudly trying to drown out Father Bob by quoting the Bible. Father Reece started:

"Submit yourselves therefore to God. Resist the devil, and he will flee from you," he intoned from James 4:7, repeating the phrase over and over. And then slicing the verse in half—"Resist the devil, and he will flee from you!" And finally turning it into a charge: "He will flee from you; he will flee from you; he will flee from you." He extended these two sentences into five-minute chants.

When Father Reece's voice gave out, Father John and Father Patrick picked up the proselytizing. They took turns trying to shout down the blasphemous rantings of Father Bob. It was exactly what O'Malley, and I had wanted to occur when we discussed his initial plan. If I had only remembered Thessalonians. *Make sure that nobody pays back wrong for wrong, but always strive to do what is good for each other and for everyone else.*

To get rid of the cacophony, and accelerate our prisoners' breakdown, Centeno and Accardi wanted to take their Bibles away. I convinced them that part of the process had to be a spiritual one, and the Bible would help them get there.

We now had a new problem. It was Accardi's idea, but Centeno, the de facto second-in-command at this point, was "all in," to use his phrase. They had each taken a side of Hannigan and dragged him to the underground. They all got into the elevator together which led ten meters down to where the priests were. We had a generator and a backup generator and enough fuel for three months. The plan was for us to leave in no more than two months.

Next to the elevator was a pulley system, like a dumbwaiter, that could be used to take supplies up and down if we needed to reduce electricity, also a spiral staircase that led down.

Miggy and I took the spiral staircase to the bottom.

By the time we arrived, Hannigan was already awake. He was slowly regaining his ability to stand as he looked back and forth at Centeno and Accardi.

Hannigan's feet stopped dragging as he planted himself, showing he could stand.

He took a wobbly step forward as both Accardi and Centeno stepped back and leveled their guns at him.

"So, your plan is to leave me here with the sodomites?" I had to strain to hear Hannigan's voice. He was very weak.

That's when his adrenaline kicked in. "Ha, you sons of bitches? Is that the plan?" Hannigan's voice got louder.

No one spoke as Hannigan stared at the two biggest threats, Accardi and Centeno. I could tell he was looking for an angle, and I instinctively stepped back, initially pulling on Miguel's arm to pull him back with me until he forcefully pulled his arm away and pulled out his own gun.

Hannigan then turned to Miguel and me and scoffed at Miguel. Not sure if he scoffed because he underestimated Miguel or as a sign that he thought he could take him even with his gun.

"Well, then let's do this. Let them free," Hannigan said as his eyes widened with rage. His quick recovery disturbed me, seeming unnatural. He turned and looked around at the cages. "You ready for me, you child-molesting fucks? You fucking abominations!"

Hannigan then turned to Accardi and Centeno again. "Come on. Let's do this."

Accardi said, "Liam, you know it's not like that, but you pulled a gun on us, you crazy son of a bitch." Accardi was trying to keep it light. I had forgotten that Liam was Hannigan's first name.

"So what are you telling me?" Hannigan stared hard at Accardi before shaking his head and putting his hands on his thighs to stabilize himself. The adrenaline was quickly leaving his system.

"Just want to give you a day or two," Accardi said, ending with a smile. "You know, to get your head straight."

"Nah, man. I'm straight," Hannigan said. "We all got to go somehow and killing some of these fuckers with my bare hands, hopefully will be enough to save me."

Accardi frowned at that.

"You realize we are all cursed right?" Hannigan said.

"Cursed?" Centeno parroted.

"Yeah, cursed," Hannigan answered flatly. "You think O'Malley's death leaving us all high and dry is coincidence or the fact that we are now stuck here without a boat is coincidence? Not to mention, Eddie Rodriguez? Are you telling me that is coincidence, also? I mean, come on."

Centeno stared hard at Hannigan. "So what is your plan, then, Hannigan? Do we just split up whatever money is remaining, abandon our plan, and try to run away from the law, the Vatican, and who knows who else until we get caught or die alone somewhere? That's the righteous thing to do?"

Hannigan laughed. "Righteous?" He looked down again, trying not to get sick and continued, "There is no fucking righteous. We are damned regardless. Don't you realize that? Don't you? You stupid sons of bitches."

I hadn't realized how quiet it was. Father Bob had stopped his blasphemous ranting, allowing the other three priests to stop trying to shout him down with Bible verses.

Father Bob must have listened intently to every word. "You are right. You are right, Liam. Let us out and let's finish this. We are all doomed. Let's embrace this." He only barely more than whispered.

"You will be first." Hannigan leveled his eyes at Father Bob who quickly stopped. He believed Hannigan.

Hannigan walked to one of the empty cells with Accardi, Miguel, and Centeno, following two to three meters behind him. Once inside, Hannigan grabbed the Bible off the bed and threw it out of the cell toward me, daring me to talk. I had nothing to say.

Accardi said, "I will be back in the morning with something to eat. There's a case of bottled water in the corner."

Hannigan sat on the bed and watched us leave.

As the elevator doors closed, I turned to Accardi. "Eddie Rodriguez? The cop? What's he got to do with anything?"

CHAPTER TWENTY-SIX
Changes In Latitudes. Changes In Attitudes

EDDIE

I had been trying to reach my dad for over a week and a half. He had pulled this game on me a few times in the past. The silent treatment was a ruse, not a punishment. He was looking for me to prove I still cared for him by driving out to check on him. The first two times it made me feel pretty good. It seemed like proof that I was important to him. But I still told him to answer the phone. I didn't like worrying. When it happened the third time, I began to rethink things. He was bored and lonely and I was the only one who responded.

I had been stuck with him for two of my worst years... seventeen and eighteen. I had to listen to his rants while Paul was living it up in Maryland and Steve was away at college. I never wanted for anything, like food or clothes, no thanks to the old man. Steve, then Paul, would make sure to buy me what I needed. I had zero sober adult supervision my junior and senior year of high school. I was stuck with a rum-soaked zombie until I graduated and went upstate to college to get my BA. Not long after joining the force I was stuck with him again.

I had plans with the boyfriend and another couple on Saturday. They recognized me from all the bad-cop stories I generated; at least that's what they said. But I had to wonder if Grant had told them. Their questions made me feel like a spectacle. They weren't trying to get to know me. It was a form of voyeurism for them, going through my mistakes as a cop. I told myself I had to see my dad the next day, so I opted out when the three of them wanted to go clubbing. I told Grant to go ahead. He wasn't happy with me.

I left to see my dad in Connecticut around 10:00 a.m. Sunday.

As I approached the front door, I heard the TV playing. I knocked. I didn't hear anything except the muted ramblings of some sitcom. I thought of calling the police. I shouldn't have to be the one to see this. No matter what I did, this moment would be etched in my brain forever. I was a cop for God's sake. I straightened myself up and knocked again, harder this time. No response. I went for the key to the front door, in my pocket.

"Hello," I heard through the door.

I was surprised to hear him, not sure if I was pleasantly surprised. I had been thinking I would finally be able to put this chapter of my life behind me.

"Hello!"

I scolded myself for being happy he might have died. "Hey, Dad. It's me. You weren't answering your phone and—"

"Hello." I heard him say again. He probably couldn't hear me over the din of the TV.

Louder, this time, I yelled, "Dad, it's me. I'm coming in."

No response but the studio audience laughing in the sitcom.

"Dad!" I yelled loudly.

"Hello. Who the hell is there?" He sounded more scared than angry.

With that, I put the key in the lock and let myself in.

He squinted his eyes. He was trying to recognize me from his grimy fabric recliner through the smoke and filth. His glasses were nowhere in sight. "Paul?" he said meekly.

I responded sarcastically, "Yes Dad, Paul. I drove up again as I normally do weekly but this time for an additional unexpected visit. I just can't stop thinking about you and was overwhelmed with concern, so I figured I'd surprise you. I'm here to pick you up, pack up your stuff, and have you move in with me." I slowed my speech and lowered my volume as I reached him in his chair.

"Paul?" he asked again, then he meekly turned his head away from me and looked over to the crowded table with a lamp in the center. It was overflowing with used, phlegm-filled tissues, a giant ashtray stuffed with cigarette butts, and his portable spittoon —a large cup he would hawk into—which was filled to the brim.

The damage to his lungs produced a milky soup which he used to dislodge into a toilet or sink. Those days were gone. There was another white mug next to it which must have had coffee in it once but now was bone dry with black stains.

"No, Dad. Not Paul."

"Oh, it's you." He was disappointed. But that's okay. So was I.

I couldn't be angry. I had to step over some dirty dishes to reach him and when I did, he smelled awful. "Dad?" I wanted to get eye contact from him.

He looked up at me, glassy-eyed. "Eddie?"

There was a warmth in his voice. Or maybe I just imagined it that way. I bit my lip to stop any waterworks on my part. I looked down at him. I saw he had soiled his pants. Suddenly, the smell became overwhelming.

"Give me a second, Dad. I'll be right back." I turned and headed for the front door, quickly slamming it behind me, fighting the gag reflex.

And losing.

I knew my first call would be a waste of time, but I made it anyway. It would be unlikely for me to get him, and even if I did, he had no ability to help. He was barely hanging on himself.

"Eddie?" Steve, my only real brother, answered. He sounded so eerily like my dad, for a moment I thought I might be having a nightmare.

"Yeah, Steve. It's me. I need your help."

"Eddie. Eddie!" Steve sounded frantic already, and I hadn't even told him the news.

"What is it, Steve? Everything okay?"

"I know I should have told you, but I moved down to Boca."

"Boca?"

"Yes, Boca Raton. Florida," Steve replied. He was trying to slow himself down. "I see Mom everywhere, Eddie. Everywhere." Now Steve was crying. It was noon. He was already soused. This call was a giant mistake on my part.

Steve was like a clone of my dad, if my dad had never met our mom. His first marriage was an auto-implosion; it was entirely his fault. He cheated on his wife, did some bad stuff at work, did hard drugs, everything he could possibly do wrong.

His second wife, Diane, saved him. He married her and became a stay-at-home dad, taking care of her two daughters. Three years later, she left him because of his lack of ambition. She had to have seen this when they got married, but she must have thought she could turn him around.

Ever since then, he stayed in Northern New Jersey near where they had lived when they were married. He tried to win her back until she put a restraining order on him.

I wanted to hang up, but I had to ask: "What do you mean, you see Mom everywhere?" I said through gritted teeth.

"Oh, Eddie. Grandma Marjorie died. She left me their house, and there are pictures of Mom everywhere." He was sobbing.

My mom's mother died and left Steve their house and probably more, and he didn't even let me know. What a fucking selfish asshole.

I had to get off the phone. "Sorry to hear you got a free house, Steve. I got to go."

I tried Paul but got his voicemail, and oh, what a voicemail I left.

I guess I am doing this on my own.

I went back inside. "Can you stand?"

"I don't know, Eddie. Can you help me up?" He was scared.

I grabbed him by his right arm, trying to pull him up, but he felt so frail I grabbed him by the left arm also. I was worried I would dislocate one of his shoulders. His legs weren't giving him any support. He stood there shaking, trying to stand. He had lost so much weight. I put my hands under his sweaty armpits and slowly let him drop back into the chair.

"I am going to have to call someone to look at you, Dad."

"No, no, you are not, Eddie!" he roared.

"Yes, I am!"

He looked down in his lap before raising his eyes to me sadly. "If you think that would be best, Eddie. Then that's what you should do."

I called 9-1-1, and they took him slowly out of the house to the hospital. He responded to the questions from the EMT, but as soon as they arrived, he wouldn't say a word to me. He wouldn't even make eye contact.

———

At the hospital, they gave him fluids and cleaned him up. They sent me back to his house to get some clothes. They were going to be keeping him for a while. As I drove back to his house, Paul called.

"Hey, Eddie, sorry I missed your call," Paul said quickly.

"No, you're not. Trust me this was something you didn't want to deal with."

"What?"

I got him up to speed on where things were with Dad. "He can't live alone anymore, Paul. You're the money guy. I need you to figure it out."

———

To his credit, he did. By the end of the week, Paul had moved my dad down to a nursing home near his house and work in Maryland. Heidi, his assistant, was able to find someone to drive my dad down from the hospital. He didn't even bother to ask me if I could do it.

Paul then hired a Connecticut attorney to work with some local people to clear out the house and put it up for sale. I offered to walk through the place and grab anything valuable. The service did the rest and left us with forty separate cardboard boxes of belongings which Paul had put in a local storage center not far from where Dad had lived.

Paul might be self-absorbed, but he got shit done. Lord knows what it must have cost. I'm sure it would be taken out of the estate, but it was worth it.

When I called up Steve, he bawled incessantly, but he sure as shit didn't offer to help with anything. He said he was barely hanging on in Boca, and I couldn't imagine how all of this was affecting him.

I had gotten a call from Agent Murray checking in about a week ago. I received another while driving up to the storage unit in Connecticut after things were settled with my dad's old home. I let the call go to voicemail. If I didn't check the boxes that were in storage now, I wasn't sure when I would.

I had told my boyfriend that I wanted to go up by myself to the storage shed in Connecticut on Sunday. I wasn't sure if it was as simple as me being embarrassed by this part of my past, or that I just didn't want to have to answer questions about my dad and family. I was very good at staying focused on what I was doing when I was doing it. I didn't like mixing my work, family, or free time.

I was going to spend Thanksgiving with Grant and his family upstate in two weeks. Things were looking somewhat serious. By the time the holiday season started, I wanted to have whatever I found in the boxes behind me.

It took me about two hours to get to the storage center after slogging through the remains of a three-car accident on 95. My dad had settled in Bridgeport after leaving the city, once New York's biggest fan, now a bitter enemy.

My hatred was more localized. I put it onto the Yankees when my mom died. I had blamed the Bronx for her loss. The Yankees were collateral damage being that the stadium was less than ten blocks from where she died. I had been a regretful Mets fan ever since. I tried to switch back to the Yankees once I realized the stupidity in blaming them for the loss of my mom, but I couldn't help myself. The Mets had stuck with me ever since.

I checked my phone when I arrived at the storage place. Agent Murray left yet another message. This time she wasn't asking me to call; she was telling me.

CHAPTER TWENTY-SEVEN
Friendly Fire

EDDIE

"Officer Centeno is no longer a cop," Agent Murray began.

"And?"

"That's it. I just thought you should know. IA finally was able to get him."

"So are you saying I should be worried? He might be out for revenge? Something like that?" I was surprised I wasn't more amped up. It was probably the bumper-to-bumper traffic to Connecticut that kept me from fully thinking about having a crazed mafioso hunting me.

"Like I said, I just think you should know."

"Thanks, Agent Murray. That's great. I appreciate the call." I was getting ready to hang up when I heard her speaking.

"Fergusson, the son, was down in Miami for a week. He supposedly was asking questions. He's back in New York now."

"Sorry, I missed some of that. You still want me to try to cozy up with Brady Fergusson? Don't you have anything else? No other angles?"

"I'm still not officially on the case, Eddie. With Brady Fergusson, you already met him. Just invite him to lunch and see what he has to say."

"Just call him for lunch? Yeah, that will go well. As you know, getting to know Brady Fergusson falls under the broad scope of things that I keep trying to remind you are not in my best interest. I mean, between my current job, my old precinct, and now Centeno possibly going native. Does that sound like a good idea to you?"

She didn't answer.

"That's what I thought. Thanks for telling me about Centeno." I hung up.

The code Paul had given me worked for the gate to enter the storage center. I had been expecting a sprawling field of single-story buildings, but this was a small campus of three five-story towers. My dad's belongings were in the second building on the third floor.

I entered the code for the storage room and saw eight stacks of white cardboard boxes. They were very similar to the boxes we'd use for long-term storage of case files back when I was a cop. We called them banker boxes at the precinct.

Most of the boxes were filled with old household items like my dad's old plates, pots and pans. I didn't ask Paul, but I assumed that these boxes were anything they couldn't sell or something that had sentimental value. Paul had told me to leave whatever I didn't want in the storage shed and he'd take care of it.

Up until the twenty-third box, all I found was trash. Even his old salsa and soul records, which might have some value, were stained and worn and seemed destined for the dump.

Box 23 was filled, however, with something of value: Memories. Right on the top was the photo album from my mom and dad's wedding. There was a second album, too. One my mother must have assembled. It had pictures of her and her babies, school portraits of me and my brothers, including Paul. Even though he was not hers, she always worked to include him. There were also a few outdoor shots of an excursion to our borough's great landmark: the Bronx Zoo. We looked happy in most of the shots. I found myself feeling both pleased and sad at the same time. I put the albums aside. Down in the box, I found my mom's birth certificate. I found the rest of our birth certificates, too. I put them aside, figuring I'd send them to Paul.

It stank of smoke, but there were memories here that me and my brothers should sort through. I put this box on one of the dollies to take down to my car.

Later, I found a small jewelry box. It had a gold wedding band, a few rings with unidentifiable stones, and three silver bracelets. I remembered the bangles jangling on my mother's wrist as she shook a thermometer to take my temperature when I was ten. She didn't believe I was sick. I had a 101 fever. Funny the things that stay with you, buried deep.

I found two old sweaters that were in good shape, and a suede jacket that must have been from the sixties. Also, some menus from the restaurant and some ledgers my dad kept. And some files marked *Personal*. I didn't have time to look through them now, so I'd take them with me. But other than that, there was nothing I wanted, which was funny, because everything was here —even the disgusting mug that my dad had spit in for all those years. The people who packed the place up were certainly professionals.

I put everything in two boxes—one with my dad's stuff and one with items for me and my brothers—placed them on a dolly and rolled them out. Heading to the elevator, I remembered my dad had a small coin collection which I hadn't seen. It probably was sold with the other valuables. Or maybe the packers weren't that professional.

I loaded the two boxes into the trunk of my Lexus. My dad's life had been narrowed down to one box, maybe three feet by a foot and a half. The other box was all that remained of the childhood of his three sons. I shut the trunk and sighed.

Once I got home, I intentionally stacked the boxes stinking of smoke close to the entrance of my condo. Seeing them daily would demand my attention until I got to them.

Two days later at work, I got a call from an unknown number. "Hey, this is Brady Fergusson. We met at the police service for my father. Please give me a call when you can." *Fucking Murray.* I relistened to Brady's message three times. "Please give me a call." I didn't like the sound of that. But I told myself I was being paranoid and called him anyway.

He answered on the second ring. "Hey, Ed, thanks for getting back to me. I feel kind of weird calling you."

"Uh, no problem, Brady. What's on your mind?"

"Do you have something to tell me?"

"Um, I don't know, Brady. What do you mean?"

"Are you into the Jets or something else?"

I didn't know what the hell something else meant. *Was he talking about the investigation? Did someone tip him off?* I thought about staying silent. I'd gotten burned so many times by speaking too quickly. But in the end, I went with the truth: "I've been a Jets fan forever... unfortunately."

"Yeah, I feel the same way. But I talked to your captain and found out you were gay, then I thought maybe that was what was going on."

"My captain told you I was gay!" I was pissed. "Well, I'm dating someone now, Brady, so I'm taken. Sorry."

That confused him. "Oh, wait. That's not what I'm saying. I'm married. I mean, I'm not gay… not that I have an issue with that at all. Oh shit. I'm not offending you, am I?"

"No. I'm not offended. It's just life in the semi-righteous world we live in."

Brady jumped at that. "That is so true!"

I had to admit, I kind of liked this big knucklehead.

"Hey," he said. "I heard that other cop, the one that gave you the evil eye in church, got fired?"

"Yeah. I heard that, too."

There was a pause. "Still, I couldn't help thinking you wanted to talk, and not just about the Jets."

I kicked myself. This wound was self-inflicted. I had opened a door telling him to call me about the Jets and now here I was.

"I should have been more up front with you, Brady, but with what happened to your dad and all the cops there and your mother crying, I didn't think it was the right time."

"Sure, I get it."

"But you are right. You read me well. You should be a cop, not a fireman."

"No fucking chance!"

I couldn't stop being a cop, even though I no longer was one, no matter the cost. "Well, Brady. I did want to talk. I could be totally off-base with what I put together regarding your dad, Accardi, the older Centeno, and Juarez. I'm not even sure what I think I know. The last thing I'd want you to think is that I am speaking badly about your dad or really any of these people."

"Uh-huh," Brady answered back but sounded uncertain.

"And I don't want to accidentally dig up some old wounds for you or create new wounds with whatever is going on with your dad."

"So you don't think he's dead, do you?"

I wasn't jumping on that hand grenade yet. "Well, what do you think?"

"No. I don't think he's dead."

That stunned me. "I agree."

"And if he's not dead, what does it matter to you? You're not even on the force."

"There's an enormous amount of pressure around a case that might have involved your dad. If we talk about anything, you have to promise me not to say anything to anyone. I'm serious. I'd be worried about not only my safety but yours and your family's. It's probably best we don't talk, to be honest."

Brady was silent for a second, then said, "There is something going on here. That young-gun cop was named Centeno, and my dad is pals with a Centeno. Everyone is acting odd. I think it would make sense if you came over. I'm less than thirty minutes from the GW Bridge. I have a few things I want to show you, and I'd be interested in what you have to say."

I could see the George Washington Bridge from my balcony. We set up a time to get together for Wednesday at seven, after I got home from work.

CHAPTER TWENTY-EIGHT
False Pretenses

EDDIE

On Tuesday, I decided to go through my dad's box of stuff.

I made three piles, one for each brother, and put a few menus and ledgers in each one. I opened the files marked *Personal*. The first one contained divorce documents from his first marriage, which probably wouldn't do anyone any good.

I untied the piece of string that kept the thick and aged second folder closed.

Inside were documents related to the murder of my mother. She had been shot in the front of the second restaurant my father opened in the Bronx. I looked at a yellowing article from the *New York Post*. Even back then, a murder in broad daylight would rarely make the front page. This story was buried inside: no picture, just an article mentioning my mother's name and a brief quote from my father, saying that "He was devastated." That was the right term.

He had written down notes about what had happened in a small notebook with a thin red plastic cover. I remember these being popular when I was very young. Inside were the names and phone numbers of the officers who initially responded to the call, Daniel Connolly and Michael Spencer and then later the homicide detective, Liam Hannigan, who handled the case. He had written notes about all three of them.

The pages documented my dad leaving messages and getting no responses or bad responses. Connolly, he wrote, made a comment about the mob taking up all of their time.

I looked closely at that page. My dad had a section circled repeatedly. It was a quote. "That's right, sir. You are correct. We are spending all our time working to help the Mafia." When I read it, as a former cop, I could hear the sarcasm bleeding through the page. To my grieving father, he had taken it to heart.

I looked at the notebook. It was an attempt to keep track of something by a man who was ill-equipped for the job.

I imagined my dad frantically showing this notebook and clippings to anyone who would listen. I remember him saying the newspapers were paid off, and I imagine it was thoughts like these that made him believe those in power were choosing to ignore him.

There was more in the notebook, but he carefully muted his racism with phrases like "as they are known to do" and the like. He used these euphemisms both to describe the Black attackers and the Irish cops. This, in his mind, was the official document of how he and the love of his life had been wronged. This was going to be how he found her killer and avenged the lack of action from those in power.

It was getting late and I was getting sad. I left the piles out and went to bed. But I realized I needed to call Grant to tell him we were off for tomorrow night. Even though I could see him at work, I should have told him as soon as I knew.

I had made it a habit not to lie to the people I dated. So I might have been too blunt.

"I'm helping out on an old case of mine and something's come up for tomorrow."

There was silence. Then Grant said, "Eddie, you're not a cop anymore."

"I know. But this is important. It's hard to explain but I feel connected to it."

"What does that even mean?"

I laughed. "I don't know, but you know me, I have a certain stubbornness. Remember, you told me that was something that made me different."

Grant didn't share the humor. "You need to choose your priorities."

"Come on, Grant. I was a cop for years. This is it for me. I mean, we are talking about some random Wednesday night. Cut me some slack."

"I've been cutting it."

"Well then, I guess you should sever it."

"Consider it done."

Click.

I would once again be single during the holidays. I was angry with myself, but I refused to be controlled.

Rockland County, where Brady Fergusson lived, was dotted with towns like Pearl River where a bunch of mostly Irish cops and fire-fighters who were unable to afford the city raised their families and celebrated their Irish heritage with one of the best St. Paddy's Day parades around. I got there slightly before seven and met his wife, their four-year-old boy and two-year-old girl.

He grabbed a six-pack of Budweiser from the fridge, and we headed into his small, barely finished basement.

Brady popped two beers open as we sat in two plastic lawn

chairs that he used for seating around a foldable plastic table with metal legs.

"So what's made you so unpopular with your old precinct?"

I laughed at his bluntness.

I took a sip of the beer, missing my Dos Equis, and said, "I can be a bit of a hothead, so some of it is that. On the other hand, I was working a case that people in city hall, One Police Plaza, and the archdiocese wanted to end."

"That's not telling me much."

"There's a lot of threads that need to come together for any of this to make sense."

"Try sewing, Eddie."

His bluntness was making me uneasy. "So, not just the case I was on, but from what I heard, all the missing priests were potential pedophiles. People with a history of some sort."

Brady nodded at this.

"It gets odd because there was an old priest who was also considered a pedophile, Father Tony, who comes from Italy to New York City right around the time that the priests start disappearing. Then Father Tony goes missing. At that point, we get word that the Vatican gives the green light to go after him, saying that he is a pedophile, and he might have something to do with the other priests' disappearances. Normally, the expectation is that they would cover for him. You know, they spent decades trying to keep this stuff in-house."

"So what do you make of that?"

"I'm not sure. It's just interesting. There's another thread. The big hedge-fund billionaire, O'Malley—the guy who went missing at sea? It turns out he had a relationship with Accardi. They were either high school buddies or frenemies, depending on who you ask."

"My dad said they were buddies."

"Interesting." I had decided not to connect Brady's dad to any of this. But maybe he would do it for me. I was also going to leave out anything about Angel Centeno just in case any of this conversation ever got back to the psycho nephew. I would let him fill in the blanks for me.

"Accardi was very interested in the priest investigation. He sought me out to ask about it. Then, the next thing I know, my friend Miguel Juarez has buddied up to him. One week later, they happen to all die in a boat accident? I mean, the whole thing is odd."

Brady stared at me for a second and put down his third beer. "You forgot to include my father."

"I didn't forget him. It's just an awkward conversation."

"To say the least, Eddie," he breathed out.

Was that the first time he called me Eddie? Maybe he just heard from my old captain that was what I went by in the past? Or maybe…

"Why did you invite me over here, Brady?" I had to ask. If he was going to beat the shit out of me or threaten me, doing it in his basement with his wife and kids above was an odd move.

Brady sighed. "Okay, Eddie. I think it is time that we are both honest with each other. Do you think you can do that for me?"

I think I nodded, but I couldn't be sure.

CHAPTER TWENTY-NINE
Confession

EDDIE

Brady finished the third Budweiser and popped open a fourth before starting. I was only about a quarter of the way into my first, so I wasn't concerned about us not splitting the beers fifty-fifty.

"Eddie, I haven't been honest with you." He paused. "I know that you worked on the case all the way back before I met you in the church. I was in the back because I had been waiting for you to arrive, and when I didn't see you, I walked to the back before the service began, figuring I could feel you out before I made any of my own decisions about you. Centeno was staring down both you and me when he left the church that day."

I didn't dare say a word, so he continued.

"I was given specific instructions not to talk to you from people at the precinct but also directly from Renato Centeno. Centeno is still connected with the Mafia. I'm just not sure how much pull he has, and he's pissed at me for not hating you as much as he does. I wanted to make my own decision. Needless to say, I am putting myself at risk by even talking to you."

"I could say the same."

"So, I have to ask you a couple of questions. First one, what do you think about Agents Murray and Cooper with the FBI? Second, what do you think is happening? Say that it involved a group of cops and concerned citizens removing some pedophile priests from their parishes; how would that make you feel? Would it change your opinion about anything?"

I took a large sip of the Budweiser and felt nauseous. I had no idea how to respond to either of those questions.

"I have to tell you, Brady, for starters, I am not thrilled that you know about the FBI agents. Also, it seems there are a lot of powerful people trying to cover this up. As for whether the people being abducted are regular citizens or pedophile priests, my first thought is that it is something probably best handled by the justice system."

Brady pushed the remainder of his fourth beer away and focused on me. "Well, that was almost a completely honest answer."

"What do you mean by that?"

"Well, I know you are still talking with the FBI, for starters."

"How the hell could you know that?"

Brady tried again. "Eddie, I need to know what your angle is here. There are things I can use some help with, but I don't feel comfortable with everything I say getting back to the FBI. I mean, I've shown my hand to you already.

"What you would think about the cops getting rid of some pedophile priests is important because it certainly seems there are bits of evidence pointing in that direction. I don't know anything for sure, but my first priority is to look out for my dad.

"I don't have much more except that I think my dad is not dead, and if I am right on that, then he probably got caught up with

Accardi and Angel Centeno. My only goal is to get in touch with my dad and make sure he is okay."

I took a moment to absorb what Brady said. As for how he knew I was working with the FBI still, well that seemed simple all of a sudden. He must have heard it from Renato who had just recently threatened to kick my ass or worse. "The problem I have is I am worried about young Centeno and the police. However, unlike you, I am not protected. I was hung out to dry. I need to keep the FBI around because I don't want to wind up with two bullets in the back of my head over some bullshit where I am just trying to do the right thing."

"Eddie, I get it. I am not part of some conspiracy here. My concern is getting my dad home safely to my mom and family. Centeno, or René as he was called before he turned thirteen and started having everyone call him by his last name, knows more about what is going on than I do but doesn't share anything with me. All he tells me is that you have a vendetta against him and his whole family, and you are on the pedophile priests' side because you are gay. Sorry about that."

"It's not you that's the asshole. No reason to apologize."

"I knew René Centeno when we were kids. Accardi had made an effort to keep in contact with the rest of the Centeno family after things went bad with Angel, back in his cop days. He was probably worried that the family was going to have him whacked."

Brady continued, "I'm not sure if Accardi was ever officially part of the mob, but he was Italian, and I am sure someone gave him orders to watch over Angel once he joined the force. I think Accardi quickly became fond of Angel. Believe it or not, he could be a likable guy when he wasn't being crazy. Accardi already knew what happened to Angel when he was a kid. He was a cop in the precinct when it was going down, so he already had a soft spot for him, especially after a second cop's kid got molested, and it was pretty clear that Angel's story was true.

"Now and then, Accardi would have a cookout or something like that and Anthony Centeno, his son Emilio, and his grandson René would come with him. I was stuck entertaining René while the adults talked. It was all complicated and a little hush-hush, especially after Anthony Centeno supplanted his brother, Angel's father, Salvatore, and moved up the pecking order in the mob because Angel had been such a disaster. I think this only cemented René's interest in his 'good for nothing' Uncle Angel.

"My dad met all types of interesting people through Accardi. However, he kept the Centeno family apart from the rest of them.

"I'm sure you wouldn't be surprised to hear that recently Danny O'Malley had been hanging out with my dad and Uncle Sandy, more than he had in years. I remember Uncle Danny stopping by around the holidays, now and then, when I was younger, dropping off ridiculous presents to me. He did the same thing with Accardi's kids, before things went south with Accardi and his wife.

"Once Uncle Danny hit it rich, we saw him less and less, but my dad and him, and especially Accardi and him, were still close. At first I thought that since he was so sick, O'Malley was just hanging out more with old friends. At this point, though, I think it is safe to say that they were working on something big.

"O'Malley has the resources to put a plan like this together, not to mention the interest. I take it you know that he was molested by a priest as a kid also, right?"

I just nodded, wanting to keep Brady talking. *The motive and the means*, I thought. It also wasn't lost on me, "O'Malley has..." If René Centeno did hear that O'Malley was dead, this was one of the things not being shared with Brady.

"Anyway, I know it sounds crazy, but with his and Angel Centeno's past and the priests disappearing all at the same time, it would be coincidence enough... but then to top it all off, there was the return of Father Tony."

"So what do you make of Father Tony?" I asked.

"Yeah, I guess you might have missed something. I know you know about what happened with Angel Centeno? Renato wanted to have you killed when he found out that you were bringing that story up again. What I guess you didn't know is that Father Tony, earlier known as Anthony Morelli, is Angel Centeno's uncle."

I stared, stunned.

"Yeah, this is where some of the bad blood between the precinct, the church, and the Centeno family started. They all worked together to allow Father Tony to leave, which left everyone unhappy, especially Angel Centeno, who believed his uncle was innocent.

"The broader New York Mafia was getting a lot of heat from what was happening with the Centenos, and it wasn't like the families were all unified back then. First, the Centenos had to get the police and the church to work together to get Father Tony shipped out of the country to the Vatican before charges were filed. And then after that, they had the whole Angel Centeno thing, where he then claims to be molested by a priest and then goes rogue by joining the police independently and writing off his Mafia family.

"The upshot was that the other families wanted new leadership, and Salvatore Centeno, Angel's father, needed to be replaced. Once Angel went rogue, stopped checking in with his dad and joined the police force, the leadership of the Centeno side of the family was moved over to Anthony Centeno, Salvatore's brother, Angel's uncle, and René Centeno's grandfather.

"I think Angel spent more time in church and became an altar boy because he missed his uncle after he was sent to the Vatican. Instead of getting closer to God, less than a year later, he gets molested by Father Donovan.

"He called his uncle, Father Tony, in Italy and he tried to help, but it came across hollow. You know, Father Tony saying, *I know I was accused but I was actually innocent,* on the one hand, while then saying, *I am positive Father Donovan is guilty because he is being accused by my nephew.* I take it you know what ended up happening to Father Donovan?"

I nodded. "Stabbed forty times. Homicide unsolved."

Brady nodded back. "When Angel said he was molested, the Centeno family knew how pissed he was and thought he was just lashing out because the Church sent away his favorite uncle. The authorities all rallied behind Father Donovan, and Angel's dad believed the church instead of his own son.

"This destroyed Angel. He decided to go to the one group that he thought was actually looking out for him... the cops. He finished high school and aced the police department exam as soon as he could. Obviously, the Centeno family was not happy.

"But nobody was happy. Angel was caught in the middle. Then after just a short time on the force, his partner's murder happened. To say the way his partner died was suspicious would be the understatement of all time. There were tons of accusations, but it all came back to one person. The cops and the mob worked it out and both cut ties with Angel. From there, he moved as far away as possible, slumming it in California, and ends up in jail in Chino.

"It didn't get much better for him once he got back to New York. Getting caught up in bullshit extortion schemes and low-level drug beefs. Uncle Sandy and my dad covered for him for a while until finally they gave him an ultimatum. He was doing some serious shit, and people were getting hurt."

Brady faded out with that. He then sat back, crossing his arms, demanding I say something.

He was right; he had told me a lot, but whatever I gave him couldn't damage my relationship with Agent Murray... at least not yet. With that being said, it was Murray who wanted to put me in this situation anyway! *If both Brady and I were looking for his dad, and his dad is with the rest of the cops and the missing priests, then I was still helping the feds anyway, right?*

That sounded sort of right.

"Okay, Brady. Here's what I know. First off, O'Malley had some sort of yacht that was renamed and repurposed, and it appears to have made some extensive trips far out of Florida.

"Also, and this might be why your dad had to leave quickly, I believe O'Malley really is dead."

"Dead? I thought his family just assumed he was lost at sea or something. For there to be some master plan, O'Malley needs to be the one in charge, right?"

I had to watch what I said. "First off, there was an overheard conversation that might have indicated O'Malley died. I can't give you too many specifics on this, but it helps with the rest of the theory. This is pure speculation, but what if O'Malley planned on taking the fall on whatever was going on with the priests? He was dying anyway, and supposedly he had been molested by a priest. So he sets up this plan to punish the priests somewhere. It can't be in the States, and you obviously can't ship them by air; even private jets would be easy to track. So, they make up the lost-at-sea story, refit his yacht, and use that for transportation."

"Yeah, but to where?"

"Well, here's where we start throwing darts... potentially: the Maldives."

"The Maldives? Where the fuck is that?"

"It's an island chain close to India." I didn't want to get into why the Maldives were suspected. That was all FBI shit. I shouldn't have even said it.

So I changed the subject. "If you think Angel Centeno and the other cops were friendly with Father Tony, could Father Tony be helping to capture the other priests? Could he have masterminded the whole thing?"

Brady smiled wryly at this. "I don't know. It's all thin."

"Yeah, so what about how you seem sure your dad is still alive? Is that just being optimistic, or do you have a theory?"

Brady laughed weakly at that. "My dad had a medal of Saint

Christopher on a silver chain that he would wear on long trips. He kept it in a drawer with his cuff links and his dad's old watch. When I was going through his stuff in Florida, the medal was missing. Like I said: it's thin."

Now Brady had shifted to "had the medal" instead of "has the medal." He was losing faith, and I could see why. Barney could have grabbed the medal and set off on the trip and, even then, so what? It's not like a Saint Christopher medal makes you invincible. They still could have been sunk in that storm, or even if that didn't get him, the priests could have rebelled by this point. God could have hit their fucking yacht with a thunderbolt. There were a lot of bad possibilities.

I had a plan. Not necessarily a good one, but at least a plan. "There's a few questions we may be able to get answered to see what we have. First, what do you think of René Centeno and his mob connections? René likes to boast like he is connected, and it sounds like there is a good chance that he joined the force with the blessing of the family. It would be good to know if it is just the cops and the Church or if the Mafia is also involved with working on keeping this quiet."

Brady's face flushed when I said René. "Don't fucking say that."

I didn't realize until then how worried Brady really was about the young Centeno and his temper and possible connections.

"What?"

"That's it with calling him that name… I'm sorry I used it. It's just what I called him in the past. He's a dangerous individual. If it gets out that I told you that… Let's just agree we don't need him any more pissed off than he already is. Agreed?"

"Yeah, okay."

Brady continued, "Renato Centeno is not going to talk to me about whether or not the Mafia is involved with this. Obviously, this is up their alley. They are mostly old-school Catholics and for whatever issues you have with the Mafia, they historically don't look kindly on little innocent kids getting fondled.

"That said, I was always led to believe that Angel Centeno was written off at a young age. I mean, if things were good with him and the family, why wouldn't he have just rejoined the family business after he got bounced from the NYPD?

"As for Renato Centeno, it's possible, but in terms of the Mafia hierarchy, he's still pretty young to be making demands on anything, especially something involving having people killed.

"All right," I agreed. "That's probably a dead end for now. How about Florida and all the stuff that was done at the docks? Any friends down there? Can you find out what your dad was doing?"

Brady nodded slightly. "If I do that, you need to firm up what you have about the Maldives or whatever else you can get from the feds. Deal?"

It was getting late. I nodded my head in agreement.

VIGILANTE PRIEST VII
Lust

FATHER TONY

Accardi and Centeno went down to visit Hannigan in his cell around eight the next morning and found him asleep. They fed the other prisoners and came back up, hoping to let Liam sleep it off.

I was impressed that Hannigan could sleep at all. Although Father Bob seethed quietly, the three priests were still reciting the Bible in rotation. Father Patrick continued even while Accardi and Centeno pushed his tray into the cell, but everyone was much quieter with Liam with them.

Miguel and I went down at lunchtime, and Liam was up… barely. Hungover and bruised badly. Liam frowned at the grilled chicken and peas we had brought. I thought I detected a tremor from his left hand. "I don't need this shit," he snarled.

He hobbled to his toilet and began vomiting.

"Bring me some Mahia or whiskey or even a few beers." Liam struggled to get the words out.

Neither Miguel nor I knew what Mahia was, but we knew it was not in the cards.

"Time to dry out, amigo," Miggy said.

We left the food tray and Liam's muttered curses behind.

By lunchtime the next day, Hannigan was shaking uncontrollably and hadn't eaten a thing. I warned Accardi about the delirium tremens. Sex abuse wasn't the only vice known to priests. We had many drunken priests, and I had visited the Monastery of Sobriety, an old lodge near Verona where we sent many to dry out and reform. My host had told me about the d.t.'s. Once they set in, a third of victims die of heart attacks. "No other addiction is so lethal," he told me.

Accardi got Hannigan to agree that if he brought down beer in a plastic cup, Hannigan would eat his food. But Hannigan demanded Mahia. Mahia was the clear liquid we had toasted with before the event that caused Hannigan to be thrown into this hole. I looked it up later. It was made by fermenting figs.

Hannigan returned to how he was when I met him, slippery. He was smarmy when Miguel and I brought him his meals, drunk off the clear liquid we were giving him now on a steady basis.

We found his stash in the pantry. There were cases of the clear liquid with a case or two of rum. Seeing the booze made me glance over to the entrance where the full case of Irish whiskey that we brought for O'Malley was. It had been left unopened.

Hannigan would coo different niceties to Miguel and me when we brought him lunch. Accardi and Centeno would go for both breakfast and dinner. Today Hannigan said, "Once again, sorry about that, you two. As you can see, I am good to go. Why don't you let me out?"

When we weren't there, we could see and hear him torment the priests, via the security cameras. Hannigan knew about these, but he was either so crazed that he wasn't thinking about them or he truly didn't care.

What Hannigan said was both equally vile and threatening.

While none of us trusted Liam, it was decided we couldn't keep him locked up forever. The next morning, Accardi and Centeno would talk with him. We would watch to see what happened, but the bunker ten meters below the ground wasn't meant for him.

———

Next morning, Miguel and I were eating breakfast in the gorgeous tropical morning sunlight. It was beautiful out on the pier with no boats. There was a gentle breeze. The fronds of breadfruit and palm trees swayed. A jacaranda tree exploded with purple flowers, contrasted by the orange flowers of birds of paradise which were lethal to eat. The smooth ocean seemed to stretch toward eternity from our sandy beach.

Accardi and Centeno surprised Miguel and I by coming out and meeting us on the pier. They had only been underground for around ten minutes. They certainly hadn't delivered breakfasts to the priests and Hannigan.

Accardi said, "Can you both come with us?"

They led us to the security room, with its phalanx of video monitors.

"Look at him. The motherfucker is just sleeping like a baby."

"Sorry about that, Father Tony." I assumed he was apologizing for the profanity.

Ironically, Miggy added his own. "Holy fucking shit."

I gazed at the screen. It took a second to understand what I was seeing. "Dear God. Is that blood?"

Accardi was looking at a different set of monitors. Father Charlie was waving his arms wide at one of the cameras but not talking. Father Michael had been in the cell adjacent to Liam's. His slumped body, arms through the bars, seemed pinned to the front of the cell. I looked closer at his arm, or rather, his left wrist. His hand had practically been slashed off.

Hannigan must have lured Father Michael over to the barred wall separating them and stabbed him to death with one of the broken Mahia bottles that were littering the floor.

Shocked, I could only think of the victim and the witnesses. "All of them are under duress," I said. "They must not have slept all night."

"Come on, Father Tony," said Centeno. "Enough with the sympathy. They deserve zero compassion."

I knew what he was saying. This is what we signed up for. This was the point.

"It's just that..." I started, but I didn't know where to go. "Never mind. You are right, of course."

Centeno turned his eyes toward Accardi. "Everything's being recorded, right?"

Accardi shrugged for a second, tapped some keys, then said, "Yep. Looks like it."

The files were being saved in ten-minute MP4s. All broken down neatly. There were longer files that were broken down hourly as a redundancy but they were lower quality.

"Give me a second, and I will pull up last night and see what happened."

Centeno sat at the master control desk and looked away from Accardi and said more to himself than anyone else, "I have a better idea. Let's keep this going."

With that, he pushed a clear red button. We all watched different screens as all of the cell doors below us clicked and then popped open.

———

"Goddamn it, Centeno!" Accardi roared, rising and running outside.

I followed him.

Accardi got to the entrance to the underground bunker and pulled on the door. It was locked. This must have been part of the protocol of unlocking the cages. We ran back to the security room.

"Goddamn it, Angel. Hit the override for the entrance. We got to get in there."

Angel didn't move.

On the monitor, most of the priests ran and huddled together at the farthest point from Hannigan, waiting to run up the staircase if he got close. It was Father Bob who realized that the unlocking of the cages hadn't woken Hannigan. He first checked on the departed Father Michael. I was stunned that the same man who seemed terrified of Hannigan days ago wasn't scattering like the rest.

Father Bob then looked into Hannigan's cage and saw the broken bottle lying next to him just inches from his right hand. Father Bob decided to grab an empty bottle that had been tossed haphazardly close to the side of Hannigan's cage, instead of going into the cell for the one by his hand. He pulled it through the bars and then quickly scurried off to be with the majority of the priests near the staircase. Father Bob then proceeded to break the bottle on the metal stairs.

"We have to stop this," Miguel breathed out. "Hannigan is one of us."

"He made his peace. You heard him," Centeno responded coldly.

"Nah, this ain't right," Accardi said. "I need you to unlock the hatch so we can go down there and sort this out."

"I don't think that is a good idea," Centeno responded calmly.

"I'm not asking." Accardi walked over and stared hard at Centeno.

Things were moving fast now. Father Bob said, "This is it, my brothers. You see what he did to Father Michael. We are all vulner-

able now, especially our elderly, like Father Julio and Father Paul."
Father Julio was one of the silent priests

Father Timothy and Father James, the two other silent priests
followed behind Father Bob: Father José and Father Stephen behind
them.

Centeno and Accardi were talking, but I couldn't hear them
because I had been straining to listen to Father Bob, and now I was
watching five of the priests walk toward Hannigan's cell.

"If you are going to do something, you have to do it right now,"
I pleaded with Accardi.

Accardi looked over at Centeno, but Centeno refused to move.
With that, Accardi slammed his hands on the table and watched
with the rest of us.

They had made it to Hannigan's cell.

Father Bob held the broken bottle with both hands above him
and then plunged it into Hannigan's exposed neck. Hannigan
quickly jerked up and spun his head backward to see what he was
dealing with. The turning of his neck caused him to bleed worse
than the initial stab by Father Bob.

With a wild sweep of his arm, he half pushed, half threw Father
Bob up against the end of his cell. Hannigan's bare foot crunched
into the broken bottle he had used to kill Father Michael.

Father Bob had used all his will to hold on to his weapon and
now clumsily stabbed at Hannigan's chest as Hannigan wrapped his
meaty hands around Father Bob's throat.

"I'm going to send you to hell," Hannigan gurgled through the
blood in his throat.

The other four priests who had been standing there stunned
finally jumped into action. Father José and Father James each
grabbed one of Hannigan's arms. If they were having an effect at all
it couldn't be seen on the video.

Father Timothy and Father Stephen each grabbed one of the
empty bottles. Father Timothy used the blunt weapon to hit

Hannigan over the head but while trying to wedge himself between Father José and Father James, he wasn't hitting with enough force to even break the bottle.

With one final jerk, Hannigan slammed Father Bob's now lifeless body against the bars, then tried to turn toward Father José. The blood that was flowing out of his neck now appeared to be slowing. With the struggle, he had lost a lot of blood. Father José and Father James together threw the weakened Hannigan to the ground. Hannigan tried to get to his hands and knees but instead fell back against the barred wall of his cell. It was at this point that Father Stephen arrived with his own broken bottle and started stabbing Hannigan in his exposed chest.

Father Stephen screamed loudly as the others backed away and watched.

After a while, he stopped, backed away, and sat on Hannigan's bed, looking at his hands.

We decided that the cells would remain open from this point forward. No one said anything to Centeno about what he had done.

Centeno, Accardi, and Miguel dragged the bodies of Father Bob, Father Michael, and Hannigan into an area at the very end of the underground bunker. I was left in the control room in case things went awry. Accardi showed me how to seal off areas, open different doors, and keep an eye on everyone through the various cameras. No expense had been spared.

As for the underground area, besides the cells, there was also an area for eight others. If for some reason we had to go underground, we had a place where we could live relatively comfortably. There was food, water, and basic supplies that could handle eight people for up to six months if we shut down the use of the outside generators to all other areas. There was also another control room where we could continue to monitor the prisoners.

This area had locked automatically when the cells were opened. There was a numeric keypad that could be used to enter a code to get in, which none of us had, but it was just as easy to open it from the main security station aboveground if we needed that section for a reason.

This was not where the bodies were being dragged. The bodies were dragged to a room behind the staircase and close to the elevator. There was a blue door that opened to a small area with a closet. Inside were four loose-fitting, blue industrial-grade laboratory suits installed with breathing equipment. Accardi and Centeno entered and donned two of the suits.

After putting on the suits, they opened a hermetically sealed door that led to the "removal room." In the room was a two-meter-deep pit. On the side of the pit was a large blue container with white powder in it. The three bodies were rolled into the pit, and the white powder was shoveled liberally on top of them.

Afterward, Accardi and Centeno exited the room, made sure the door resealed correctly, took off their suits, and rehung them. Then Accardi turned a nozzle on the side of the wall that started the water, which came through a spigot halfway up the pit inside the removal room.

The nozzle was to be left on for fifteen minutes. This gave me time to follow the list of questions that were left behind. I was able to see and talk with Accardi and Centeno from the control room. I asked if either of them felt dizzy or nauseous. I then had them check their entire body for burns. The questions were to be asked in five-minute increments for a total of three times. Afterward, Accardi turned off the nozzle and left the room.

This was hard on all of us, including the prisoners. The prisoners pleaded but surprisingly did not fight back against Accardi, Centeno, and Miguel. I doubted that the prisoners would be able to beat the three of them even though there were ten of them remaining. They were all exhausted, some more than others; four were barely able to stand.

That night at dinner, at the same table where Hannigan pulled his gun to start all of this, we decided that one of us should stay up and watch the monitors to make sure nothing broke down. The cells were open now, and we wondered if the docile behavior by the prisoners was a ploy.

I offered to stay up and watch for the first night. Besides the others' concerns that the prisoners might escape, I also couldn't help but be worried about the prisoners themselves. I was uncertain. I knew I was committed to the plan but I did not want any unnecessary suffering.

Father Patrick tried to recite the Bible alone but couldn't continue and ended up falling asleep, sitting. The two others who had been reading, and the four older priests made no attempt to stay up at all.

By two in the morning, only Father James and Father José remained awake. They were talking about what they should do, but they both agreed it would be difficult to overpower us. They started talking about trying to take care of the older and less-healthy priests. I admired their compassion. Then I wondered why they never cared for their victims. Some sins can only be atoned with Christ's forgiveness. And even then, as priests, we were not exempt from the wrath of God.

I crossed myself and prayed away such wayward thoughts. I was a compass. O'Malley's plan, so logical, so inspired, and so just, had left me unable to navigate the world I had entered. I was spinning, unable to find a true north that let me know exactly where I stood—with God, the Church, and myself.

I decided to look at the stored videos, particularly the one involving the death of Father Bob and Hannigan. I would look at what happened to Father Michael later.

The whole thing lasted less than five minutes, and on the second viewing I noted something. After Hannigan killed Father Bob and broke free briefly from Father James and Father José, I could see clearly now that he was looking toward one of the cameras. He opened his arms up as if to say, "Now! You have to help me, now." Shortly afterward, he slumped to the floor.

I found myself watching this a few times and focusing in on his eyes. I could see the urgency, the shock, and then the sadness all within maybe fifteen seconds.

I turned my attention back to Father James and Father José who were holding each other, terrified.

I was snapped out of my stupor by a flashing orange light and a monitor that none of us had really paid attention to. It was the dock. A boat was approaching.

Too confused to know how to use the speakers for our sleeping quarters, I briskly walked there, waking everyone.

Accardi and Centeno quickly got dressed and ran to the dock with their weapons and flashlights. Miguel was close behind. Struggling with fatigue, I couldn't keep pace.

But soon I heard Accardi yelling, "We have the boat surrounded. Identify yourself."

Centeno then added, "Quit fucking around or we will shoot!"

Miguel said something in Spanish that loosely translated to a mixture of what both Accardi and Centeno had said.

I hid behind a copse of pine trees, twenty yards from the dock.

"Hey, it's me! It's me!" I heard from the boat and could immediately tell who it was.

As he was tying the boat to the dock with Accardi's help, Barney looked over at us. He was sobbing. "I'm so sorry. I know I let all of you down. It's just... it's just that..." He slowed down as he looked us over. He could tell something was wrong.

"Oh God, what happened?" he finally said.

CHAPTER THIRTY
Hit and Stay

EDDIE

Anyone of any real importance had the week off for Thanksgiving at BDQ. I was told that I could choose whatever days I didn't want to work and figure out coverage with the rest of the guard station. Now that things were over with Grant, I wasn't going away. So I decided to work the three days before Thanksgiving.

On Monday night, I had separated the things in my dad's box and had it mostly figured out. I decided to go through the binder folder piece by piece. Most of his random scribblings were concerned with the mob connection to my mother's death, with references to newspaper articles about the Mafia and police corruption. Then I found an entry that made my knees buckle, and I sat on the floor.

All it said was, "The Centenos?"

Remembering the name when I was young, I assumed the Centenos had some made men in the family back then as they did now, but they weren't ever the head of the Italian Mafia in New

York, so Centeno would not be the first name one would think of when they thought of the mob.

One page later, he had the name Centeno and a dollar amount with a date next to it. The first amount was fifteen hundred dollars and the second was two thousand dollars. Between the other notes and the book, it looked like my dad was being extorted. Seeing the dates and the amounts listed made his notebook seem less like the ramblings of a person crazed with grief. These entries were more like legitimate evidence.

But evidence of what?

I had a restless sleep before heading into work the next morning. If I had found the notes with the Centeno name on them earlier, I would have just taken off, but I didn't want to call at midnight the night before I was supposed to come in.

Work was slow Tuesday, so it was easy for me to go into the back room to make some calls.

I left a voicemail for Edna James at IA to give me a call.

I made my second cup of coffee in the Nespresso machine they had for us and enjoyed my drink for a few moments before making my second call.

"Glad you called, Eddie," Agent Murray said.

"Yeah, hey, Brady Fergusson and I got together last week." I paused, waiting for her response.

There was none, so I continued, "Anyway, he didn't have anything definitive, but it certainly seems like he is close to what we are thinking about this."

She still didn't say anything, so I blurted, "That's about it."

"Did he say anything about the money?"

"What money?"

"What about Hannigan? Did he mention Officer Hannigan?" she continued, not answering me.

"Hannigan? Who the hell is Hannigan?" I said.

"Eddie, I unfortunately can't tell you everything, but I would ask about Hannigan. I believe this would be important to you, especially."

"Why would that..." I froze, remembering. I was seeing my dad's handwriting in my head. "Wait. Officer Hannigan? Like, Officer Liam Hannigan? Like, one of the cops who worked on my mom's case?"

Bill, one of the guys on the security team, walked in. "You may want to keep it down, Eddie."

"Keep it down. What the fuck! Don't tell me to keep it down, Bill. Murray, what the fuck does this have to do with anything? Answer me!"

Before she could say anything, Bill said, "Excuse me, Eddie. I think you should take an early lunch."

"Fuck you, Bill." I couldn't slow down.

Bill patted his hands downward in the air, trying to get me to calm down.

I was about to say something and quickly realized he was right. I hung up on Murray. "Shit, Bill. Sorry about that. It's just... it's just... Well, I just found out something that... I apologize. Give me a few minutes. I'm cool."

Even though I was technically Bill's boss, cursing a blue streak was not the BDQ way. I needed to keep things tight.

"No problem. I get it. It's the holiday season!" he laughed.

"You got that right. Sorry," I said again. Then my cell rang. It was Edna James. "Ah, shit. I've got to take this."

"I'll leave you to it. But try to keep it down, boss. If someone walks in here and hears that..." Bill frowned, making his point.

I picked up on the fourth ring. "Hi, Edna."

"You okay, Eddie?" Ms. James asked.

"Yeah, I'm okay. What's up?"

"You called me. Are you calling about Centeno?"

She was right. I was calling about Centeno, just not the one she expected.

I answered, "I am." If she has an update for me on that prick Renato, that couldn't hurt for me to know, either.

"Have you heard from him? What did he say?"

"Nope. So far, he's let me be."

"Thank God. I probably should have checked in with you sooner."

"Actually, it's the uncle, Angel Centeno, I had some questions about."

I told her I wanted to know what Angel Centeno got involved in when he got back from California. He would have been in his early forties, and he would have needed work. I also told her about my mom's case and my dad's ledger.

"I know it sounds crazy. But either directly or indirectly, my dad crossed paths with Liam Hannigan, a homicide detective, and somebody in the Centeno family. I don't know what kind of files you have access to—or if there were any files on these guys back in the day—but if you could do a look-back, I'd really appreciate it."

With us both concerned about the young Centeno, I was hoping she would give me a little assistance in exchange for me keeping her in the loop. I was pleasantly surprised when she said she'd let me know if she found anything. She couldn't give me anything confidential, but she could potentially find something that had already been disclosed.

"Of course, Eddie. I take it you know that I spoke with Officer O'Neill."

"John?" I felt a surge of anxiety. "Why the fuck would you do that?"

Edna James paused. "Ex-Officer Centeno was a problem, Eddie. I needed to get him out. It would have been irresponsible for me not to have him removed."

So you hung him out there for Centeno to... to what?"

She didn't answer, so I continued, "Do you have a fucking conscience, Edna?"

"He was going to have to talk to someone anyway."

"What the fuck does that mean?"

I could tell she was thinking before she spoke. "The FBI called, saying that they had on good authority, that someone in the precinct had potential information on the missing and assumed deceased Daniel O'Malley. John came forward. Confidentiality was assured. But I understand there was a breach."

"A breach? What the fuck does that mean? You know I'm dealing with this psycho, and now you throw some poor guy into the mix that might not even have heard what he thought he heard."

"I'm sorry, Eddie. I feel bad about involving John."

"Yeah, you tell yourself that. I gotta go."

FBI. Fucking Murray!

I left work. It wasn't much of a struggle to get permission to go home early. I called Murray from my car.

"Murray." I could sense a touch of emotion there. She knew I was angry.

I was so pissed off. I didn't even know where to begin.

"Your move, Eddie." She prodded. That was the wrong thing to say to me.

"Hold the fuck on."

I pulled my car over to the right lane and snapped on my blinkers. Traffic was fairly light being it was the Tuesday before Thanksgiving. I was far enough down the block that I should be easily spotted after people drove through the preceding stoplight. I was not willing to drive through city traffic during this conversation.

"My move, huh?" I began. "Okay, how's this for a move? I want you to give me one goddamn good reason I should ever help you with anything ever."

"Because you know it is the right thing to do."

"The right thing to do," I parroted back mockingly. "Really. Well, when the fuck are you going to do the right thing? I just heard you outed my friend John. Don't you give a shit about anyone? You realize he's supposed to be getting married soon? I mean, seriously, why the fuck would you do that to him?"

"I didn't do anything to him. He volunteered—confidentially."

"Except every fucking thing about O'Malley and the priests have all types of ears that we don't know about, listening in. So why would you think John would remain secret?"

"I'm not the fucking mole, Eddie."

"That's no excuse. You're not the mole, no shit. You are the opposite. You don't tell me shit, do you? For example, what the fuck do you know about my family's and the Centeno family's relationship, or how the hell does one of the cops who was working my mom's case come into play?"

I stopped there. I was willing to wait weeks to hear her response.

"You are not going to like this. It is not only complicated, it's also anecdotal and third-party."

"Try me."

"Okay. The record states that your dad accused the Centeno family of extortion, but only once, and this was after what happened to your mother.

"Now, while the Centeno family did have control of your dad's part of the neighborhood, there seems to be a pretty good feeling that the family was not involved in your mom's case. For one, the two assailants that got away were 'colored' as the report read. Even though it was not unheard of for the Mafia to use Black people as enforcers, if they were looking at sending a message, the message would have come through clearer if the perp was Italian."

She always impressed me by her depersonalized way of speaking. It took me a second to get back to being pissed at her.

As I was about to speak, some asshole laid into his horn behind me. He must have seen my head and, realizing I was in the car, he wanted to make me move no matter why I had my blinkers on. It had started to rain slightly, and I couldn't make out much from my rearview mirror, but this guy picked the wrong guy at the wrong time.

"I gotta go," I said to Agent Murray.

I got out of my car and saw the honking asshole was a cab driver who had stopped far enough behind me that he could easily get around. I pointed to my blinking hazard lights. "See these lights? When they blink, it means go the fuck around me."

The cab driver got out. Any normal person would have just pulled around me. But he wasn't normal. "You think I'm blind? My fare wants to be let off where you stopped."

I'm not sure exactly what I said, but it was definitely something I shouldn't have.

At that point, an Audi plowed into the back of his taxi, driving it to within an inch of my Lexus.

"Ha!" I laughed and turned back to my car.

It was at that point the Middle Eastern cab driver unleashed a right hook to the side of my head.

Ten minutes later, I was in the back of a cop car. Handcuffed.

I remembered something I heard from a captain at the police academy. A lesson I had heard and understood but, like a fucking idiot, never adopted.

"Most assaults and murders happen not out of premeditation, but because of sudden actions that spur reactions. If you create a situation by calling someone out or challenging them, you instantly lose control over that situation—because you may have just forced someone to react. And you can never predict how they will react."

In other words, to avoid conflict, don't initiate it. Don't fucking engage.

"What's the charge, Officer?" I asked.

"Assault. Disorderly conduct."

"He fucking decked me!"

"Also, potential hate crime. He says you called him a camel jockey, terrorist, and Muslim motherfucker."

The cabbie had embellished a lot.

If something like this happened in the Bronx, it probably would have just been a standard fender bender with a few people exchanging insurance information. But I was in Manhattan. And an asshole cabbie sandwiched by an Audi and Lexus was going to be done by the numbers. I was now wrapped in a whole new legal nightmare. The hate-crime charge was totally bogus. But I knew how that worked: the cabbie was trying to tee me up for a civil suit. *Jesus.*

With New York's new stringent hate-crime laws, the accusations of racial slurs were more damning than the disorderly conduct charges. I blew my one call on Agent Murray. She helped get me released on my own recognizance, picking me up in her black Crown Vic.

"There's a power bar in the glove box if you are hungry, Eddie," Agent Murray said as if she were picking me up from the gym.

"Do you want to know what happened?" I asked.

"I think I have a pretty good idea," she shot back.

My seven hours dealing with the police had not relaxed me. "This shit is your fault. If you'd just be straight with me and let me—"

Someone started talking behind me. We weren't alone in her car. "Hey, it's not—"

"What the fuck?" I turned sharply to see behind me, my heart racing.

"Jesus, calm down, Eddie. It's just me," Agent Cooper said coolly, looking at me with concern.

"Why the fuck didn't you say something when I got in the car, you fucking troll?" I seethed.

Cooper laughed.

I was losing it. "What the fuck is this? Where the hell are we going?" We were heading away from my condo.

Agent Murray breathed out. "Relax, Eddie. I am taking you to your car. I got that taken care of, but you have to calm down. You are no good to me—"

"No good to you! No good to you!" I was in a full rage. I couldn't form another sentence.

"Or," Agent Murray emphasized as she continued, "or more importantly yourself. What are you doing right now?"

I looked around. I looked at Murray, and then I looked at Cooper.

I felt myself relaxing, if just slightly. "Okay, okay, Murray. I need answers."

CHAPTER THIRTY-ONE

Crimes and Misdemeanors

EDDIE

It was almost nine. Murray had called ahead to make sure that someone would still be at the impound to release my car.

"This isn't going to be a short story, Eddie," Murray said as I was noticing a fresh scratch on the back of my Lexus.

"What?" I fired back, distracted.

"Can you meet tomorrow at the bureau?"

"What? You know I still have a full-time job that doesn't involve dealing with your bullshit."

"I take it that's a no."

"Yeah... that's a fucking no." I opened my driver's door, looking back at her. "How about the next day? Thursday?"

"You mean Thanksgiving?" Cooper answered for Murray.

"Yeah, Thanksgiving. I won't be celebrating this year."

Murray frowned at that and looked at me concerned. "Eddie, listen. This seems to be taking a toll on you. If I were you, I would spend Thanksgiving with family. We can get together on Friday if that would work."

"Friday will be fine." The office would be closed that day anyway.

The next day, Wednesday, I got two calls while at work. The first one I received on my cell was from a Detective Harrison who wanted to go over my charges and make sure that I was not planning on leaving the city. The other was from one of BDQ's corporate attorneys, Mr. Steinem.

I called the police back first. "I am surprised they have a detective on this case," I said as calmly as I could in the back room, behind the front desk at BDQ.

"Well, Mr. Rodriguez, we know you are an ex-cop with some previous offenses on your record. We want to make sure things are done thoroughly and fairly. It doesn't make anything easier because of your history with the other traffic incident and now you hitting a cop."

What? "Hitting a cop? What do you mean by that?"

"Well, Cadet Brown said that you assaulted him, specifically that you threw a cup at him."

"Assaulted him?" I roared. "You have to be fu— You have to be kidding me. Your cadet was goading me. He called me a racist. I'm Latino, for fuck's sake."

"Well, that might be, Mr. Rodriguez, but we need you to show up on Monday to be formally charged, regardless."

I tried to stay calm. "So, this little prick… Excuse me. So your cadet can call me a racist and make fun of me for getting in an incident with a Black teen earlier this year, which ultimately led to me no longer being a cop, and nothing happens to him, then he can claim that he was assaulted by a friggin' Styrofoam cup? Does that make any sense to you?"

Harrison sighed. "I don't know how productive this conversation is going to be, Mr. Rodriguez. If you are not here on Monday, we will put out a warrant for your arrest."

I hung up and left a message for the corporate attorney. My next call didn't go much better.

When Mr. Steinem called me back, he called me on the main front desk number. I couldn't figure out how to transfer the call, so I was stuck talking with him with the two other guards next to me.

After he let me know who he was, I shot back with the obvious. "Why are you calling me?"

"Well, Mr. Rodriguez, I know you were arrested yesterday, and we need to discuss what that means for you and how this looks to BDQ." The arrogance in Steinem's voice was palpable. I could tell he felt dirty even talking with me and especially over something so tawdry.

"How do you know about that?" I shot back, happy that the other guards were walking away to give me some space. *Have you ever talked to someone and immediately hit it off like you were old friends? This was not one of those times.*

"BDQ is a powerful company that carries a lot of weight. It is in the company's best interest to know things. It is also important for a company with BDQ's reputation to keep an eye on some of our more *interesting* employees." He was leaning into his arrogance.

"Well, I—" I tried to interrupt.

Steinem didn't let me. "Whatever witty retort you may be thinking of or whatever you want to add, please don't." He sighed. "I have directions here to drive with you down to the station at eleven o'clock on Monday. I will be assigned as your lawyer, and I will do my best to protect both you and the firm. For the firm, I will be paid well, as I should be. My work with you will be pro bono."

"You know what. I think I will just defend myself or get my own attorney," I seethed.

Steinem laughed. "Well, I can't force you, but if you decide to do that, please contact Mr. Kennedy in HR; maybe you will make it easier for us to handle this issue. I will see you in the building lobby at ten thirty sharp on Monday, Mr. Rodriguez." With that, he hung up the phone.

I bought a twelve-pack of Dos Equis and a rotisserie chicken after leaving work on Wednesday. I vowed to spend Thanksgiving alone, pissed off at the world.

The silence became deafening by noon on Thanksgiving, so I flipped around and found a channel showing an old Woody Allen movie. I liked the old shots of New York and how a certain level of irreverence used to be allowed.

After picking at the chicken that I reheated in the microwave for Thanksgiving dinner, I ended up splitting Dad's things into three separate piles. Paul's was by far the biggest, mine was the second, and Steve's was the smallest, because fuck him. He got a house and Lord knows what else and was still unable to take care of himself.

I kept my promise by finishing off the twelve-pack and sitting on my couch, crying, mumbling, and telling myself to get my shit together.

I arrived at the FBI office at eleven thirty on the Friday after Thanksgiving. Murray met me at the entrance.

"Good afternoon, Eddie," Murray said with a bit of anger. I was supposed to have been at the FBI office at ten.

"Not really."

Cooper was waiting for us upstairs in a conference room. I sat down, and Cooper tossed me a bottle of water from across the table.

Murray was angry. "Eddie, you realize that this is for your benefit, and we are doing you a favor, right?"

"What?" I matched her anger.

Cooper jumped in. "Eddie, we both appreciate what you've been doing and are trying to do. We wanted to clear up any misunderstandings. But as we said Wednesday night, we are on a bit of shaky ground here."

I met Murray's gaze and scoffed. "What the fuck do you want me to say?"

"I want you to stop being such a little bitch."

With that, I jumped to my feet. I stared at Murray hard.

Murray kept eye contact the whole time. "What are you going to do, Eddie? Are you going to take a swing at a female FBI agent in an FBI building a few days after being charged with assaulting a cop—"

"That's bullshit, and you know it."

"Eddie." She paused. "Look in the mirror. You're supposed to be the good guy. We are trying to go after criminals who are beating, torturing, and potentially killing people, and instead we are spending a majority of our time with your crap."

"Fuck you."

Murray continued to look at me coldly. "Yeah, fuck me. You do realize I am not the enemy, right?"

I couldn't think. I leaned back.

Murray continued, "Sure, people will let you down, and there are a fair number of bad people in the world, but you need to keep your eye on the ball. Let's try to keep focused."

I tried to say something, but now I was not sure what to say. I defaulted to humor.

"Is this an intervention or an investigation?"

"Both. But you are trying to change the subject."

"The subjects are related. Tell me about my mom's murder."

"Now, I am willing to go through what we have, but I would like a commitment from you that going forward you will prioritize things that we can influence and change, and deprioritize things that we cannot."

I shrugged. I was embarrassed, and as usual she had a point.

Murray got up and left the room. Cooper said, "Hey, Eddie. Listen, I get it. All Murray is saying is that we are on the same team."

"Okay."

He frowned, then continued, "What's happening here is big. Murray is all in on this. She is taking a lot of heat. As you might imagine, she's got other things she is supposed to be doing. This case is not being viewed as a priority. You realize she has to keep the bosses informed. Imagine her explaining one of her best leads is some guy who gets fired as a cop. Then she has to bail him out of jail. I mean, on a case she's not even supposed to be working on."

Cooper had a point. "Okay," I said again.

Cooper nodded at Murray, and Murray reentered the room.

"All right." Murray joined us at the table. "This is what we have."

CHAPTER THIRTY-TWO
Useful Idiot(s)

EDDIE

Murray began. "So, Eddie, like I said, we are working with a lot of old notes and connecting the dots from conversations, and more importantly, Cooper's accounts, from talking with a few retired officers. The point is we are still not entirely sure of most of what I am about to say."

"I get it."

"What's this?" I smirked knowing what it was.

"Sign and date on page twelve and twenty-three," she said coldly.

I signed not knowing how many of my rights I had given up.

"To begin, this stays among the three of us." She made eye contact.

I didn't even have to speak. She could tell I was about to erupt.

"There's a chance that Angel Centeno was involved with your mother's murder."

"Go on."

"It looks like the Centeno family had influence in the neighborhood where your dad's restaurant was. But we've found no reports of the mob running extortion schemes or protection rackets in the neighborhood at that point.

"But someone who was around back then speculated that Angel Centeno went rogue when he got back to New York after doing time in California. There were rumors he got involved with fencing and burglary operations with no Centeno ties, however it's not like the local residents were aware of this.

"Even if they were, he was a known character. The stories of what happened while he was a cop were varied, but they always arrived at the same conclusion—don't mess with Angel Centeno.

"We found a report that says a warehouse we believe he operated burned down. If it was his, all his fenced goods went up in smoke. Regardless, around this time, a source says he started to lean on local businesses for protection money, using his last name, his image as a tough guy, and some local muscle.

"The story we heard was at some point your dad refused to pay, and Angel sent some non-Italians to talk with him and things went sideways. According to the old-timer, Angel just wanted his muscle to scare your parents, especially since he was doing this without the blessing of the family. Gunfire would also bring heat from the police. His mistake—if this version of events is true—was giving two high teenagers with nothing to lose and everything to prove, a pair of guns."

"Why didn't the fucking cops do something? I mean, if this story is around now, it must have been around then, too. I found notes from my father naming the fucking Centenos." I knew the answer. If half of what I heard was true back in high school, the Centeno family would have had a lot of juice with the force back then. Unless it couldn't be avoided, they weren't going to press in situations like this.

"Well, Eddie, as you know, the Centeno family was pretty protected by the local precinct back then.

"And then there's Liam Hannigan," Murray ended.

"Right, you are going to love this, Eddie," Cooper added.

"I'm not *loving* any of this."

"Sorry about that, Eddie. Not what I meant to say. It's just that it gets pretty messy. Liam Hannigan is an interesting guy. I don't have all the details, but Angel and him got into a dustup before Angel was accused of popping his partner all those years ago.

"The working rumor is that Angel was banging Hannigan's wife. I mean, Hannigan was substantially older than her, and Angel was, I don't know, five or so years younger than she was. Not sure if Angel was intentionally trying to embarrass Hannigan or if Hannigan's wife was some sort of player."

Cooper looked over at Murray, but if she was offended, she wasn't showing it.

"Anyway," he continued, "there was a large function up in the Catskills in the old police camp with a bunch of the New York City precincts and divisions. Angel and Liam start trading blows, and then different cops from the two precincts, Angel's and Liam's, start going at each other; supposedly, Accardi and even Barney Fergusson took a few shots.

"This created some bad blood between Bronx Homicide and Accardi's Fort Apache precinct."

Cooper looked down for a second, reading his notes. "One of the rumors that went around was that one of Liam's kids is actually Angel's. Now listen, this is really, really thin. But, it potentially answers some questions for us.

"Here's the interesting bit. When Angel comes back to town and starts going all Scarface on his own, Liam vouches for him. Liam filed the report that helped to clear Angel not only from some of the more minor things but also from being a suspect in your mother's murder."

"Why would Hannigan try to help Centeno?" I questioned.

"Right! Yeah, this is where things started getting fishy. I mean, Accardi, and by proxy, Fergusson, looking out for Angel the whole time made sense. They even flew out to Cali once to see him while he was doing time, but Hannigan…"

My bullshit detector was on full alert. "So, wait... am I missing something? You two are just looking out for me and going over stuff about my parents with FBI resources, just to be nice?"

Cooper laughed. "Yeah, something is missing all right. Hannigan."

"Yeah, some fucking clear answers are missing."

"No. You don't understand. I'm saying Hannigan is missing."

"What?"

"Yeah, Hannigan. He's MIA, too. Along with Accardi, Juarez, and the others."

"Hannigan is missing? I mean, I guess it could be related, but why?"

It was my old pal Murray to the rescue. "It's not just Hannigan. It's also millions of dollars that are missing."

Cooper said, "O'Malley hired Hannigan to run a portion of his security a year or so ago."

I shook my head. "I still can't get over O'Malley glomming on to these low-rent cops."

"Well then, you are going to love this. Shortly after bringing on Hannigan, O'Malley puts fifty million dollars into a numbered account where only the two of them have access. Once O'Malley is presumed dead, the account is zeroed and Hannigan disappears."

"Shit."

Cooper nodded. "Yeah. O'Malley's accountants had made clear their concerns about the joint account shortly after it was established and O'Malley blows them off, saying he is setting up an emergency account, in case anything ever happens to himself or his family. But with all his other trusted people, why choose Hannigan? Something is off.

"Anyway, at this point, everyone just assumes Hannigan must have the goods on O'Malley, something with pictures and little boys or girls. You know, some shit like that. With O'Malley's money, it's not like the fifty mil changed anything materially, so everyone just moves on from it.

"This is a good find, but a dead end, since no one involved with O'Malley's businesses had any connection with Hannigan. However, I do a search on the computer, and I find one of Hannigan's sons is on the force serving in a precinct right here in Manhattan. So, I decided to pay him a visit.

"You want another water?"

Cooper had noticed I was done with mine. Before going to the fridge to grab three waters, one for each of us, he tossed a tape recorder on the table.

"Old media," I joked.

"Yeah, we already digitized it. Anyway, you aren't going to believe this," he promised, then went to grab the waters.

The first voice I heard was Cooper's: "Thanks for talking to me today, Officer Hannigan. As you know, we are concerned about your dad and just want to try to find him."

"You don't have to sweet-talk me, Agent Cooper. I know why you're here, and it isn't about my dad."

"Okay, then. Why do you think I'm here?"

"I was surprised when you told me about the numbered account, and I am smart enough to know that the O'Malley connection has us talking today.

"My mom is going broke battling stage IV colon cancer, and my dad is running all over God's green earth. He told me he was doing good works for O'Malley, but then he disappears. Or at least stops answering his cell phone. Who does that? I figured he was probably dead, along with his boss. But then you told me about the money… fifty million dollars, and my mom is about to lose her house? I don't give a shit if they are divorced. That's cold-hearted."

Hannigan kept going. "I was glad for him hooking up with a powerful man like O'Malley, especially after things went bad with him with the force. You know with him supposedly on the take and shit like that."

Cooper made eye contact with me as we were listening to the tape. I could just see him critiquing the interview. His best option was to stay quiet. This kid was giving him all types of information.

"I have to think my dad is still alive. He told me he had a fake passport and was flying to India right before he went missing. The fake passport didn't make any sense. I mean, unless he was already planning to take the fifty million, right?"

We listened to the tape whirl for about five seconds before Cooper's voice came on: "So, what else did he say?"

"Nothing directly. But what about everything else? I mean, something had to be going on. First, my dad goes missing and then that boat with Centeno and the other cops. It's like the entire O'Malley police posse was being erased," Hannigan blurted. *Bingo!*

"So, your dad was friends with the cops from Fort Apache?" Cooper tried to keep it conversational.

"Yeah, especially Accardi and Centeno. The three of them had an on-again, off-again relationship, but they always seemed connected. They all were involved with O'Malley one way or another."

Cooper clicked the tape off and looked at me.

I was lost. "So why would Hannigan be hanging around the guy who was banging his wife? There's something wrong with your thesis."

"You think?" Cooper grinned. "But that's your takeaway? Really? This is a witness who confirms his dad was working with O'Malley and that he recently flew to India."

"So what's special about India?"

Murray walked over with an iPad. "Take a look." She had circled the Maldives in red and started zooming out. North of the Maldives was India.

"Come on, Eddie." Cooper grabbed the iPad from Murray and started pointing at the zoomed-out map. "First, Perth, where O'Malley was last seen before we were told he was presumed dead. He could travel northwest to the Maldives, then we know the yacht got refitted in Cape Town, which is where you would have that work done if you were continuing west to the US. Now it looks like before any of this, Hannigan showed up in India for some unknown reason, which is the closest major country to the Maldives. If not there, do you have any better suggestions?"

I didn't.

CHAPTER THIRTY-THREE
The Things We Do For Family

EDDIE

I ate lunch with Cooper and Murray and left. On the drive back to my condo, I started feeling heavy and alone. Not being a cop was having a bigger effect on me than I expected. When I was a cop, there was always something going on. I was always being invited to one event or another. At BDQ, I was an outsider.

It also was cramping my dating style. Being a gay cop was part of my identity, now I was just another gay suit working for money. Not much intrigue to that.

I decided to make some calls.

"Hey, Eddie, what's shaking?" Paul answered his cell.

"Not much, Paul. Just wanted to wish you and your family a belated Happy Thanksgiving," I said.

"Yeah, no problem. The kids would have loved to talk with you. Did you get my message?"

"Yeah, sorry about that. I got busy."

"Good for you, Eddie!" Paul shot back. "Hope you are having fun up there in the big city. I miss the place."

Paul was trying to be nice. I better keep it short. "How's Dad?"

"Bitter and sober. One is related to the other. But he looks a hell of a lot better."

"Hey, thanks for taking care of him. I will check in with you soon."

"Sounds good, brother."

He didn't even have enough time for me to say goodbye back. I knew I was being a prick, but for someone who manages millions of dollars, he didn't have great people skills.

Edna James was next. I left a voicemail. I knew I should call Steve also, but Jesus, he was heavy lifting.

I hadn't checked in on John in a long time, so I tried him next.

"Harro," he answered.

There must have been a problem with the line. "Hey, John, it's Eddie." I waited and didn't hear anything, so I continued, "I think there might be something wrong with the line." Still nothing.

I hung up and called back.

The phone was picked up immediately. It was a woman's voice. "Eddie?"

It must have been his girlfriend or shit, probably his wife at this point. "Oh, hey. Sorry, uh..." I couldn't remember her name.

"It's Debbie. It's fucking Debbie," she screamed into the phone.

I didn't know what to say to that, so she continued, "Johnny can't talk to you right now; he is still recovering. Besides a fractured skull, he also had to have his jaw reset."

"What?"

"That psycho Centeno jumped him right in the middle of Central Park. He came out of the blue and tackled him, then started slamming his head into the ground. The kick to the face was what got his jaw."

I couldn't respond.

"Eddie?"

I was going to make both Centenos pay, the uncle and the nephew, if it was the last fucking thing I did.

"Yes?"

"Listen to me." Debbie paused for effect. "If you ever, and I mean ever, had the slightest affection, care, friendship, whatever for Johnny, I need you to make a promise to me.

"I need you to promise that you will never call us again. That you won't bump into us accidentally. That if you see us, you'll walk the fuck away in the other direction. You, Eddie. You. You are toxic. Johnny is a good man. Screw that. Johnny is a great man. He wants to do the right thing, but you, you, Eddie Rodriguez—you are poison."

I shouldn't have but I placed the call anyway.

"Murray," she answered flatly.

"Why didn't you tell me Centeno fucked up my friend?" I was back at my condo, but I drove past the entrance.

"What?"

"What? What! How many lives do you fuck up in any given day? I mean, besides mine and everyone I've gotten involved with you?"

"You are talking about John O'Neill?"

"Yeah, John O'Neill. The guy with the wired jaw."

Murray bristled. "I'm not sure what else you want me to say. I—"

"What else to say? When were you planning on telling me he got tuned up? Was it just not imp—"

"What are you talking about? You already yelled at me about this a few days ago."

I got it now. "At that point, I only knew you sold him out. I didn't know he got fucked up."

"Well, now you know the whole story."

"The whole story! I can't believe—"

Edna James was calling me back as I was completing my circle back to the entrance of my building.

"You know what, fuck you." I hung up on Murray.

"Hey, Edna, thanks for calling. Can I call you back? I am just pulling into my garage."

The signal got lost as I went underground.

It was three fifteen in the afternoon. I grabbed a Dos Equis out of the fridge, humming the tune, "It's five o'clock somewhere... You know what? I don't give a shit."

"Thanks for telling me about what happened to John O'Neill."

She did not pick up on my sarcasm. "Oh. Why, yes. Once again, sorry about that, Eddie. It is awful."

She had changed a lot from her days as the ice queen back in the precinct. She continued, "So, I'm returning your call. Is now a good time?"

"You know what? Now isn't..." I paused. *Wait.* I was remembering what I had asked her to look into the last time we spoke. "Actually, now is fine. Thanks for getting back to me." I did a 180 from rage to faked calm.

"Okay, then. It does look like there is an Angel Centeno connection to what happened with your mother."

"Go on."

"As for Hannigan, he seemed to have a taste for payola."

"What?"

"He might have taken bribes." She paused. "You know, Eddie, I'm trying to help you out here. While it's not illegal to record this conversation without my consent, it would be highly unethical."

"What?"

"You heard me, Eddie. Don't play stupid with me!"

"Yeah, yeah, I'm not recording you."

"Well, good. What happened, anyway? You ask me to look into this for you, and then you don't answer your phone? You have to be smart enough to realize that it is probably not in my best interest to talk to you about this, right?"

I was still stung about John getting tuned up, but she was right. "Yes, I understand."

She breathed hard, then continued, "Hannigan might have taken cash from the Centeno family and other bribes, but that wasn't the reason he left the force."

"Why was he fired, then?"

Edna said quietly, "Well, he appeared to have been covering for his buddy Angel when your mom got shot, Eddie. Also, he didn't technically get fired. He—"

"I got it. He was given the ability to resign like they do with most cops. Anyway, what do you mean Centeno and Hannigan were buddies?"

"Well, I guess you must be getting information from other people, then. Do you know about Centeno and Hannigan's shared history?"

"That Angel was banging Hannigan's wife, yeah," I said flatly.

"What?" Edna responded sharply.

Shit. Ugh. "I am sorry, Edna. That Centeno and Hannigan's wife were having an extramarital affair." I should have realized how PC she was.

"What? Wait. What did you say?"

I tried again. "That Angel Centeno was having an improper—"

"What the fuck are you talking about, Eddie? Do you think that Angel Centeno was having sex with Hannigan's wife?"

"Uh-huh," I answered, although really I had no idea.

"I have found no record or source about that. Who told you that?"

"Never mind. Cops are always telling bullshit stories like this, always with some sex angle. You know that, Edna."

"It was even more outrageous than that. Couples and affairs, at least that's consensual. No, it all had to do with Angel Centeno being... I can't believe I am about to say this. You promise me you are not recording this, Eddie?"

"Yes. I promise."

Edna continued, "Well, it all had to do with Angel Centeno being molested by a priest."

"Yes, I know that. I just don't—"

"Let me finish." She paused, then continued, "So Hannigan's godson was the one who accused a different priest; this priest happened to be Angel's uncle."

Tony Morelli, the Vatican priest, I thought but didn't say. I remembered being involved in old cases where BICs, Bronx Irish Catholics, would be involved. Now and then, we would see perps going out of their way for godsons and goddaughters. It was considered a huge deal to be made a godfather or godmother back in the day. A lot of them would treat their godkids as if they were their own son or daughter.

Edna kept going. "So, many years later, Liam Hannigan and Angel Centeno end up going at it during some big police event. Somehow the two of them put two and two together, and Liam was pissed that his godson's molester, who happened to be Angel's uncle, got away while Centeno's molester ended up ultimately getting killed.

"From what I understand, shortly after the fight, Liam Hannigan found out from his godson that he had lied about Tony Morelli,

Angel's uncle, all those years ago. Supposedly, the little brat had a problem with the young priest catching him smoking or something like that."

"Wow."

"Anyway, after that, the two of them became friendly. More importantly, it started Hannigan's relationship with Accardi, who eventually helped Hannigan get his gig with O'Malley.

"So, have I done enough for you, Eddie. Are we officially even?"

I almost said yes, but that gave me an opening. "Well, yeah, just one last thing. I have been getting some strange phone calls from the same number over and over again. I am pretty sure it is Centeno. Can you give me his cell number so I can make sure?"

There was a long pause. Edna sighed and read Centeno's cell number to me.

"We are even, Ms. James. Thank you."

I wasn't sure what I was going to do with Centeno's cell, but it was good for me to have.

I decided to call Steve before settling in for dinner and a movie at home.

"I don't think you understand, Eddie. They are after me." Steve sounded terrified.

"Have I missed something, Steve? Who are they? And why are they after you?"

"I don't know!" he screamed.

Even for him, this was odd. Usually, his rants were of the my-life-is-so-unfair variety. Paranoia was a new flavor.

"You need to promise me. You need to promise me you will come down here."

"If you don't know who is after you, how am I going to know?"

I paused. It was a long shot, but I should ask. "Has anyone asked you about me? Did they want you to give me a message?"

"You? Why would this be about you? They are everywhere! You're a detective! When they call, you can tell them."

"They call?"

"I can hear them in my dreams. It's so awful"

"Are you high, Steve? Or off your meds?"

"I need you here, Eddie!"

Ugh. Just what I needed. I would be getting time off from BDQ for the holidays. Maybe I would drive down and see Paul and then continue south to Steve. Get some sun and maybe even check out Miami. If I felt adventurous, I could nose around and see if I could find out anything regarding the missing cops.

"Well?" Steve sounded desperate. "Eddie?"

"Sure thing, Steve." I tried to settle him. "I will make it down. I just need to figure out what my holiday break looks like."

"Holiday?" Steve shot back. "No, I need you here now. I can't... I can't... wait. I got to go." Click.

"Always good chatting with you, Steve," I said to myself.

VIGILANTE PRIEST VIII
Envy

FATHER TONY

I realized now that the loss of O'Malley hadn't just damaged Hannigan, it had damaged all of us. With no leadership, there was no trust. I thought everyone would be happy to see Barney and to have a boat back. But even Accardi was looking at Barney skeptically.

Accardi told Barney that Hannigan was dead. Then Barney confessed that Hannigan had given him the green light to go into O'Malley's room, where the rest of us were told not to enter out of respect for our departed friend, and that's where he found a secure phone.

"I called Brady, my son. He told me to get the hell out of here. But I realized I was putting everyone in a bad position."

After Barney said this, everyone except me went to O'Malley's room. I went to the security office to check on our captives.

Eerily, Father James and Father Julio were looking back at me into the camera. They were reciting the Lord's Prayer. How nice that they were seeking solace in the most basic and beautiful of our supplications. Then, as so often happened when I found myself sympathizing with these men, I rebounded with the opposite thought. Did they pray after they had committed the most vile of sins. Or did they bathe in contentment after their savage, evil assaults on the innocent and trusting? For a moment I thought of asking them through the microphone.

The damage these vile men had caused was incalculable. They had violated the holy trinity of trust among Christ, his soldiers, and his flock.

I was interrupted by Centeno and Barney yelling at each other.

"So you're telling me that Hannigan told you about the phones?" Centeno snarled.

"I know how it looks. Don't ask me why!"

"I know why. Because you were bitching about having to come all the way in. He knew you. He was buying an ally. Or trying to."

"He said what he said," Accardi added, more as a reflexive action of sticking up for his partner than actually believing him.

"Well, that's bullshit. Hannigan didn't trust any of us. The first time we were all relaxed he pulls a gun, but right before that he gives a sat phone that none of us know about to Barney just before Barney skips on us. You telling me Hannigan didn't want something?" Centeno spat.

"Why wouldn't he have given Sandy the sat phone? Him and Sandy were better pals than you two." Barney didn't respond, so Centeno turned his attention toward Accardi.

"Sandy? What the fuck is going on with you? We have a problem here." Angel stared at him.

"Yeah, we do," Accardi responded.

No one said anything while waiting for Accardi to say something further.

"My mind is on a different problem," Sandy finally said. "Hannigan didn't happen to tell you what the plan was for us to finally get off this island when we are all done—did he, Barney?"

Barney shook his head no.

I looked over at my nephew, Angel, and he once again, looked like the scared boy I had seen when he was young.

"Wait.. well, why does it matter? You know the plan, right, Sandy?" Angel asked.

"No, I don't know the plan, you asshole. Why would I know the plan?" Sandy glared back at him.

"So, Barney, when you were chumming it up with Liam, he didn't tell you anything about the final plan to get off the island? And as for you, Sandy, why the fuck wouldn't O'Malley have told you the plan?" Angel said, going back and forth between the two of them.

Accardi couldn't make eye contact with any of us. "It wouldn't have made any sense for us to know those details until we were in the final phase on the island. It would have been a liability if one of us would have gotten detained. It was the right call. No one could have anticipated that both Liam and O'Malley would be dead."

"Well, that just doesn't make any sense. This isn't on me," Angel protested.

"This is absolutely on you," Sandy responded. "If you hadn't opened the cells, Liam would still be alive."

"Don't put this on me. This all started when Barney abandoned us. If not for that, we wouldn't be here now. This is on him," Angel said, turning his head toward Barney,

"What are we going to do?" Miguel asked.

"I don't know. We have to think about it. Talk it out," Accardi murmured.

I looked around the room. Barney was looking away toward the door. He wanted to be anywhere else.

Centeno wouldn't let it go. "Hannigan wouldn't have gone native if not for you abandoning all of us."

"Fuck you, Centeno!" Barney shot back.

"Come on, gentlemen, let's discuss it in the office. You're coming, too, Miggy." Accardi put his arms around Barney and Centeno and led them out the door. Miguel patted me on my back and offered me a smile before filing out behind them.

The office?

I woke up to shouting. It was the priests. They had gotten close to the camera near the staircase. This one was the most accessible. All of the cameras had microphones:

"Hello, is anyone there?"

"Dear God, they've abandoned us!"

My eyes couldn't focus as I tried to snap myself out of my stupor. I reflexively looked at my watch and realized it was nine o'clock, an hour later than we normally fed them breakfast. I wasn't sure how they were keeping time down there. I didn't remember any clocks, but somehow they knew.

I wandered out into the sunlight, squinting my eyes. The few hours I had slept were uncomfortable hours.

When I entered the main open area where we dined, I quickly got my answer on what "the office" meant. Accardi and Centeno were passed out on the table. They had broken into the whiskey, and each had a partially filled glass in front of them. A disheveled Barney waved his hands in the air when I walked in, telling me to keep it down for his sleeping friends, assuming they were all still friends. He was in the kitchen making breakfast. We still had some eggs, and he had defrosted some bread and bacon.

I peered into Miggy's room and saw him sleeping restlessly on the top of the covers of his bed.

"Good morning, Father Tony." Barney smiled.

His eyes were glassy, but he seemed relatively sober.

I walked over to him and kept my voice low. "Thanks, Barney, but we need to feed the"—I paused for a second trying to think of a better word but not finding one—"prisoners."

"Okay, okay," Barney said as he was wrapping up cooking. He frowned as he split the four eggs he had put on the one plate for himself and put two on a plate for me. He split the rest of the food he made, then pointed to one of the empty bedrooms. I grabbed my plate, poured myself a cup of coffee, then followed him into his room.

Each room was identical, more or less, with a king-sized bed and a small desk and a chair. Barney sat on his still-made bed, and I sat on the chair.

"Wait, you haven't slept?" I asked.

As if on cue, he yawned and grabbed the coffee he had placed on the floor next to his feet.

"I've had a bit on my mind," Barney replied.

I didn't say anything, so he continued, "At first, I was feeling guilty about how we no longer have a plan to get off the island. However, for me, my life ended when I left Florida. I can't imagine living my remaining days without my family. After stewing in guilt and feeling sorry for myself... There's a lot here, Father, besides my getting cold feet. I mean, I am the only one besides you who would be considered a practicing Catholic. You can still find me at church most Sundays. Accardi stopped decades ago, as did Miggy.

"I've given this a lot of thought and I am losing faith in what we are doing here."

He paused, waiting for me to respond.

Beware of false prophets, which come to you in sheep's clothing, but inwardly they are ravening wolves. I couldn't tell him what I really felt. I had a duty to support him. "We are doing the right thing, Barney. This rampant behavior... this pestilence... needs to be exposed, and unfortunately leaking a list of priests to a newspaper would not bring the necessary level of attention to this abom-ination."

"Okay, but even if I agree with you there, why not document that from the priests? Why not interview them and force them to answer questions?"

"Well, that wasn't the plan we discussed," I responded, giving a nonanswer. "The plan was to see how they would react once confronted with the enormity of what they had done, when they were no longer protected and any chance of absolution removed. Think of the victims." I tried to end with some punch.

"Okay." Barney stared at his plate and continued to eat.

I hadn't answered his questions. I had failed him. I would have to figure out how to better respond.

We finished our meal and prepared breakfast trays for the pris-oners. Barney started telling me about what he had talked about with the others.

First, when he arrived in Malé after taking the last boat, he was waved at by someone who was also not native to the Maldives. Whoever it was must have recognized the boat and thought Hannigan was pulling up because both Barney and Hannigan were of a similar size. The person frowned and went over and started talking to two young men, more boys than men. Barney decided this must be the guy, Thaddeus, who Hannigan had told us was his and O'Malley's local contact for supplies.

Second, Barney went over the call with his son, Brady. Barney said the phones O'Malley purchased were special. An outbound call would first go through West Bengal, a known area for telephone scammers, and then bounce to a New York number with either a 212 or 917 area code, so it would appear like a local call. If someone tried to call the number back, it would connect to a local person in New York City who would have no idea why they were being called.

Because of all the security measures, Barney's call with Brady was even more difficult. There was a three-to-five-second delay on both sides, and they found themselves talking over each other. There were a few pieces of information that Barney had received before hanging up within the three-minute window that O'Malley had set to use the phones even though we felt pretty sure the call couldn't be traced.

Brady said René Centeno was on the run. He had disobeyed orders and now he was on his own. Angel had given him the location of the island, so it was possible he would be coming our way. He said he hoped not; René's presence would not help things.

Brady further stated that the FBI was still on the case and that it looked like they were connecting the dots. Everyone was distancing themselves from Accardi and the rest of us at this point: the mob, O'Malley's New York connections, even the O'Malley's family themselves.

Lastly, Barney told me that he had run into one of the crew who had abandoned us on the island. Barney doubted that this run-in was accidental. The crew member apologized to Barney about what they had done and then told him they had been working off orders from the New York mob.

He left Barney with a foreboding message: "The bosses in New York want to make this very clear. This ends with Accardi, Centeno, Father Tony, and you (Barney). If or when you get caught by the feds, you take full responsibility for the operation. They know where your families live, who your friends are, and it won't just be the New York families that will be after you. There are a lot of powerful people with a lot to lose. All of you need to get your stories straight." With that, the old crew member left a hundred-dollar bill on the table in front of Barney, covering his drink and Barney's and leaving the extra change behind.

"So, it sounds like they don't even know Miguel is with us?" I was surprised that this was the first thing that came to mind.

"I guess not," Barney replied.

"So what did you do after that?" I asked. There was still time that hadn't been accounted for since he left.

Barney's shoulders slumped. "I don't know. Not much. I walked around and found someone who would tell me the name of the guy at the dock... Thaddeus. Besides that, I just tried to think of a plan. I knew I needed to come back to the island at this point, especially since I had the only boat."

The two of us had walked back to the security center with all the cameras. After checking things out, the plan was for me to hand the trays to Barney who would put them on the dumbwaiter and let the prisoners separate them.

As I closed the security door behind me, Barney turned his head to me. "Wake the others."

"What?"

"Now!" Barney yelled quickly, raising his hand to his head.

I looked at one of the monitors, and now I could see the blood. I must have missed it when I first woke up, but now it was clear. There was so much blood.

CHAPTER THIRTY-FOUR
Self-inflicted Wounds

EDDIE

I forced myself to go out on Saturday and woke up in an apartment down in Chelsea. The room was almost all white, glowing with the sunlight coming through the window. It had to be midday. Everything hurt.

I could faintly hear the noise from the street below, but there was no noise in the apartment.

My first task was to find my phone to gauge the time and, second, to find out who was with me or had been with me. I made a mistake by sitting up too quickly and found myself running to the bathroom where luckily the door was open, as I barely made it to the commode.

I laid my head on the cold tile floor, promising myself to never drink again. I could feel the icy sweat on my body. It was sticky and thick on my hot skin.

Eventually I surfaced. My clothes were in the bedroom on top of the radiator. My phone and a note were on a circular dining room table in the small apartment.

Had a great time, Eddie.

I am sorry I had to run. Feel free to grab anything you want out of the fridge.

Looking forward to getting together again sometime.

It wasn't lost on me that there was no phone number and not even a name on the yellow notepad. There were no papers of any kind sitting around. I wondered if whomever I had spent the night with had cleaned up things before he left or if he was just a neat freak.

I walked out into the briskness of New York City heading into the last few days of November and waited for my Uber. *The buzzer didn't list a name for apartment 3C.*

I spent the remainder of Sunday recovering and trying to recall my hookup from the previous night. I kept drawing blanks and swore to stop drinking. I slept restlessly, not just because of the brutal hangover; I was due to be criminally charged on Monday.

I met Mr. Steinem in the lobby the next day at ten thirty sharp.

He stood there in his two-thousand-dollar suit, looking me up and down. He was bigger than I imagined. I expected a skinny, affected, elitist nerd. This guy was built. He had to be six foot four and weighed as much as your typical NFL linebacker.

"Ah, Mr. Rodriguez. It is so nice to meet you. I was worried that you were going to take your own advice and defend yourself."

"Fuck you," I responded flatly.

Steinem enjoyed that. "Oh, was that going to be your opening statement to the judge? You are as witty as expected." He turned on his heel, walking outside to the busy Manhattan street where a limo was waiting.

"Well, I am no fancy lawyer like you, Mr. Steinem, but don't you think it is racist as shit that the first Latino you see in the building you assume must be me? Do you not think Latinos are smart enough for finance?" *Fuck this guy.*

He opened his arm widely in front of the limo so I could get in first. He faked a look of shock on his face before responding. "Oh, Mr. Rodriguez, I am not the one who is being accused as a racist here. I can go over some of the notes and affidavits of this case, or would it be easier for me to go over your previous case where you ran over a different person of color? Regardless, you might not realize this but the files I get do contain pictures. I was given the pleasure to see your handsome face before we met."

"Are you saying that because I am gay?"

He completely ignored me.

Once we were settled in the limo, he said, "Privacy, please." With that the driver put up the glass that was opened between us. Shortly after, Steinem put a mask over his face.

I hadn't put a mask on in months. The COVID restrictions had been removed for a while.

"Sorry, I don't have one," I fake-apologized.

"No need," Steinem said curtly. "As you are probably aware, your services will no longer be needed at BDQ."

I actually was more surprised than I should have been. "Really?"

"Yes, really," Steinem replied. "Eddie, from what I understand you had a very simple job to do at BDQ. However, it seems that you have not been able to do it."

"Wait. Are you telling me this is not about the car accident? This is about—"

"I'm not telling you anything except what you must already know."

The car was getting close to the precinct. I poked my finger into

Steinem's chest, enjoying watching his eyes grow big. "I am nobody's monkey, Steinem. You hear me?"

Steinem grabbed my hand and began to squeeze tightly. "Listen, Mr. Rodriguez. As much as I would enjoy kicking your ass, I am not paid to do that. I am paid to defend you. In this one... and I mean one... instance. That said, if you ever put a finger on me again, you will lose it. Am I clear?"

He released my hand, and I quickly brought it back to my chest. Before I could fully think of what to do, the limo had stopped. We were at the precinct.

He glared at me for a second, and the door of the limo opened.

When someone like Steinem walked into a precinct, it would always get attention. When it happened at Fort Apache, we knew some drug dealer, rich kid, or other slimeball had gotten the golden ticket, a get-out-of-jail-free card. Now, here in Manhattan, I was that asshole.

I wanted to pop him in his fucking jaw right in the middle of the fucking precinct. *Fuck this. I was done.* I wasn't joking with him about not being anyone's monkey anymore. I was serious. *Fuck everyone.* I should have made him lose teeth in the limo. I was still stewing when they read the charges.

The charges were steep. I could get five years. Five fucking years for this penny-ante crap. I mean, for what? For calling some guy bullshit names I'd call anyone, not even racial slurs? This was crap. Six months was for assault with a Styrofoam cup. *The world is fucked.*

Up to that point, Steinem had done most of the talking. I had to jump in. "So, you are telling me Cadet Brown wants to press charges on this shit? No professional courtesy for a fellow cop? No understanding that you don't kick someone when they're down? None of that? That's how you do things here?"

The detective running the case looked back and forth at me, then at Steinem, twice. He was stunned that I had said anything.

Steinem, however, looked amused.

The detective looked over at me, dejected. "Well, Mr. Rodriguez, I'm not sure what you were expecting. If you want to apologize to him, you could do that. I mean... I don't know Cadet Brown too well, but—"

I was so angry I felt like I had left my body. "Apologize? Apologize! That's what you want me to do, you fat fuck? I should be the one apologizing?"

With that the detective shoved his shirt farther into his pants and huffed. He ignored me and looked over at Steinem. "Mr. Steinem?"

That angered me more. "Yeah, Mr. Steinem. You. You suck. Do you have anything you would like to add? Anything else you could do to help?"

"No, Eddie. I think you are doing great," Steinem responded sarcastically.

That was it. I snapped. I jumped out of my chair and lunged at him. My swing was ineffective as he backed up just in time, but I was able to grab him by his shoulders.

Within seconds, three more officers were in the room. One had grabbed my right shoulder. It was at that point I realized the gravity of my situation. I was really losing it.

I sat back down. I almost started crying, but I wasn't going to give any of these assholes that satisfaction.

I was having a hard time focusing. Almost in the distance, I could hear Steinem and the detective talking. I heard Steinem say firmly, "I'm fine, and no, I don't want to press charges."

I then heard a soft voice: "Eddie. Eddie?"

It was Steinem. It was so out of character, I was stunned. He actually looked concerned. This made me sink. I wasn't angry anymore. I felt lost.

We walked into a small interrogation room with a table. The blue-Audi guy was going to be interviewed by Steinem. The detective had already taken his statement.

As we sat there waiting, Steinem kept repeating, "Just relax, Eddie. What happened, happened. We will work with it. Just stay calm."

I cursed myself. I had managed to make such an ass out of myself that I had humanized the bloodsucker.

The blue-Audi guy was wearing a nice enough suit but that wasn't what got my attention. It was the button he wore which said, "Stronger Together." I hoped, initially, this would help me. But then I thought about the three offenses I was facing. The official transcript said I called the cabbie a foreigner, I had told him to go back home, and I had said he was speaking gibberish, while mimicking his accent. I had been so angry, all three charges could have been accurate. Blue-Audi guy might totally hate me.

I wanted to say, *Come on, really. That's a hate crime?* But this was not the person to say that to.

Steinem asked if the blue-Audi guy had heard me and the cabbie yelling at each other. He explained that once his car was done plowing into the cab, he looked up from the accident and saw me go sprawling. The Audi guy came across as nervous and uncomfortable.

"So I can't speak to what started it. But I did hear Mr. Rodriguez as he got up and rushed the cabbie, I mean, Mr. Rahman."

"And what did Mr. Rodriguez say at that point?"

"He said something to the effect of, *Hey you fucking douchebag, what the hell is wrong with you?*"

"So he didn't mention the cabbie, Mr. Rahman's ethnicity?"

"No."

"Could you see Mr. Rahman's face from your car?"

"No. Not at first. Of course, I got out of the car as soon as I could. I felt awful."

"So you couldn't see Mr. Rahman's demeanor? And if Mr. Rahman had said anything in my client's direction, would you have heard it from your car?"

"That's hard to say."

I had to jump in. "I am sorry if I offended him. But you know, he was the one who hit me first."

He looked back at me sadly. "I know, Mr. Rodriguez. I just can't support this type of vitriol. I mean, words create violence."

I blurted, "Well, he said some terrible things to me also."

"Like what?"

"I can't remember," I mumbled. I really couldn't.

Steinem was looking at me again; however, this time there was no humor. He was concerned.

I decided I better wrap up. "I appreciate your sensitivity with language. I am gay and Latino—"

"Latinx," he interrupted.

"Yes. Yes. Latinx," I agreed, even if I never quite understood the distinction. "That's fine. I mean, my point, though, is that I am gay and Latinx. I have suffered verbal abuse because of who I am. But when someone cold-cocks you, good manners are not the first thing on your mind. Of course, I was angry. First, the guy sits on his horn, then he punches me in the face."

"Did you see that punch?" Steinem asked.

"No. I crashed. My head jerked forward. I stupidly tried to put the car in reverse, as if that could help, and then I saw Mr. Rahman and heard the end of the attack."

"So you didn't hear Mr. Rodriguez say any of the things that he is being accused of."

"Why no, but based on—"

I thought for a second but couldn't help myself. "I don't want it to seem like I am profiling or anything, but I can pretty much promise you that the cabbie is a Republican. I mean, you understand. It's just a different mindset."

His eyes got big, and then he stared at me. "Well, that would be his choice, right?"

Steinem ignored me. "I want to thank you for coming in today and telling us what you observed."

"No problem. And I want to apologize. I feel like I set off this unfortunate chain of events with my driving."

The judge hit me with a ludicrous two-hundred-fifty-thousand-dollar bail, which Steinem said BDQ was prepared to post on my behalf. The company would pay for my defense. "Do not leave the state," he told me. "BDQ is representing you as an act of good faith. They can tell me to drop your case at any point in time. Do not put me in the position where I have to do that, Eddie."

The case was scheduled after the holidays on January 24.

CHAPTER THIRTY-FIVE
Toxic

EDDIE

On the drive back, Steinem had asked me if there was anything at the office I wanted. I had forgotten, among all the chaos, that I had been fired. I hadn't brought in anything personal to the office. It wasn't like I had my own space. I was either at the front desk when people walked in or in the shared break room behind it. With that, he asked me if it would be okay if I just headed directly to the elevator to get my car. He made a judgment call that he didn't want it to be the typical formal process with security.

I noticed a voicemail from Murray on my phone to go with the four missed calls I had gotten from her before heading down to the garage.

While I appreciated her checking in on me to see how things went, I wasn't sure if I wanted to let her know how badly I fucked up. It wasn't lost on me that I was still looking for her approval. She was important to me.

Everything works in threes, and for today it started by me

getting fired, followed by looking down the barrel of five years in jail. I knew my call with Murray was going to be unpleasant, but this was the least of my problems.

I replayed everything I had done wrong. The "anything you say or do could be held against you" line when you are read your rights was burning my brain. I can't believe I went after my own attorney during my interview. Regardless, I obviously wasn't going to do any time on this bullshit. *I mean, right?*

Even so, after the shit I pulled, this was not going to just get swept under the rug. I'm going to get some probation or shit like that, and it is going to be on my record. The only fucking thing I've done is security. How the fuck was I going to get another gig with a racial incident on my record?

I tried to listen to the radio, but I was too amped up.

"Hey, Eddie. It's Amanda. It's important that we talk immediately."

Finally, a voicemail worth saving. It was the first time she had left me a message with her first name.

I wondered if she already knew how badly I screwed up this afternoon.

I waited to get home before dialing her back.

Instead of answering her phone with Murray, as she had countless times in the past, she answered, "Eddie?" She was concerned.

I supposed I disappointed her. "Hey, listen, Amanda. I know it went bad but I'm better now. I will keep a calmer head going forward."

"What?"

Was she looking for an apology? That's fine, she had a point. It was long overdue. "Hey, I'm sorry. I'm a hothead. I am a master of self-inflicted wounds."

There was silence on the phone for a few seconds before Murray responded. "Eddie, I'm not sure what you are talking about but I am calling about Edna James."

"Edna James?" *Where was this going?*

"Yeah. She's dead, Eddie."

I tried to talk but couldn't.

"Eddie?" Murray had waited a few seconds.

"Yeah, okay. I'll call you back." I couldn't process this.

"Eddie, it's important that—"

I couldn't. I just couldn't. I hung up the phone.

So, obviously, this had to be Centeno. This wasn't some sort of coincidence. I quickly jumped to John. *Did they get him? Is someone looking out for John?*

I jumped off my couch and ran to the door of my condo and checked if it was locked. For years I didn't bother locking it. I mean, who would be crazy enough to break into a cop's house? I also locked the door on my balcony.

I knew it would piss Debbie off, but I called John regardless.

It rang five times and went to voicemail.

"It's Eddie, as I am sure you are aware. Listen, I am trying to stay out of your life or lives. It's just... it's just that it's Centeno. It looks like he might have done something awful, and I am worried for you and John. You should call the precinct and see if they can have someone placed at your—", I hung up.

I decided to call my old boss. This was getting out of hand, and I didn't want John to be overlooked.

"Captain Broward," he answered formally.

"Yeah, right. It's Eddie, Eddie Rodriguez."

"Well, Mr. Rodriguez, you really should have called on the main number so we could record it. I am required to call you back on a landline. Can I call you back now?" Broward sounded formal, nervous, confused.

"Yeah." I was unsure if this was a brush-off. I needed a fucking decoder ring to follow the emotions of this asshole. *Stay cool, Eddie.*

I waited for five minutes for him to call me back. It doesn't take that fucking long for him to get a recorded line. I grabbed my second Dos Equis from the fridge and fought the urge to call him back.

Finally, my cell phone rang with an unrecognized New York number. "That took a long time, Captain," I answered.

"What?" a gruff voice answered. "This is Detective Bradley from Homicide."

Detective Bradley? I didn't recognize the name. The Homicide division was separated from the 41st Precinct as it was in all of the boroughs. They had their own building and operations, but still we referred enough cases to Bronx Homicide that I should have at least recognized the name.

I figured Captain Broward was treating me by the numbers at this point. He guessed I knew about James's murder, then instead of calling me back, he had just booted me to Homicide. I wasn't his problem anymore. So, the question was what Homicide had I been booted to. *Where had Edna been killed?*

"So, Detective Bradley, I take it you aren't from Bronx Homicide, as I forwarded a fair number of cases to them when I was at Fort Apache. Which borough are you calling from? Manhattan?"

I got no response from Detective Bradley.

Typical dick homicide detective. "Anyway, like I was trying to tell Captain Broward, we need to get someone over to Detective John O'Neill's house. Unfortunately, John lives in the Bronx."

"Why?"

"Because he might be at risk, that's why."

"Why would you think he would be at risk, Mr. Rodriguez?"

"Because of fucking Centeno, that's why. Jesus." *Is no one thinking this through?*

"Okay, Mr. Rodriguez. I will have someone look into this. In the meantime, I need you to come down to Manhattan Homicide. Do you have the address?"

"I don't, but I can figure it out. When do you want me there?"

"Immediately, if possible," Bradley replied.

"I'll be there in an hour." I dumped the remaining Dos Equis, grabbed a power bar from the cabinet, and headed back down to my car. Not sure how I was going to help get Centeno, but I would do everything I could for John and Edna.

I had eaten a big breakfast and skipped lunch. Now it was nearing four and I was starving.

I found myself reflexively driving to the pizza place where Edna James and I had gotten together. It was more or less on the way to the Manhattan Homicide building where I was to meet Detective Bradley. I could eat a couple of slices in the car on the way there.

I luckily found a spot outside and ran in with only one person in front of me. My eyes settled on where Edna and I had sat, now eerily empty. The counter guy gave me a Diet Coke while I waited for my two slices. I popped the top and stared at the empty table.

At Homicide, things moved fast at first. I dropped Detective Bradley's name and told them my own. I was placed in an interrogation room.

I waited. I practiced deep breathing for a while, replaying my interactions with René Centeno. Nothing but constant hostility.

I looked around the sparse table and at the two-way glass. I felt a cold chill as my brain started working again. What was the point of me being here? Why wouldn't they have just taken my statement over the phone?

I should have asked those questions ninety minutes earlier.

Looking down at my phone, I saw the missed calls from Murray. Now would be a good time to call.

"Eddie? Why did you hang up your phone?"

"I'm at Homicide."

There was silence.

"Murray?" I asked.

There was a long pause. "I will debrief you when you are done."

I had figured out why I felt like a caged animal. I wasn't here to help with the case. I was a suspect.

CHAPTER THIRTY-SIX
Monkey Business

EDDIE

Detective Bradley came in with another detective who didn't introduce himself. Bradley started with reading me my rights and telling me that it would look bad if I wouldn't talk to them or if I got an attorney.

"What do you think I did?" I responded, trying to stay calm.

"What do you think we think you did?" Bradley responded.

I knew it was a technique, but it came across childish. "Well, this is Homicide."

"It is."

I knew I was innocent, but I also knew that there were forces set against me. I thought of Steinem; he was the obvious person for me to call. He was already retained for me through BDQ on the other case.

However, I thought this was odd. Why not just ditch me and let me fend for myself? Initially, I thought so they could keep an eye on me and make sure I didn't say anything about BDQ, but what if this was some elaborate setup, and they were going to have control over the attorney who I was relying on? I doubt they'd be involved with what happened to Edna, but still, what if the plan was to give me a crappy lawyer who would remove me as a problem.

I could call Paul, but he hadn't been in New York in forever; he'd just be picking a name out of a phone book. Of course, I could go with the public defender, but what if he was able to be influenced by the people who were pissed at me for my work on the priests' case?

I called Murray again. If anyone could help me with this question, it would be her.

I felt myself sink as my call went to voicemail.

I called Steinem next. It might be the wrong move, but at the end of the day he was already helping me on one case. And when I thought about it, he seemed like he had enough money not to be bought where he would intentionally sandbag me. I also doubted his ego could handle rolling over on a case.

I left a voicemail for him on his main number.

I was confident that he wouldn't be calling me back anytime soon, and hopefully Murray would get back to me beforehand. Bradley told me Homicide had twenty-four hours to hold me if they wanted, and that is what they planned on doing. A great way to spend the last minutes of the longest Monday of my entire life.

I spent the night in a holding cell inside Homicide. My phone died in the middle of the night, but I was alive the next morning.

A guard arrived around ten in the morning and took me to a small room with a phone in it.

I was told Steinem was on hold for me.

"Mr. Rodriguez," Steinem said.

"Yeah, I am not sure if you are up to speed on where I am and what is going on," I said in a calmer voice than I expected. My nerves were pretty much shot, and with the lack of sleep, I could break at any moment.

Steinem quickly answered, "Well, it's important for you to understand that BDQ would not want to be involved in a murder case. It is bad optics for a company that wants to protect its image."

"So, you are saying you can't represent me?"

Steinem paused before speaking. "Since you are no longer a BDQ employee, the expenses of the new case would not be covered by them. I am still working with you on your other one, and if there are expenses that overlap to this one, then BDQ would be willing to cover those through their case."

What a tortured way of speaking, I thought. *Wait.* "I am sorry, but what are you saying? Are you saying that you can't defend me in this new case?"

Steinem said flatly, "I am saying that my costs would not be covered by BDQ for this."

"But you would take this case if I wanted you to?" I fired back.

"Well, if that is your preference, but my costs would be a thousand dollars an hour. I am sure that would be out of your ballpark," Steinem answered, quickly adding, "No offense."

Ha, no offense! Please. I still wasn't sure of something. "Wait, it sounds like you are trying to talk me out of hiring you as my attorney, but you are not telling me flat out that you won't take this case. Why is that?"

Steinem took a moment before responding. "Well, the public defender is required to give you a vigorous defense. I am available if you'd like, but with my costs, I would imagine that—"

I think I figured it out. "Does BDQ want you to take my case, but you don't want to take it?"

"BDQ wants me to take your case. I imagine they want me to continue to keep an eye on you. However, they are not going to cover my costs being that this is a murder charge. They don't want

BDQ to be attached to this directly. So, you see, it's probably better for you to go with someone else," he growled.

This is my guy. "Sounds good, I would like you to defend me."

"Are you sure?" Steinem sounded incredulous.

"Absolutely," I said. This was the surest thing I knew in a while.

"I will be there within an hour," Steinem responded, then immediately hung up.

So, BDQ wanted someone to watch over me. Was this only about BDQ, or was this linked back to the missing priests' case? I hoped I was right about Edna James not being killed by BDQ or one of the powers that be who were trying to cover up the missing priests' case, but I couldn't be certain.

If this were true, having Steinem nearby might be a good thing, regardless. If not, I wanted to spin this in a way that however they were trying to protect either of the Centenos, it was going to quickly become not worth the hassle.

Regardless, Steinem clearly did not want to help me. This was what I wanted to see. He was not bought completely. He would do what he was told, but he didn't appear to be corrupt. At least I hoped I had read this correctly.

They took me to an interrogation room to wait for Steinem.

When he arrived, he seemed pissed at me and the rest of the world.

"Here are the forms I need you to sign before I can agree to work with you." He slapped some documents on the table, and threw down a pen.

"Great to see you again." I couldn't help myself.

"I am going to need a twenty-thousand-dollar retainer to begin," he practically snarled.

"No problem," I replied nonchalantly. "If you can get me out of here, I can get you a check when we get back to my condo."

Steinem was obviously good at what he did, and he had figured out my mental gymnastics. "Okay, Eddie. Let's do this. You don't say a fucking word. You hear me?"

"Yep." I smiled, pleased this bulldog was working for me.

Steinem was not amused. "And don't smile. It's not funny. This is homicide. No mistakes. *Do you understand?*"

He took a breath, then continued, "I've dealt with these two before. I don't have to be Perry Fucking Mason as long as there is nothing that I am missing."

The only thing I knew about Perry Mason was that his middle name wasn't Fucking.

Steinem turned from me and growled toward the guard who was standing inside. "You. Leave."

The guard looked like he was going to protest but then walked out.

Once the door closed behind him, Steinem said, "So, did you do it?"

I quickly responded, "No."

Steinem grabbed me firmly by my wrist. "I am not fucking around here. Did you do it?"

"What the fuck, man," I said. His grip was tight. He was staring at me, unflinching. I returned the gaze and said, "No."

He walked away from the table, pulled down the cuffs of his jacket, and straightened his tie. Then he yelled at the guard through the door. "Send them in."

CHAPTER THIRTY-SEVEN
Contempt

EDDIE

Steinem put a recording device on the table, turned it on, and asked each of us to speak clearly, stating our names and who we were.

I said, "Eddie Rodriguez," making sure not to smile. Bradley and his partner, Daniels, identified themselves, too.

"Why is my client here?" Steinem said.

Daniels coughed. "Because he is being charged with the murder of Edna James."

"Okay. So, why is my client here?"

"What do you mean?"

"You are saying that you are charging my client with the murder of Edna James. That is within your capacity. I am asking, why is my client here? What evidence did you have that made you believe that my client was most likely the culprit, and what made you assume he was a flight risk who needed to be held overnight?"

Daniels looked over to Bradley, so Bradley said, "Well, first, your client left evidence with his DNA at the scene. As for a flight risk, given your client's growing criminal record, we figured that was a necessary precaution."

Steinem looked over at me. "You thought it was necessary to put an ex-cop in a holding cell where he could have theoretically been in proximity with other homicide suspects that could know he was an ex-cop?"

"He was put in his own holding cell."

Steinem wrote down a note, then asked, "What DNA evidence?"

"There was a beer bottle that your client left behind on Edna James's counter with his DNA on it."

With that, Steinem dropped his thousand dollar pen on his notepad. "A beer bottle?"

Bradley answered, "Yes, a beer bottle."

Steinem stared at Bradley hard. "What other DNA evidence did you find?"

"None." Then quickly added, "None yet."

Steinem looked at his pad for a moment, then back at Bradley. "Then what other evidence do you have, period?"

Bradley looked at his notes. "Well, we know that René Centeno and your client were spending a lot of time together, and they seemed to have some shared interests—"

"What? What did you hear? Who could possibly think—"

Steinem didn't even say a word to me. He just looked at me. I'd never seen a look like that. It displayed such utter contempt at my stupidity for even engaging while he was sitting next to me.

Steinem turned to the detective. "Tell me why you think that René Centeno and my client are friends?"

"There are a few things."

"Oh, I have time. Proceed."

"Well, first we know that your client chased Ms. James out of an official police function just a few weeks ago."

I smirked and shook my head at this.

Steinem ignored me. "Go on."

"Then he and Centeno not only had a conversation in the precinct before your client was fired, but right after, the two were spotted down the street a few blocks having another private conversation. Publicly the pair made a show of pretending not to like each other."

So someone was watching me and Centeno when he threatened me and my family after the church service for Accardi, Juarez, and Fergusson. I needed to find out who that was.

"Okay, we'll get back to that later. What else?" Steinem said.

"Well, we found an odd note in Ms. James's notebook listing Eddie's and Centeno's phone numbers, saying she was going to see if they had placed any calls to each other."

I looked over at Steinem. Edna must have jotted something down when I asked her for Centeno's cell. I imagined she was going to check to see if he had called me, since that was what I claimed might be going on.

"Eddie, we can discuss this later if you want to add something," Steinem said.

I risked nodding. It wasn't actual speech, so I figured I was safe.

"Do you find it odd that my client would leave a beer bottle with his DNA in plain sight and not leave other traces around the crime scene?" Steinem asked.

"I've seen odder."

"From an ex-cop?"

Bradley didn't answer.

"What type of beer?" Steinem asked.

"Dos Equis."

Had Centeno broken into my house?

Steinem had already thought of this as he turned to me. "Eddie, do you have Dos Equis at your house?"

I nodded yes.

"Detective Bradley, do you have a picture of the bottle showing any identifying marks such as expiration date or batch number? I'd like to check it against what my client has in his house."

"Sure, Mr. Steinem. We would be happy to go to your client's house with you."

Steinem looked back at the detectives, then said, "I would like a few minutes alone with my client."

The two detectives looked at each other, thinking of what to say, but after a minute got up and left me and Steinem alone in the room.

After I explained in detail as clearly as I could about what the detectives would find in my apartment, Steinem asked if there were materials or evidence there that would support my innocence. "Well, there's plenty of evidence that Centeno and I did not get along."

I explained that the box of my father's notes was still there with references to Centeno, albeit the older uncle, Angel Centeno. I told him briefly about John O'Neill, who both James and I were told was attacked by Centeno. But I asked Steinem to use him only if things got desperate. "His fiancée hates me, and he might hate me, too, now," I explained. Finally, I mentioned that Agents Murray and Cooper of the FBI were also aware of Centeno and the threats he made to me. "I mean not to mention pretty much anyone else in my old precinct would tell you me and him didn't get along—if they told the truth."

As Steinem was looking at leaving the room to get the detectives back, I thought of one last thing.

"How long does Rohypnol stay in your system?" I blurted.

Steinem stopped in his tracks. "What?"

I quickly went through the story of what happened Saturday night. It was embarrassing, but it made sense. I do remember quickly going from buzzed to blacking out and waking up the next morning.

"The answer to your question is the effects last about twelve hours, and it stays in your system for around five days, if I remember correctly. Wait, are you claiming you were roofied the night of the murder, you stupid son of a bitch?" Steinem snarled.

"It's embarrassing. I'm not certain."

"Being embarrassed is much better than being convicted."

I sighed. Steinem was an enormous prick, but that was what I was paying him for. "Even if I got roofied, how can I prove that's how the bottle showed up at Edna's house? I don't even remember where I was or where I left from, the morning I woke up."

"Do you typically use your credit card in bars? Did you take public transportation home, compared to a cab or an Uber? If the latter, there would be clear documentation. We might even track down video footage of the scumbag who doped you. Also, we need to get you a blood and urine test, A-S-A-P. There may be residues that can help us."

"Ah, shit. I hate needles."

"You hate needles? That's your response?"

Steinem took a step toward me. "Mr. Rodriguez, I don't give a shit if they shoot one billion volts through you so you boil in your own juices. However, I am damn good at what I do, and I don't want to be left in front of some judge with my dick in my hand just because you might be a *yittle* ashamed of having a few too many beers or afraid of an *ouchie*." Steinem finished his diatribe, talking like a baby.

He was so over the top. I laughed.

Shockingly, he laughed back.

He then looked at me with what I could only describe as kindness. "Listen, Eddie, it seems that you are getting fucked here… and not in the good way. I don't think Tweedledee and Tweedledum there decided to keep you locked up overnight completely on their own. I can all but guarantee that there will be a few more curveballs before we get through this. We need to have things lined up and have our own cards to play, in case it gets messier."

"Okay."

The two of us went over a few more details, then invited the detectives back in the room. We were going to negotiate for a limited search of my condo with both myself and Steinem present.

CHAPTER THIRTY-EIGHT
Uncertainty

Eddie

It ended up being more than the four of us. There were five others who were clearly from forensics.

The first fight we had was because the detectives wanted me to drive to my place with them instead of Steinem. This went on for a while but was clearly a nonstarter and they gave up.

The second disagreement was over the scope of the search. Since this was voluntary, Steinem wanted to be able to stop the search and gathering of evidence. We agreed that unless something was clear and obvious evidence, regarding Ms. James's murder, Steinem could stop the search after the initial gathering of evidence from the kitchen and dining room.

The last argument was over what was technically the kitchen and dining room considering the open floor plan in my place. Steinem literally made them go through a blueprint of my condo, which they pulled from an online database and highlighted the sections that would be reviewed.

After a late lunch, it was almost four before I got into Steinem's car for the ride over to my condo. On the way, we stopped at Steinem's doctor's office on Park Avenue and I gave blood. I was impressed. Steinem was a full-service lawyer. I wondered how much of the twenty-thousand-dollar retainer was used up. No matter, I would have to call my brother Paul and get more cash from the trust.

You never realize how dirty your home is until you have a group of forensics experts searching through your stuff. They took a few other pieces of trash out of the receptacle besides all the empty Dos Equis bottles. I was a little embarrassed that I hadn't separated my recyclables from my normal trash like I normally did. I was letting everything go. I wasn't sure but thought I remembered somewhere that not separating my recyclables might be some sort of misdemeanor. *That would be something to go to jail for, wouldn't it?*

I protested when they took all the remaining Dos Equis out of my fridge. "Can't you just take photos?"

It was a lighthearted joke, but no one laughed.

The whole thing was surreal.

I could see the irritation on Steinem's face when they finally got around to Dad's things; they just picked the boxes up and booked them as evidence. I had thought they overstepped the agreed-upon area of the search, but I wasn't sure and didn't want to seem more suspicious by demanding the boxes not be taken. Steinem demanded a photograph of every document in each box.

They put a bunch of small fibers into plastic bags and checked the walls, counter space and handles for prints.

It was over in three hours. Detective Bradley asked if I could leave with them and not stay in the condo until they went through the evidence. I was told it would be better if I stayed at a friend's house, so any evidence in my condo wouldn't be corrupted. I looked over at Steinem, and he shook his head no, so I responded to Bradley accordingly.

As previously agreed upon, Steinem and I would get together with the detectives two days from now back at Homicide to go over what was found.

Tomorrow—Wednesday—I would meet with Steinem at his office to go over things based on what they might or might not find.

I thought of calling a friend over to spend the night but decided against it. I did use the chain on my condo door which I hadn't used since I moved in. I barely slept waiting for the moment when René Centeno would come busting through my door. If not for the chain, I don't think I would have slept at all.

Steinem changed his mind and decided to come to my condo on Wednesday afternoon. Apparently he had a rich client in New Bedford, so I was on the way. I was almost certain he had thought about the optics of how it would look for me to be coming into his posh law office.

"Eddie, the detectives shared their theory on what happened and a few other things," Steinem began.

"So they think they have Centeno's car on video outside both Edna James's condo in Inwood and your condo here." He paused, wanting me to speak.

I didn't need to be prodded. Inwood was just north of my neighborhood. Centeno could just go straight down Broadway for twenty blocks to get to my building. He could easily have gotten back and forth to both of our places in plenty of time. *This was the whole case, right?*

"So that's it, right? Obviously, Centeno killed James." I paused for a moment, the anger building regarding her death. "Then he came over to my place to finish me off, but instead of finding me, he came in here and grabbed a bottle to set me up."

Steinem stared at me for a second, reading me, before responding. "Well, two things. First, they tell me they have a pretty clear video feed from in front of your condo, and Centeno never entered. Also, they spotted you outside of Edna James's condo."

He arched his eyebrow accusingly.

"You know what? Fuck you. Give me a moment." I had to think. "So this maybe goes back to somebody roofieing me."

"Do you remember what he looked like?" Steinem said.

"I don't know. I mean, if I saw a sketch or a photo of him, maybe. I think I met someone who was familiar. But it's really vague. Wait, I think that was early on. That might be a dead end. I remembered leaving him and going out to the dance floor. Then I used the restroom at some point. I mean, if he drugged me, he just drugged me and walked away and found me later. How fast does that shit work?"

"I don't know. What's the last thing you remember?"

I walked through things. "The last thing I remember... the last thing I remember..." I was straining. "I mean, I see flashes. Leaving the club. Arriving at a condo. I can't imagine someone spiking my drink and driving me to freaking Inwood without me noticing. And then dumping me in Chelsea. I just don't know." I was embarrassed but also getting scared.

Steinem sat back for a second on that. I could see he was thinking. "Okay, we are going to have to work on your response to this. If you blacked out, just say you blacked out."

Steinem was still looking down. He looked up at me about to continue, then looked back down again before saying, "So, this is a problem if you are outside of Edna's condo, especially if you don't have a reason or you were blacked out then."

"Okay... so?"

Steinem didn't answer and instead shifted back to the prosecution's case. Their theory was that Centeno realizes he could get spotted outside of James's condo, so he decides to abort going after James and instead goes to my condo to tell me that I need to take out Edna James. I get drunk to build up the nerve to do so and then go there and kill her. Afterward, I realize what I had done and head as far away as I can think of to drink more, so I can have an alibi that I was nowhere close.

"If this is their case, and we can prove you were roofied, the case will have enough holes to drive an eighteen-wheeler through. Let's hope your test comes back positive. Also, we need the address of where you woke up. There could be more video footage there."

The test for Rohypnol or similar substances came back negative, which meant either someone used a more exotic substance to drug me, or I was just blacked out, drunk. The way things had been going for me, the second option was clearly a possibility.

Thursday with the detectives brought more questions than answers.

"So, per your request, we checked to see if Mr. Rodriguez's house was broken into. This came up negative," Detective Daniels said.

That doesn't mean much," Steinem said. "It's almost impossible to be able to notice if a lock has been picked."

Neither Bradley nor Daniels responded to that.

"And it looks like there was disinfectant used recently throughout the kitchen and dining room," Daniels continued.

Both Steinem and I looked at each other.

"What is most concerning is what is in the boxes." Now it was Bradley who was speaking. "It looks like your family has a long relationship with the Italian Mafia. Can you tell me—"

I saw red. "*A long relationship?* Those fuckers killed my mother."

Bradley went on. "I understand that, but that isn't the point. The point is now—"

"Now! Now, fucking what?" I roared. "You have to know this is bullshit. Did you check in with Agent Murray on this to see what my relationship is with this Centeno or any fucking Centeno, for that matter? If there was a Centeno that was killed... then... then you would be harassing the right guy. I mean, if that was the case —" I stopped talking. I saw Steinem staring hard at me.

"So, you admit that you and Centeno had a relationship?" Bradley followed.

Steinem jumped in at this point. "Listen, Detectives. I can assure you that we can prove beyond a reasonable doubt that my client and René Centeno did not have a friendly relationship."

"What about this?" Bradley looked down at his yellow pad of paper. "What about this Agent Murray person?"

Steinem thought for a moment. "Eddie is assisting the FBI on a case that is separate—"

"I wouldn't say—"

"Eddie!" Steinem glared at me, then turned his attention toward the detectives. "We will have to see what Agent Murray and her colleague can share. A lot of things are confidential with the two of them. Due to the severity of these charges, I am sure a certain degree of latitude can be provided but only to the point where my client doesn't have additional legal issues for potentially disclosing confidential information."

Detective Bradley frowned. "I'm not going to let the FBI—"

"I think we are done for today."

I followed Steinem out of the room, leaving Bradley and Daniels sitting there confused. I was confused also.

CHAPTER THIRTY-NINE
Pretender

E<small>DDIE</small>

In his limo, Steinem explained why he cut things short.

"We are not going to aid the prosecution. I know you think you were damaging the prosecution's case by showing how you and René were enemies, but when you start making emotional threats on the entire Centeno family, this helps them establish a mindset capable of murder." *The asshole had a point.*

Steinem needed to figure out how René Centeno could have gotten into both of our buildings without being tracked. Steinem was going to thoroughly review all the video evidence that the detectives and their forensics team had gathered.

"I really think Agent Murray could just destroy their case, too," I said.

"I'm hoping she will, but as of now she's not returning our calls. As you suggested, she's between a rock and a hard place if her boss warned her off the case and she ignored him. Murray might get dragged in soon, regardless. The Centenos are a known Mafia family. If they start connecting René Centeno's killing of someone in Internal Affairs to their larger operations throughout the city, it would be an enormous win for them. The feds might file RICO charges—Racketeer Influenced and Corrupt Organizations."

"I know what RICO is."

"Right, but the point is this might hook into the broader New York Mafia."

Steinem had kept me out of a cell so far, so I was happy with his work. At best, I would have had to post bail if not. As of now, they just asked that I not leave the borough of Manhattan. Steinem agreed this was a fair compromise.

It took two weeks until Steinem and I met with Bradley and Daniels. What they had was clearly circumstantial bullshit. From the video to the timeline to the beer bottle that was left behind, it would be very difficult for them to make a compelling case against me. Especially under the *beyond a reasonable doubt* bar that is given in criminal cases.

Steinem wasn't sure what was worse: the video where we thought we spotted Centeno or the video of *me*.

Steinem had enhanced and broken down two different sets of videos from both locations, highlighting the parts that were germane to the case.

He began with what he thought was Centeno.

"If you look at the time-stamped section outside of Edna James's condo, you see a rabbi walking alone up Cooper Street. If you notice around fifteen minutes earlier, we see Centeno's car coming from the opposite direction. I believe Centeno's car was parked on the other side of 204th Street outside of the field of view of the camera." Steinem pointed to a screen on the wall in one of Homicide's conference rooms.

"So you're saying a rabbi whacked James?" Bradley scoffed. I stared hard at him, wishing it was him that Centeno would have visited. It was hard for me not to say anything.

"In a sense, yes," Steinem said dismissively, then continued, "Now, look here. Once again, there is Centeno's car. This time on 181st Street, right at the split before you would turn to go into my client's building." Steinem clicked his laptop. "Then, here. There's the rabbi again."

"Oh, I see." Bradley mocked Steinem. "So are you saying that a rabbi killed James, or are you saying that Centeno dressed up like a rabbi and killed James?"

"I don't care which one. I am saying, do your fucking job. This is obviously a person of interest. Either Centeno is talking with this individual or Centeno is this individual. Regardless, it is pretty odd for the same rabbi to be walking alone both times at both sites, right?"

"Well, yeah, but this is New York City. Not only that, look at the map. You have Yeshiva University, what, five blocks from your client's house for Chrissake, right? So what, because a couple rabbis in a couple locations decide to walk on their own, and all of a sudden they are the primary suspects?"

"You are not listening to me. There aren't two separate rabbis."

"You are certain that they are the same rabbi? How in the world could you say that?" Bradley looked proud to be holding his own with the high-priced lawyer.

"I figured you'd say something like that. I have a letter from the video forensics experts Sipacum Group, saying that with ninety percent accuracy, they can assure that is the same person." Steinem produced a letter from his briefcase.

Bradley looked at it briefly, then tossed it toward Daniels.

"So what else?" Bradley continued.

"What type of analysis did you have done that shows the person you have listed as my client on the tape you sent is actually my client?" Steinem questioned.

"Do you have a point you want to make?"

"Sure. You are saying that my client is the guy with the leather jacket with rhinestones? Am I correct?" Steinem pointed at the screen.

"Yes, that is what I am saying."

"Did you have anyone match my client's height and build with this person, because I had Sipacum take a look at this also. Do you want to see the results? I take it you have no corroborating footage to provide facial recognition."

Neither detective responded, so Steinem continued, "The person may be a woman with short hair or someone who is transgender. My client doesn't own a jacket encrusted with rhinestones. To help me understand your thorough research, what is there about my client that would make you believe this might be him?"

I couldn't help myself. I let out a snicker.

Bradley happily turned his attention to me. "Do you have something to add here? Can you assure me that this isn't you? Or are you still sticking with your story that you were somewhere down in Chelsea, which might as well be on the fucking moon? You still can't give a direct statement, can you?"

"How's this for a direct statement?" I began. "I think you are a fucking bigot." Steinem put down his pointer and said, "Eddie."

I continued anyway, "Do you think I would ever wear something like that? You are assuming that just because I am gay. My sexuality isn't the only thing that defines who I am. Why didn't you pull my—"

"Eddie, knock it off!" Steinem interrupted.

"Pull your what? Pull your what?!" Bradley said, rising out of his seat.

"Pull his Uber receipts, Detective Bradley," Steinem replied calmly. "Do you have anything else you want to say to my client?"

Bradley sat back down.

Steinem continued, "I have a copy of Mr Rodriguez's Uber activity. I can get a letter from Uber's corporate department if you'd like."

Detective Bradley looked over at Daniels who flashed an *I told you so* look. Bradley looked at his papers for a second, then finally blurted, "Yeah, you should probably do that."

"Detective Bradley, when I met with you the first time, I stressed my disappointment in you and your partner's treatment of my client. Specifically, how he was kept overnight while not a flight risk, and on flimsy evidence. Today, I could argue that you are intentionally trying to demean him because of his sexuality."

Detective Bradley gave a mocking frown back.

Steinem continued, "If you continue to pursue my client on a criminal charge he clearly did not commit, I will go after you, your partner, and this office civilly. Do I make myself clear?"

Bradley surprisingly smiled at that. "Crystal," he responded.

"Okay, do you have anything else that you want to tell me or my client today?"

Bradley's smile widened at that. "Yes. This case is being passed off to the FBI. Besides the murder of Edna James, they are going to look into your client for obstruction of a federal case and other racketeering activities. They are going full RICO on this, and your client is right in the center of it all."

CHAPTER FORTY
Double Agent

EDDIE

Steinem asked for us to leave once he found that my case was being moved to the FBI. These two were just wasting our time. They would handle some aspects of the flimsy murder case, but my real use was for the feds going after the New York mob. *Where the fuck was Murray with all this?*

I had wanted to ask the detectives what they meant about me obstructing justice with the FBI. I had basically blown up my entire life to help the FBI. Steinem said he wouldn't have trusted their answer anyway.

"Those two clowns wouldn't know the specifics. The feds are not going to tip their hand to the NYPD. Never in a million years."

Steinem said he would look into it. He told me explicitly not to call either Agent Murray or Cooper. He wanted to feel them out and see what he could find before I reached out to either of them.

I should have listened, but I didn't.

I ended up leaving a short but terse voicemail for Murray.

"Thanks for looking out for me. I'd appreciate a call back if that wouldn't be too much to ask."

I was happy with myself that I didn't leave anything worse.

Steinem called me the next day. "So, they want you to come on Tuesday next week. Unfortunately, I will not be in town."

"By 'they,' you mean the FBI, right?" I said, feeling sick to my stomach.

"That's correct. Long story short, they have a lot of levers they can pull on a RICO case like this."

"So, here's what I said back to the feds. I told them I would see what I could do on getting you to appear Tuesday. It's two days before Christmas so they realize this is a big request for what seems to be a fishing expedition. I said we would work on getting you there on that day, but if my client, you, comes in, under no circumstances, will anything regarding the murder of Edna James be discussed. Would you be comfortable with that?"

"So what the fuck are we going to talk about, then? The weather?"

"They want to push this RICO angle and your relationship with the Centeno family. "You don't think Agent Murray would set you up, do you?"

I thought for just a second. "No, but I still don't think it is a good idea for me to go in there alone." At this point, I wasn't sure of anything.

"Of course, I've got it taken care of. Like I said, I think this is just a fishing expedition. Let me know what works and I will stop by your condo with my associate, Clyde Monroe. He is a smart lawyer. And he'll be there to shut things down if it goes the wrong way. Just don't go off on any tangents. If you are unsure of a question, look over at Clyde and he will take it from there. You'll be fine. Our goal is to help the feds and make clear you have only been trying to aid an investigation."

It was eerie heading into the FBI not knowing if I was a suspect or an informant without either Murray or Cooper to guide me. Clyde Monroe was a reassuring and distracting presence. Hearing the name, I figured he would be another patrician lawyer like Steinem, but with Southern roots. He was not. He was a northern white guy, about ten years older than me, who spoke Brooklynese, and was weightlifter huge. Their law firm must own a gym. Even in his tailored suit, his biceps bulged against the fabric.

"You are a very intimidating babysitter," I said, standing close to where I had seen Agent Murray the first time.

"Steinem said you need continual supervision."

"I'm sure he told you I'm my own worst enemy."

"That and more. The game plan is to find out what the FBI wants and give it to them. Let me be very clear, Eddie... Is it okay if I call you Eddie?"

"Sure."

"Do not lie to FBI investigators about anything. If you are unsure of something... a date, a conversation, the weather... do not state it as fact. Say you can't remember. Lying to an FBI agent is a crime. They use this crime like a pair of pliers... to squeeze informants. Any problems, you are feeling uncertain, you think you want to bolt, just turn to me, and I will take care of it. Got it?"

"I hope the fuck so."

They made me put my phone in a soft bag that snapped shut. Steinem and Monroe had warned me about this beforehand, so while I was put off by it, I was not surprised. Not sure what she was officially, but some lady who worked for the FBI had dumped me in the conference room Murray had brought me to. *Coincidence?* She offered Monroe and me a bottle of water, then left us.

Clyde Monroe and I sat there in silence until I felt like the walls were closing in.

I had thought about it earlier, between my conversation with Brady Fergusson in the past and the fact that my brother Paul had been a big basketball fan in his youth. I remember him taking me to a few games when he lived in the city. "Are your parents big New York Knicks' fans?"

"Why do you ask?"

He seemed totally stunned by my question. So I began to explain, "Because two of the greatest—"

"Are you talking about Clyde Frazier and Earl 'the Pearl' Monroe? Yeah, I remember the stories. They were fans, but that's not where I got the name from. My dad was Clyde also."

"Oh, well, still not a bad name to have."

"Not at all, but I sure would have preferred to have their jump shots instead." He gave me a kind smile. I think he could tell I was nervous.

I really liked this guy. I hoped his being here was a good omen.

It was a little over thirty minutes later when Agent Williams and Agent Smith came in and introduced themselves. Agent Williams was white and had a blond buzz cut. At first, I thought he looked like a skinhead that you'd see in the movies except dressed in a fancy suit. Especially with the tat that was partially hidden behind his pressed white dress shirt but extended to the back of his right hand. As he had turned to close the door after letting his partner in, I could see the real reason for the short haircut was the smooth circle of male-pattern baldness on the top of his head.

Smith, on the other hand, was a dark ebony, ripped muscles straining beneath his tight suit. Both men had an edge. But while I had been potentially attracted to Agent Murray, I was 100 percent attracted to Agent Smith. He reminded me of one of my past boyfriends, only more attractive and more successful.

Agent Smith began. "Thanks so much for coming in today, Mr. Rodriguez. Either of you need another water?"

I was shocked by the soft edge from Agent Smith. I realized this was most likely a good-cop play.

"No, I'm fine. Why am I here?"

"Well, we are just looking for you to connect some dots for us," Agent Williams said.

"Okay."

"While we appreciate the help that you were offering Agents Murray and Cooper, we are confused why you hid Detective O'Neill from them. Then Detective O'Neill ended up almost getting killed, allegedly by Centeno. We also wonder why you failed to mention your odd connection with the Centeno family, Sandy Accardi, and the Fergussons. I mean, we read the notes on the case, but a lot of those dead ends end with you." Williams stared at me.

"Let's go, Eddie." Clyde stood up.

This was bullshit, just like Steinem had warned me. "What... did... Agent... Murray... say?" I stressed every word.

"Let's go." Clyde had walked behind me now and put his hand on my shoulder.

Agent Smith said, "No, it's not like that, Eddie. Just give me a second, Mr. Monroe. This isn't really about your client. Agent Murray thinks you've been helpful. Cooper does, too. She, just like us, is just confused about things, like why you would hide your conversations with Brady Fergusson from her, and why wouldn't you bring up O'Neill immediately to try to protect him from Centeno, and why did Accardi seek you out when it looks like you had no relationship with him up to that point?"

I had answers to all these questions, but I didn't want to slip up by saying something I would regret later. "What do you think I've done?"

Clyde patted my shoulder. I assumed asking questions couldn't hurt me.

Williams answered, "This is what we think, Eddie. We think that Angel Centeno was involved in the death of your mom, and we think that you know something about the New York mob and these missing priests. And we finally think that you're concerned for your family and your own safety because of your history with the Centeno family. We think you are scared and getting squeezed to cover for them. That's what we think."

"Okay, we're done here. Stand up now, Eddie," Clyde interrupted.

Williams looked over to Smith when the lady who brought me to the conference room, initially, knocked on the door.

Agent Smith opened the door wide.

Agent Williams visibly changed gears. "Okay, Mr. Rodriguez. We appreciate what you have given us so far. At this point, we would like to get you back with Agents Murray and Cooper, if that would be okay."

I hadn't given them shit.

"Unfortunately, Mr. Monroe, we can not allow you to sit in on this meeting."

"Well, then, my client isn't going. Let's go, Eddie."

I needed to find out what was going on. I knew both Steinem and Clyde were going to be angry, but I needed to know. "It's okay, Clyde. I got this. If anything doesn't feel right, I'll just walk."

Clyde wasn't happy, and I was sure he was worried about the raft of shit he was going to get from Steinem, but this was my decision.

Agent Smith said, "If you wouldn't mind coming with us, we will take you to a room to wait for them."

CHAPTER FORTY-ONE
No Apologies

EDDIE

The agents brought me to a smaller conference room, opened the door, and told me to wait inside. I was not alone. There was a stocky, balding man seated at a table with three blank pads, two pens, and a half-finished water bottle. I sat four seats away from the man in a spot with my own pad and pen.

"Where's my lawyer?" I wanted Clyde Monroe at my side.

The other man didn't answer.

This was bullshit.

I was thinking it, but the stocky man said it for me: "What the fuck is this?"

"I mean, seriously," the stocky man asked again. "What the fuck is this!?"

I had no answer. Instead, I came up with three questions of my own: Who was this guy, how far up the Mafia food chain was he, and what did the FBI tell him about me?

They had told him something, because he stared at me with palpable hatred.

I doubted I was going to be killed in the FBI building, so I stared back. This was his move. I certainly wasn't going to talk first.

After about a minute of me staring into those dead, dark eyes, the stare-off came to an end. He finally opened his mouth.

"Okay, Ed. What do you want?"

"What do I want?" I parroted back. I was trying to buy time.

After giving me another thirty seconds, he spoke again, angry vitriol coating every word. "I am not sure what game you are playing here, Mr. Rodriguez. As you are aware, I am a private citizen who tries to contribute to the community where I can. I am not sure what confusion you have about myself or, more importantly, my family members and their friends, but regardless, I look forward to helping you get less confused."

"What have you been told about me?"

"Do you think this is some sort of game?" The man leaned toward me, putting his weight on his elbows and meaty hands. He was old. It was hard to judge his age, somewhere between fifty and seventy. But it wasn't his ambiguous age that concerned me, it was those eyes. They were a dark void and they looked familiar.

"You're a Centeno!"

He growled, "You are finished. Leave and get my attorney."

When no one came, I started rambling, "I'm not sure what is going on here. But I think we are both on the same page here. I was put in a room with you, and I am fairly certain for this specific reason: The FBI is fishing here, and I am pissed that they are trying to use me, and of course, you. I mean, I've never met you before.

They are obviously trying to get one of us to say something they can use, even though there is no connection between either of us."

I stopped there hoping to lower the temperature in the room. I threw my arms open wide showing him that I had laid my cards on the table. I had nothing to hide.

With that, he stood. His anger had multiplied, and now he was staring down at me. "You little fuck! You are telling me you have no part in any of this? You are just some sort of rube put here in front of me to... to what? I will tell you something, Ed." He spat when he said my name. "You have pissed on the names and reputations of colleagues and members of my own family. You've been digging up old stories about my cousin... but I have to tell you something, Ed. Those things were nothing compared to this. Now, you want to blame my son for this, for something you did. You have made some serious miscalculations, Mr. Rodriguez. Those... those mistakes will have consequences. Severe consequences."

I stood up and backed up a step. "Your son? Did you say your son? You son of a bitch. Let me tell you something about your son."

"WHAT DID YOU FUCKING SAY?" he roared.

I was stunned—by the sheer volume of his voice and the realization this was a guy who had the resources and certainly the mindset to cause me real pain.

With that, an old friend stormed into the room. It was Agent Murray. "Come with me, Eddie. Now."

I felt dizzy as Agent Murray and Agent Cooper rushed me out of the room back toward the conference room.

Behind us, I heard someone yelling, "Hey!" By the suit and the anger, I would bet that was René Centeno's dad's attorney.

The three of us were still standing as Murray slammed the door to the conference room with Cooper and I already inside.

She turned to me sharply. "Goddamn it, Eddie. Why couldn't you just stay quiet? Do you know who that was?"

I was so angry and confused I couldn't get my bearings. "René Centeno's fucking father, thank you very much!"

"That's right, Eddie, Emilio Centeno. Do you have any idea the type of resources someone like that has? He is the heir to the Centeno family and his father is approaching ninety. He is right at the doorway to take over that arm of the New York Mafia."

"Are you fucking kidding me? You are mad at me."

"We had it all set up for you. All you had to do was be surprised to be in the room with him. You didn't have to confront him! Shit!"

"Didn't have to confront him? Did you listen to that son of a bitch? He sure as shit knew who I was as soon as I walked in there. Why didn't someone let me know what the plan was?"

"We couldn't. Cooper and I had to be interviewed for hours over how we were handling you, especially with all of the trouble you had been causing and then... then after, I was reprimanded. I suggested this would be a good way to show you don't have a connection with the Centeno family."

I sat down overwhelmed by the bunch of shit just dumped on me. "So, you throw me into a situation blind and then blame me for the outcome? Are you nuts, Murray? Now what do I do? If the Centenos were planning on leaving me alone before, well, that's not the case anymore."

Murray looked over at Cooper and her shoulders slumped.

But Cooper piped up. "Maybe, Eddie, maybe not. This might have saved your ass. Emilio knew about you, Eddie. He knew everything. But now he knows we know. And if anything happens to you, we've got him on tape threatening you. So maybe this was good. Maybe we need to step back and see it from a fresh perspective."

I sat there shaking my head, trying to process everything. Clyde Monroe cracked open the door and I waved him in.

"What is this? What did I miss?" Monroe glared at Cooper and Murray.

"Welcome to the most fucked-up post-mortem since JFK was shot," I joked, still somewhat in shock.

"None of what he said is admissible. He did not agree to anything."

"It's fine, Mr. Monroe. I think we can safely say that Mr. Rodriguez didn't say or do anything that could have hurt his case," Cooper said.

"Can I get that in writing?"

Cooper ignored the question.

"Hey, Eddie. I get it." Amanda Murray was talking in a much softer tone. "I apologize if you think we handled it wrong. But Cooper makes some valid points. You should know you can always call me or Cooper's number; however, we will have to record all calls going forward. We are forbidden to be the point people working with you anymore, so this does change our relationship a bit."

"You mean the type of relationship where you try to figure out different ways to fuck me over?" I said with an odd smirk. I was angry, but part of me was sad.

"You did good, Eddie," Cooper added.

Amanda walked over and squeezed my shoulder. "I want you to come through this okay, Eddie. You can do this."

They assured me the FBI would be tracking Emilio and the rest of the Centeno family closely. I was not officially removed as a person of interest but unless a red flag popped up, I should be okay for now.

They couldn't make a call on whether I would be charged for the murder of Edna James. That would be handled by Manhattan Homicide.

"It's wrapped up," Clyde said. "It's clearly Centeno."

"Well, if something goes wrong, and you need a character witness, I'm here," Murray said, her eyes probing mine.

"Thanks," I said, shaking their hands.

I exhaled in the elevator and tried to keep my shit together. I felt more scared and alone than I had in a long time. Murray had been a lifeline. A constant in months of madness. I found myself making excuses for the lack of emotion from Cooper and Murray as I left; maybe it was because the conference room was being videoed or maybe it was just that I cared for them, especially Murray, more than they cared for me.

I did the math. All I had remaining in my life at this point were my three family members, and I was as distant with all of them as I had ever been.

VIGILANTE PRIEST IX

Tempus Fugit, Memento Mori

FATHER TONY

I had replayed the video so many times that I could quote it word for word. It all began with Father Charlie arguing now against the fact that priests were imprinted separately after ordination and that we could fall the same as a lay person. My words had affected him, especially after finding out that one of the boys he had victimized had later killed himself.

"We are no longer the sons of Aaron," Father Charlie had said to Father Reece.

This had infuriated both Father Reece and Father John, two of the Bible study devotees. All three of them, Father Patrick being the third, had become very close since being thrown together.

Father Reece protested, "The priest is the highest among his brothers. The consecrating of the oil of God is on him." He had shortened Leviticus to make his point.

Father Charlie stopped for a moment and almost walked away but instead turned toward Father Reece and Father John, staring at each for equal time. " 'The time will come when they will not endure sound doctrine: but after their own lusts shall they heap to themselves'."

Father Reece grabbed Father Charlie, placed his leg behind him, and tripped him. Father John began screaming at Father Charlie, kicking the fallen man and calling him a demon.

Father Julio, who had observed this scene, slowly walked away, went to his room, and got in his bed.

Father James and Father Timothy moved to stop the two priests who were both kicking Father Charlie. They pulled them away, and Father Charlie slowly got to his feet.

Father Reece and Father John's eyes were wide with shame for what they had done.

Father Timothy, a fellow silent priest, went into Father Julio's room to let him know that the chaos had stopped.

No one had paid any attention to Father Stephen, who picked up the broken bottle he had used to stab Hannigan.

"You will be judged!" Father Stephen roared before plunging the glass into Father Charlie, who was still unsteady.

"Dear God. This is it," Father Stephen said next.

From there, chaos erupted.

This is when Father James started screaming for help in front of the surveillance camera. When I first watched the tape, I thought that Father Stephen had been screaming with him in unison, but no. Father Stephen had screamed, "You are false!" before stabbing Father James in the back and knocking him hard, headfirst into the concrete ground.

Father Timothy stared seemingly frozen in fear and held Father Julio's hand.

When I ran to wake the others, I foolishly thought that Barney was going underground to stop the killing.

Father José hearing the screams of his friend Father James, tried to overpower Father Stephen, but Father Stephen was much stronger. He raked the broken bottle across Father José's smooth face. When Father José reached for his face, Father Stephen stabbed the bottle deep into his neck.

Father Patrick who had been sitting in his room reading his Bible, rocking back and forth and waiting for things to end, walked out and declared, "Stephen is right. If you do not have faith in our salvation, then you are a cancer among us."

The feeble Father Paul interjected, "We need to show contrition for what we've done."

"Show contrition?" Father Patrick questioned. "We have all paid for our sins. We have all paid for our sins here and now. I will no longer suffer piously. We have paid for our sins."

Father Paul quoted the Bible back, " 'Be alert and of sober mind. Your enemy the devil prowls around like a roaring lion looking for someone to devour.' "

This stunned Father Patrick as he took a step back.

Father Stephen looked possessed. He picked up Father Paul's brittle body and threw him hard to the ground. You could hear the cracking of bone and the thud of flesh as he landed. "So be it!"

Father Patrick, horrified, screamed, "You must stop!"

Father Stephen turned on him and stabbed him furiously in the chest until Father Patrick dropped to the ground.

Father John and Father Reece had been standing there in shock since attacking Father Charlie.

Father John was the first to move as he tackled Father Stephen by his legs, knocking him to the ground. The bloody bottle shard broke in his hand as he hit the ground.

Even with this, Father Stephen quickly turned Father John around on the ground, pinning him and scraping the remaining broken glass chunks that were stuck deep into his right hand across the soft parts of Father John's face, blinding him and cutting the inside and outside of his mouth before tearing into the front of his throat.

Father Reece kicked Father Stephen sharply in the head, but it wasn't enough to stop him. So he continued to kick him, not always fully connecting.

Father Timothy finally exited Father Julio's room and began kicking Father Stephen from the other side. Mostly with glancing blows.

Father Reece finally connected squarely into Father Stephen's throat. Father Stephen choking now, fell, clutching his neck with both hands. Father Timothy and Father Reece continued to kick Father Stephen until Barney and Accardi arrived, pulling the two away from his lifeless body.

It wasn't until that moment that Father Timothy had noticed his friend Father James was still moving. "Help him," he pleaded, breaking his long silence.

In the end, only Father Reece, Father Timothy, Father Julio, and Father James survived, however Father James was barely alive.

Father James had deep wounds. Besides the wounds, he sounded like he had a punctured lung and he had been concussed. I squeezed out the broken glass, and poured alcohol over the open wound. Then I gave him antibiotics. But we doubted he'd survive.

After we cleaned up the carnage and Accardi and Centeno got rid of the bodies, we had a long conversation. "This was not right," I said, "We are down to four, maybe only three. We should just let the others go and view our mission as completed. We have cleared the church of a great stain."

"We cannot," Accardi said after I pleaded with them all.

I was no longer scared of the remaining four. I convinced Father Reece to discuss the Bible instead of just reciting it. Father Timothy wouldn't speak with me. I believed he thought his oath of silence was protecting him, since he and the other priest, Father Julio, who remained quiet, had not been harmed so far. Father James would likely be dead soon.

I spent most of my time with Father Julio. The more I looked at him, I began to think of him as an older version of me who had committed a terrible sin. He had started balding and had more gray, but our facial features and our mannerisms were similar. We had other things in common, too.

I was fluent in Spanish as well as Italian. But Father Julio would only talk to me in Spanish now. Italian and Spanish are similar, of course, but he didn't want to make it easy for the others to listen to what we were discussing. He had either not thought of or realized that Miguel was fluent in Spanish also. We mostly talked about his parish back home and his stories as an orphan growing up in the system until he became a priest, hoping the Church would prove to be a family of sorts.

He mentioned his "experiences" with the young boys. He said they were born out of loneliness and too much wine. I hid my disgust. "How many?" I asked.

"Three. Four." Father Julio was quiet. "I'm not sure anymore."

I was sure that was a lie. When we were making our list of targets, three was a big number for Accardi. Three reported instances was the sign of a serial predator, he said. Men like that must pay. One false charge had nearly ruined my life. And I remained a pariah, until I was forgotten about in the States.

I thought of my mother. How she died of heartbreak when I was accused. Falsely accused. And how my father, left alone, drank and died, stumbling into traffic. Both dead before last rites could be received. These were some of the realities that motivated me. They could be added up. They could be acted upon. These priests had violated the holy trinity of trust between Christ, his soldiers, and his flock. Even so, what about my sins now? *There is only one lawgiver and judge, he who is able to save and to destroy. But who are you to judge your neighbor?*

Accardi had insisted on grabbing Father Julio. He was the last one we took before leaving the United States.

After three days of my questions and frequent visits with Father Julio, Centeno had had enough.

"Father Tony, you know how this ends, right?" Centeno said.

"I do."

"You know I can understand most of what you are saying." Centeno stared at me.

"I have nothing to hide."

Centeno got closer to me. "Let me make this more clear. I am ordering you—"

"Hey, look alive, everyone. We have visitors," Accardi interrupted. We had been spending the majority of our time crammed into the security station together with the monitors.

There was a boat approaching. I assumed it was the bad news I had been expecting, but I went out with the others, regardless. We were all armed and took positions as Accardi had laid out earlier.

It was the bad news I expected. Renato Centeno introduced himself to me entirely differently than I was prepared.

"You must be Father Anthony." He got around to me, shaking my hand, after giving a hug to Accardi, Fergusson, and his Uncle Angel, as well as a nod to Miguel.

He then looked beyond me and asked, "Where's Hannigan?"

"Things haven't been going well, Renato," Angel said.

"Well then, I wish I had better news." René followed. He was going to continue and then turned toward Accardi. "Wait, so what happened to Liam?"

Accardi simply said, "He got out of hand, and he needed to be handled. It went downhill from there."

René grimaced and sighed. "So, there is a BOLO, be on the lookout, for all of you except Miguel. Hannigan was on the list, too, and so, I imagine, am I."

"Okay, that's good to know. Very helpful." Accardi turned to Miguel. "Miggy, are you comfortable taking the boat to Malé for supplies? Barney and I can help you with the controls."

Miguel nodded but looked uncertain.

"If you don't feel comfortable, we can figure another way."

"I got this, Sandy. Just don't want a breakdown in the middle of nowhere, okay?"

"You'll be fine, and we will give you one of the sat phones just in case."

René jumped on that. "Phones?"

"Yeah, we have a few useful supplies that O'Malley left us."

René nodded and continued, "Anyway, the BOLO isn't the worst of it. The feds seem like they are putting together most of the missing pieces. I don't think that they are as far off as you'd like. I tried to close off as many loose ends as possible, but I wasn't getting—"

"Don't act like you did us any favors," Angel interrupted. "You went rogue."

"It wasn't like that. I swear," René protested.

Nobody said anything. And nobody looked at the new arrival.

"Yes, I might have gone a little overboard, but I tried to close as many threads as I could that might lead back to us. I didn't realize the bosses would react the way they did."

René stopped, looking around for support. Not seeing any, his anger rose. "Don't fucking judge me. None of you were there. I had to make a call."

This time Angel did speak. "Okay, René, what's done is done. You are with us now."

"So, show me around. Let me know how I can help." René wrapped up, seeming less threatening than I imagined.

All of us walked together, cautiously watching René. No one really trusted him, not even his uncle. We'd read the headlines out of New York. An IA woman murdered. A precinct cop beaten within an inch of his life. Centeno, tied to both victims, had gone AWOL. When Angel wondered if René was behind it, Accardi said, "If it walks like a duck, quacks like a duck, and looks like a duck, it's your fucking nephew."

Now we knew for sure.

René remained mostly quiet looking at the sleeping quarters and the food supply. He only finally perked up when we got to the security room.

"So, wait. What's this?" René sounded disgusted.

"What do you mean?" Accardi said.

"There's still what... four of them remaining? What gives?"

"What do you mean?"

I could see the rage and darkness in René's eyes. He paused before speaking. "Uncle Sandro." Sandy wasn't his real uncle but to a certain degree had raised him. "It's just that we are out of time. We need to finish taking out the trash and jump."

We all heard this.

"Tempus fugit, memento mori," I mumbled to myself. They used to put this phrase in grandfather clocks. "Time flies, remember death." It was ascribed to the great Father McGivney who founded the Knights of Columbus, but was really taken from the Gospel of St. Luke. It deals with my Savior Jesus discussing murders under Pilate. *Was I any better than the late Roman governor?*

Everyone had continued talking while I got lost in my head. What would Jesus think about this? What would our prisoners write about their lives and our treatment of them, if we gave them paper and pen?

"Well, that's my opinion," I heard René say, bringing me back to the present. "Let me down there and I will finish this."

"That's not the way it is supposed to work," I said.

René looked around for support and once again found none.

"I don't get it. Looking at the number of priests left, I think you made your point. If we leave now, the remaining priests will starve or kill themselves. You didn't blow through all of O'Malley's money, did you? If not, it's time for the exit plan, right?"

"Hannigan was the only one with access," Angel said.

"What do you mean by that? Access?"

"I mean only Hannigan and O'Malley were on the account and only Hannigan and O'Malley knew about the exit plan. That's what I mean."

"What?! You all are looking at me sideways, calling me a fuckup. When you killed the only guy who had access to the money, you also killed the only guy who knew what the plan was to get us the fuck out of here?"

None of us had a response for this.

René shook his head. "That doesn't make any sense. If you are trying to keep money secret, it's not like either of them would have given the bank their passport. Did Hannigan have to call in? Was there computer access? Do you at least know the bank? As for the exit plan, have you searched the computers? Looked around for any notes, coordinates?"

"It doesn't matter, Renato," Accardi said. "You don't understand. We made a commitment to O'Malley. We are on board until the end. We are all at peace with this."

"Yeah, you all look at peace," René scoffed.

Accardi stared hard at René. "Renato, this is hard work, but we are all committed. We didn't ask you to come here. You still have money of your own. If you are not in this with us, I am sure we all understand."

Everyone nodded their heads eagerly, hoping that the volatile René Centeno would be taken out of the equation.

René paused. I could swear I saw the fury rising from his soul to his face. He then turned away for a second. I assumed he was trying to compose himself. When he turned back, he gave us a sheepish grin.

"All right. I guess we will all be sharing a cell together soon enough," he said. "Just like the pedophiles you all seem so intent on coddling."

He sat at a computer station and brought up some screens that we hadn't seen before. "Looks like you have about twenty terabytes on the dark web." René looked around. Seeing the blank stares, he continued, "It looks like there is a switch to make all the videos go live through various social media and dark websites. I can't make out what the trigger is, but I gather, it must be when all of this gets shut down."

René paused for a moment. "Look here. There's a letter, in a PDF format, and a video message from O'Malley claiming all culpability. Looks like there are spaces available for any of you to add video messages if you'd like. I can activate that surveillance camera there." René pointed to a circular device embedded in the wall.

Miguel asked the obvious. "How do you know all this… stuff?"

René laughed. "Well, first off, there is a Word document with some general instructions. Then, no offense, but my generation grew up with social media and video blogging. Finally, I did some computer work when I worked in Manhattan for a few months. Nothing complicated, but looking for documents and videos was the main part of the job.

"I'm telling you the right thing to do is let me down there. I don't even need a weapon, and I will finish this for all of us." René flipped back to the video feeds before looking around the room again at all of us. "If not that, let me tinker around with the computer a bit, and I will see what I can find. I mean, right here it looks like there are a few other cameras on the island. If you'd like, I can have one of the monitors cycle through them so we can make sure nothing sneaks up on us, right?"

Accardi watched the young Centeno click away, and sure enough, one of the monitors started to cycle through various video feeds at different parts of the island. There were even cameras in our sleeping quarters. Accardi looked around and Angel nodded. "Sure thing, Renato. See what you can figure out."

The computer equipment had been mostly useless for the rest of us.

As we all walked out of the security room, René said, "I'll grab my remaining stuff out of the boat, then do a deeper dive into the system. I might even get lucky and be able to find O'Malley's money or something about the exit plan. Did Hannigan and O'Malley have any other computer devices, like a laptop, tablet, or even a cell phone?"

"We'll show you their rooms when you get back," Accardi said.

When René was out of sight, Accardi turned to the rest of us. "I know. I don't trust him, either. Still, if he can help us access the money or potentially find O'Malley's exit plan, if nothing else, it gives us more options."

My mind went through the idea of there being hidden explosives in the sleeping quarters or some sort of poison gas that could be released. I laughed to myself. Accardi and Angel were basically family to René, and even if that weren't the case, what would be the point of doing something like that even if he could. If he wanted to leave, he would just take one of the two remaining boats and leave us. My lack of faith in him reflected my own lack of faith in my convictions. I felt ashamed.

CHAPTER FORTY-TWO
Targeted

EDDIE

I had slept through a call from Paul earlier in the day and hadn't gotten out of bed until two. I didn't want to answer any questions about what I had done all day, so instead I left for Connecticut to spend Christmas Day with my mother.

There were more people than I expected at the cemetery, luckily none within eyeshot after I parked my car and lay next to my mother.

The snow was mostly gone, but the grass was still crisp and cracked beneath my weight as I sank down beside her grave, feeling the wetness bleed into my jeans.

I closed my eyes. I felt dizzy from last night's bout of drinking alone, and the sense of sadness washing over me didn't help.

I woke up with my legs stiff and my hands numb. This was a good way to get sick. "Eddie, you fucking moron, focus."

I thought I had woken up on my own, but while trying to stand, the buzzing in my pocket began again, the vibrating sending shocks of pain through my leg. I gingerly reached into my pants. I was shocked to see it was Agent Murray. She had already left a voicemail.

On the way back to my car I shook my legs every few feet to get the blood moving and to get my jeans to stop sticking to me.

I started the Lexus, turned on the heated seat, and set the heater on high.

"Eddie, give me a call immediately." That could mean anything.

"Eddie?" Murray answered. "Where are you right now?"

"I'm visiting my mother's grave in Connecticut. Is that okay?" I had no patience left.

"John and Debbie O'Neill are dead."

"What?" I couldn't process what she was saying.

"John and Debbie—" she started again.

"I heard you." I was numb. "What are you telling me?"

"It seems like Renato or his dad are tying up any loose ends.

"I need you to head to the local police department. Cooper will let them know you are on your way." She paused. "Do you see any troublesome-looking people or vehicles around?"

Driving to the Bridgeport Police Department, I kept an eye out for New York license plates in my rearview mirror. I kept waiting for someone to ram me or pull up beside me and take a shot at me, but nothing happened.

I told Murray I needed to call my brothers to let them know they were in possible danger, but she told me explicitly not to do this. They were probably safe as long as they were not aware of anything regarding the priests' case or the Centenos. Anything I said to them would only put them at more risk. There were not enough resources to offer any sort of protection for them so the best way to keep them safe was for them not to know anything.

A couple of hours after waiting in a conference room in the police department, I was picked up by a pair of federal agents. They disabled my cell phone, removing the battery and sim card. They gave me a burner phone to use with Agent Murray's number and a central number for the FBI programmed in.

They were concerned someone within the police department was tracking my movements via my cell. The concern was that they could give my location to the Mafia.

I was put up in a Connecticut hotel for four days. I gave the agents the key to my condo, and they gathered up a suitcase full of clothes and toiletries as if I was going on a trip. They even got my six-pack of Dos Equis out of the fridge. Twice a day, agents would call me and ask me if I needed anything. They didn't want me to order anything, so they would pick up food and drop it off to me.

The story had blown up in the national news. The mayor had stepped down and was looking at possibly being indicted on racketeering charges. There were at least four Mafia hits that had taken place that had made the news, and my friend John and his wife were not included in the four. They were withholding the names at this point, but one of the deceased was a cop, and the other three were potentially involved in organized crime. I could only hope that the Centenos didn't have the backing of the other families and were getting whacked for making waves.

The New York tabloids ran stories about the two missing New York priests as if they were killed by the Mafia, but I knew, as did the feds, that it was more complicated than that.

The feds assigned to me were no longer Murray and Cooper. They were Smith and Williams now, the two who had briefly interrogated me before dumping me in a room with Emilio Centeno.

I had to repeat all I knew to them, but this time they were much more interested in the details of what I knew about Accardi and the Centenos.

At the end of the meeting, I was advised to stay in Connecticut for the foreseeable future.

After playing by the feds rules for five days, I was finally allowed to call Steve on Tuesday, the day before New Year's Eve. Smith and Williams drove me back into New York to a rest stop before handing my cell phone back to me so I could make my call. Regardless, I was unable to reach Steve. I left a message and called Paul.

"Hey, Eddie, how's it going? Everything okay?" Paul sounded amped.

"Things are fine, Paul. How are you?" I was robotic with my answers. Not sure what to say and what not to say.

"Good. Good. Just busy." He must have been thinking he hadn't made it clear enough that he was too busy to talk to me by the way he answered the phone. This time he left out any ambiguity.

"No problem. I hear you, Paul. I'll let you go." I hung up the phone.

I couldn't do this. I certainly didn't want to get into it with Paul with two agents staring at me the whole time.

Paul immediately called me back on my cell phone.

"Hey, Eddie, you sure everything is all right?"

"Yeah, Paul. Sorry if I was short, but you said you're busy."

"Yeah, I know I'm always busy. How you doing anyway?"

"True. I'm okay. Just lots of changes going on up here. Not sure where my head is lately." I thought that sounded neutral enough for him not to worry about me.

Paul laughed. "Yeah, me also. You remember that novel I had been writing for the last seven years or so?"

I vaguely remembered him having different hobbies, writing being one of them. "Yeah, I think so."

"Anyway, it turns out it was crap. I decided to go in a different direction, and I've been busy with a new project lately. I think I really have something good here." He responded with an energy that stole what little remaining strength I had.

"Sounds good, Paul. You keep it up." I hung up again, and this time he didn't call me back. The agents drove me back to the same Connecticut hotel.

I was told by Agent Williams, I had gotten a voicemail from Steinem on Monday. It was almost a week since talking to my brother Paul. Steve had not called me back.

To keep me safe, only a limited number of FBI personnel knew I was under their protection. With the NYPD potentially being compromised, they weren't taking any chances.

We once again drove across the state border back into New York —another precaution in case my phone was being tracked—and parked in a McDonald's lot. If anyone was tracking my phone, we wouldn't be here long enough for them to reach me, and we were intentionally choosing different, spread-out locations, so it would be hard to figure out where I was staying.

They asked me if I wanted anything, so I got my normal cheeseburger meal with a Diet Coke. Smith and Williams both just drank their bottled waters, even after I offered to buy them Happy Meals if they would leave me alone in the car to make some calls. They would not.

I called my brother Steve first. I couldn't leave a message because I didn't know when I would be able to use my cell phone again. I decided to ask the agents to check in on him for me.

I then got Steinem on the phone.

"Well-played," he said.

"What's well-played?"

"You got me to call you. Usually it's the other way around. I'm not sure if you are upset about my unavailability to meet with the FBI, or if you were trying to pull some sort of power move by not calling and checking in on the status of your case, but regardless, here I am."

"I liked Clyde Monroe just fine. And whatever happens with my case happens."

"Very Zen, Eddie, but you can't fuck around with this. Have you been watching the news lately?"

"Yeah, I have been watching the news. It doesn't look good."

"That's your take, Eddie? You should probably go somewhere for a while," Steinem said.

When I didn't say anything, he continued, "Well, obviously neither the FBI nor the NYPD was playing straight with us. I can't make promises formally, but if I can't get these charges to disappear, based on the bullshit they pulled, not to mention setting you up for a civil case, I am less of an attorney than I think."

"You seem so humble. Are you sure you can handle that type of pressure?"

"Fuck you, Eddie. I'll call back when I have something."

CHAPTER FORTY-THREE
Ambush

EDDIE

Steinem was good at his job, and part of his job was reading people. He had picked up that something was off with me. Before I could hang up the phone, he said, "Wait, what is going on with you, Mr. Rodriguez? Is there something I should be aware of? Have you been drinking?"

Steinem had jumped to damage control. He wasn't exactly sure what he was dealing with.

"It's complicated." I felt a dose of pleasure by putting this smug prick on his heels.

"Complicated," Steinem repeated. "Do you still want me to be your legal counsel? Are you currently considering or active in any cases involving me, my firm, or BDQ Investments? Are you in some state of duress where you do not feel comfortable discussing things with me?"

"Lots of questions there… Counsellor," I replied.

"Eddie? My main concern is that you are in trouble. Are you in trouble, and if so, can I help?" Steinem sounded believable.

"Yeah, I am okay." I was going to say his first name, but I didn't know it. I laughed to myself at the fact I hadn't even gotten a business card from him or gone through the headache of looking up his credentials online.

The laugh made Steinem nervous. "I can be in contact with powerful resources if you need them. I would like to meet with you —hold a second." I heard him clicking away at a computer. "In three hours, in the pizza place that you were in with your old friend. That would put us at six oh four, so let's say six on the nose, okay?"

"Can you hold a second?" I asked and heard no response.

The FBI agents had been staring at me the whole time.

"Do you think—"

Williams abruptly said, "Hang up the phone."

I started to speak.

Williams then followed with a quick and forceful, "Now!"

I blinked and instantly clicked off.

Steinem immediately called me back and I let it ring.

"I need to see my lawyer."

"Not happening," Williams shot back.

"I'm not asking."

"Fuck!" Williams returned. "Do you have any idea..." he started but didn't finish, then said, "Okay, call back Steinem. Tell him you are under FBI protection but you can meet with him tomorrow. Get him to commit to a time after four p.m. We will give him an address in Manhattan to meet that we deem safe. Got it?"

I did.

I called back Steinem and told him what the feds told me.

Steinem refused to believe me at first.

"You think I'm making this shit up? You called me because you see everything I'm involved in blowing up. People I know are dropping like flies. So the feds came to get me! You should watch your ass, too, now that I think about it. I'm fucking toxic!"

Steinem refused to believe me and demanded to talk to one of the agents. Agent Smith talked with Steinem, and after a two-minute conversation, he convinced Steinem. When the phone was returned to me, Steinem said, "Okay. If I am supposed to be there at four, let them know it needs to be no more than fifteen minutes from my office or I might be late."

———

The next day I was picked up in a black van, and I sat in the back with Williams and Smith.

"I feel like an Amazon delivery in here," I joked.

Neither Smith nor Williams laughed. Instead, Smith said, "How are you holding up, Eddie?"

"Hanging in there, I guess. How are you doing? How does this case rate for excitement?"

"We've both had worse gigs; trust us."

"I'd love to hear your tales. Got to be better than walking a beat in the South Bronx."

The rest of the ride down was very friendly. Williams and Smith traded funny FBI war stories. Drugs stored in a septic tank, a perp pissing himself intentionally in the back of Williams's car, claiming he had not been allowed to use the bathroom, a stakeout at the Canadian border in February at ten below zero when a deer set off the trip wire and blew the job. For me, it made the trip the most fun that I'd had in weeks.

———

It took me a second to realize where we were after they opened the back of the van and I stepped out. We were in a large garage, but looking at the plates and vehicles I quickly put it together. We were in the garage of the FBI building in Manhattan. The one I had now been to multiple times.

This wasn't good. "I thought I was meeting with my attorney," I said coldly.

"You are, Eddie. No problem. He should be here shortly. Let's go upstairs," Smith said.

I was placed in a small conference room with no phone and no clock and two bottled waters. I was halfway through the first when Steinem came bursting through the door.

"Don't tell me how to do my job! You are a junior FBI agent. You are out of your depth." He was yelling at Agent Williams who followed closely behind him.

Williams was hot. "You are a corporate suit playing defense attorney, Barry. I am fairly certain I understand this better than you." I had to assume Barry was Steinem's first name.

Before he sat, Steinem made eye contact with Agent Williams who had let in Agent Smith and two other people I didn't recognize. I could tell Steinem was thinking but he couldn't help himself. He gave a wry smile, then said, "You could not begin to fathom the depths of what I know, *Andy*."

Agent Williams cocked his head to the side and then quietly said, "What the fuck did you call me?"

Steinem realized he had shown too much of what he knew and quickly adjusted. He didn't sit because Williams was beginning to walk around the table toward him. "Listen, that was poor form, Agent Williams. I shouldn't have said that."

Smith grabbed Williams by the shoulder with a firm thick hand, but Williams kept speaking, his voice having changed completely, "Nah, man. That ain't right. There's something wrong here. How could he possibly know that? This is a problem." He turned and looked past Smith at the two other agents who had walked in, but if they had any authority, they weren't showing it. They looked unsure and waited for direction.

I began to think about the sliver of Williams's tattoo that had stuck out slightly below his pressed white shirt, and I found it morphing in my head into a neo-Nazi symbol. I remembered thinking he looked like a skinhead when he walked in the first time I saw him. Whatever he was in the past, Steinem seemed to know, and this had Williams clearly on edge.

After a few more backs-and-forths, Steinem worked his magic and was able to change a glaring, standing Williams to a less-threatening, glaring, sitting Williams.

There was a lot of paperwork pushed toward me, and then came the ultimatum.

Smith spoke to me in a quiet voice, "Listen, Eddie. We are willing to settle both your criminal and civil charges."

"Civil?" This was the first time I had heard of any civil cases being thrown at me.

Steinem spoke next, trying to keep things light under the weight of the glaring Williams. "Yeah, Eddie. I didn't want to stress you out, but both Mr. Rahman and Cadet Brown are suing you."

"*Suing me?*"

"Yeah, besides the damage to his car, Mr. Rahman is also suing for soft-tissue damage, psychological—"

There was always someone trying to get at me. "So, basically bullshit. So he's looking at making a payday over this, and I take it the cadet found out and had the same idea. Well, fuck that. I am—"

Smith said, "Eddie, you need to understand both of these people are viewed as respectable individuals—"

"Respectable." I snorted.

"Yes, Eddie. Both are *viewed* that way; whether they are or are not doesn't really matter. Both have clean records. Cadet Brown coaches a youth basketball team in his free time, and Mr. Rahman has given his number to at-risk women and driven them to the Manhattan police station to get away from their abusive spouses on multiple occasions. These are facts that would come up if you were to be part of a civil suit."

For whatever good I did as a cop, I didn't even round up my change for charity when given the option at the grocery store. They had a point. "Okay, so what are you saying?"

"My point is that we can make it all go away. We can make it easy for you. We can work with the local police and handle the criminal side and come to your aid on the civil side."

"Oh, ain't that just swell. So glad to have the FBI on my side. You all have made my life so much better since getting involved with you. Cut to the chase; I'm waiting for the and or the but."

"Eddie," Steinem said. "They want you to wear a wire."

Smith said, "We are dealing with powerful people here and powerful organizations. If we want indictments, we need to be able to lay things out clearly. We need to know what is going on with the ex-cops, one of your original theories. We think the easiest target is Juarez."

"Juarez, like Miguel Juarez? Well, I haven't seen him in forever, and I don't think he is the guy you want anyway."

"If we could set up a call with you and him, would you be willing to work with us?"

I didn't want to screw Miggy.

Smith continued, "Tell him you left BDQ, and your family is no longer around and that you miss him. Just get him talking. Let him know you are looking to help him out. With any luck, he might let you know what he and the ex-cops are up to. If the conversation doesn't go that way, push the angle of just wanting to catch up and letting him know you are there for him."

"Sounds like a shitty thing to do to a friend."

"We think Juarez is a small fish and is being used as a pawn.

He's not our main interest. We are hoping to get him talking to lead us to something bigger. You know the broader Mafia, Accardi, Centeno, the mayor, potentially even O'Malley if he turns out to be alive."

Steinem said, "Hey, Eddie, listen. I think this is a good deal. Juarez is the smallest fish in that sea and very likely is looking for an exit. If half the shit that is being leaked out is true, you'd be doing him a favor, not to mention cleaning up all your legal troubles. If these cases go forward, and they find out you have a trust fund, it could get really ugly. Believe me."

I told myself that I was doing this to help Miggy, but I didn't trust anyone at this point, including myself. "Let's do it."

Williams remained seated as we all exited the room with Steinem second to last and me last. Williams was still upset about the earlier interaction with Steinem. "Not everyone should be defined by one action," he said. "If you put in the effort, you should be given the opportunity to improve over time and not be defined by a short period of your life."

Nobody commented. I wondered if he was talking about himself or Juarez.

Or me.

CHAPTER FORTY-FOUR
Hunted

EDDIE

I was told by the FBI not to leave my condo under any circumstances. Ever the lawyer, Steinem told me that technically they can't force me to stay in my condo; I only couldn't leave the state based on the deal he made. With the amount of shit going down, it made sense to stay indoors for now. Williams gave me a cell phone number to call If I felt threatened. He said someone would be at my condo in five minutes. I knew this was bullshit. It can take five minutes to get up the elevator.

They had me write a letter designed and dictated by profilers and shrinks at the bureau to appeal to Miggy. I wrote it out in my own hand. It was a pathetic, *I miss you* note sprinkled with Spanglish. I'm not sure if I wanted it to work or not. Either way, it got rid of my legal hassles.

They sent this letter and a special burner phone to a contact in India who was going to try to use a local asset to get the phone to Miggy in the Maldives. They supposedly had spotted Miggy picking up supplies in Malé, the capital, and the only major city in the sprawling group of islands.

While I felt bad setting Miggy up, it sounded like they might be right. From what I was hearing from Steinem, Murray's thoughts about the priests seemed accurate, all the way down to the Maldives. If Accardi, Centeno, and the others were keeping priests trapped on some island in the middle of nowhere against their will, I couldn't imagine Miggy being on board with this.

When I asked Williams and Smith about Agents Murray and Cooper, they gave me nothing. "We're your guys, Eddie," Williams said.

"The only reason you're my guys is that Murray kept me in the game," I said. "She could piss me off, but she worked her ass off."

Left to my own devices, I rarely strayed from watching the news, stopping briefly once on ecotourism in Ecuador and a boring ninety-year-old Turner Classic comedy. Slowly, the national news was connecting more pieces. A number of priests had gone missing. Some of them were rumored to be pedophiles. A story ran that the NYPD had kicked the case up to the FBI. My old police captain, Broward, the mayor, the O'Malley family, everyone had no comment for the press. The mob, my biggest fear, disturbingly enough, wasn't making the national news.

I figured it was only a matter of time before my name would surface.

This had to be a field day for the Steinems of the world with everyone lawyering up, I imagined.

———

It had been five days since I had talked to him, and I found myself happy to hear his voice. I was starting to go a little stir-crazy being locked up in my condo twenty-four seven.

"Hey, Eddie," he began. His voice sounded strange. That couldn't be good.

"Hey, Bar—" I was getting ready to playfully call him Barry when I changed course. I hadn't liked the way he sounded. "What's going on, Mr. Steinem?"

"I regret to inform you that I can no longer be your attorney," Steinem blurted.

I should have seen this coming, but I was still stunned. "What?"

"I'm sorry, Eddie. The cases are pretty much settled. I have all the documents signed that you need. As long as you work with the FBI and do your part, you should be good."

"Well, that's fine if everything goes smoothly, but when the fuck does anything go smoothly?" Without Steinem, I'd have no one looking out for me.

"I know, I know." Steinem was flustered. "It's just that there's a lot going on, and I have other cases that are starting to press on me. When I took your case, I thought—"

"Who's the monkey now, Barry?" I seethed.

Steinem replied coldly, "I will do what I told you I would do, Mr. Rodriguez." He paused. "And Eddie, fuck you." With that, he hung up the phone.

I told myself that Steinem had put up a fight, but I couldn't be sure.

I got more bad news the following day when I was picked up by Agent Smith and Agent Williams in a Cadillac. "So, there's a news story about to break citing you as a key informant, Eddie."

"What? They have my fucking name?" This was bad.

Agent Smith responded calmly, "Yes, but they've agreed not to use it. However, they will be reporting that someone is working with the FBI that has knowledge about the NYPD case. It would be surprising for Juarez not to get wind of this, and if that happens, well…"

"So, what are you telling me?" I felt cold.

"Not telling you anything at this point, Eddie. I mean, at least not about the plan for the case. It's just that if you had been forgotten over the last couple weeks, now you might be a target again." We had driven around in a circle and were outside my condo again.

Smith wrapped it up. "If you need anything at all, during the day, call me or Williams. If you ever feel like you are in danger at night, call the number that you were provided. As of now, we just want you alert."

I watched the Cadillac go down the block and turn right out of my view, leaving me to my thoughts. I wanted to enjoy the fresh air, but I didn't feel the crispness of the January air. All I felt was exposed.

———

Three days later, I got a hard knock on my condo door, followed quickly by, "Mr. Rodriguez, I need you to let me in." It was Williams's voice.

"Everything okay?" I couldn't see clearly out of the peephole. I think I could see one of Smith's broad shoulders to the left of Williams.

My old cop instincts kicked in. There was something off about Williams that had never sat straight with me, especially since his interaction with Steinem. "Can I see who's standing next to you?"

"What?" Williams screamed at the door.

Agent Smith came into view, putting himself in front of the peephole. "It's me, Eddie."

I jiggled the lock and let the two agents in.

Williams yelled at me as I let him in. "What the fuck was that?" He was hot.

Maybe it was just my nerves, but I could tell something was off.

Agent Smith turned to Williams, giving him an angry look and said to him, "Come on, man."

Agent Williams frowned, and his face reddened before turning to me and saying, "Hey, I apologize, Eddie."

Now I was really nervous. Something was definitely strange.

"What's going on, you two?" I was missing my NYPD-issued Glock 19.

"We need you to pack a bag, Eddie. We have a green light. We are sending you to the Maldives."

I was happy things were in play, but my stomach soured. Something had changed.

CHAPTER FORTY-FIVE
A Time To Kill

EDDIE

I sat in the back seat of a Town Car with Williams, while Agent Smith sat up front next to the driver.

"What the fuck is going on, Williams?"

"We are heading to Kennedy."

"That's not what I'm asking."

"You got her, Dan?" Williams turned to Smith.

"Yeah, I got her," Agent Smith said, futzing with his phone.

"All right, then."

"We have a call for you." Agent Smith handed me a cell phone.

"Hello," I said.

"Hey, Eddie." It was Agent Murray.

"Fuck," I responded. "The constant bearer of bad news." I paused, stating the obvious. "So, Miggy is dead. You finally found a way to kill off someone else I know."

"No. It's not that." She sounded upset.

"Hey, Amanda." I wasn't trying to be disrespectful. I was trying to be a friend. She shouldn't take credit for this one. "Listen, he went into this on his own. I tried to warn him. Something felt off, but he had to know—"

"It's not him, Eddie."

"What?" I shot back. John was already dead.

"It's your brother."

I could feel my heart stop. I wanted to know which one, but I couldn't respond.

"It looks like a professional hit. I literally just found out," Murray said after waiting a couple of seconds for me to respond.

"Which brother?"

"Paul."

I stayed silent looking out the window at the busy streets of Manhattan and thinking how much smaller my world was becoming by the day.

"Eddie?"

"Yeah," I replied, numb.

"I requested the case, and I think they are going to give it to me. I will get you justice."

With that, she hung up the phone.

Justice. The word swam around in my head. *What is justice? When has anyone ever felt joy from justice?*

Williams said, "Eddie, I'm sorry about this; we just got word from Amanda... Agent Murray, on our way to get you." He paused. "This looks big. Nothing is one hundred percent, but it looks like it might be the Russians, not the Italians who went after him."

I could tell he was trying to temper his excitement at the potential size of this case with having to tell me the bad news. "This is really big, Eddie. If this involves both the Italian and Russian Mafia working together, we are talking about something on a scale we haven't seen in decades."

I initially was irritated, but I found it hard to stay mad. I felt alone more than anything. "How'd they do it?" I finally mumbled.

"Professional hit. Double tap." Smith made a snap decision to rip off the Band-Aid and just be blunt.

"Centenos?" It felt like someone else was talking for me as my eyes lost focus watching the car lights blur as the sun had begun to set.

"Hmmm… hard to say, but probably not." Smith was looking forward now, avoiding eye contact with me. "Something involving both organizations would have to be done from the top, you would think."

"Right," I whispered.

Williams turned to me then. "You have an opportunity to blow this wide open. As you know, it is not just the New York priests. There are a lot of people who you will be helping."

"Yeah, a lot of greasy pedophiles," I breathed out.

"Well, we can't be certain," Williams said. "Just because someone is accused of something doesn't mean they did it."

"Nah, they did it," I said. "O'Malley with all his money and connections wouldn't do this on a hunch. He had all of this laid out, and he would be certain about his targets."

"Well, maybe." Williams looked down at his iPhone but thought better of it and turned to me. "Regardless, you are doing the right thing. If it turns out the priests are pedophiles, well then, we will get them also… but we will get them the right way… in the courts."

"I don't give a fuck if they are being skinned alive." Suddenly, I was furious. "Do you think I give a fuck about a bunch of priests that abused kids, especially as a gay man?"

Williams turned uncertainly toward Smith.

Smith took over. "Well, Eddie. I think what Agent Williams is trying to do is get you in a good mindset. I mean, this is going to be dangerous work you have signed on for."

"No shit," I sneered.

Smith turned away from me for a moment, realizing that he should just let me grieve.

Williams felt forced to respond. "Hey, Eddie. I'm on your side." He smiled, trying to look friendly, but instead came off as insincere. "All we are saying is that it is better if you can go into this with a purpose. You know, something that can drive you that makes you feel like you are doing the right thing."

I looked down at my hands for a moment. "Oh, I have a purpose."

Williams gave an approving nod.

"My purpose is revenge."

Before getting on the plane, I left a second message for Steve to check in on our dad. I told him to call me immediately. I didn't want to leave a message about Paul on his voicemail.

Without being able to get him, I was assured by Agents Smith and Williams that they would have someone check in with my dad and track down Steve. I would get an update when my plane landed in Mumbai before continuing on to Malé.

I made a promise as I got on the plane. No matter what happened, I was going to find a way to kill Angel Centeno and René Centeno. There was no way I was going to let them slip justice with their sleazy high-powered lawyers. I had no one at this point. My dad was dying, and my remaining brother, Steve, was too far gone. I would do this one good thing for myself and my mother.

CHAPTER FORTY-SIX
Somnambule

EDDIE

As the plane lifted off, I felt my system crash. The adrenaline that had been running through me was unsustainable.

I tried to remember my brother's smile. He was gifted with those Irish good looks. His eyes would sparkle with emotion. However, my mind kept on changing to what he did for a living. He had gone over it with me a few times, but the way I remembered it he tried to get Wall Street to bankrupt companies. I think he called it "selling short." It could have been his own sleaziness that got him on the radar of the Russian mob. If the Italians said something about him, maybe that just gave the Russians another reason. I couldn't believe that I alone had gotten him killed. I shook this from my head and forced myself to think about why I was on the plane.

I replayed the FBI game plan. The success of the plan seemed to swirl around this mysterious contact in Malé. He had supposedly befriended Miggy at one of the shops he ran, and he had convinced

Miggy to schedule his visits so that all requested supplies were in stock. Specifically the medicines and bedding seemed to be a problem. This appeared way too convenient. There was something I wasn't being told.

I would be met in Mumbai by an Interpol agent and put up in a hotel for two days while they set things up with this contact. Besides helping with narrowing down Miggy's schedule, the contact seemed relatively confident about the island where Miggy and the rest were encamped, or at least close enough. The hope was that Miggy would show up after I arrived, and I would wrangle my way back to the island. If not, the contact and I would charter a boat or a puddle jumper and get me to the suspected island that way.

Once I had a clear visual of the compound and of any of the principals, such as Accardi or Centeno, and was able to determine with some confidence where the priests were being kept, I was supposed to call in on the sat phone to begin the cleanup operation. This whole thing was probably written on the back of a fucking napkin.

Thinking it through, I had to laugh. Nobody had told me how I was going to explain why I was there to Miggy. What the fuck was I going to tell him? *Oh, I was just in the neighborhood?* I figured I would just level with him. Interpol and the feds were onto them. You need to cooperate.

But that seemed nuts, too. He had gone all in with his cop pals. He would likely go out with them, too.

I had other logistical questions. What if I was searched? What if the sat phone was taken from me or damaged? The answers I came up with were clear. I was collateral damage for the feds and anyone else looking at a big win for their law enforcement career. I laughed derisively to myself as the plane accelerated for takeoff.

Mostly as I slept, I dreamed of my dad. Not the old, withered wreck of a man, but the younger version, the guy who took the family to the Caribbean every year. It was a disturbing dream. I tried to remember our previous holidays and thought back to when I was eleven, when we went on our last trip—to Jamaica. My dad and mom were having a hard time keeping the threads together.

I remembered the juxtaposition of the placidness of the Caribbean blue waters to the tension surrounding me and my family. It was a mockery of where we were as a family versus the others frolicking in the water. After that, there were no more trips.

We finally touched down in Mumbai after fourteen hours in the air. I was dizzy and stiff getting off the plane. No one should remain seated for that long. I heard stories about jet lag, but I would have been disoriented regardless. Adding to that disorientation were my expectations about India. I had imagined that Mumbai would be a Third World country with children in tattered clothes begging for rupees as I tried to elbow through the squalor to my luggage.

Instead, Mumbai Airport was efficient, clean, and sleekly modern. All signs were in English besides Hindi, making it easy for me to maneuver down to customs and then to the baggage claim where I was going to meet my contact.

It was 2:00 a.m., and the airport was practically empty, which made it very easy to spot my contact who was holding a sign for *Jones*. I grabbed my small bag that I had checked, and we headed out into the city.

I was put up in a Marriott Hotel, where once again I was surprised. From the outside, it looked like a palace. Inside, it was a mix of old-world architecture and modern luxury. I felt like an idiot. The digital revolution had transformed China from a nation of starving peasants to a country of exploited workers and filthy rich, cutting-edge techies. Why wouldn't India be the same? This place had old colonial poshness plus new money plushness.

I wanted to go to sleep when I finally got settled, but I had made the mistake of looking at my phone and seeing messages. Nothing from Steve, one from Agent Smith asking me to text him when I landed, and a couple from Agent Murray asking me to call. The voicemail she left had that flat voice that I was becoming accustomed to. It was a voice that foretold more bad news.

I texted Smith that I had checked into my hotel.

It was now 3:44 a.m., local time. I didn't have the energy for Murray at this point. I barely got my teeth brushed before collapsing on the bed. There was nothing planned for me the next day. I had been given the card of my Interpol contact. If I left the hotel I should be aware of pickpockets, but besides that I should be relatively safe.

I woke up right at noon. I hadn't shut my curtains properly, and I had lost the battle against the unrelenting sun.

I got dressed and I called Murray.

It rang three times before it was picked up. "Hello?"

That was a very unMurrayesque answer. "Hello, Agent Murray?"

"Speaking." I heard her cough, and then I heard something click. "Eddie?" She was becoming alert.

I had figured out what had happened. "Oh crap. Sorry about that. I hadn't thought of the time change," I mumbled. "It's twelve thirty-four in the afternoon here. What time is it there?"

"Two oh five," Agent Murray mumbled back. She must have been rounding the minutes or something.

"Hey, listen, you want to just call me back?" I wasn't sure I wanted to hear what she had to say anyway.

I could hear a sink running as she responded. "No, Eddie. That's all right." She paused for a second, then turned the sink off. "I'm sorry to tell you. I have more bad news."

I didn't have many people left. "Okay," I responded.

"Yeah, it's your dad, Eddie. He passed away yesterday. Also, we still haven't been able to reach your brother. We had someone stop by his house to check on him and the door was left open. When they walked inside, it didn't look like there was anything wrong except for the door being left open." Murray was monotone.

I wasn't surprised about my dad. The loss of his favorite son was probably the last straw. I wanted to ask whether he had been told about Paul to complete the picture of what I imagined happened, but how would that help? I decided to focus on my last surviving relative.

"So when you say the door was open, do you mean the door was unlocked, or do you mean the door was actually open?" I once again felt detached as if someone else was talking for me.

"Yeah, Eddie. Open, like not closed. Unlocked wouldn't have been as big of a red flag. We are working on getting his cell traced and should hopefully have something soon. Would you have told anyone about him living in Boca? His driver's license and public records still have him listed in Jersey. When we checked the Jersey property it was locked, and his mail was being held at the post office. It looks like no one has checked on that place in a while." I could hear her walking around, and it sounded like she had finally settled in a chair somewhere. Her breathing was labored.

I was feeling tired already and I had just started moving. "Nah, not that I know. I mean, he inherited that property from what I understand. Are you telling me he never stopped his payments on his place in New Jersey? I think he was renting there. I don't think he owned the place."

"Yeah, that's the way it looks," Murray said. "Hey, listen, Eddie. I will get back to you if I hear anything. Is that okay?"

She sounded a little irritated. It made sense since it was the middle of the night there. "All right, Murray, thanks for your help. I will see what I can do on my side. Wish me luck."

Agent Murray didn't wish me luck. She just hung up the phone. I'd have to feel sorry for myself on my own.

I ordered a light lunch in the hotel and picked up a free local paper before heading back to my room. I tried to pick up the flavor of the place. They used strange words like crores and lakhs to describe large sums of money. Then the sports pages were about cricket matches. I didn't understand a damn thing about overs and wickets, either. But other than that, English was English.

After a few hours, I dressed business casual and wandered out into the city for dinner. Other than our trips to the Caribbean, I had never been overseas and that was a long time ago. I needed to clear my head.

My hotel building and the nearby sightseeing historic spot Gateway of India were more than a hundred years old. But the surrounding area was very modern and cosmopolitan. Sure, there were women in saris, and tons of men on bikes, and strange, three-wheeling minicabs, but the big-city energy was everywhere. There were plenty of skyscrapers, everyone was walking and talking on cell phones, and the traffic was insane.

The pedestrians didn't give a shit about anyone driving through the streets. People would constantly just dart in front of the slow-moving cars or walk right beside them on the street. *Try that shit in Manhattan*, I thought to myself.

Yelp didn't work, but I was able to sort restaurants through Trip Advisor and the top-rated place nearby was a Japanese restaurant. I was lucky to get into the packed place. Walking the street, many were still wearing masks. I hadn't even thought about asking what the current COVID situation was here.

While enjoying the excellent food, I found myself looking around at the crowd. Watching the businessmen, groups of young women dressed up to go out on the town later, and of course, couples.

By 9:00 p.m. I was exhausted and looking at going to sleep. I was supposed to get a call the next day around eight in the morning with instructions for the day, most likely involving a flight to Malé.

I hadn't heard back from Murray, so I had to assume she didn't have an update about my brother, Steve. I should have been more upset about him, but he had been so flaky lately that I wasn't confident this had anything to do with the Centenos. The timing was bad but the last few times I had talked with him... I mean anything could be true.

My head hit the pillow and I was out.

The phone rang at 7:50 the next morning. It was a go. I was booked on a 3:00 p.m. flight. I lay in my bed until noon before packing and then walking outside to get lunch, not sure if I would ever be back in India again. This time I didn't use any service to tell me where to eat. I looked at a busy restaurant which had more locals than tourists and that is where I went.

My mouth was on fire, but the food was fantastic. I was hoping the gurgling in my stomach would stop before I got on the plane leaving for Malé but it didn't. I was pretty sure it wasn't just the curry. Probably also because from this point forward, I would be on my own.

The Maldives hadn't sanctioned Interpol to harass their citizens or visitors. The government had a healthy skepticism of imperialism and foreign overreach. And, of course, on the other hand it allowed some people with colorful and questionable backgrounds a place to spend their vast wealth. I am certain this is one of the reasons the presumably deceased O'Malley had chosen the place.

Right before boarding the plane, the Interpol agent who had

picked me up earlier handed me five hundred dollars for expenses. "Great," I said, pocketing the cash. "This won't even cover my funeral expenses."

He gave me a blank stare as I turned and entered the gate for departure.

We lifted off and banked south. I would be in Malé in two and a half hours.

VIGILANTE PRIEST X
Wrath

FATHER TONY

There were many things my friend Danny O'Malley had said, but this had been haunting me, "They should see that they abandoned their vows, their duty, their God. They should realize the pain they have caused. Not just to their victims, but to the entire church. You, Father Tony, have suffered for their sins. Christ's flock has suffered. The Holy See—it cowers and protects the evil in its ranks in order to protect itself."

I found myself defending the current pope and most of the Vatican in my response. "It isn't the entire Vatican. It isn't even the pope. This is being handled by a few powerful cardinals as well as the cowardice or blindness of the rest of us, including myself, that can sense the truth. We are all to blame."

O'Malley had been a bright, energetic speaker. Fueled by passion. By love for the church.

I had added, "If they die, we will be killers."

"No. We will leave them alive, but wounded. Just like they left their victims. And when they perish, they will face the same judgment we all face."

"Are you not worried about facing that same judgment?"

"My motives are pure and for the greater good."

His initial plan when he found out he was dying was to remove the stain from my name in New York and throughout the church, but this shamed me into telling him about the list of actual, proven pedophile priests. After that, he moved quickly, sharing his idea with his old friend, Accardi. He would fund everything and take the fall. Justice would be done. The priesthood was not a sanctuary for deviants who would pile sin upon sin with their betrayal of trust, of the Church, and the Holy Trinity. "Let no man do what these men have done. And let no man protect them!" he boomed when I asked complicated questions.

In the end, he came to me again. I was to be the key man. The lure and the cover. A Vatican priest touring America, what could be more innocuous?

The best-laid plans had been mislaid.

René rekindled our sense of survival. He was young; he was strong. And every one of us wanted to believe what he was selling: That we could escape our current situation without being killed or jailed for the rest of our lives. René hadn't arrived at the island empty handed. He had over three hundred thousand dollars in cash. He wasn't clear about how he had so much. In all likelihood he had stolen it from the family. With that amount of money, maybe we could retrofit our small boat to take us somewhere after our remaining prisoners were no longer alive. René also had the potential of finding the initial plan that my friend O'Malley put together for us and even get us access to the remaining money. I felt ashamed to be worrying about such things.

The first complication was that René had only rented his boat as a one-day rental since he thought we would leave as soon as possible. René believed he had turned off the transponder shortly after getting it and now he could scuttle the rental boat in open water. This would leave us with one remaining boat. That was not going to happen.

Hannigan's death had complicated things. We needed to find some of O'Malley's money and hopefully his exit plan if we had any chance of not getting arrested. We all had some cash remaining, but not enough to create new lives for all of us even if René shared his cash. Not to mention, no matter how little he liked it, we had to stay until the last priest had perished. René begrudgingly agreed, saying "I guess we will all share a cell together."

The first move, then, was to return René's boat. We weren't sure if the transponder was actually off or the boat could have another tracking device on it. We didn't need any additional complications.

Since, per René, everyone was on Interpol's radar except Miguel, Miguel returned René's boat. Barney, René, and Angel picked him up quickly and headed back to our island. Accardi wanted René nearby in case there was any complication with someone else returning the boat. Angel said he was coming along to catch up with his nephew, and Barney was there in case there were any complications with either boat. René had to see we didn't trust him.

While they were gone, Accardi again chastised me regarding getting close to the remaining priests, especially Father Julio.

"Father Tony," he said. "Building bonds with them is not making it any easier and is delaying the inevitable."

"I know," I said.

"These men, they deserve what they get. Don't you believe that?"

"I'm afraid that sometimes I am not sure," I admitted. "The

Bible takes great pains in teaching that only God should judge and not man."

"We are not judging them, Father. They are judging themselves. We have done our best to let their own evil spread among them. You befriending them is cruel."

"As a priest, I am taught to comfort, but I hear your words. I will try not to intercede any further."

The next day, Miguel returned to Malé alone and sought out Thaddeus to arrange some sort of schedule for weekly supplies. Barney had given him a description of the man who he believed had mistaken him for Liam weeks ago. René was surprisingly generous with covering the costs of things.

Barney was right and Miguel found Thaddeus. There were sourcing issues with our order. Miguel had to make a few trips. On his third trip, he returned looking grim.

Miguel had been approached by a local who knew who he was and handed him a letter. The letter was from the New York detective Eddie Rodriguez. All of us were upset, but René was somewhere between terrified and out of his mind with rage.

"I knew I should have killed that motherfucker. I had so many chances."He then looked over at all of us. "So this doesn't change anything?"

None of us responded.

"Does it?" he roared.

Angel went to put his hand on René's shoulder, and René quickly slapped it away.

Barney and Accardi both took a step back and went for their guns. Miguel started to go for his when René said, "Okay, okay. I am not going to do anything, you jumpy sons of bitches." René let out a forced laugh. "Just give me a moment."

"How about this? What if you ask them?" René looked at each of us.

"Ask them what?" Accardi shot back.

René said, "You know, ask them how they want it to go down. Their deaths, I am saying."

All of us looked at René, stunned.

René continued, "No, seriously. I mean, that's the point, right? They all have to go. All of you seem to be sympathetic to these fucking pedophiles. Or whatever you want to call them. My point is… my point is if I was them, I'd want an option. I mean, if they want to go sooner, let them. We could do it with guns. I think we have drugs in the medical station that could do the trick. My point is we give them the option."

Accardi stroked his chin. He had aged and grown a little wattle that he had begun tugging on recently. "Interesting."

Barney added, "Yeah, I agree. I mean, that's what I would want." With that, René smiled and put his hands up as if this were obvious.

Barney continued, "Would you be comfortable asking them, Father Tony?"

This was going to be on me. I had become the instrument of death. I felt myself pulled in two directions. The initial one was to honor O'Malley. To do what he set out to do. But I had always been uncomfortable with the torture aspect. Death was one thing. Suffering another. I looked at each man and surprised myself. "Okay. I will do it."

René looked around and smiled. "Okay, then you all head down there, and I will keep an eye on all of you from here in case you need anything."

None of us liked the sound of that.

Miguel said, "Well, I need to set up the boat if we are going to have it fitted for all of us to potentially leave this island, and I could use some help."

Barney chimed in, "Well, that falls under my expertise, I guess. I still don't know how we are all going to fit on the boat."

René smirked at that. "All right, you assholes. I get it. You still don't trust me."

With that, both Accardi and Angel protested, but René waved them off. "Listen, I get it. I can be a bit of a hothead. I will help Miguel unload supplies and organize the boat. It makes sense to get that much done tonight, but it's almost seven, and you haven't fed the priests yet, so I don't see why we would start retrofitting the boat at this time. We're better off doing it early tomorrow morning and only if you get all the priests to agree. Otherwise, we are just messing with the boat for no reason. Right?"

Barney said, "So you're saying you don't want me up here with you and Miggy to unload the boat?"

René breathed out, exasperated. "I am saying, Father Julio probably isn't that formidable, and unless Father James had some sort of remarkable recovery, he's not tough, either; however, the other two... I mean, one of them could get the jump on Accardi or Angel while Father Tony is talking to Julio or James.

"Father Tony is going to have to have a pretty direct conversation with all four of them. They might look at this as their final chance for escape. If you trust me less than them, I guess you should just have Father Tony go down there alone, and all of you stay up here, guns drawn." René finished, sounding more angry than sulky. We all went down, except for Miggy.

This was a mistake.

I was talking with Father Julio when the lights went out. He was the last one I spoke to. None of the others had taken the offer.

"René, quit fucking around!" Angel screamed at the closest camera, trying to get René to turn the lights back on.

I was frozen in fear. I reflexively grabbed Father Julio's hand. We were sitting on his bed next to his food.

I had been brutally honest. I told each man the same thing. That they had been chosen because of their vile actions. That O'Malley wanted them to be here until they died. Over time, something was going to happen: they could get injured, they could be killed by one of the others who had gone insane, or they could starve to death when we ran out of food. That was the plan. But now, O'Malley was dead, and there was a change of heart. We would kill them, however they wished to die. Or we would continue as things have been. Their choice.

Father Reece said, "God have mercy on your soul, Father Anthony."

I wasn't sure if Father James heard me. He hadn't eaten in the last couple of days. When I thought about it, I wasn't sure about the last time I had seen him awake. He lay there sleeping while I talked to him. He was not going to last much longer.

I could hear Barney, Accardi, and Angel yelling out in the corridor.

I released Father Julio's hand, telling him I would return.

Accardi and Centeno were banging on the door at the top of the spiral staircase. "What happened?" Barney asked.

"I think you know what happened," Accardi snapped.

"So what does that mean for Miggy?" Barney responded quietly.

"Aww… No. We shouldn't have left him up there alone with that psycho." Accardi breathed as he and the rest headed down the spiral staircase again.

I looked away. There were other emergency lights throughout, but we felt very vulnerable. All eight of us were trapped together, four of them, and four of us.

I started to wander slightly away seeing where the other emergency lights were, but not straying too far from the group when I heard Angel raise his voice: "Wait. Fuck you, Sandy. Did I miss a vote or something?"

"What? Do you think if *you* were planning things, this wouldn't have happened?"

"Maybe. And that's not even the point. The point is how come it is always you barking orders? We've been listening to you blindly the whole time, and look where it got us."

"What do you have in mind? Do you want to invite more of your family members to help? That seems to be working out."

"You know that wasn't on me, you son of a bitch."

Barney piped up, "Are you two kidding me? Come on. Keep it together. Let's look around."

Our nerves were affecting us, not to mention the priests, but everyone listened to Barney and it paid off.

We found a keypad that led to the area with the underground security cameras, food, and bedrooms for us.

"This is the answer," Barney said.

We all agreed and started entering different number combinations that we thought might relate to O'Malley. It was a standard-looking keypad with the letters written below the numbers but with *QZ* under the one. There was an asterisk and a number sign. We tried *omalley* with the keypad and then tried using the asterisk for the apostrophe in O'Malley. That didn't work. Without knowing how many digits there were in the code, this was nearly impossible. We did figure out that the pound sign acted as an enter for the code. But all we got was a three-red flash, never the green light we were hoping for. This was something else Hannigan had died with, the code to this area.

Which gave me a thought, however unhelpful. "Do you think René figured out a way to access O'Malley's bank account and possibly the exit plan?" *For the love of money is the root of all evil.*

I shouldn't have said that. Everyone looked at each other

angrily, but surprisingly, it was Accardi who couldn't keep his mouth shut, "What do you think, Angel?" he seethed.

The cells could only be locked electronically from the security station aboveground. Most likely there would be similar controls in the security room underground if we could figure out the code. Since we couldn't lock the cells, we didn't feel safe sleeping.

We stayed up for another six hours before needing to take a break. It was Barney's idea to have Accardi and Angel take the first break. We went to two of the empty adjoining cells, and I sat next to the bed while Angel slept, and Barney did the same for Accardi. It was doubtful the two old friends would do anything to the other but it wasn't worth the risk. They would each sleep for five hours.

I woke up to a gunshot. I must have fallen asleep and dropped my gun. Father Timothy must have snuck in and grabbed it. He had shot Angel. Angel was clutching his throat and gagging. The blood was oozing out in dark black in the low light.

Father Timothy had turned the gun on me, but instead of pulling the trigger, he put his finger over his mouth telling me to keep quiet.

Barney and Sandy were already turning toward our cell as Father Timothy opened fire on them. I covered my head with my arms, frozen. I think I saw Father Reece was in the room with Barney and Sandy, but I found myself covering my eyes in abject fear.

Almost immediately, I heard more gunfire, either Sandy, Barney, or both were firing back. The shots rang out for an endless amount of time. I felt a sharp pain in my left arm. I had been hit.

When the shots finally stopped, I slowly stood, not sure what to do next. Father Timothy and Sandy were dead. As I walked out of the room, I sliced my foot on a large piece of broken glass. I had on boat shoes and the glass cut me right through the right shoe. It was one of the broken bottles of Mahia which I thought we had cleaned up from before. Father Timothy and, as I would find out later from Father Julio and Father Reece, had hidden broken bottle pieces in the cells.

Barney was still alive. Sandy Accardi had been shot twice. The killing shot was to the head. Father Reece had hidden behind the massive Barney Fergusson and had been stabbing him in his back with broken glass as Barney had been shot three times in his torso. Barney, at some point, must have turned on Father Reece. By being surprised, he had forgotten about his gun and instead killed him with his bare hands.

I found myself detached, thinking that Father Timothy must have fired guns in the past. It would make sense with him growing up in West Virginia and ending up in Tennessee.

Barney was bleeding heavily and having a hard time talking. I had to sit down first to get the broken glass out of my foot and then could only move slowly, having to keep pressure on my bleeding left arm also. I walked past him as he looked at me sadly, but I would be no good to him unless I could stop the bleeding from my foot and arm.

I looked over and saw Father James still lying in bed. Father Julio had walked out of his room and immediately put his hands up when he saw me. I pointed at him and he went back into his room.

I grabbed two pillowcases from the two closest empty rooms and used them as bandages for both my foot and my arm. I was surprised that my arm had only been grazed. I was in tremendous pain.

By the time I had gotten back to Barney, he had slumped to the ground with his eyes closed. His breathing was shallow. There was nothing I could do for him.

I thought about taking off his Saint Christopher medal that I was

wearing and putting it around his neck, but I could not. I was terrified, and he was out of time.

Unless I figured out the code to the other rooms, the remaining
three of us were going to die down here: Father James, if he wasn't
dead already, Father Julio, and myself.

I went back to the box.

O'Malley was always deeply religious. I was hoping my answer
would lie there. We had discussed Romans at length. With Paul's
dispute with the false teachers and how there was a parallelism with
what we were doing, but every iteration I could think of wouldn't
work. I used an asterisk as an apostrophe in Romans, even though it
doesn't have one, I added the two years that were disputed when it
was written either 57 BC or 58 BC. I even entered years from the
Hebrew calendar to correspond, but then I had one last thought. The
phrase that he said to me before we agreed on starting all of this:
Romans 6:23. I typed in romans followed by 623, and the green
light came on. *For the wages of sin is death.*

Now at least we had access to the section with the additional
food and supplies while still being trapped underground.

Father James and Barney were dead, but I would keep Father
Julio alive as long as I could. There was no way for me to escape,
but at least I would be able to survive for months down here,
waiting to tell my tale, and more importantly, give my journal to
someone with all the details that I had shared with O'Malley so
long ago.

CHAPTER FORTY-SEVEN
The Art of Making Friends

EDDIE

My imagination of Malé was completely different from reality. I had expected pristine beaches with only local restaurants and few foreigners. But once I crossed the bridge, separating the airport from the main city, the first thing I saw was a Kentucky Fried Chicken. I laughed. My taxi driver asked what was so funny.

"Ah, nothing," I said. It was easier than explaining.

I noted that it wasn't just the Americans who had influenced the local culture but also the country that I had just left. The Indira Gandhi hospital showed that India held some sway here also.

The big thing missing here was the beach. From where I had picked up a cab at the airport, and as far as I could see, no beach. The whole island seemed surrounded by a rocky seawall which went right up to the highway with no way of entering the beautiful light blue water. Malé had more of a city feel than a resort atmosphere.

I got a text on my phone after settling into my room in Malé.

"Meeting is set for ten p.m., meet at the Queen's Lounge." I was surprised by how tired I was.

It was only 7:00 p.m., and the island wasn't that big. I figured I should get something light to eat, something familiar. I headed to the Kentucky Fried Chicken which was only a few blocks from the hotel.

Afterward, I walked to the Queen's Lounge from the KFC. The sun was down and it was a perfect evening. I walked past the lush landscape of Sultan's Park and a mosque, and then the capital building which was decorated similarly to the mosque. I had mixed views about this. I had a serious boyfriend whose Muslim family disowned him when he came out. So I wasn't a huge fan of fundamental religions of any type. But this seemed right. Since the Inquisition, the West, the Soviets, and the Far East had been invading Muslim countries and setting down rules for the locals to live by. It was nice to see the Malé people showing some cultural sovereignty in order to counteract America's fast-food franchises.

It was nine thirty when I arrived at the Queen's Lounge.

I was expecting a seedy bar, but the place had more of a night-club feel except darker and creepier. There were three things that were making me feel that way. The first was a definitive Muslim vibe. This made me feel Islamophobic and like a bit of an asshole.

The second thing was the décor. The whole place was red and black. I'm sure it was meant to look plush and formal, but it gave off more of a mob feel. I could easily envision a bunch of bosses sitting here smoking cigars and discussing business.

The final thing was that the place was too quiet. It might have been a weekday, but I thought Malé was a resort. *Where were all the drunken tourists?* The only ones at the bar were a couple of lonely, scantily clad women.

The hostess at the front desk gave me a big smile. It faded when I mentioned I had a reservation with Thaddeus.

She took me into the main section, a large room with a stage at the end. A short man who looked more like someone from Mumbai than Malé, stopped her, and they exchanged a few words. "I am Amir, the maître d'," he said. "Welcome to the Queen's Lounge."

"Thank you."

"We don't want any trouble, sir."

"What?"

"I mean no insult. It is just that we are a simple, peaceful business. We cannot be involved in anything." He was being deferential, too much so. *Who the fuck was this Thaddeus that I was meeting with?*

"That's great, because I'm involved in wanting a beer," I said. "Is Thaddeus waiting for me?"

"No, sir. Not yet. Let me show you to a private room." He wanted to get away. His forehead was glistening from sweat.

He led me up a flight of stairs, which opened onto a balcony overlooking the stage. Along the front wall were three doorways.

He opened the door to the last room, and I was surprised by the juxtaposition of the room to the expansive openness from where we came. This room couldn't have been more than fifteen feet square with no windows. There was a table with four seats crammed around it.

I sat down with the back of my seat having barely enough room for someone to get around me.

The maître d' didn't leave.

"Can you get me a Dos Equis and a water please?"

"I'm sorry, sir."

"Oh, sorry about that. Can you send in the waiter or waitress or server?" I wasn't even sure if I could order food here.

"Oh no, I would be happy to get you a drink; you want a beer, Kingfisher?" He was looking down.

I should stay sharp. "Just water please. Bottled preferably."

"Sure."

As I was sipping my Perrier, Thaddeus arrived.

The first thing I thought was that there was no fucking way this guy's real name was Thaddeus.

He was of average build and didn't look local. The Maldivians I had seen so far were very dark-skinned Asians. This guy was more Mediterranean, potentially Moroccan. He wore a thick gold chain and had the top four buttons undone on his Tommy Bahama-looking shirt.

"Happy to finally meet you, Eddie." His accent was thick, but beyond that I couldn't place it. When Thaddeus smiled, I saw a missing tooth on each side. One had been replaced by silver, the other by gold.

"Yep," I replied. I had no idea what to say to him.

"So, it doesn't look like your friend Miguel is coming back here anytime soon."

"That's too bad," I said. "Have you seen him?"

"Briefly. Last week. How did you end up coming to our fair island anyway, Monsieur Eddie?"

Having never been to a confidential-informant school, I wasn't sure what to say. Reflexively, I reached into my pocket for my phone, and Thaddeus sprang from his seat and grabbed my arm.

"Hey!"

"What are you doing?" I felt the moisture of his breath near my cheek, and I began to feel claustrophobic. No worries of COVID here. I was missing the safe-space rules that we had in the US.

"I'm checking my phone, if that is all right, Thaddeus."

He released my arm. "Sorry. A man in my position can't be too careful."

I frowned as I clicked the button on my cell phone bringing up the home screen. No signal. I should have guessed.

"For both of our protection." Thaddeus flashed his metallic

smile. "Please do not unlock your phone. It is best for both of us if this conversation is not recorded."

"Oh, is it?"

"I do not understand. I have been nothing but professional. You have to understand that I am putting myself in great jeopardy by even being involved with you and there is this"—he paused and almost spat out his next two words—"this distrust."

Just get me to the fucking island. "Listen, Thaddeus. I don't mean to offend you, but the very first thing you told me was that our whole plan is fucked."

"How do you mean 'fucked'?" Thaddeus had sat back down and now looked at me as if offended. I was having a hard time judging this B-rated Bond villain. *What the fuck had the FBI gotten me involved in?*

"I mean my friend. You know, Miguel. You were supposed to have him here so I could talk some sense into him and save him from whatever bullshit is going on."

Thaddeus nodded at this. "Yes, this is unfortunate." He paused before continuing. "I don't think things are going well on the island."

"You think?"

He ignored my sarcasm. "Yes, that is what I think. Miguel seemed like a good man. I could sense he was nervous." Again, he paused before continuing, "Like you."

"What, that I am a good man or that I am nervous?"

Thaddeus sat back deeply in his seat and sipped some clear liquid from a very interesting large, purple glass. It could have been vodka, Zima, or lighter fluid. Whatever it was, Thaddeus had been drinking it for a while because his face didn't change at all with the big swigs he ingested.

"You are funny. I imagine we could be friends."

"I'm not looking for friends, Thaddeus. I'm looking for Miguel."

"I thought he was your friend?"

"Touché. Yeah, he is. But you know what I mean. I'm here on business."

Thaddeus took another swig and let out a measured laugh. "We are on the same team here. I mean, what would your mother think of you talking like this to someone who is trying to assist you?"

"She's dead."

"Okay. Your father?"

"He's dead too."

"To your parents, then, Monsieur Eddie." With that, he raised his glass and finished off the remainder of his clear liquid.

"Listen. We have a job to do. Let's just get it done. I know that you are being compensated well for this, so let's not act like you are my pal." His eyebrow arched at this, so I decided to lean in, hoping to gain leverage. "I know more than you think. Do you think I would come here half cocked, not knowing what I was getting into?"

Thaddeus surprised me with his biggest smile yet. "I am impressed. I was worried what your reaction was going to be. You are so relaxed. I was told that this was going to be a surprise."

I reflexively pushed my seat back getting ready to stand. *What did he mean?*

Before I could move, Thaddeus had already pulled out his pistol and was pointing it at me. "I was told that this would be an awkward encounter, Monsieur Eddie. Like I said, I am impressed. I thought you were only being spoon-fed the smallest details from the police, but for you to have the resources to know what the Mafia in New York had planned for you also. Well, bravo."

Thaddeus had held a gun many times before. I could tell by his casual nature. However, I did see an opening. For some reason, he was holding it too loosely. I only had one shot at this, so I better make it count.

CHAPTER FORTY-EIGHT
Dead Man In Paradise

EDDIE

Thaddeus slowly backed up in his chair, then spoke once again, calm and measured. "You don't look right, Eddie."

He had backed far enough away that I couldn't reach the gun cleanly from a sitting position. I had missed my window. I would have to wait for another opportunity. It didn't appear as if he were done with me yet. If he was going to be chatty, I could use that to my advantage while I waited for another opportunity.

"Well, sorry, that's the way I look when someone is pointing a gun at me." I thought of my police training. Stay calm. No sudden moves.

"I understand you are worried. I would be if I was you, trust me, but what are you thinking? Don't lose your nerve now."

What the fuck? Things had taken a turn into the surreal. "What do you mean? Is it not loaded?"

"Of course it's loaded."

He then surprised me by turning the gun around and handing it to me with the barrel now facing him.

I took it and sat shocked.

I couldn't believe it. I pointed the gun at Thaddeus. "Okay, you made the right decision. Now, stand up and open the door. I will call Interpol, and we will get this all sorted out. I promise to be very positive in my report to them. You are right, you have been nothing but pro—"

I stopped mid-sentence at the broad smile on Thaddeus's face. Obviously, he wouldn't hand me a loaded gun.

I hadn't noticed until he handed it to me, the gun was a Glock 19 very similar to the one that I used on the force. It was a slightly older model but still something I was very comfortable with. Why the smile? Was the gun filled with blanks? I couldn't risk popping the clip to see. I pointed it to the ceiling thinking of pulling the trigger to check.

"Hey! What are you doing?" Thaddeus panicked.

"Don't worry, I am not going to deafen us both by shooting a blank into the ceiling." I assured him.

"Blanks? There are no blanks."

"Wait. What?"

"Listen, Eddie. I don't understand," Thaddeus almost whispered. "You are making this more difficult than it needs to be."

I had to figure out an exit. Based on my conversation with the Indian guy who I assumed was management, I didn't think the staff was going to support Thaddeus, and the local police would not want to get involved in shooting a civilian for this scumbag. I would just have to stay in control until the local police arrived.

"Yeah, real sorry I didn't say just kill me. The last thing I'd want to do is make you look bad in front of your mob friends. I mean, seriously, what did you expect me to do when you handed me the gun?"

With that, Thaddeus's demeanor completely changed. He now looked utterly confused. "What?"

I repeated, "What?"

He then looked at me with his hands spread wide. "Do you think the Mafia wanted me to kill you?"

Was he trying to play some sort of mind game on me? "Yeah, that's why you were pointing a gun at me."

Thaddeus was flustered now. "Pointing? Well, yes, but... didn't you tell me you knew what I was going to say to you?"

Hold on. "No, I think I said I knew more than you thought I did."

Thaddeus got comfortable in his seat again. "Put that down for a moment." He pointed to the gun.

I kept the gun ready but slid it and my right hand below the table.

Thaddeus continued, "I don't think you understand. My Mafia friends, as you call them, wanted to let you know that you have a green light."

"A green—" I didn't finish. "Go on."

Thaddeus smiled. "Yes, a green light. They can't officially sanction the killing of a Centeno, but they wouldn't mind if you or I took care of one. There won't be any repercussions from them, if you take out Centeno or anyone else remaining on that island at this point."

"Got it. So the New York Mafia has had enough of the Centenos and anyone connected to them?"

"All of your problems are with them, yes? Not with the rest of the families?"

I thought for a moment and nodded. With everything going on with the cops and the mayor's office and the Vatican, I could see how this made sense. The Centenos were bad news.

Thaddeus continued, "They don't want any blood on their

hands, but if you prune a few branches that might make their life easier. In return, they will do their best to back your story with the authorities and make sure you are protected.

"The plan, Eddie, is for you to look on the ground after you get twenty to thirty meters into the island. They want you to act like you find it on the ground. The gun is clean and untraceable."

"Okay, will do. I doubt that a satellite would be able to pick up me doing this and... wait, if they have satellites that strong, and if they can check on me in real time, then why don't they just use the satellites to see the bad guys doing stuff to the priests and arrest everyone?" Like I said, this plan had been written on the back of a napkin.

"Satellites?" Thaddeus shook his head. "No. Drones, not satellites. There's no way they could track them well enough through the tree cover. The agents are going to be parked offshore around five kilometers or so. Since this isn't being sanctioned by the Maldives government, it's a very small operation." He then looked me in the eyes. "I thought you said you knew more than I thought?"

I wondered who the hell Thaddeus was. *Interpol? Maldives secret agent?* I had no clue.

"I think I might owe you an apology," I said.

"Never apologize in this business, Eddie!"

"I didn't."

———

Thaddeus picked me up at my hotel at nine the next morning, and we drove to a small dock. Thaddeus led me to a sparkling new Yamaha speedboat, *The Big Mirage*.

"Yours?" I asked.

"A friend's. Nine hundred horsepower."

The number was meaningless to me, but it sounded like a lot. I whistled, like I was impressed. I stored my backpack in a side cabinet. Inside, I had the 9mm Thaddeus had given me, a change of clothes, toothbrush, passport, and two liters of water.

Thaddeus punched some coordinates into the GPS, and captained us out of the port. But once we were two hundred yards out, he got a call. He motioned me to take the wheel, pointed at the dashboard screen, and moved to a seat in back. I didn't understand how he could talk over the three roaring outboard motors, but he was yelling in what sounded like French.

Watching him from the captain's seat, heading southeast, I realized how much I would have hated him if I didn't like him so much; some scumbag who could be hired by the highest bidder to do whatever dirty work was necessary in some forgotten end of the world. I mean, compared to this asshole I was Dudley Do-Right.

This guy is out openly working with the mob, and I get fired because of the appearance of some shit. *Unbelievable.*

He tried talking to me over the roar of the motors, but it was too annoying. From the way it sounded, we would be able to talk when we got to the relay point.

He had switched from drinking his clear liquid from the purple glass to straight out of the bottle. He had brought four bottles and placed them in a cooler next to him. It seemed like a lot. He had offered me some before we had untied the boat and headed out on the open sea. I had declined but was now regretting it, thinking that I was approaching certain death in a couple of hours.

We reached the relay point without any interruptions. There was a smaller boat there waiting for us, and we pulled up next to it. *It must have supplies for our incursion onto the island.* We had spotted only one other boat in the last hour.

"Okay, okay," Thaddeus barked into the phone before hanging up and turning his attention to me.

He resumed the conversation we were having before we left Malé. "I still can't believe you thought your friend Miggy was taking some sort of plane to see me." His voice had become slurred. The clear liquid finally having an effect. "I mean, you would have to have someone clearing logs and making sure the air traffic control was paid. No, my friend, that is not what you would do."

"It's great to be learning all this from such a successful international criminal."

There was something oddly relaxing about being around Thaddeus. I couldn't place my finger on it. He gave off an aura. It made you feel like everything was going to be all right.

"No, no, my friend. You are wrong on all counts." Thaddeus looked over the expansive empty sea and smiled broadly, breathing in the air before continuing, "I wouldn't say successful. I get by. As for international, ha! You can't do what I do and be international. You have to be, how would you say, the big fish in the small bowl to be successful. You need to have contacts and backup plans. You can't do that if you are bouncing around from country to country."

With that, Thaddeus finished off one of the bottles of clear liquid, then tossed the empty bottle into the ocean. I frowned as I watched it float.

With that, he laughed and continued. "As for criminal, what does that even mean—'criminal'? I don't hurt anyone unless it is absolutely necessary. I'm an intermediary. A go-between. A fixer. And I don't support anything where innocents are being hurt."

I wanted to believe him.

"What about the priests?"

"What do you mean by 'priests'?"

"You don't watch the news much, do you?"

After saying this, I hadn't seen an update on any of the local TVs which were mostly on BBC for news.

Was it possible he didn't know? Maybe he was telling the truth. He was just a day-jobber for Interpol. Or was it the New York mob he was working for? Regardless, to not have someone from Interpol protecting me and instead just using a contractor, I knew what that meant. This operation was intentionally being kept small. Small enough where if anything went wrong, it could be dismissed. As for me, I would just be written off.

He was confused but laughed. He then reached into his cooler and grabbed what appeared to be one of the last two bottles of clear booze. He must have tossed one of the empty bottles overboard when I wasn't paying attention.

He loosened the cap and I reached for the bottle, "You mind if I have some of that?"

Jesus, if he drank from that bottle first and I took a swig after him, COVID would be the least of my worries.

He frowned and said, "You sure?"

"Yeah, if you don't mind."

He sighed and tossed me the bottle. Luckily, I caught it, surprised he would throw the bottle containing the precious fluid and risk it being smashed.

I took a big swig. My mouth and throat burned. It tasted like rotten bananas mixed with cheap tequila.

"What the hell is that?" I winced, moving my tongue around trying to get rid of some of the taste.

"Mahia," Thaddeus said proudly.

"Well, thanks for warning me."

"Hey, no one has taken care of you better than your friend Thaddeus. Do you think the Mafia cares if you live or die, or your friends at Interpol... What about them?"

"What about them?"

Thaddeus shook his head. "Sending you to that island alone with nothing but your penis exposed?"

There was a lot wrong with that sentence. "Penis exposed? You mean nothing but my dick in my hand?"

"Yes. Whatever. My point is the same. What kind of plan is this?"

"Yeah," I breathed. "Wait, what do you mean alone?"

"Sorry, my friend. I was told to bring you here. This is a one-man job."

CHAPTER FORTY-NINE
Sheep To The Slaughter

EDDIE

We transferred to the waiting boat, and Thaddeus explained the basics of it to me and how he had gotten it from Hannigan before selling it to Interpol. Hannigan had given it to Thaddeus to bring supplies and medical help to the island when O'Malley had gotten too sick to be left alone. I'm sure Thaddeus, the slippery son of a bitch, sold the boat to them for a fortune. He even went as far as telling them that the two boats, the one he got from Hannigan and the one remaining on the island, were identical.

Interpol decided to use this boat so that if someone spotted me, they would hopefully just think it was Thaddeus. However, they didn't explain how I would be any less fucked if they thought I was Thaddeus and then figured out it was their favorite ex-cop.

Anyway, they had looked the boat over and were surprised that there were no electronics. They figured the only reason that would be, is because Centeno and friends didn't want to get snagged out in the open water once they ditched the island. A boat without electronics would be off the grid. Interpol also thought while on the island, they could be monitoring boat traffic. O'Malley definitely had the type of cash that could have bought that type of equipment.

It seemed simple enough. After I pulled up the anchor, I wouldn't have to worry about it again. The plan was for me to be guided in by Interpol and just drive the boat up as close as I could to the island. Once the boat got stuck in the sand, it would no longer be my responsibility. They would pick me up from the island regardless of how things went down.

Interpol was keeping track of the people on land and would try to place me away from them. Once Thaddeus left, I was going to get additional, hopefully better, instructions.

"Hey, Eddie. Hide the gun now. Put it in the back of your pants," Thaddeus said quickly after getting done showing me the basic boat controls.

I quickly grabbed the gun out of the backpack and put it in the back of my pants, making sure the safety was on beforehand.

As I was getting ready to ask why, I saw Thaddeus turn away toward his boat and wave into the sky. I couldn't see it, but he must be waving to one of the drones he talked about earlier.

On cue, his phone vibrated and he picked up.

"Okay, okay," he barked.

He popped open a white panel for storage below the wheel of the boat and took out what looked like a fancy waterproof walkie-talkie with a clear cord, earpiece, and mic.

After handing it to me, he said, "Don't put it in yet. Once you talk to whoever is on the other line, I can't talk to you again."

"Are you good?" He nodded firmly to me as I shrugged in response.

Thaddeus laughed at that and got back on his boat.

"I wish you well, my friend." Thaddeus smiled and started the engines.

Then before leaving, he reached into his cooler and tossed me the bottle of clear liquid, leaving him with only one remaining. "For you, my friend."

This time I was not as lucky, and the bottle shattered against the far wall of my small boat.

I frowned and he frowned back.

With that, Thaddeus left my life presumably forever.

My nerves had been frayed, but now I was practically shaking. There was no way out of this now, so I took a deep breath, then put in the two-way earpiece and attached the clear mic to the top of my T-shirt. I then tucked the line under my shirt and put the dark black, cell phone-sized device in the back pocket of my pants. I stared at the knob for a moment and then clicked it on.

"Hello," I said out into the void.

I got a quick response. "Hello, Eddie. This is Agent Jones. Can you hear me?"

I laughed, responding to the clear Indian accent. I couldn't hide from my emotions at this point. I was so nervous I could feel my heart pounding.

After not hearing anything else, I said, "Yes."

"Good. Start the boat and steer to heading two hundred and seventy degrees. You can tell what direction you are pointing by the white bubble. Do you see it?"

"Okay, got it." My knees felt weak, standing, but I was too nervous to sit.

"Very good, Eddie. Speed the boat up to twenty knots but no quicker. We have a lot to discuss before you get there.

Most of what was discussed was how I was going to approach the island and get around once on land. My responses were short.

"Relax, Eddie. We haven't seen any movement on the island since the drones went active."

"That's reassuring," I said. "I think."

"It should be. I'm watching you now. You just scratched your ear, and you seem to be kneeling."

"I guess I crouched down when the island came into view."

"All right, see that thin stretch of sand near the tree line?" Agent Jones was guiding me in.

"Yes. How about the drones? Do you see anything?"

"Like I said, we haven't seen any movement since we started monitoring the island."

"If the island is abandoned, why not just send some locals to check it out rather than me? I mean, I know the Maldives government isn't really cooperating, but…"

"Like whom?"

This irritated me, not sure if it was the cold, impersonal use of proper English that pissed me off or because there were lots of options that didn't involve flying me from New York City to the far edge of the world.

"Well, Thaddeus, for starters."

"You need to slow down."

"What?"

"The boat. The boat!"

"Fuck!"

I decelerated, but the high tide kept the boat moving forward.

"Turn parallel to the shore, Eddie! You're doing fine."

"That's nice of you to say. Oh shit!"

I heard the sandpaper-dragging sound of the boat hitting bottom.

"Was this part of the plan?" I asked out into a void with no response.

"Hello!" I panicked.

"Yes. Yes. All is good, Eddie. Walk in, stay low, and hit the tree line."

My waterproof Panama Jacks weren't going to do me much good in knee-high water. As I sloshed toward land, I checked the low center of my back for the gun. I wasn't sure if I wanted someone to be on the island, like Centeno, or if I just wanted it to be empty. I felt exposed.

No doubt the dense knot of trees and bushes posed a problem for drones. But for humans, it was no big deal. The copse of palms went on for about one hundred feet. There was crabgrass and thorny bushes, but Central Park had denser foliage in some areas.

I could see through to a group of buildings. There was something that looked like a shed to the right, a medium-sized building about the size of two mobile homes straight ahead, and then a larger building to the far left.

I relayed the buildings to Agent Jones and then asked, "What do you want me to do?"

"Slowly walk with your hands high in the air but not too slowly, at a measured pace toward the smallest building. If anyone sees you, make sure you show them that your hands are empty and let them know you are here to see Miggy and you want to help. That should buy you time."

"I don't like that plan. These fuckers want to kill me."

"We've gamed it out, Eddie. It's what we do. Trust me. Head toward the building to the right. And lower your voice. I can hear you fine."

There was no way I was going to walk around with my hands up. My right hand had been playing around my lower back with the top of my Glock like a security blanket. I pulled it out, flicked off the safety and held it close to my thigh.

I stepped into the breach, moving quietly, my eyes darting everywhere.

"There is a camera pointed at the door to that building. I can see it hidden in a palm tree about forty feet from the entrance."

"Go to the door but knock first."

"Knock? Are you serious?"

There was no response.

"Fine. If they shoot and kill me will you be shortly behind?" I could feel the bile in my throat.

I walked to the door and noticed the mechanism was a little fancier than I expected. "It looks like it is locked. There is a small red light on the top of the keypad."

"Okay," Agent Jones responded.

I was about to knock when Agent Jones interrupted, "Wait! Don't knock. Go to the smaller of the two remaining buildings and see if the light is red or green on that door."

I would have to walk through a rather open stretch to get there. "All right, keep an eye on me." I moved quickly. The Glock was getting slippery in my hand. I switched it to my left hand, drying my right hand on my shirt.

"It's a green light."

"Okay, then knock."

I knocked and counted to fifteen, noting another camera built in at an angle right above the left side of the door. There was no easy way to push the door open and get to the side before someone could open fire.

I surprisingly felt a strange calm. "Okay, should I go in?"

"Give it a few more seconds," Agent Jones stated. He was clearly muting me now and then.

After what felt like ages, Agent Jones responded, "Okay. Go in."

CHAPTER FIFTY
Righteous Kill?

EDDIE

The smell was overwhelming as I opened up the door. The corpse had been there for weeks it seemed. I saw the black stain on the floor and another black stain on the wall behind me. To the right was a bank of monitors that were still active. I didn't see any movement on the monitors, as they cycled through different cameras every few seconds. I knew the right thing to do was to look at them to see what I could find, but I couldn't help but spin back toward the body.

The size was right. The body was only partially lying on its side. I gently pushed it over on its back with my foot. It was definitely him. Someone had killed my friend Miguel.

I ran out of the building and got sick outside.

"Eddie! Eddie? Have you been shot? You okay?"

"Yeah. It's Miguel. He's dead," I breathed. "Give me a second."

I looked out at the clean, newly built concrete buildings and the view of the trees and the water. Someone put a bullet in Miggy's head. And whoever did it was probably here.

"Are you sure it's a dead body?" Agent Jones said.

"Yes, I am certain," I replied, still trying to get grounded.

There was a long pause and then, "Eddie, how are you?"

I headed back into the building and scanned the monitors. I didn't see anything for a moment, and then I finally focused. There were so many dead bodies lying around. It was devastating to see. Then I noticed what appeared to be the last surviving captive who was dressed in priest garb. He was moving from room to room around the dead. "Dear God," I said out loud.

"Eddie?"

"I'm looking at a bank of security cameras. There's a priest who's still alive. It looks like everyone else is dead."

"Okay, Eddie we have enough, we are coming to get you."

I quickly looked at the system. The computer screen had fairly easy-to-follow instructions. It looked like only one building was locked down. There was no natural light coming through to the cameras that were cycling. Based on the size and lack of windows, I clicked the switch that was connected to what I thought was a shed when I saw it earlier. The light turned from red to green. This was no shed; this was an underground bunker.

I ran back outside now, heading for the shed bunker.

I could feel the beating in my head from the adrenaline.

The voice in the earpiece wouldn't stop talking: "Eddie. I am telling you to stand down. We won't be able to talk to you if you go underground."

I had been played. "Are you telling me you knew they were underground all this time?"

Agent Jones responded coolly, "Well, of course. Why else would we need someone to go on the island?

"We will be arriving shortly."

I ripped the earpiece out.

I opened up the door to the bunker and stepped to the spiral staircase leading down.

I was surprised to hear two voices talking in a foreign language. By the time I reached the bottom, I heard "Arrepentido" and then the crack of a gunshot.

I had an angle on the shooter in the cell standing above the body. I fired three quick shots, hoping it was a Centeno. But when my target slumped to the floor, I realized that wasn't the case.

"Who are you?" I yelled as he looked at me with fading eyes.

He was stunned but finally said, "Father Julio."

I had killed the last surviving priest.

He surprised me by trying to stand.

"Hold on. Hold on," I implored.

I then ran upstairs, putting the headset in my ear.

"Agent Jones?" I said out into the void.

Agent Jones was frantic. "What did you do? What happened? Why did you remove your earpiece?"

"It's over, Agent Jones," I whispered back. *I had managed to kill the sole survivor.* I couldn't let anyone know this. "This is it. I looked around and they are all dead."

I ran back down to be with Father Julio. He was fading. There were tears pooling in his eyes.

"I have a confession," he said.

"Okay," I said, holding his hand, waiting to hear about his behavior with his young congregants.

"I am not Father Julio," he breathed out.

I released his hand and studied his face. I didn't recognize it unless...

"I am Father Anthony. Father Tony. The Vatican priest," he blurted out. "I am the one who started all of this."

"What?"

"This act. What we did corrupted all of us. My last act until now was thinking of myself. I killed Father Julio. I killed him thinking I would be able to take his place and go free. That was never part of the plan. I have failed."

At this point, he moved his hand slowly to his neck and pulled out the medal he was wearing. It was a medal of Saint Christopher. My father had worn one like it which he had gotten from his father when he had left Cuba.

"Just relax. Someone will be here soon." I stared at him. This was all on him.

He started to close his eyes and then they opened wide. "No, no, I need you to do something for me."

He coughed from the exertion but continued, "My journal. My journal has everything. Get it from my room in the big building." The big building which I hadn't visited yet.

"Okay, okay, I will get it."

"Go now!" Father Tony roared, blood spilling from his mouth in clumps. "There are too many who don't want to know the truth, but the world needs to know, or all of this was for—"

With that, Father Tony slumped lifeless to the ground.

When I came back aboveground, Agent Jones was once again frantic. "Eddie, stop moving around. We need you to stay put. There still might be other dangers."

"Copy that," I said. *What could possibly be in that journal? I had to see it.*

"Hey, unfortunately, I have to go to the bathroom, Agent Jones."

"Fine. We will have eyes on you. Just go and then come back. And leave your mic on. Head into the palm trees where you arrived and then come back into the center of the three buildings."

"Yeah, that's not going to work, not that type of bathroom," I shot back.

He then said something that sounded like "God He," or maybe "Gandhi," before, "Listen. I need you to stay put."

"Yeah, that's not going to work for me."

"Well, it is going to have to, Mr. Rodriguez. Wait until we arrive, and you can take as much time as you need. Once the island is clear, we can escort you to a facility," Agent Jones said firmly.

"Nope, not going to wait," I replied and then pulled out my earpiece again.

When I got to the entrance to the main building, I put my hand back on the Glock. Maybe there was a Centeno remaining; regardless, I needed to be cautious.

The place was filled with bugs and the smell of rotting food. Clearly, no one had been in here for a long time. I kept a wide arc from the kitchen and made my way to a series of rooms. There was only one with a priest's garb in it, so I marched in and opened the drawer of his nightstand and there it was, his journal.

This was it. It had dates and names; even cardinals and bishops were listed. Most of the priests were in the United States, but this problem was global. As Father Tony wrote, the sinners had been protected and often moved. But there had been no justice, and without justice and fear of justice, the Church remained damaged and vulnerable to more cycles of sin. They had covered it up for years, and while the incidents had all but stopped in the last couple of decades, that didn't make up for the cover-ups in the past and all the families who never got justice.

Father Tony wasn't complicit. It said right on the first page that he was falsely accused, but regardless, the old theory that I had discussed with Agent Murray months ago looked to be true. He was out to undo the past crimes of his Church. He was a vigilante priest.

I rubbed my prints off Thaddeus's Glock and tossed it on Father Tony's bed. I was going to have to hide something new in the back of my pants. The Moleskine-sized journal was a perfect fit.

On my way outside, I had an idea. I walked through the fetid kitchen trying not to look at the bugs or the rotting food. I wanted to be sitting in the sand with a six-pack of beer when Agent Jones arrived. All I could find was an unopened bottle of Mahia. The same poison Thaddeus had given me on the boat. I grabbed it and twisted off the screw-top.

When I got back to the center area, I put my earpiece back in.

"I'm back," I said. "Sorry about that call of nature."

"If you move before we get there, you will be jailed for interfering with an active Interpol crime scene. Do you hear me?"

"I do."

"What were you doing in there? What did you find?"

I thought for a second. "Two-ply toilet paper. Pretty good."

There was no response.

"And I needed a drink, so I found a bottle of Mahia." I held the bottle high in the air.

To finish the act, I gulped two swigs as loud as I could, one for Agent Murray who had gotten me into this mess and one for Thaddeus who had introduced me to this poison. Then I quietly spilled out half the bottle, and loudly I collapsed onto my back as if I were sunbathing on the beach.

I waited for Interpol to arrive.

CHAPTER FIFTY-ONE
Eddie Rodriguez

EDDIE

Twenty armed men in khaki pants and shirts and blue berets swarmed the island.

Agent Jones and a fellow officer stood over me.

I took another large swig of Mahia, wanting to play up my shot nerves to hopefully limit his questioning.

"Stand up and turn around," he said.

I could feel the sweat pooling around my lower back causing the leather of the vigilante priest's journal to stick to me.

I completed a full circle, hoping my shirt provided cover.

From where I was standing I could see a team of the Interpol agents with forensic kits, body bags, and moving boxes. They were dragging out the computer equipment onto the sand. Once in the open space, another team started to strip down the computers and remove the hard drives.

Agent Jones turned around and yelled, "Agent Sharma, come here! Bring your wand."

"What the hell is all this? I did my part. What else do you want from me?"

Agent Jones ignored me. He reached up and removed my earpiece.

"The transponder."

I retrieved it from my pocket and handed it to him.

I turned my head to the underground compound and saw they were bringing out bodies.

"So, I saw that my friend Miggy was dead."

"Oh, Mr. Juarez."

"Yeah, *Officer* Juarez," I spat back. "What about the rest? Did you find the Centenos and Accardi?"

No response. He turned to talk to an agent carrying a black medical bag.

It looked like they were erasing the hard drives. Someone had been paid off.

"Scan him," Agent Jones barked at Agent Sharma in his khaki uniform.

Agent Sharma waved the security wand across my front and sides and then asked me to turn around.

As he was scanning me, now from behind, I roared at Agent Jones, "Hey, Jones! You owe me! I come here as a civilian to do your job. You can at least tell me whether or not the Centenos, Fergusson, and Accardi are alive or dead, right?"

Jones ignored me, but Sharma called out, "He's clean."

Jones approached. "Good. I can't answer your questions, Mr. Rodriguez, as this is an ongoing investigation. However, we greatly appreciate your service and courage."

What a prick.

Then he asked Agent Sharma to give us a minute.

He waited for Sharma to depart, and said, "I'll confirm it when I get back to Malé. This place is a mess. But it looks like we found the retired cops."

454

"No, Renato?" I asked. "He's younger than me."

With that, Agent Jones's eyes narrowed. "No, why? Did you spot him? Do you know if he is here somewhere?"

I shrugged and shook my head no.

Thankfully, Agent Sharma then asked me to follow him to a boat to be taken off the island.

I grabbed my bottle of Mahia. I was getting a taste for it or maybe it was just settling my nerves.

When I got to Malé, I was quickly taken by two Interpol agents for a late dinner of fresh seafood. It might have been the best food I had ever eaten. Or maybe being alive can activate your taste buds. I never removed the journal from my lower back. I planned to keep it there until I was on the plane back to New York. After coffee and dessert, I was taken back to my hotel room and asked to stay put for the evening. I was flying to India tomorrow morning and then back to New York City.

A few minutes after the Interpol agents left me, I received a call.

"Congratulations, Eddie. I hear you acquitted yourself well," Agent Murray said.

"Come on, Amanda. Acquitted myself? You can do better than that." I laughed at her.

"I'll do better when you are back here."

Not sure if I was just overwhelmed, but I found myself getting emotional. "Hey, I'm serious, Agent Murray. No matter what you think of me, I have all the respect in the world for you. You are important to me. I haven't met anyone like you before. You are a good person, and I wish I could be more like you. I consider you a friend." I felt my eyes watering.

There was a short pause before she said, "You also, Eddie." She paused again. The "you also" could have been a response to any of several things I had said to her. "Be careful. I look forward to seeing you when you return."

The phone clicked and I frowned. I rubbed the moisture from my eyes and leaned back on my hotel bed.

Staring at me on the small table in my room was the almost empty bottle of Mahia. It was still relatively early, around 9:00 p.m.

I kept nipping at the bottle until I decided to go out. I was surprised, but not unhappy, to recognize one of the dockhands I had seen when I was with Thaddeus. I took it as a sign to see my friend one last time before I left his life forever. The dockhand made a quick call and set things up. I arrived at the Queen's Lounge at nine thirty. The journal was now sticking firmly to my lower back.

I asked the short Indian man if Thaddeus was there.

"He just got here! You have excellent timing."

"Eddie, my friend." Thaddeus smiled, but not brightly enough to reveal his metal teeth. "This is a surprise."

"I thought we each deserved a celebratory drink."

"Mahia?"

"Sure."

With that, Thaddeus smiled broadly back at me and waved the man away dismissively.

Thaddeus grabbed me a clean glass from a cabinet I hadn't noticed before and filled it to the rim. In the cabinet was also a stash of a couple more bottles of Mahia. Thaddeus obviously used this room frequently.

"I was told to talk with you." Thaddeus looked at me seriously. "You know, before you left."

As I took a sip of the Mahia, I tried to gauge Thaddeus. He was too slippery for me.

"Okay," I laughed.

"I was going to tell them you were too well-guarded by our police friends for me to talk with you." Thaddeus smiled thinly.

"Okay. I thought you would be happy to see me, you fucking pirate," I laughed.

"You have me mislabeled, my friend. I'm just a simple businessman. And speaking of business, did you bring my gun back?"

"Nah, unfortunately, I had to ditch it on the island."

He nodded and took a large swig. "Collateral damage, I guess. So, everyone was dead, huh?"

I didn't say anything. Spooked that he knew way more than he should... as usual.

He wouldn't speak until I answered. "Yeah, I guess so."

"What about Renato?"

I paused for a moment. "No, not him."

"You are getting good at this, Eddie." Thaddeus now smiled widely, revealing both of his shiny teeth.

"I took care of him earlier." Thaddeus held his glass up.

I clicked it and said, "You what?"

"Before you even met me, my friend. Remember, you were not the only one given a green light on Centenos. I was told not to let you know. My New York associates wanted you to remain, let's say... motivated."

He opened an app on his phone. "Look," he said.

René Centeno lay crumpled on the floor in a pool of blood.

"Good," I said, but the transactional nature of the killing made me uncomfortable.

"I shot him on his boat, sailed out, and gave him a burial at sea."

"I can put in a word with our friends back home, and make sure you are compensated for the dirty work on the island," Thaddeus continued

My discomfort was making me angry. "Thaddeus, you have no

idea. I was the first one to flag the whole thing! That fucker killed people to try and silence me."

"Breathe, Eddie. You are here. You survived! Now go and be a returning hero."

Thaddeus sat back in his seat. "It's good, eh?"

I looked at the clear liquid in my glass. It was. "Aye," I said back.

"To you, my fellow pirate," he said, standing. This was my cue to leave. He obviously had other plans.

I raised my glass to him and stood up, getting ready to exit.

The journal had dug itself deep into my lower back at this point and was becoming quite uncomfortable.

I pulled it from the back of my pants and started heading toward the door.

"What's that? A Bible?"

"Oh, nothing," I said. Then I reconsidered. "You might get a kick out of this."

Thaddeus quickly looked it over, his eyes wide.

"I know, right?" I said proudly. "The whole operation, the book of sinners."

Thaddeus paged through the book, scanning just like I had when I found it.

"Sit back down."

Shit. *The businessman in front of me had glimpsed a new opportunity.* He paused from his reading and banged out a text. *I guess his phone did work in this room.*

"I didn't expect you to start reading chapter and verse, Thaddeus." I reached out to take the book but he pulled it back.

"Relax, Eddie," Thaddeus said, taking a sip of his Mahia, then offering to fill my glass. "Just give me a moment."

I tried to open the door and realized it was locked. "Quit fucking around, Thaddeus."

Thaddeus's phone buzzed and he looked down at the screen.

Suddenly, he stood up and whipped his gun out from the back of his pants, pointing it at me.

"Eddie, Eddie!" Thaddeus was practically crying. "Why didn't you just leave when you should have? Why did you do this to yourself... and to me?"

We had done this dance before, but it felt different this time. There was no misunderstanding here.

I tried to remain calm. "Hey, Thad, listen. I don't have any interest in any of this. I could care less if—"

The two shots to my chest from his gun stopped me from continuing. I hadn't noticed the silencer until now.

I was in shock, but the pain was coming.

"I'm sorry, Eddie." I looked into Thaddeus's eyes and saw the sadness.

The next shot to my head stopped the pain.

CHAPTER FIFTY-TWO
Damage Control

INTERIM MAYOR ANTONIO LOPEZ looked down at the cards that his press secretary had put together for him and continued reading, "Without the tireless efforts of our own New York Police Department and the Federal Bureau of Investigation, especially the local New York division, we would not have been able to root out the corruption among not only both of their organizations, but also throughout our own government.

"It is an important reminder that we must always be vigilant. Those in government and law enforcement are held to the highest level of responsibility. We are here to protect and serve. It is incumbent on us to act decisively when we find anyone who is not living up to the high standards necessary to allow that level of trust."

The mayor looked over at the head of the FBI, who gave him a nod and a smile. The FBI head, John Matthews, was flanked by the regional head, Robert Nguyen, and two of the agents who had been working the case.

With that, the mayor turned back to the crowd. "This has been a difficult time for our city and our country. No one is above the law. Whether you are a wealthy family from Wall Street, like the O'Malleys, or a wealthy family working with our public sector, like the Centenos, you are not above the law. If you are law enforcement, like former officers Accardi or Juarez, you are not above the law. Even if you are the mayor of our great city, you are not above the law."

He then looked over at a three-by-five card with a list of reporter's names and their publication or network next to them. "I will now open the forum for questions."

He started with a local. "Jerry?"

"Jerry Weinberg, *New York Post*, can you give us an update on Antwan Martin, the unarmed teen who was shot by a cop last night?"

"We would like to keep any questions today within the scope of this case."

"Are you serious?"

"Yes. Next question. Charlie Tucker?" Mayor Lopez responded, choosing a national network.

"Charlie Tucker from CNN. Are we supposed to believe that the Centeno family acted alone on this? Without the blessing of Don Abatantuono? Also, there has been a serious lack of specifics on what actually happened. When will we be getting operational specifics on what happened with Renato and Angel Centeno, not to mention the head of the family, Emilio Centeno?"

Mayor Lopez smiled. No one in the crowd smiled back. "Well, there's a lot of speculation going on there. I mean, first, Mario Abatantuono has never been implicated directly with organized crime. There has obviously been speculation."

With that, the mayor looked over at the FBI director, who had already begun walking toward the microphone.

Director Matthews straightened his suit and began. "We are well aware of the allegations involving Mr. Abatantuono. If he, or, for that matter, any person in power does anything that is provably illegal, we will take appropriate action. As for Angel Centeno, he was found dead on the island. Renato Centeno is presumed at large at this point. We are trying to track down Emilio Centeno for further questioning but have been unable to locate him thus far, and at this time have no proof of his involvement. There is a two-hundred-and-fifty-thousand-dollar reward for any information that leads to us locating either of them."

Charlie Tucker continued, "So, we are left to believe that all of this had to do with Angel Centeno being molested when he was young, and even though his attacker was found dead, he, out of the blue, calls up his long-lost uncle—what was his name again..." The reporter looked down at his notepad. "Oh, right, Anthony Morelli... who, if I am reading this correctly, had been accused of molesting someone also. Then this Father Morelli identifies other priests who might be pedophiles, calls Dan O'Malley who funds the operation, recruits some elderly cops, the mayor's office, and a few FBI agents. And then there's the disgraced cop whose mom just happened to be shot by someone working for Angel Centeno decades ago. This all seems very hard to believe."

Director Matthews frowned at this. "I don't believe there was a question there."

Charlie Tucker didn't respond.

Director Matthews looked out into the crowd. "I have been in law enforcement for over forty years. I can assure you that most of the time the simplest answer is usually the right answer. Even though it would be much more interesting for a celebrity or politician to have had someone killed, it is much more likely the husband did it because the wife was cheating on him. You look like a nice young man. I am sure you will have a great career as a news reporter, but not everything is a conspiracy."

"Thank you for that, Director Matthews. You are just looking at only getting the truth out and have nothing to hide. That is what you are saying, right?"

Charlie got no response. "I am pretty sure that was a question, Director Matthews."

"Yes. Of course, Mr. Tucker. Now I believe you have had enough time. I believe the polite thing to do would be to allow other reporters to ask some questions."

"May I ask just one more?"

"No."

Director Matthews looked at the three-by-five card with the reporters listed on it and made the decision that he'd only be getting to about half of them.

Charlie asked his question anyway. "If you have nothing to hide, wouldn't it make sense for us to ask questions to the actual agents who worked the case?"

Next on the list was a local reporter. "Rebecca Saunders from WZRB?"

"Rebecca Saunders from WZRB," she repeated.

"Yes, Ms. Saunders?" Director Matthews asked, impatiently.

"I have a question for either Agent Cooper or Agent Murray."

"Well." He paused and looked back at the regional director. "I am not sure if the agents have been properly briefed on certain aspects of the case that need to be kept confidential until all remaining suspects of any wrongdoing have been prosecuted."

The crowd was silent.

Matthews looked over toward the regional director again. "Bob?"

Bob looked over at Agent Murray, who did not hesitate as she walked to the microphone.

Agent Murray strode up as the director reluctantly took a few steps back.

"What is your question?" Agent Murray asked the reporter.

"What do you think about the Centeno"—Rebecca was forced to pause and look at her notes—"the Centeno-Rodriguez connection? Do you think that there is anything else there?"

Murray paused before answering. "Rodriguez. Edward Rodriguez. Eddie was a hero. He went beyond the call of duty working on different aspects of our case. He put himself at risk to further our case and was the lynchpin in bringing things to their conclusion."

"Wait, did you say 'was'? I thought Mr. Rodriguez was still considered missing."

"Well..." Agent Murray paused.

With that, Director Matthews stepped forward. He attempted to take the microphone from her but feeling her bristle, he paused and opened his arm up, asking permission. Agent Murray glared but stepped back. "The whereabouts of Mr. Rodriguez are unknown, and while his involvement in this case was vital, he had some unfortunate behavior in the past that makes it probable that he might have gotten into some trouble outside of the scope of the case. Angelica Black, RVN?" Another National Network.

Agent Murray tried to get to the microphone, but the director ignored her and waited for the next question.

"Angelica Black, national correspondent for RVN, my question is for Agent Murray."

"I think we've received a response from Agent Murray already. What is your question?"

Angelica Black was a well-respected reporter with over twenty years of experience, winning multiple awards. "Director Matthews, this case has been riddled with the smell of a cover-up. I would suggest you let Agent Murray answer some questions. It is my understanding that she has been an FBI agent for many years. I am sure she can be trusted to not divulge anything that might be damaging to your case. What do you think?"

The director looked toward Agent Murray with his teeth visibly gritted. "I don't think that is fair to you. What do you think, Agent Murray?"

Agent Murray walked to the microphone. "I would be happy to answer more questions, Director."

The director stood less than an arm's length behind Agent Murray.

"So, what do you think of Eddie Rodriguez's past? I have been told that he had been involved in some racial incidents previously and had been asked to leave the police force. Do you think he got himself in trouble?"

"I know of those reports and can only talk about the Eddie Rodriguez I know. Eddie Rodriguez was a good man or is a good man, if he is still alive. He always was respectful to me and others. From my dealings with him, he wanted to do the right thing. He wanted to do the right thing to the point where it probably got him—"

Agent Murray hadn't noticed the beeping and ringing of different devices in the crowd and onstage, but she did notice Ms. Black ignoring her.

"Ms. Black? Ms. Black?"

Angelica Black held her finger up in the air. She wasn't listening to her. She was listening through her earpiece. Someone in her newsroom was redirecting her. "One moment, please."

"My question... Uh-huh. Yep. Got it. I have a question for"— Ms. Black paused, smoothing out her suit and smiling—"for Director Matthews."

Director Matthews tapped Agent Murray on the shoulder as she was speaking: "It is important for all of you to realize Eddie Rodriguez was a good man. He did things that might not ever—" No one was listening to her.

Director Matthews once again opened his arm up and smiled now at Agent Murray. Agent Murray reluctantly backed away from the microphone.

"Yes, Ms. Black," Director Matthews said before quickly

following with, "And this will be the last question. All of us need to get back to tie up the remaining threads of this case."

Ms. Black smiled wryly. "Thank you, Director Matthews." She paused, pushing her earbud in her ear and shaking her head. "Okay. So, files have just been dumped on multiple sites, including Wiki-Leaks, Facebook, Instagram, Substack, I could go on." Ms. Black smiled broadly as she waited for a response.

"I don't like to deal in speculation," Director Matthews responded coolly.

Ms. Black said, "I can respect that, but it appears there are extra-ordinarily detailed records here. Let me read the first paragraph, if I may: 'It has been a hundred and sixty-eight hours, exactly seven days, since there has been an uplink from the computer array in the Maldives. This lapse has triggered an automatic data dump. If you have received this package, please immediately copy it to your local drive, and then make an additional copy to an external drive. The information in these documents will be extremely damning to many powerful people disclosed within. I, Daniel O'Malley, with the help of Father Anthony Morelli have put together a detailed record of the systematic cover-up of the Catholic Church involving decades of abuse to their congregation. Both Father Morelli and I are devout Catholics and believe in the love and redemption offered through the belief in Jesus Christ. We fervently pray that this does not cause disillusionment in the teaching of our Lord and Savior, but instead only removes the corruption of man from his Holy Word.'" Ms. Black paused for effect.

"Well, I guess this information will need to be reviewed by the appropriate organizations. Thank you all for your time." Director Matthews quickly turned away but not before Ms. Black made her last statement.

"You are mentioned in the documents, Director Matthews." Ms. Black stared at the director.

Director Matthews made a half turn back toward the podium but then quickly turned back and walked briskly away.

EPILOGUE

WEEKS HAD PASSED; the Vatican had briefly responded, saying they were taking the matter very seriously but had remained silent until today.

The website that was used to crowdsource information, the thousands of accusations, and the broader Vatican scandal was a daily story on the news. People familiar with the different accused priests were able to upload their own documents and information to further add validity to that which Father Morelli had put together.

Many victims came forward to tell their stories. Many priests were indicted. No politician and no person in law enforcement was indicted on criminal charges. The evidence was circumstantial. Even Director Matthews, who was mentioned as a friend by Cardinal Uelichar, could not be criminally indicted. His sins were done cleverly by redirecting the FBI's attention. However, after much civil pressure, Director Matthews stepped down to take early retirement due to personal reasons.

There was substantial civil backlash. Many politicians, law enforcement, and others who had been part of the cover-up retired early, moved, or were shunned by society.

The pope was frail and fading. This would be his final Ash Wednesday, of that he was sure. His aides had suggested moving the event to the Vatican's Nervi Auditorium, but he insisted on greeting the faithful who flocked to Saint Peter's Square.

"'Pray for us, for we are sure that we have a clear conscience, desiring to act honorably in all things,'" the pope began. He wondered if this Bible quote would be unnerving to the audience. He was speaking in his native Italian, but he was being translated throughout the world.

"These words, from Hebrews 13 are as important today as they were when first inscribed. They will be the Church's solemn commitment from this point forward." He paused. "The Holy See has been attacked from within and without. Gangsters, thugs, crippled sinners who prey on the most vulnerable of our flock—they have caused this crisis. But my beloved institution is also to blame. We desire to act honorably in all things. But it is easier said than done. I was heavily pressured to protect the Church and to defame Father Morelli and his accomplices. I will not do this.

"I have reviewed the written documents, the recordings, and the videos that have been left behind. I must act honorably. We all must. Though it pains me, I must authenticate their veracity, and I must tell the truth.

"In 1960, Cardinal Borgnino started a group that looked into these accusations and took it upon himself to handle these matters internally. Over the decades, this strategy has been passed down. The current and final caretaker of this information was Cardinal Uelichar. Father Morelli, who had been falsely accused of the most heinous of sins, was given access to the written and electronic documents that had been stored in our most sacred house, the Vatican.

"These documents showed that a wing of our Church, hoping to protect itself, adopted a strategy of containment. This, Father

Morelli concluded, was not acting honorably. Eventually, he decided to act. Efforts to stop Father Morelli were not successful. Continuing this misguided strategy of containment, the documents and electronic files kept here in the Vatican were destroyed. This was done to protect me as pope and more importantly to protect our Church as a whole. I wish this had not been done.

"The cardinals who knew about this strategy have been identified. Their lives, going forward, as with the rest of the Church, will be based on transparency and rooting out any remaining indiscretions within our great Church whether of this sort or other misuses of power.

"Cardinal Uelichar has written an impassioned piece that all of you by now have seen. It goes into great detail how he, the three other cardinals, many bishops, monsignors, and other representatives of our Church did what they did to protect the Church, God's Church, and the countless innocents who would be caught within the net of distrust that these crimes have created.

"While I am sure they believe this wholeheartedly, I am left with the somber thought of all of those who have been injured by our Church. I cannot abide that there can be a higher duty to the Church than to protect our most vulnerable, our children.

"*For God gave us a spirit not of fear but of power and love and self-control.* We cannot be afraid of the reprisals of the public, and we especially cannot be afraid of our own congregation.

"As the living embodiment of God's Word, we are not celebrities or politicians looking for the adulation of the many. We are instead, and from this point forward, will be examples of God's grace in man. We will live our lives nobly, and when we do falter, we will face the consequences without fear.

"'For God so loved the world that He gave His one and only Son, that everyone who believes in Him shall not perish but have eternal life.' Penance must be paid.

"Mr. O'Malley and Father Morelli have laid bare the sins of our

Church. Mr. O'Malley having been injured by one of our priests and Father Morelli being falsely accused and brought into an underbelly of secrecy, since he was viewed as a fellow violator, gave both of them the motivation to do what they did.

"While I certainly do not condone the kidnapping of priests and their eventual deaths, revealing the sins of our Church will hopefully be cathartic and allow us to move forward in a more loyal representation of God's Word.

"There is clear evidence that priests were moved around to other churches and for the majority of the time moved out of contact with the public, especially the young; however, this did not always occur, nor did it punish nor rehabilitate these priests.

"The evidence was also clear that whenever possible, local and sometimes higher-level pressure was put onto governments and law enforcement to keep quiet about these incidents. I have no illusions that what was kept inside the documents within the Vatican was not all-inclusive.

"Any priest who is still alive and was listed in Father Morelli's documents will be investigated. If charges are substantiated, they will be defrocked. They will no longer be priests of our Church. As for the bishops and cardinals mentioned, I have told them the penance that I plan to impose, and I asked them to join me. We must bare our sins and humbly ask for forgiveness from the public for our failures.

"I will not consume any food until I hear God's Word, letting me know that it is time. I will live only off of water and sugar. I am eighty-nine, and I do not want to die, but if it is God's will, so be it.

"I am planning on setting up a tent in Saint Peter's Square for the public to view our act of contrition. This is the least that I and the Church can do. I love all of you. Please pray for us."

The pope didn't end up alone in Saint Peter's Square. Many fasted, whether accused or not. It was seen as an act supporting the elderly leader of the expansive Catholic Church.

Catholics around the world joined the fast from their own homes. Others flew in, many sharing that the pope's act had inspired them, and even cured them of disaffection. Wayward Catholics like Colin Dunphy from Dublin, Ireland, now aged sixty, flew in. Dunphy never told the local police or his family about the advances of his local parish priest. "In many regards, I'm still a ten-year-old victim of fear and shame," he told a newsman at the scene. "I can finally once again truly love my Church. It is the fragility of men, not the teaching of our God that has been put to the test."

Only one of the accused cardinals joined the pope. Cardinal Uelichar and the two others praised the courage of Pope John but said that God had told them to pray for forgiveness on their own, and it would be a distraction from Pope John's sacrifice if they joined.

By the time Pope John died on the third day, only the ones praying and supporting remained. The agitators who had come to mock the Church and the countless who had come making financial demands of the Church had already left.

Five had decided on the twenty-fifth day of fasting that they would stay for forty days as a show of commitment and faith to their Church. By the fortieth day, only four people remained: one of the accused bishops, two young priests, and Colin Dunphy. One of the other accused bishops had died.

Including the pope, ten in all died over what became known as the Great Fast.

On Easter Monday, forty-one days after the Great Fast began, a young steward who had worked personally with Pope John appeared on Italian TV. What he said would quickly hit the national news.

He had told the news station that he possessed a sealed envelope with a letter inside from the recently deceased pope.

The steward was clearly nervous on television, but he gathered his courage and tried to speak clearly to the attractive newswoman. "I would like everyone to see this envelope." He held the envelope by its sides, revealing the papal seal at dead center.

The steward nervously handed it to the newswoman who, as instructed, gently moved her fingers around the seal to show that the envelope had not been opened and was sealed tightly. Afterward, she handed the envelope back to the steward who then broke the seal and unfolded the letter.

The steward read slowly and deliberately, having to repeat himself a few times: "If you are hearing this, it was God's will for me not to survive. I am not saddened by this. I call on all of you, whether parishioners, local priests, and especially our Church leadership to look into your hearts and souls and more closely follow our God's path.

"We had become the bureaucracy that our Lord Jesus despised. We do not control righteousness nor should we hold contempt for anyone. We shall be simple shepherds once again caring for our flock, instead of exalted dignitaries looking for adulation. For those who exalt themselves will be humbled, and those who humble themselves will be exalted.

"Also, we need to reconsider some of our precepts and why they exist. It was our Lord God who said, 'It is not good that the man should be alone; I will make him a helper fit for him.'

"Scholars, for years, have questioned the Second Lateran Council. It is unnatural for someone to live his life alone without the support of someone bound to him or, for that matter, her. We need good leadership who are willing to follow God's core tenets, no matter what their gender or interests are, as long as they know love. Anyone who does not love does not know God, because God is love.

"The world is in crisis. As leadership in God's Church, we preach the importance of faith and how faith will get our flock to the kingdom of heaven. We preach hope and to constantly be positive in our world and forward-looking.

"We need to, first and foremost, preach love, love in all of its many wondrous forms. So now faith, hope, and love abide these three, but the greatest of these is love.

"Let us realize the importance of God's Word and use love as the rock of our Church. Love first for our shared God, but secondly, for all of humanity, our community, our friends, and our enemies. Love endures all things. Love never ends.

"I love all of you deeply, and I will be with you always. I will be watching you all with your Lord God above, surrounded by your loved ones who have gone before you. Love first, love always."

The Church changed deeply from that point forward.

The message moved from rhetoric and reflection of biblical texts to the daily act of living life in the footsteps of Christ. Heeding the words of St. Francis, the focus shifted; instead of being teachers of doctrine, the message for all was to be an instrument of peace and love and kindness.

Thank you for reading, Vigilante Priest. We hope you enjoyed getting to know Father Tony and Eddie. If you did enjoy reading Vigilante Priest, we'd appreciate it if you'd help others find it too.

Recommend it: A few words to your friends, book groups, and social networks would be fantastic.

Review it: Please tell your fellow readers what you liked about this book by reviewing, Vigilante Priest.

ABOUT THE AUTHORS

JOE GALLAGHER - AUTHOR

Joe Gallagher lives in Mount Airy, MD with Dena and two of his kids, Ryan and Lilli. His eldest child, Andrew, is a college graduate and has started his own life journey. In addition to his writing, Joe is an active member of various communities that keep him busy.

DAN BOWDEN - AUTHOR

Dan Bowden is the son of an NYPD detective. He holds a teaching degree and worked part-time at a Catholic Church. He lives in Tinton Falls, New Jersey with his wife, Sandy. Dan has two sons, Brian and Bobby and two daughters-in-law, Melanie and Nikki. He is the proud Grandpa to five wonderful grandchildren, John, Bella, Abby, Robert and Jojo.

Made in the USA
Monee, IL
12 July 2024

a5ec5a39-31e0-4c1a-abce-a0f08967b44bR01